THE PLAGIARIST GAME

CLIFTON WILCOX

WINDWARD PUBLISHING

Fredericksburg, Virginia

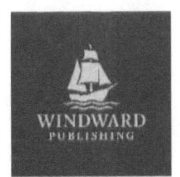

Print ISBN: 978-1-969770-16-6

EBook ISBN: 978-1-969770-15-9

Hardback ISBN: 978-1-969770-17-3

Published by Windward Publishing LLC., Fredericksburg, Virginia.

Library of Congress Cataloging in Publication Data

Wilcox, Clifton

The Plagiarist Game

Windward Publishing, LLC

2026

DEDICATION

Dedicated to the margins, where the most dangerous ideas are written.

TABLE OF CONTENTS

BOOKS BY CLIFTON WILCOX

Non-Fiction

Scape Goat: Targeted for Blame

Groupthink: An Impediment to Success

Bias: The Unconscious Deceiver

Witch-hunt: The Assignment of Blame

The Fall of the Kingdom of Northumbria

Witch-hunt: The Class of Cultures

Road to War: The Quest for a New World Order

Envy: A Deeper Shade of Green

The Rise of the Nazi SS

The Horrible Void Between the Trenches

Fiction

Cool's Last Stand

Where Despair Comes to Play

The Monuments Must Bleed

Keeper of the Fallen Ages

I, Monster

Harvest of Eyes

The Case Against Jasper

Crimson Plume: The Song of Corvus

Framed in Love

Echoes of the Forgotten

Blacktop Harvest

PROLOGUE

THE FIRST LINE

The words were already written before she realized she was going to die.

They floated through Clara Bellweather's mind with quiet, terrible clarity—not screamed, not panicked, but composed, as if someone else were reciting them inside her skull.

A silence deep did reign...

She tried to breathe. Water lapped softly against stone somewhere nearby. The night air was cold enough to sting her lungs, sharp with autumn rot and the faint sweetness of fallen leaves. Elmwood University slept behind her—lit windows, distant laughter, the soft illusion of safety. The world of lectures and footnotes. Of margins and meaning.

She had spent years studying tragic endings.

She had never believed she would become one.

Her back pressed against something damp and unyielding. Stone. Moss. Her palms slid uselessly when she tried to push herself upright. The ground was wrong beneath her—too soft, too slick, as if the earth itself were breathing.

"Please," she whispered, though she did not know to whom.

A shadow detached itself from the dark.

Not rushing.

Not frantic.

Patient.

The figure moved with deliberate care, like a scholar approaching a lectern. Clara's mouth opened, but no argument formed. No brilliant defense. No theory. Every quote she had ever memorized abandoned her. All that remained was the sickening awareness that she had been led here. Chosen.

"You studied them," the voice said calmly. Close now. Cultivated. Almost kind. "The broken girls. The beautiful endings."

Something brushed her fingers.

A flower.

She recoiled, a sob breaking loose as she recognized the pale petals, the scent—clean and funereal. The irony was so precise it felt engineered.

"Ophelia had water," the voice continued. "Juliet had sleep. Antigone had the earth. Every story gives them a final element. A proper one."

Tears streaked down Clara's face. "I didn't mean— I was only—"

"Studying," the voice finished for her. "Yes. So was I."

She felt hands at her shoulders. Not violent. Certain. Guiding her backward.

The sky tilted. The stars fractured.

Cold surged up her spine.

Her breath collapsed into her chest as the pond took her.

The shock of it erased sound. Thought. Even fear. Water filled her ears, her mouth, her nose—an intimate invasion. Above her, the surface trembled like warped glass. Leaves drifted. The world distorted.

She kicked. Once. Twice.

Then a pressure at her back. Steady. Unrelenting.

In the chaos of her failing body, her mind did the only thing it had ever been trained to do.

It reached for words.

She saw them—not heard them.

Ink on vellum

Elegant. Controlled.

And in my soul, a silence deep did reign...

Her fingers clawed. Touched fabric. Something smooth. Cool.

Paper.

The darkness thickened. Her limbs weakened. The water stopped fighting and began to carry.

The last thing Clara Bellweather felt was not terror.

It was comprehension.

The hands released her.

She drifted.

Above her, somewhere beyond the trembling surface, the figure remained long enough to arrange the final details—to tuck the rose, to place the card, to perfect the image.

A scholar's work.

A writer's hand.

A beginning.

Because stories, after all, always start with a body.

CHAPTER 1

THE FIRST OMEN

The biting autumn air, sharp with the promise of frost, did little to quell the creeping unease that settled over Detective Maria Richards as she stepped onto the grounds of Elmwood University. It was a scent that spoke of decay, of nature's inevitable surrender, but today, it was overlaid with something far more unsettling – the metallic tang of fear, the acrid undercurrent of something fundamentally wrong. The university, usually a vibrant tapestry of intellectual pursuit, a symphony of rustling leaves and hushed academic discourse, felt muted, its usual energy stifled by an invisible shroud. Gothic spires, normally stoic sentinels against the sky, seemed to sag, their shadows lengthening with an unnatural haste, clawing at the manicured lawns and the weathered stone pathways.

Maria's gaze swept over the scene, her senses on high alert. The air, usually alive with the murmur of students and faculty, was now thick with an anxious silence, broken only by the hushed, urgent tones of uniformed officers and the distant wail of a siren. A knot tightened in her stomach. This was more than a routine call; it was a disruption of the natural order; a dissonant chord struck in the heart of academia. The very architecture of Elmwood, with its ivy-choked walls and arched windows that seemed to hold ancient secrets, felt like a witness holding its breath, a silent observer to a tragedy that had shattered the veneer of intellectual serenity.

Her destination was the university's ornamental pond, a usually picturesque spot where students often sought quiet contemplation amidst the meticulously maintained rose bushes and weeping willows. Today, however, the water's placid surface was marred, its reflection of the overcast sky fractured by an event that defied the tranquility of its setting. The scene was a stark tableau, a deliberate and disturbing disruption of nature's gentle artistry.

As Maria approached, the hushed murmurs of the gathered officers intensified, their faces grim. The air grew heavy, not just with the scent of decay, but with the palpable presence of death. Even from a distance, the scene was undeniably theatrical, a chillingly deliberate arrangement that screamed of something far more sinister than a simple accident or a crime of passion. It spoke of intent, of a twisted narrative being played out against the backdrop of scholarly pursuits. The usual crispness of autumn was replaced by a chilling stillness, as if the very trees were reluctant to shed their leaves, fearing what lay beneath. The ivy clinging to the university's venerable buildings seemed to tighten its grip, as if trying to absorb the unfolding horror, or perhaps, to hide it. Maria felt a familiar prickle of unease, a premonition that this case would be unlike any other, a tangled knot of intellect and depravity that would demand more than just forensic expertise. It would demand an understanding of the stories that lay hidden beneath the surface of this esteemed institution.

The body, submerged in the shallow waters of the ornamental pond, was a stark departure from the usual serene beauty of Elmwood University. Clara Bellweather, a name that now carried the weight of a brutal end, had been found amidst the gentle sway of the weeping willows and the vibrant, yet fading, hues of autumn foliage. Detective Maria Richards, her senses honed by years of navigating the darkest corners of human behavior, felt a cold dread seep into her as she surveyed the scene. It was more than just the shock of a young life extinguished; it was the chilling artistry, the deliberate staging that spoke of a mind deeply disturbed, yet terrifyingly in control. Clara's eyes, wide and vacant, stared unseeing at the overcast sky, a silent testament to her final moments. The wilting rose, its petals a faded crimson against the pale canvas of her skin, was clutched with a rigor mortis-induced grip, a macabre flourish that Maria recognized with a sickening lurch. This was a scene ripped from the pages of a dark romance, a tragic echo of a literary figure whose fate had been sealed by love, loss, and a watery demise. The juxtaposition of the pristine academic setting with the stark reality of murder was jarring, a violation of the sanctuary of learning that Elmwood was meant to represent. The usual hum of scholarly activity was silenced, replaced by the hushed, urgent tones of the investigation, and the palpable fear that now permeated the air.

The meticulous arrangement of Clara's body was the first thing that truly unsettled Maria. It wasn't a chaotic mess of limbs and torn fabric, but a deliberate, almost graceful, positioning. Her body lay partially submerged, her limbs arranged with a chilling precision that suggested careful planning. The wilting rose, placed with such care in her hand, wasn't just a random object; it was a symbol, a deliberate allusion. Maria's mind immediately flashed to the tragic tale of Ophelia, the Shakespearean character who met her end in a watery grave, surrounded by flowers. The connection was too potent, too deliberate to be a coincidence. This killer wasn't just murdering; they were telling a story, weaving a narrative of despair and betrayal through their gruesome artistry. The pristine façade of Elmwood University, a place usually associated with intellectual rigor and the pursuit of knowledge, was now irrevocably marred by the brutal reality of a life brutally extinguished. The very architecture of the campus, with its gothic spires and ivy-clad walls, seemed to loom heavier, casting longer, more ominous shadows that seemed to mirror the darkness that had descended upon the institution.

Maria knelt by the edge of the pond, the cold, damp air seeping into her. The water, usually clear enough to see the smooth pebbles beneath, was now clouded, disturbed by the grim discovery. She noted the way Clara's simple, yet elegant, dress clung to her pale skin, waterlogged and heavy. The stark contrast between the lifeless body and the vibrant autumn colors surrounding it was a painful reminder of the life that had been so cruelly snatched away. This was not a spontaneous act of violence; it was a performance, a chillingly deliberate statement crafted by a disturbed mind. The wilting rose, even in its decay, held a disturbing beauty, a morbid romanticism that sent a shiver down Maria's spine. Her gaze swept over the scene, cataloging every detail, every nuance. The scent of decaying leaves, the rustling of the willows, the distant caw of a crow - all these sensory inputs were meticulously filed away, potential threads in the unraveling tapestry of this crime. The quiet contemplation usually found by this ornamental pond was shattered, replaced by the stark, brutal reality of a life ended with such calculated theatricality. The university's reputation, built on decades of academic excellence, now hung precariously in the balance, tainted by the blood that stained its pristine waters.

The onlookers, a somber assembly clustered at the edge of the cordoned-off area, whispered amongst themselves, their hushed tones a stark contrast to the usual vibrant energy of the Elmwood campus. Their faces, a canvas of shock and morbid curiosity, were turned towards the pond, towards the grim spectacle that had brought their academic pursuits to a jarring halt. The gothic spires of the university, silhouetted against the bruised, grey sky, seemed to loom larger, more imposing than usual. The ancient trees, their branches gnarled like arthritic fingers, cast long, distorted shadows that stretched across the quad, mirroring the growing darkness that was beginning to envelop the university. These shadows seemed to writhe, to whisper secrets, to carry the weight of the unfolding tragedy. Maria felt a strange sense of being watched, not just by the anxious crowd, but by the very fabric of the university itself – its venerable buildings, its ancient trees, its hallowed halls that had suddenly become a theater of death. Her gaze drifted from the scene of the crime to the faces in the crowd. A flicker of recognition, a gut feeling that defied logical explanation, began to coalesce within her.

This murder, she sensed, was not a spur-of-the-moment act of violence. It was meticulously planned, a chillingly deliberate performance orchestrated with an almost artistic intent. The literary allusion, the poetic fragment, the pristine yet brutal nature of the crime scene – these were not random elements. They were pieces of a puzzle, deliberately placed. Her mind, trained to dissect complex scenarios, began to sift through the torrent of details, seeking patterns, connections, a logic that lay hidden beneath the surface of this horrific display. She knew, with a certainty that settled deep in her bones, that this case would demand more than standard investigative procedure. It would require a deep dive into the very soul of the university, into the minds of its inhabitants, and into the dark, often hidden, world of literary obsession.

The scent of decaying leaves seemed to cling to her, a constant reminder of the mortality that had been so brutally exposed, and the enduring mystery that now lay at the heart of Elmwood. The hushed whispers of the onlookers were a prelude to the deeper, more insidious secrets that the university held, secrets that Maria was now compelled to unearth. The tranquil beauty of the ornamental pond, once a sanctuary for students seeking solace, had become a chilling monument to a violent end, a stark reminder that even in the most serene of settings, darkness could take root. The wilting rose, a symbol of lost love and faded beauty, was not merely a prop; it was a taunt, a declaration of intent from a killer who understood the power of symbols and the allure of a tragic narrative. Maria felt the weight of the task ahead, the intricate web of deceit and depravity she would need to unravel, all while the ghost of Ophelia seemed to linger in the rustling leaves and the still, dark water. The intellectual heart of Elmwood had been pierced, and Maria knew this was only the beginning of a descent into a world where art and murder intertwined with terrifying precision.

The vellum felt impossibly cool against Maria's gloved fingertips, a stark contrast to the humid, clinging air that bore the scent of decay and damp earth. It was small, no larger than a playing card, and tucked so deliberately beneath Clara Bellweather's rigid hand, nestled amongst the wilting crimson petals of the rose, that it could easily have been missed by less scrutinizing eyes. But Maria Richards's eyes missed little. Her gaze, trained to dissect the minutiae of a crime scene, had snagged on the unnatural stiffness of the victim's fingers, a rigidity born not just of death, but of a clutched object. And there it was, a sliver of ivory against the dark, saturated fabric of Clara's dress.

With the painstaking precision of a surgeon, Maria used a pair of fine-tipped tweezers to gently ease the card from its resting place. The vellum, surprisingly thick and of a quality rarely found in everyday stationery, resisted for a moment, then surrendered with a faint, almost apologetic rustle. As she carefully lifted it, the weight of it in the evidence bag felt disproportionate to its size, laden with unspoken significance. Unfolding it revealed a surface of pristine, unblemished ivory, marred only by the elegant, impossibly fine script that flowed across it. It was calligraphy of a rare and exquisite kind, each stroke deliberate, controlled, and imbued with a chilling artistry. The ink, a deep, almost black hue, seemed to absorb the muted light, lending an air of somber finality to the words it formed.

Maria's breath caught, a sharp, involuntary intake that was swallowed by the oppressive silence of the quad. She recognized the script, or rather, the *style*. It spoke of a meticulous mind, a hand guided by a deep appreciation for form, a mind that saw the act of writing not merely as a means of communication, but as an art form in itself. This was not the hurried scrawl of a panicked individual, nor the clumsy printing of someone trying to mask their identity. This was a deliberate, calculated flourish, a statement designed to impress and intimidate in equal measure. The contrast between the refined elegance of the writing and the brutal reality of the scene it accompanied was jarring, a disquieting juxtaposition that sent a fresh wave of unease through Maria.

Then, her eyes scanned the words themselves. A single line, extracted from some forgotten corner of poetic despair. The syllables, even in their written form, seemed to carry a heavy weight, a melancholic resonance that echoed the tragedy unfolding before her.

"And in my soul, a silence deep did reign, where love's sweet song became a mournful strain."

The quote. Maria's mind, a vast repository of literary knowledge, accessed the obscure files with a speed that belied the shock coiling in her gut. It wasn't from any of the commonly anthologized poets, not a line that would spring readily to the lips of a casual reader. This was something deeper, something more esoteric. A forgotten sonnet, perhaps, or a verse from a lesser-known epic, chosen with deliberate intent. The sentiment itself was a lament, a profound expression of betrayal and the crushing weight of disillusionment. It spoke of a profound inner desolation, of a once-cherished emotion curdled into sorrow.

This was no random act of violence. This was a message. A calling card.

The implications slammed into Maria with the force of a physical blow. The killer wasn't merely killing; they were curating their crime, imbuing it with meaning, crafting a narrative that would resonate with a specific audience – or perhaps, with themselves. This wasn't just about ending a life; it was about making a statement, about announcing their presence with a chillingly poetic flourish. The Ophelia allusion, she now realized, was merely the overture. This vellum card was the true prologue, a dark introduction to a story the killer intended to tell.

And then, beneath the quote, almost an afterthought, was a symbol. Tiny, intricate, and utterly alien. It was not a signature in the conventional sense, no initial or name. It was an emblem, a stylized mark etched with the same fine precision as the calligraphy. It was sharp, angular, yet possessed a certain unsettling fluidity, like a coiled serpent or a predatory bird's talon. Maria felt a prickle of unease creep up her spine. This symbol was not just decorative; it was a brand, a mark of ownership, a unique identifier that the killer clearly intended to be recognized, or at least remembered. It was the seal on a terrifying pact, a silent promise of more to come.

The elegance of the script, the obscure beauty of the chosen verse, the enigmatic symbol – all of it coalesced into a single, horrifying realization: this killer was intelligent. Terribly, disturbingly intelligent. They possessed a mind that was both analytical and artistic, capable of orchestrating such brutality with a chilling detachment, and then, of memorializing it with a flair that bordered on the theatrical. This wasn't a crime of passion; it was a meticulously designed performance piece, with Clara Bellweather as its tragic, unwilling centerpiece.

Maria carefully secured the vellum card in a sterile evidence bag, the faint rustle of the plastic a mundane counterpoint to the profound disturbance it represented. She looked back at Clara's still form, the wilting rose, the muddied water, and the encroaching shadows of the Elmwood gothic architecture. The scene, already horrific, had now taken on a new, sinister dimension. The initial shock had given way to a chilling intellectual puzzle, a labyrinth of intent and symbolism that Maria was now tasked with navigating.

The implications rippled outwards, touching every corner of the serene, academic environment. Elmwood University, with its hallowed halls and cultivated intellect, had become the stage for a meticulously crafted murder. The scent of decaying leaves, which had seemed merely seasonal moments before, now carried a more potent, foreboding fragrance, a perfumed harbinger of the darkness that had taken root within its manicured grounds. The whispers of the onlookers, previously a murmur of shocked disbelief, now seemed to carry a new, fearful undertone. They were witnessing not just a crime, but the unveiling of a predator's manifesto.

Maria's gaze swept across the gathering of students and faculty, their faces pale and etched with a mixture of horror and morbid fascination. Among them, she searched for anything, a flicker of recognition, a misplaced detail, a subtle anomaly that might betray the presence of the mind that had orchestrated this macabre tableau. The killer had deliberately invited attention, not through brute force, but through the insidious power of suggestion and artistry. They had left a calling card, a cryptic message delivered in the language of tragedy and obscure poetry. It was a challenge, a gauntlet thrown down at the feet of the authorities, a dare to decipher the twisted logic that had led to this point.

She knew, with a certainty that settled deep in her gut, that this was not an isolated incident. The Ophelia allusion, the carefully chosen quote, the enigmatic symbol – these were not the random acts of a disturbed individual. They were deliberate choices, pieces of a larger puzzle deliberately placed to sow discord and confusion, and perhaps, to hint at a pattern. The killer was sending a message, not just about Clara Bellweather's death, but about their own twisted worldview, their perception of love, loss, and betrayal. This first, cryptic calling card was a promise of more to come, a chilling preview of the dark narrative that had just begun to unfold within the venerable walls of Elmwood University.

The quiet beauty of the ornamental pond, once a serene reflection of the changing seasons, was now irrevocably tainted, a watery grave that held not only the victim, but the first chilling whisper of a killer's dark design. The wilting rose was a symbol, yes, but the vellum card was the signature, the undeniable proof that beneath the veneer of academic respectability, a profound and terrifying darkness had found its voice. Maria felt the immense weight of the task ahead, the intricate tapestry of deception and depravity she would have to meticulously unravel, thread by painstaking thread, all while the lingering scent of decaying leaves seemed to whisper secrets of the rot that festered beneath the polished surface of Elmwood.

This was more than a murder investigation; it was an excavation of a fractured psyche, a descent into a world where literature and violence became inextricably intertwined. The killer had announced their arrival, and their chosen medium was death, seasoned with an unsettling intellectualism that promised a truly terrifying challenge. The elegance of the script, so at odds with the brutality of the act, was a siren's call, drawing Maria into a deadly game of wits, a game where the stakes were nothing less than life itself. The symbol, etched with such deliberate care, felt like an eye, watching her, daring her to understand. It was the signature of a predator, one who understood the power of symbolism and the intoxicating allure of a tragic narrative.

The vellum card, now safely sealed, felt like a physical manifestation of the killer's intellect, a testament to their ability to orchestrate such horror with a chillingly artistic hand. Maria's mind raced, sifting through possibilities, searching for any connection that might link this carefully constructed scene to a motive, a perpetrator, or even a future victim. The quote, *"And in my soul, a silence deep did reign, where love's sweet song became a mournful strain,"* resonated with a particular poignancy. It spoke of a profound emotional void, a life where love had soured, transforming into a deep and abiding sorrow. Was this a reflection of the killer's own internal landscape, or a commentary on Clara's life, a twisted judgment passed upon her? The ambiguity was unsettling, a deliberate veil cast over the killer's true intentions.

Maria carefully documented the placement of the card, the precise angle of the rose, the subtle indentation on Clara's palm where the vellum had rested. Every detail, no matter how seemingly insignificant, could be a crucial piece of the puzzle. She recalled the hushed, almost reverent, tone of the responding officers, their shared sense of awe at the sheer theatricality of the scene. This was not the messy, desperate violence they usually encountered. This was something else, something that spoke of a mind steeped in the dramatic arts, a mind that understood the power of symbolism and the enduring impact of a well-crafted narrative.

The symbol itself continued to nag at her. It was unlike any insignia or emblem she had encountered in her years on the force. It was abstract, yet undeniably potent, evoking a sense of ancient, primal power. It could be a sigil, a marker from some obscure tradition, or perhaps, something the killer had devised entirely on their own, a personal brand designed to instill fear and elicit recognition. The very act of etching it onto the vellum spoke volumes about the killer's desire for acknowledgment, their need to leave an indelible mark on the world, and on the minds of those who would investigate their crime.

As the forensic team meticulously worked around her, their movements precise and methodical, Maria stepped back, allowing herself a moment to absorb the broader implications. The calling card was more than just evidence; it was an invitation. An invitation into the killer's world, a world where death was a canvas and tragedy was the medium. It was a gauntlet thrown down, a challenge issued to the established order, a taunt directed at the very institutions of law and order that sought to apprehend them. The killer had revealed themselves, not by name or face, but by their intellect, their artistic sensibilities, and their chilling disregard for human life.

The weight of the case settled upon Maria's shoulders, a heavy, suffocating cloak. She knew, instinctively, that this would be no ordinary investigation. It would demand a different kind of approach, a willingness to delve into the less tangible aspects of human psychology, to explore the hidden currents of obsession, resentment, and literary fascination that might drive such a meticulously crafted act of violence. The vellum card was the first thread, a single, delicate strand that promised to lead her into a labyrinth of dark secrets, a maze of literary allusions and symbolic gestures, where the line between art and murder was blurred into a terrifying, indistinguishable whole. The scent of damp earth and decaying leaves seemed to intensify, a constant, unsettling reminder of the fragile boundary between life and death, and the chilling realization that this was only the beginning. The killer had made their introduction, a cryptic calling card delivered with chilling precision, and Maria knew, with a growing sense of dread, that the performance had only just begun. The chosen quote, speaking of love's sweet song turned mournful strain, echoed in her mind, a somber melody playing out against the backdrop of a brutal reality, a stark testament to the darkness that had infiltrated the tranquil grounds of Elmwood.

The murmur of voices, usually a low hum of academic discourse that punctuated the air of Elmwood University, had congealed into a palpable wave of hushed dread. It was a sound that clung to the damp, cool air, a collective exhalation of shock and morbid curiosity that coiled around Maria Richards like a shroud. The quad, typically a vibrant hub of scholarly pursuits, a verdant expanse where students debated philosophy and professors contemplated the cosmos, now felt charged with an unnerving stillness, a silence that was far more potent than any uproar. Each hushed syllable, each furtive glance exchanged between the assembled faculty and students, was a testament to the fear that had unfurled its dark wings over the hallowed grounds.

Maria's gaze swept across the faces; a panorama of pale visages etched with a complex tapestry of emotions. There was horror, raw and unadulterated, evident in the wide eyes and slackened jaws. But beneath that, a darker current flowed – a morbid fascination, an almost irresistible pull towards the spectacle of tragedy. It was the same instinct that drew crowds to a public execution in centuries past, the unseemly allure of witnessing a life extinguished, especially when it was punctuated by such deliberate, artistic flair. These were the intellectuals, the custodians of knowledge, yet here they were, drawn into the primal theater of crime, their reasoned minds momentarily overshadowed by the sheer, visceral impact of Clara Bellweather's demise.

The whispers were not mere gossip; they were nascent theories, nascent fears, coalescing into a chaotic, unformed narrative. They spoke of Clara Bellweather, of her quiet dedication to her studies, of her seemingly unremarkable life, now brutally punctuated by an act of savage artistry. Some whispered about her recent research, a seemingly innocuous exploration of medieval poetry that, in retrospect, now seemed fraught with unspoken significance. Others, their voices barely audible above the rustle of leaves, speculated about her personal life, searching for any hint of a clandestine affair, a hidden enemy, a secret that might explain such a violent end. The theories, though varied, shared a common thread: a desperate attempt to impose order on the senseless, to find a rational explanation for an act that defied all logic.

Maria caught snippets of conversation, fragmented and laden with implication. "Did you see the card?" a woman's voice, strained with disbelief, whispered to a man whose face was ashen. "The writing... it was like nothing I've ever seen."

"And the quote," another voice, deeper and tinged with academic gravitas, added, "I can't place it. It's not a common verse, not something from the usual canon." The recognition of the obscure nature of the quote only served to deepen the mystery, to elevate the killer from a mere brute to an enigma, a perpetrator with a disturbing literary bent.

A young student, her face buried in her hands, sobbed softly, her grief a stark counterpoint to the hushed intellectual speculation. Her despair, however, was quickly overtaken by the pervasive atmosphere of unease. "She was always so kind," the student choked out between sobs, her words lost in the general murmur. "She would never... she didn't deserve this."

Maria's attention was drawn to a knot of professors standing near the entrance to the library, their tweed jackets and professorial air doing little to mask the fear in their eyes. They spoke in low, urgent tones, their gestures sharp and agitated. One of them, a man Maria recognized as Professor Allen Fry, head of the Comparative Literature department, ran a hand through his thinning hair, his face a mask of bewilderment. "It's... it's almost a literary statement," he murmured, his voice barely audible, as if he were still trying to process the words on the vellum. "The choice of verse, the symbolism... it's deliberate. Calculated."

The mention of symbolism brought Maria's attention back to the enigmatic mark etched onto the vellum card. It was a detail that gnawed at her, a silent question mark in the meticulously crafted narrative. This wasn't just a murder; it was a performance, a staged event designed to provoke, to shock, and to leave a lasting impression. The killer had not only taken a life, but they had also attempted to script the aftermath, to imbue the tragedy with a meaning that transcended the immediate act of violence.

As the forensic team continued their meticulous work, their white-clad forms moving with an almost reverent slowness around Clara's body, Maria found herself drawn to the periphery of the gathering crowd. She wasn't looking for clues in the obvious places, not anymore. The calling card had changed the nature of the investigation entirely. She was now searching for the *mind* behind the madness, the intellectual architect of this macabre masterpiece. She scanned the faces, searching for any flicker of recognition, any subtle sign of an individual who might possess the knowledge and the inclination to orchestrate such a chilling display. Was there someone among them who understood the nuances of obscure poetry, who possessed the artistic hand to craft such elegant calligraphy, who harbored a darkness deep enough to translate abstract emotion into brutal reality?

Maria's gaze swept over the assembled faculty, her eyes lingering on those who seemed to possess a particular intensity, a sharp intellect that might mask a darker, more complex nature. Professor Allen Fry, head of Comparative Literature, his brow furrowed in deep thought, stood apart from the others, his usual academic composure frayed by the evident distress. He was a man who lived and breathed literature, a scholar whose life was dedicated to the dissection of texts and the understanding of their hidden meanings. Could such a man, steeped in the beauty and complexity of words, be capable of such brutal acts? Or was his distress a performance, a carefully constructed facade to deflect suspicion? The question hung in the air, as heavy and oppressive as the overcast sky.

She considered the possibility that the killer was not necessarily someone within the faculty, but perhaps a student, a disgruntled alumni, or even an outsider who had somehow gained access to the university's inner workings and its intellectual discourse. The quote on the vellum card, after all, was obscure. It hinted at a knowledge base that might extend beyond the immediate academic circles, or perhaps it was a deliberate attempt to mislead, to cast suspicion on those with specialized knowledge. The more Maria considered the possibilities, the more the scope of her investigation widened, stretching beyond the immediate confines of Elmwood's manicured lawns and into the vast, often shadowy, world of academic obsession and intellectual rivalry.

The sheer audacity of the act also played on Maria's mind. To commit such a violent crime on the grounds of a prestigious university, during what would have been a normal academic day, was a bold move. It suggested a killer who was not only intelligent and meticulous but also arrogant, someone who believed they were above the law, or perhaps someone who saw this act as a justifiable, even righteous, intervention. The carefully chosen words on the vellum card were not just a signature; they were a manifesto, a declaration of intent that would echo through the hallowed halls, a testament to the killer's twisted worldview.

Maria felt a growing sense of unease, a familiar but unwelcome companion in her line of work. This was more than just a case; it was a descent into the darker aspects of the human psyche, a journey into the heart of a mind that found beauty in brutality and purpose in destruction. The academic setting, usually a symbol of enlightenment and progress, had become the stage for a macabre performance, and Maria was tasked with unmasking the artist behind this terrifying production. The weight of the investigation settled on her shoulders, a burden made heavier by the intellectual puzzle that lay before her, a puzzle crafted by a mind as sharp and as dangerous as any weapon.

She took a slow, steadying breath, forcing herself to focus on the tangible, even as the intangible began to weave its unsettling spell. The forensic team was meticulous, their movements precise as they documented every minute detail. But Maria knew that the true clues, the ones that would lead her to the killer, would not be found under a microscope or in a fingerprint database. They would be found in the interpretation of the literary fragment, in the understanding of the symbolism, in the unraveling of the killer's intellectual motivations. This case demanded not just the sharp eye of a detective but the keen mind of an academic, a mind capable of appreciating the nuances of language and the depths of human depravity.

The dappled sunlight, struggling to break through the thick canopy of ancient oaks, cast shifting patterns on the grass, making the scene appear almost dreamlike, a surreal nightmare unfolding in broad daylight. Maria's intuition, a finely honed instrument that had served her well over the years, was screaming at her that this was no ordinary murder. It was a carefully constructed narrative, a chilling testament to a mind that was as brilliant as it was terrifying. The killer had left a calling card, a piece of art that was as beautiful as it was deadly, and Maria was determined to decipher its meaning, to understand the twisted logic that had driven someone to such an act. The university, a place of learning and enlightenment, had become a hunting ground, and she was now the one hunting, not just a killer, but a ghost in the machine of academia, a phantom whose words were as sharp as any blade.

The hushed whispers, the nervous glances, the palpable fear – they were all pieces of the puzzle, fragments of a story that was only just beginning to unfold, a story written in blood and ink, a story that would test Maria Richards's intellect and her resolve like never before. The intellectual elegance of the crime, its almost artistic execution, presented a unique challenge, one that would force her to confront not only the darkness within a single individual but also the potential for darkness that could fester within the very institutions of knowledge. This was not a chase; it was a dissection, a deep dive into the psyche of a killer who wielded words and violence with equal, terrifying proficiency. The poetry, the symbolism, the meticulous staging – it was all a deliberate attempt to elevate their act beyond mere criminality, to imbue it with a meaning that would resonate, that would shock, and that would, perhaps, even be admired by some twisted corner of the academic world. Maria knew that to catch this killer, she would have to understand their mind, their motivations, and their very unique, very disturbing, artistic vision. The truth lay not just in what was done, but in *why* it was done, and the answer to that question was hidden somewhere within the hallowed, and now haunted, halls of Elmwood University.

CHAPTER 2

ECHOES OF TRAGEDY

The sterile, fluorescent-lit hum of the precinct offered a stark, almost jarring, counterpoint to the morbid, blood-tinged atmosphere of Elmwood University's quad. Back in the comparative quiet of her office, the vellum card lay pristine under the harsh glare of a desk lamp, its elegant script a chilling testament to a mind that found solace, or perhaps inspiration, in the macabre. Maria traced the calligraphic flourish with a gloved finger, the words – *"Alas, I am slain."* – echoing in the silence. This wasn't a cry of desperation, but a pronouncement, a deliberate literary flourish that spoke volumes about the killer's intellectual vanity. The phrase itself was deceptively simple, yet its origin was far from common knowledge. It wasn't a Shakespearean sonnet or a Wordsworthian lament; it was a fragment from a far more obscure corner of the literary canon.

Her research had led her down a rabbit hole of Elizabethan drama, a period known for its dramatic flair and often tragic endings. This particular quote, she discovered, hailed from a lesser-known play, a tragedy penned by a contemporary of Marlowe, a playwright whose name had long since faded into the footnotes of literary history. The play, titled "The Serpent's Coil," was a convoluted tale of betrayal, ambition, and poison, a melodrama that had never achieved the widespread acclaim of its more illustrious counterparts. That the killer had chosen this specific line, from this particular play, was no accident. It was a beacon, a breadcrumb trail left by a mind that not only possessed an intimate knowledge of literature but a specific, perhaps even fetishistic, appreciation for its more obscure corners. It suggested an individual steeped in the academic world, one who reveled in intellectual superiority, who saw themselves not just as a perpetrator but as a curator of their own grim narrative. The choice of a dramatic, archaic phrase, rather than a modern idiom, also pointed towards a killer who embraced a certain performative grandiosity, someone who wished to imbue their act with a theatrical weight.

Maria felt a familiar surge of intellectual adrenaline. This was precisely the kind of puzzle that ignited her mind, the kind where the clues were not etched in bloodstains but woven into the very fabric of language. The killer had presented a riddle, wrapped in the guise of a brutal crime, and Maria was determined to unravel it. The quote was more than just a signature; it was a key, a potential window into the killer's motivations, their education, and their psychological landscape. It was a gauntlet thrown down to anyone who dared to understand, a challenge to dissect not just the act but the mind behind it.

To that end, she had arranged a meeting. The precinct's sterile meeting room, equipped with a long, polished table and a whiteboard stained with the ghosts of past interrogations, felt like a purgatorial space, a place where the vibrant world of ideas was forced into a drab, bureaucratic mold. Across from her sat Dr. Aris Gibson, a figure who, even in the utilitarian confines of the police station, exuded an aura of learned gravitas. His tweed jacket, though slightly rumpled, and the faint scent of old paper that seemed to cling to him, were a stark contrast to the utilitarian drabness of his surroundings. Dr. Gibson was, by all accounts, the preeminent scholar of Elizabethan drama at Elmwood University, a man whose life's work was dedicated to the very texts that now held the key to a murder.

"Thank you for coming, Doctor," Maria began, her voice calm and measured, a practiced counterpoint to the tension that always accompanied such meetings. She pushed the vellum card across the table. "We found this at the scene. The victim, Clara Bellweather, was murdered on the university grounds. This quote was left beside her."

Dr. Gibson picked up the card, his brow furrowing as he read the inscription. He handled it with the same reverence he might accord an ancient manuscript, his fingers delicate as they hovered over the paper. A slow nod of recognition dawned on his face, though it was tinged with a disquiet that was more academic than emotional.

"'Alas, I am slain'," he murmured, his voice a low rumble, rich with the cadences of spoken verse. "From 'The Serpent's Coil' by Thomas Kyd, though some attribute it to a lesser-known contemporary, perhaps even a ghostwriter for Christopher Marlowe. It's... an interesting choice. Rather obscure for a casual literary allusion."

Maria leaned forward, her gaze fixed on the professor. "Obscure, perhaps, but clearly significant to the killer. What can you tell me about the play, Doctor? About its themes, its context? And why might someone choose this particular line to punctuate such a violent act?"

Dr. Gibson settled back in his chair, a thoughtful expression clouding his features. The sterile room seemed to recede as he began to weave his narrative, drawing Maria into the world of Elizabethan theatre, a world of shadows and intrigue that was eerily reminiscent of the crime itself. "'The Serpent's Coil'," he began, "is a play deeply rooted in themes of deception, revenge, and the corrupting influence of power. It's a Jacobean tragedy, you see, a period that followed the Elizabethan era and was characterized by a certain cynicism and a fascination with the darker aspects of human nature. The protagonist, a disillusioned courtier named Edmund, is driven by a burning desire for vengeance against those who have wronged him. He orchestrates a series of elaborate schemes, employing poison, manipulation, and ultimately, murder, to achieve his twisted sense of justice."

He paused, his eyes distant, as if he were watching the play unfold in his mind's eye. "The line, 'Alas, I am slain,' is spoken by Edmund himself, ironically, not by a victim of his schemes, but by Edmund as he is confronting his own mortality. It's a moment of profound, self-aware despair, a recognition of the futility of his actions even as he is consumed by them. He realizes, in his final moments, that his quest for vengeance has led him to his own destruction, that the 'serpent' he has set loose has ultimately coiled back to strike him."

Maria absorbed his words, the pieces beginning to click into place. This was not just a random quote; it was a complex, multi-layered statement. "So, the killer identifies with the murderer, with Edmund, rather than the victim?" she asked, her mind racing.

"Potentially," Dr. Gibson confirmed. "Or, they might be using the quote as a form of ironic commentary. Perhaps they see Clara

Bellweather's death as a form of deserved retribution, a self-inflicted wound upon the university itself, and they are lamenting the 'slaying' of the system, or the academic purity, that she represented. Or, and this is perhaps the most disturbing possibility, they see themselves as a victim, a martyr in their own right, enacting a necessary, albeit tragic, act of 'slaying' for a greater cause, and in their own demise, they will lament their own undoing."

The implications sent a shiver down Maria's spine. The killer wasn't just intelligent; they were deeply philosophical, albeit in a profoundly twisted way. They saw themselves as a figure of tragic destiny, capable of both enacting great harm and lamenting its inevitable consequences. This wasn't the work of a spontaneous act of violence; it was premeditated, calculated, and imbued with a sense of self-importance that bordered on megalomania. The sterile environment of the precinct suddenly felt suffocating, a stark contrast to the rich, textual world Dr. Gibson had conjured, a world of ancient motives and enduring human failings.

"The play's themes," Maria pressed, "revenge, corruption, the dark side of human nature... do any of these resonate particularly with the academic environment at Elmwood?"

Dr. Gibson's gaze drifted towards the reinforced window, his expression unreadable. "Elmwood, like any institution of higher learning, is a complex ecosystem," he said slowly. "Beneath the veneer of intellectual pursuit, there are currents of ambition, rivalry, and often, profound disappointment. Ideas can become weapons. Careers can be forged or broken by a single review, a well-placed critique, or the perceived plagiarism of a rival. The pursuit of knowledge, while noble, can also be a battlefield."

He turned back to Maria, his eyes holding a deep, unsettling understanding. "'The Serpent's Coil'," he continued, his voice dropping slightly, "is also a play that explores the corrupting nature of secrets. Edmund's schemes are fueled by hidden knowledge, by the secrets he uncovers and the ones he himself perpetrates. He believes he is orchestrating the downfall of others, but in doing so, he is unraveling his own moral fabric."

Maria felt a chill that had nothing to do with the office's air conditioning. The parallels were too striking to ignore. Clara Bellweather's death was not an isolated incident, but a symptom. The killer was not just targeting an individual; they were targeting a system, or perhaps, a specific set of perceived injustices within it. "Are there any particular academic disputes or rivalries at Elmwood that might align with the themes of this play?" she asked, her voice barely a whisper.

Dr. Gibson hesitated, then shook his head. "It would be unprofessional of me to speculate on the personal lives or professional conflicts of my colleagues or students. My expertise lies in the texts themselves, in their interpretation and their historical context. However," he added, a flicker of something akin to concern in his eyes, "I can tell you that the choice of 'The Serpent's Coil' suggests a killer who is not only well-read but who also sees themselves as an agent of retribution. They are likely intelligent, methodical, and possess a strong sense of moral justification, however warped. They are not acting out of impulse; they are enacting a narrative."

The sterile meeting room, with its bland walls and functional furniture, suddenly felt like a stage. Maria was playing her part, the determined detective, while Dr. Gibson, the erudite scholar, was providing the exposition, illuminating the darker, more complex layers of the unfolding drama. He was offering her a glimpse into the mind of the killer, a mind that was steeped in the tragedies of the past and was now, disturbingly, re-enacting them in the present. The vellum card, once a mere object, now felt like a portal, a testament to a mind that found elegance in death and pronouncements in poetry. The echo of Elizabethan tragedy had, it seemed, found its way into the hallowed halls of Elmwood, and Maria knew, with a certainty that both thrilled and terrified her, that the investigation had only just begun to peel back the layers of this meticulously crafted literary murder. The play was on, and she was compelled to see it through to its bitter end, even if the final act involved confronting a darkness that had been brewing within the very heart of academia.

Maria found herself not just in the sterile confines of her office anymore, but navigating a labyrinth of scholarly research, the scent of aging paper now a constant companion to the metallic tang of the precinct. Clara Bellweather, the victim, had been more than just a name on a file; she had been a scholar, a mind consumed by a particular brand of tragic narrative. Her thesis, Maria discovered, was a deep dive into the archetypes of suffering women in Shakespeare's canon, a subject that now seemed eerily prescient. The preliminary reports from the forensic team, meticulously detailed and clinically detached, painted a picture that sent an unwelcome tremor of recognition through Maria's analytical mind. The discovery of Clara's body in the university's botanical garden, near the ornamental pond, was itself a detail that resonated with a specific Shakespearean tragedy. The initial findings mentioned fragments of flowers clutched in Clara's hand, remnants of what the botanists tentatively identified as lilies and rosemary – flora often associated with mourning, remembrance, and, in Clara's case, perhaps a desperate, final grasp at beauty or innocence.

The forensic pathologist had noted signs of drowning, but the precise circumstances remained obscured by the garden's natural elements. However, the detail that truly seized Maria's attention was the description of Clara's clothing, a delicate, almost ethereal dress, damp and clinging, suggesting she had been immersed in water. It wasn't the brutal, overt violence of a stabbing or a gunshot; it was a death that hinted at a more insidious, almost passive surrender, or at least, an appearance of it. Maria found herself comparing the scant details to the iconic scene of Ophelia's demise. Shakespeare's Ophelia, driven mad by grief and betrayal, had met her end in a brook, her floral crown floating on the water as she, too, was engulfed by the aquatic element. The imagery, though circumstantial, was potent. Were the flowers a deliberate staging, a macabre floral arrangement by the killer, or a genuine, albeit tragic, detail from Clara's own final moments? The ambiguity was precisely the kind of intellectual trap the killer seemed to be setting.

Maria requested the complete thesis proposal from Clara's academic advisor, Dr. Allen Fry, a renowned Shakespearean scholar who had initially expressed his profound grief over Clara's death. Fry, a man whose public persona was one of gentle erudition, now seemed to carry the weight of something more profound, a veiled discomfort that Maria couldn't quite decipher. His office, a veritable shrine to the Bard, was crammed with leather-bound volumes, antique busts of Shakespeare, and framed playbills from centuries past. Maria felt as if she had stepped into a meticulously curated museum, each artifact whispering tales of tragedy and genius.

"Clara was... exceptional," Dr. Fry began, his voice heavy with emotion, but also with a certain academic detachment. He gestured vaguely towards a stack of papers on his desk. "Her focus on the 'suffering heroines' was particularly insightful. She explored how societal expectations, patriarchal structures, and the very nature of their circumstances often dictated their tragic fates. Ophelia, of course, was a central figure in her analysis. Clara argued that Ophelia's madness was not merely a consequence of Hamlet's rejection, but a profound, almost existential, breakdown brought about by the erosion of her identity and agency within a patriarchal court."

He picked up a worn copy of *Hamlet*, its pages brittle with age. "She believed Ophelia's death, while presented as accidental or suicidal, was a more complex statement. Clara posited that the drowning was, in a sense, a return to a primal state, a release from the suffocating constraints of her world, an ultimate reclamation of her own being, however tragically. The flowers, in her interpretation, were not just decorative elements; they were symbolic of her fleeting beauty and innocence, of the pastoral ideal that was brutally shattered by the harsh realities of Elsinore."

Maria listened intently, her mind racing, connecting Fry's words to the crime scene details. The lilies, representing purity and sorrow, and the rosemary, for remembrance, were indeed prominent in depictions of Ophelia's death. Had the killer, in their warped interpretation of literary tragedy, sought to recreate this scene? And if so, was Clara Bellweather the Ophelia, or was the killer casting *themselves* in a more active, perhaps even vengeful, role? The thesis itself was becoming a crucial piece of the puzzle, a window into the mind that had conceived of Clara's death, a mind that was clearly steeped in the very tragedies it was now so meticulously, and disturbingly, emulating.

"Did Clara express any particular anxieties or concerns about her research?" Maria asked, pushing the envelope. "Any sense that she felt... endangered by the subject matter?"

Dr. Fry hesitated, his gaze shifting to a framed portrait of Shakespeare hanging above his fireplace. The silence stretched, punctuated only by the soft ticking of a grandfather clock in the corner. "Clara was deeply immersed in her work," he finally replied, choosing his words with careful deliberation. "She was brilliant, fiercely dedicated. Sometimes, that level of immersion can lead to... an over-identification with the material. She would often speak about the psychological toll of exploring such dark themes. She felt a profound empathy for these women, a yearning to understand their pain on a visceral level."

He looked back at Maria, a troubled expression clouding his features. "There were moments, I confess, when I felt concerned about the intensity of her focus. She spoke of how the academic world, for all its intellectual pursuits, could also be a place of intense emotional friction. Rivalries, perceived slights, the crushing weight of expectation... these can take their toll. But I never imagined... never for a moment... that it would lead to anything like this."

Maria pressed further. "The choice of *Hamlet*, and Ophelia specifically, is significant. Were there any particular academic disputes or controversies surrounding Clara's thesis, or her work in general, that might connect to the play's themes of betrayal, madness, or familial discord?"

Dr. Fry sighed, running a hand through his already disheveled hair. "The academic landscape can be... competitive, Detective. Clara's work was groundbreaking, innovative. Naturally, it garnered attention, both positive and negative. There were those who lauded her fresh perspective, and others who felt her interpretations challenged established orthodoxies. But 'betrayal'? 'Discord'? These are strong words. While academic debates can be heated, they rarely descend into such... visceral territory." He paused, then added, his voice lower, "However, Clara did have a... significant disagreement with Professor Sterling in the Classics department. Their fields, while distinct, overlapped in certain areas of classical mythology and its influence on later literature. He publicly criticized her methodology, her theoretical framework. It was quite... acrimonious."

Professor Sterling. Maria made a mental note. Another name to add to the burgeoning list of potential connections. The mention of academic rivalry, particularly when framed by the violent themes of *Hamlet*, was too significant to ignore. The killer, it seemed, was not just performing Shakespeare; they were orchestrating a narrative that mirrored the play's core conflicts, using Clara's own academic focus as a morbid blueprint.

Maria left Dr. Fry's office with a growing sense of unease. The polished disguise of academia was beginning to crack, revealing the darker currents that flowed beneath. Clara Bellweather's thesis on tragic heroines, particularly Ophelia, was no longer just a research project; it was a prophecy, a chilling premonition that had been tragically fulfilled. The flowers, the pond, the very act of drowning

– it all pointed towards a deliberate, calculated emulation of Shakespearean tragedy. The killer wasn't just leaving clues; they were weaving a narrative, casting themselves as a director in a gruesome play, with Clara Bellweather as their unwilling, and ultimately, deceased, protagonist.

Back in her office, the sterile environment seemed to amplify the weight of the literary references. Maria spread out photographs from the crime scene, the forensic reports, and Clara's thesis proposal. The images of the lilies and rosemary, so innocent in their botanical classification, now seemed imbued with a sinister significance. She began cross-referencing the flora with Elizabethan symbolism, and specifically with descriptions of Ophelia's funeral in *Hamlet*. The play mentioned rosemary for remembrance, and pansies for thoughts, but also fennel and columbines, symbols of flattery and infidelity. Violets, representing faithfulness, had "withered all when my father died." The connection wasn't a perfect match to the flowers found at the scene, but the *intent* was unmistakable. The killer was playing a game, using literary symbolism as their weapon, their signature, their very modus operandi.

Maria then delved deeper into Clara's research materials. She found annotated copies of *Hamlet*, marked with Clara's incisive observations. One passage, detailing Ophelia's mad scene, was heavily underlined: "There's rosemary, that's for remembrance; pray, love, remember. And there are pansies. That's for thoughts." Clara had scrawled in the margin: "Ophelia's fragmented thoughts mirror the fractured identity of women in patriarchal societies. Her drowning is an escape, a return to a more fluid, less defined existence." Another note, besides the description of her burial:

"The flowers, not as symbols of mourning for others, but as manifestations of her own inner landscape, her last coherent expression before dissolution."

The killer, Maria theorized, was not simply replicating Ophelia's death. They were reinterpreting it, perhaps even perverting it, through the lens of Clara's own thesis. If Clara saw Ophelia's drowning as a form of liberation, a tragic reclamation of self, then perhaps the killer saw Clara's death as a similar, albeit violently imposed, act. They were forcing Clara into the role of Ophelia, using her own academic interpretations as justification for her murder. This was a killer who not only understood literature but was actively engaging with it, manipulating it to serve their own dark purposes. The intellectual vanity that Maria had sensed from the initial quote was becoming increasingly evident.

The investigation now required a nuanced understanding of literary theory, a dive into the very texts that the killer was using as their script. Maria requested access to the university's extensive library archives, specifically the rare books collection, where Clara had apparently spent a significant amount of her research time. She needed to understand the specific editions Clara was consulting, the marginalia she had left, and any potential interactions she might have had with other scholars who shared her interests, or perhaps, her rivalries. The quad, once just a picturesque university setting, now felt like a stage set for a tragedy, each tree, each bench, each academic building holding the potential for hidden secrets and dark motives. The echoes of *Hamlet*, once confined to the hallowed halls of literature, were now reverberating through the very fabric of Elmwood University, and Maria was determined to decipher the killer's final act before the curtain fell.

The killer's gloved hand, it was theorized, meticulously placed the folded parchment beside Clara Bellweather's cooling form, a final, macabre flourish to a performance already concluded. This wasn't the impulsive act of a frenzied assailant; it was the deliberate signature of a perpetrator with a profound, and deeply disturbing, artistic vision. Maria, hunched over the initial crime scene photographs, felt a prickle of unease crawl up her spine. The paper, stark white against the damp, dark earth of the botanical garden, bore no fingerprints. Forensic analysis would be a painstaking process of elimination, a search for microscopic fibers, a trace of skin cells, anything that could betray the unseen hand. But the true enigma lay not in its physical absence, but in its textual presence.

The words themselves were a carefully chosen sonnet, a piece of verse that whispered of lost innocence and the cruelties of fate. It spoke of lilies wilting under a poisoned sun, of rosemary's scent growing bitter with remembrance, and of a brook that embraced a soul too pure for a corrupt world. The language was archaic, ornate, imbued with a melancholic beauty that was chillingly out of place in the stark reality of a murder investigation. Maria, armed with a degree in literature before she ever considered the badge, recognized the echoes of Elizabethan verse, the rhythmic cadence of a bygone era. This was no amateur scribbling; this was the product of a mind that had not only studied the classics but had internalized them, allowing them to fester and mutate into something monstrous.

The accompanying note, scribbled in a different, more urgent hand, was even more cryptic: "The scholar sought wisdom in sorrow, but found only its final, aqueous embrace. Her thesis, her undoing." It was a pronouncement; a judgment delivered with the cold finality of a divine decree. The killer wasn't merely a murderer; they were a self-appointed critic, a curator of tragedy, and Clara Bellweather was their latest exhibit. Maria felt a surge of frustration. This wasn't just about finding a killer; it was about deciphering a narrative, about understanding the twisted logic that drove this individual to stage their crimes with such theatrical precision. Each poem, each quote, was a breadcrumb, a taunt, an invitation to a deadly intellectual game.

"He's playing with us," Maria muttered to herself, her gaze fixed on the digital reproduction of the poem. "He wants us to see his genius, his literary prowess. He's not just killing; *he's writing*." The thought was both terrifying and strangely exhilarating. It meant the killer was predictable, in a perverse sort of way. If he was using literature as his script, then understanding the script was the key to understanding the author.

She requested copies of all literary works found in Clara's apartment, her thesis notes, and any research materials related to her studies. She wanted to immerse herself in Clara's world, to understand the texts that had so profoundly influenced her, and, it now seemed, her killer. The preliminary reports had hinted at a broader literary interest, but Maria suspected the killer's focus was far more specific. The Shakespearean connection was undeniable, but was it the only wellspring from which this disturbed intellect drew?

The forensic team was meticulously sifting through Clara's digital footprint, searching for any online literary forums, academic discussions, or private correspondence that might shed light on her interactions with potential suspects. But Maria had a hunch that the killer's methods were decidedly old-fashioned, eschewing the digital for the tangible, the permanent. The handwritten poem, the carefully chosen verse – these were the hallmarks of someone who valued the enduring power of the written word, someone who saw themselves as a modern-day bard, albeit one whose muse was death.

Maria contacted Dr. Fry again, her questions now more pointed. "Professor Fry, you mentioned Clara's intense focus on the 'suffering heroines.' Were there any particular poems or poetic works that she frequently referenced in relation to these figures, beyond Shakespeare?"

Dr. Fry, his voice still tinged with a professional sorrow, paused. "Clara was fascinated by the Romantic poets as well. She found a particular resonance in their explorations of intense emotion, of love and loss, of the sublime and the terrifying. Keats, Shelley, Byron – she admired their ability to capture the raw, untamed aspects of the human psyche. She often drew parallels between the passionate despair of their poetic voices and the plight of the tragic figures in drama."

"Did she ever express a particular affinity for any specific poems by these authors?" Maria pressed, her mind racing. The Romantic era was a fertile ground for themes of overwhelming emotion, of beauty intertwined with decay, of the individual battling against societal constraints. It was a thematic landscape that could easily be twisted by a disordered mind.

"There was one poem," Fry recalled, after a moment of reflection. "'Ode to a Nightingale' by Keats. She found the speaker's longing for oblivion, for escape from the 'weariness, the fever, and the fret' of human existence, deeply compelling. She spoke of the poem's exquisite melancholy, its ability to evoke a sense of both profound beauty and profound sadness. She even compared the nightingale's song to a form of eternal, unchanging beauty, a stark contrast to the ephemeral nature of human life and suffering."

Maria felt a chill trace its way down her spine. 'Ode to a Nightingale.' The imagery of escape, of a world beyond human pain, of a beautiful, melancholic trance. It was a poem that spoke to a yearning for transcendence, a desire to shed the burdens of mortality. And the killer, it seemed, was providing a tragically literal interpretation of that yearning. The idea of a killer meticulously crafting poems to fit their victims, weaving a narrative tapestry of death, was beginning to solidify in Maria's mind.

She requested a copy of Keats' poems, specifically focusing on 'Ode to a Nightingale.' The poem was a cascade of evocative imagery: the drowsiness, the opiate dream, the yearning to be "a sodden with the dew." The speaker's desire to "fade away into the forest dim" felt chillingly prescient. Maria imagined the killer, surrounded by stacks of books, poring over these verses, searching for the perfect lines to encapsulate their next victim, their next act of performative violence.

The investigation now felt like an archeological dig, each layer of evidence revealing more about the killer's complex motivations. They weren't just driven by rage or greed. This was something far more intellectual, more deliberate. The poems were not mere postscripts; they were the very essence of the killer's modus operandi, the twisted manifesto of a literary murderer.

Maria then turned her attention to one of Clara's thesis committee members and academic advisor, Dr. Billy Yale. Maria's initial interactions had been marked by his evident grief, but Maria now sensed an undercurrent of something else, something he was perhaps reluctant to share.

"Thank you for meeting me on such short notice Dr. Yale," Maria began, her tone measured, "I want to get right down to the point." Maria began watching for any change in his demeanor. "Clara's work on Ophelia was particularly detailed. Did she have any theories about Ophelia's death that deviated significantly from established scholarship? Any interpretations that might be... controversial?"

Dr. Yale hesitated, his gaze drifting to a framed painting of Shakespeare on his wall. "Clara believed that Ophelia's drowning was not simply an act of despair, but a symbolic act of defiance. She argued that in a patriarchal society that stripped women of their agency, Ophelia's final act was a desperate, and perhaps subconscious, attempt to reclaim her own narrative, to dissolve into a realm where she could no longer be defined or controlled by men. She saw it as a tragic, but ultimately powerful, assertion of self."

"An assertion of self through dissolution?" Maria mused, the words echoing in her mind. "So, in Clara's interpretation, Ophelia's death was almost a form of liberation?"

"In a highly metaphorical sense, yes," Yale conceded, his brow furrowed. "She believed Ophelia, in her madness, found a fleeting moment of true freedom from the suffocating expectations of the court. Her drowning, in Clara's thesis, was a return to nature, to a primal state of being, free from the constraints of identity and societal roles. It was a radical interpretation, certainly. Some of her peers found it overly sympathetic, almost romanticizing the tragedy."

The implication hung heavily in the air. If Clara saw Ophelia's death as a form of liberation, a reclamation of self through a return to a more fluid, less defined existence, then what did that mean for her own death? Had the killer, in their twisted emulation, sought to grant Clara this very liberation? Had they perceived her death not as an ending, but as a form of tragic transcendence, a final, albeit violent, apotheosis? The poetry, Maria realized, was not just a signature; it was a justification, a theological underpinning for their horrific actions. The killer saw themselves as a facilitator, a divine hand guiding the victim towards her predetermined, literary fates.

"And this interpretation," Maria pressed, "did it cause any particular friction within the academic community?"

Yale sighed, a sound heavy with unspoken anxieties. "There was one, a Professor Sterling found her work... problematic. He felt she was projecting modern feminist ideals onto a historical figure, distorting the original intent of the play. He argued that her interpretation softened the tragedy, that it undermined the stark reality of Ophelia's mental breakdown and its tragic consequences. Their exchanges were, to put it mildly, impassioned. Sterling viewed Clara's thesis as a dangerous example of academic revisionism."

Professor Sterling. The name was a recurring motif, a discordant note in the otherwise carefully composed symphony of Clara's academic life. Maria filed it away, a potential key to unlocking the killer's identity. The venom in Yale's description of

Sterling's reaction suggested a deep-seated animosity, a professional rivalry that might have festered into something far more sinister.

The killer's modus operandi was becoming clearer with each passing hour. They were not simply selecting victims at random, but were carefully curating a gallery of characters, each embodying a specific aspect of literary tragedy. Clara, the scholar of suffering heroines, was now Ophelia. Her death, staged with poetic flourish, was not an act of random violence, but a deliberate re-enactment, a horrifying performance art piece. The poems left at the scene were not just clues; they were the killer's dramatic monologues, their pronouncements to the world, a testament to their perceived intellectual and artistic superiority. They were weaving a narrative, each victim a character carefully placed within a grander, darker drama, and Maria was beginning to suspect that the killer saw themselves as the ultimate author, the director, the god of this unfolding tragedy. The university, with its hallowed halls and intellectual pursuits, had become a stage, and the killer was its most chilling playwright. The weight of this realization settled upon Maria, a heavy cloak of foreboding. She was not just investigating a murder; she was unraveling a meticulously crafted literary masterpiece, written in blood.

The notion that Clara Bellweather was merely a random victim, a casualty of circumstance, began to fray at the edges of Maria's professional certainty. It was too neat, too... theatrical. The poem, the note, the very stillness of Clara's pose in that damp, verdant grotto – it all screamed intent. This wasn't the messy aftermath of a crime of passion or a desperate act of robbery gone awry. This was a meticulously curated tableau, a scene set with deliberate precision, each element a brushstroke in a macabre masterpiece. Maria found herself returning to the initial crime scene photos, not just for the forensic minutiae, but for the narrative they implied. Clara, the scholar, the one who found liberation in dissolution, had been granted her wish in the most brutal, literal fashion. The killer, in their warped understanding, had provided the ultimate escape, the final, aqueous embrace.

This realization shifted the investigation's trajectory. Maria wasn't just hunting a killer; she was attempting to decipher an elaborate literary allegory. Clara Bellweather, the victim, was not an isolated incident but a character in a burgeoning, horrifying saga. The killer wasn't just taking a life; he or she were casting roles, selecting individuals who, in their twisted logic, embodied specific literary archetypes. It was a chilling prospect, one that sent a cold dread seeping into Maria's bones. If Clara was Ophelia, then who would be next? What tragic heroine was waiting in the wings of this deranged playwright's imagination? The thought was overwhelming, a vast, dark canvas of potential victims unfolding before her.

She began to sketch out a terrifying hypothesis, a framework for understanding the killer's selection process. The focus on "suffering heroines" that Professor Fry and Yale had mentioned, combined with Clara's own academic predilections, suggested a pattern rooted in literary tragedy. Maria started a new document, a private ledger of anxieties and deductions. She began by listing Clara's archetype: the tragic scholar, the one who sought meaning in the sorrow of fictional characters, ultimately becoming one herself. The reference to Ophelia, particularly Clara's radical interpretation of her death as a form of defiance and liberation, was a powerful indicator. The killer hadn't just chosen Clara for her passion for literature, but for the specific lens through which she viewed it, a lens that mirrored their own dark fascination with tragic finales.

Beyond Ophelia, Maria's mind raced through the pantheon of literary figures, the women who had captivated Clara and, by extension, her killer. There was Antigone, the defiant rebel against unjust laws, whose conviction led to her own demise. Could a victim embodying such steadfast, unwavering principle be next? Then there was Medea, consumed by vengeance, her passionate love curdled into a destructive fury. The killer might see such a victim as a twisted mirror, a reflection of their own destructive impulses. Or perhaps the doomed lovers, like Juliet or Hero, whose fates were sealed by circumstance and the interference of others. The Romantic poets, a particular obsession of Clara's, offered a rich vein of melancholic yearning and idealized, yet often tragic, love. Keats' Isabella, mourning her lover and his severed head, or Shelley's tragic figures, consumed by unattainable desires and societal pressures. Each archetype represented a potential target, a preordained role in the killer's grim theatrical production.

Maria felt a growing sense of urgency, a desperate need to understand the killer's aesthetic. They were clearly educated, possessing a deep knowledge of literature and a flair for the dramatic. The choice of a sonnet for Clara, with its formal constraints and its rich history in expressing complex emotions, spoke volumes. It wasn't just a message; it was a statement of artistic intent, a demonstration of control and sophistication. The killer was not a brute; they were an artist, albeit one whose medium was death. The carefully chosen words, the reference to a "final, aqueous embrace," all pointed to a mind that savored symbolism, that saw death not as an end, but as a profound, tragic statement.

She replayed her conversation with Dr. Fry and Yale in her mind, dissecting every word. Their description of Clara's interpretation of Ophelia's drowning as a return to nature, a primal state of being free from the constraints of identity and societal roles, resonated with the killer's actions. It was as if the killer had taken Clara's academic thesis and performed it, violently, literally. They had granted her the ultimate return to nature, the final dissolution, and in doing so, had asserted their own perceived mastery over life and death, over narrative and meaning. The killer wasn't just an executioner; they were a re-writer, a dark god imposing their own tragic ending onto the lives of others.

The concept of Professor Sterling, the academic rival, continued to linger in Maria's thoughts. Fry and Yale's portrayal of Sterling's outrage at Clara's "feminist" interpretation of Ophelia painted a picture of a man deeply invested in traditional readings of literature, someone who saw Clara's work as an affront to the established canon. Could this professional animosity have escalated into something far more sinister? Was it possible that Sterling saw Clara's interpretation not just as academic error, but as a personal attack on his own intellectual integrity? The idea of a deeply held literary disagreement morphing into murderous obsession was not entirely outside the realm of possibility, especially for someone described as having *impassioned* exchanges with Clara. Maria decided to delve deeper into Sterling's background, to examine his academic history, his publications, and any documented interactions he might have had with Clara beyond Fry and Yale's account.

The methodical nature of the crime scene, the absence of forced entry, the placement of the poem – all suggested a killer who was known to the victim, or at least had access to Clara's world without raising suspicion. This pointed away from a random act of violence and towards a more personal, albeit twisted, connection. The killer was an insider, someone who understood Clara's intellectual landscape, her passions, and perhaps even her vulnerabilities. They had moved within her orbit, observing, dissecting, and ultimately, choosing her as their next muse.

Maria's gaze drifted to a collection of classic novels on her desk, dog-eared copies of works that had seemed to shape Clara's understanding of the world. Maria thought Clara would have imagined Elizabeth Bennet's wit, of Jane Eyre's quiet strength, of Hester Prynne's resilience in the face of ostracism. These were women who, in their own ways, had navigated complex societal expectations and personal tragedies. The killer's selection process was proving to be not just about tragedy, but about the very essence of female resilience, defiance, and the inevitable consequences of societal pressures. It was a commentary on the female experience, filtered through the distorted lens of a literary admirer.

The sheer intellectual arrogance of the killer was becoming increasingly apparent. It was not about just committing murder; it was about creating an exhibition, a curated collection of tragic lives. The victim was a carefully selected artifact, imbued with a specific literary significance. Clara, the scholar, was the first piece in this ghastly gallery. Her death was not just an end, but a statement, a demonstration of the killer's profound understanding of literary tropes and their willingness to enact them in the most visceral way possible. The very act of leaving the poem, a piece of art in itself, was a taunt, an invitation to an intellectual duel. The killer wanted to be recognized, admired even, for their intellectual prowess, their ability to weave life and death into a grand, tragic narrative.

Maria felt a profound sense of isolation, a loneliness that stemmed from the unique nature of this investigation. She was not just dealing with a murderer; she was dealing with a dark artist, a self-proclaimed literary critic who used flesh and blood as their medium. The pressure to understand the killer's literary vocabulary, to anticipate their next move, was immense. It was a race against time, not just to prevent further bloodshed, but to unravel a narrative that was unfolding with terrifying speed and precision. The literary world, which Maria had always seen as a source of solace and intellectual stimulation, now felt tainted, a breeding ground for a darkness she had never imagined. The beauty of the verses, the elegance of the sonnet, were now irrevocably linked to the horror of Clara's demise, a chilling reminder that even the most refined artistic expression could be twisted into a tool of destruction.

She began to conceptualize the killer's mind as a vast, dark library, each shelf lined with the tragedies of human history and literature. They were a curator of despair, a collector of broken souls. Clara's death was a carefully selected exhibit, one that spoke to themes of intellectual pursuit, tragic irony, and the search for liberation through oblivion. The killer's motive, Maria suspected, was not rooted in any traditional sense of grieving, but in a deeply ingrained, perhaps pathological, need to manifest literary narratives in the real world. They saw themselves as an agent of fate, a divine hand orchestrating the final acts of these chosen characters.

The implications were staggering. If the killer was selecting victims based on literary archetypes, then the pool of potential targets was not random, but deeply symbolic. The killer would be looking for women who embodied certain qualities, certain narratives. Was it possible that the killer had a list, a mental rolodex of literary heroines they intended to bring to life? This thought was a cold knot in Maria's stomach. The weight of this realization settled upon her, a heavy cloak of foreboding. She was not just investigating a murder; she was unraveling a meticulously crafted literary masterpiece, written in blood, and she had to find a way to stop the author before the final, tragic act. The university, once a sanctuary of knowledge and enlightenment, had become the stage for a dark, literary drama, and Maria was now an unwilling participant, tasked with deciphering the script before the final curtain fell. The careful composition of Clara's death, the symbolic resonance of her chosen demise, hinted at a deeper, more disturbing motivation than simple malice. It was an intellectual statement, a profound manipulation of narrative, and Maria was determined to understand it, to dissect it, and ultimately, to bring the author of this tragedy to justice.

The sterile scent of disinfectant did little to mask the underlying metallic tang that clung to the air in the precinct's evidence room. Maria ran a gloved finger over a photograph of Clara Bellweather, her gaze fixed on the victim's placid expression, so at odds with the violent finality of her end. The initial report, a dry recitation of facts and forensic findings, felt woefully inadequate. It was an autopsy of a crime, devoid of soul, of motive, of the chilling intellect that had orchestrated such a macabre tableau. Maria craved something more, a deeper understanding that transcended the tangible evidence, something that spoke to the very essence of the human psyche, both the victim's and the perpetrator's.

It was this yearning that had led her to Dr. Aris Gibson. He wasn't a detective, not in the traditional sense. Gibson was a tenured professor of comparative literature, a man whose life was steeped in the hushed reverence of ancient texts and the labyrinthine corridors of academic discourse. Yet, Fry and Yale had spoken of him, a quiet intellectual with an unsettling grasp on the darker currents of human experience, someone who understood the allure and the terror of tragedy not as an abstract concept, but as a potent, driving force. Maria had hesitated. Engaging an academic in a murder investigation felt akin to consulting a cartographer for directions in a war zone. But Clara's death, so steeped in literary allusion, demanded an unconventional approach.

When Gibson arrived, he did so not with the swagger of a hardened investigator, but with the quiet, almost apologetic grace of a scholar forced to leave his ivory tower. He was a man of slight build, and just like their first meeting, his tweed jacket was more of a testament to a life spent more in libraries than on the streets. His spectacles, perched on the bridge of his nose, magnified eyes that held a disconcerting blend of intellectual curiosity and a profound, almost weary, understanding of human folly. He spoke in measured tones, his voice a soft murmur that seemed to absorb the surrounding cacophony of the precinct, leaving a pocket of quiet contemplation in its wake.

"Detective, I hope your investigation is going somewhere?" He began, offering a tentative nod, "After you spoke with Professor

Fry, he contacted me and mentioned your interest in... certain thematic elements." He gestured vaguely towards the collection of crime scene photographs spread across the table. "This is truly a tragedy." He paused adjusting his glasses. "A doctoral student with promise, her life extinguished as it seems, of a particularly... literary bent."

Maria met his gaze, searching for any flicker of unease, any hint of revulsion. She found only a calm, analytical curiosity. "Professor Gibson, thank you for coming in on such short notice." Gibson nodded and Maria began. "Here is what we know. Clara Bellweather was murdered. Her death was staged, a deliberate performance. As you know, the killer left a poem, a sonnet, at the scene. Whoever it was clearly had a deep understanding of literature, and I believe they are selecting victims based on literary archetypes." She paused, allowing the weight of her words to settle. "Professor Fry suggested you might offer some perspective on the philosophical underpinnings of literary tragedy."

Gibson picked up a photograph of Clara, her lifeless eyes staring into the distance. He turned it over, as if expecting to find a hidden inscription. "Tragedy," he mused, his voice barely audible, "is as old as civilization itself. From the ancient Greeks, wrestling with the inevitability of fate and the hubris of man, to the Renaissance masters exploring the complexities of human nature and the destructive power of passion. It is a genre that forces us to confront our mortality, our limitations, and the often brutal arbitrariness of existence."

He looked up, his eyes meeting Maria's. "Authors, for centuries, have used tragedy as a lens through which to examine the human condition. They create characters who are often noble, flawed, and ultimately, brought low by forces beyond their control – be it a cruel twist of fate, a character flaw, or the machinations of others. These narratives, Detective, are not merely stories; they are explorations of our deepest fears and anxieties. They offer catharsis, yes, but they also serve as a chilling testament to the fragility of life, the ever-present shadow of death."

He returned his attention to the photographs, his fingers tracing the outline of the grotto where Clara had been found. "The deliberate placement of the victim, the inclusion of the poem... this suggests a perpetrator who views their actions not as a crime, but as a creative act. They are not simply killing; they are orchestrating a narrative, imbuing their victim with a specific symbolic meaning."

"Exactly," Maria interjected, leaning forward. "Clara's academic work focused on reinterpreting tragic heroines, particularly Ophelia. She saw Ophelia's death not as a descent into madness, but as a liberation, a return to a primal state, free from the constraints of societal expectations and personal identity. The killer seems to have taken that interpretation and enacted it, violently."

Gibson nodded slowly, a thoughtful frown creasing his brow. "The concept of liberation through dissolution is a recurring theme in certain philosophical and literary traditions. The idea that true freedom lies in shedding the self, in returning to a state of pure being, unburdened by consciousness or the pressures of the world. Take Ophelia for instance, this meant drowning, a return to the embrace of nature. It's a romanticized notion, of course, and one that, in the hands of a disturbed individual, can lead to horrific acts. The killer, in this instance, appears to be acting as a dark interpreter, a literalist who seizes upon the symbolic and imposes it upon reality."

He picked up the sonnet; his brow furrowed in concentration as he read the carefully penned verses. "This form," he continued, his voice a low hum, "the sonnet, is a vessel of immense expressive power. It demands concision, elegance, and a profound understanding of language. To use it in this context is not merely a flourish; it is a statement of control, of intellectual superiority. The killer is not just leaving a message; they are demonstrating their mastery over form, over language, over the very narrative they are constructing."

Maria felt a jolt of recognition. This was precisely what she had suspected – the killer's intellectual arrogance, their desire to be understood, perhaps even admired, for their macabre artistry. "They see themselves as an artist, Professor. A playwright, perhaps, and Clara is their first tragic heroine."

Gibson's gaze was distant, as if peering into a landscape only he could see. "The literary canon is replete with women whose lives are defined by suffering, by injustice, by a tragic destiny. From Antigone, defying tyrannical law, to Hester Prynne, bearing the mark of societal condemnation. These figures represent not just individual struggles, but universal themes. A perpetrator fixated on these archetypes might see themselves as an agent of some grand, tragic design, selecting individuals who, in their eyes, embody these fated roles."

He paused, then added, "The philosophical underpinnings of tragedy often touch upon determinism versus free will. Is the character's fate sealed from the outset, or do their choices lead them to their downfall? Your killer seems to believe in a form of artistic determinism. They are not merely reacting; they are fulfilling a preordained script, casting individuals into roles they believe are pre-written for them. It's a dangerous permutation of literary theory, Detective, one that removes agency and culpability, replacing it with a twisted sense of cosmic justice."

Maria nodded, the weight of his words settling heavily upon her. Gibson's calm, almost dispassionate analysis was more unnerving than any outburst of fear or anger. He spoke of tragedy as a subject of academic study, yet his eyes held the grim understanding of its real-world manifestation. "Professor Fry mentioned your discussions with Clara about Professor Sterling, her academic rival. He described Sterling as someone who vehemently disagrees with Clara's interpretations, particularly her feminist readings of classic texts."

Gibson's expression remained placid, but a subtle shift in his posture suggested a deeper consideration of this information. "Professor Sterling," he said, his voice regaining its academic cadence, "is a man deeply invested in the established order of literary interpretation. He views Clara's work, and indeed much of contemporary literary criticism, as a dilution of the classics, a misinterpretation driven by what he perceives as modern, often ideological, agendas. He believes in the inherent meaning of a text, as intended by the author, and sees attempts to 're-read' or 're-contextualize' these works as a form of intellectual vandalism."

He sighed, a barely perceptible sound. "Clara's re-interpretation of Ophelia, for instance, as a figure of agency and liberation, would have been anathema to Sterling. He sees Ophelia as a pitiable victim, consumed by her love and driven mad by grief – a traditionalist interpretation. He views her death as a tragic consequence of male betrayal and societal pressures, a narrative that reinforces his belief in the inherent vulnerabilities of women in a patriarchal society. Clara, on the other hand, saw a defiance in Ophelia's embrace of dissolution, a radical act of self-determination in the face of an unbearable reality."

"So, Sterling might have viewed Clara's work as a personal attack on his intellectual integrity?" Maria pressed, the pieces beginning to click into place with a chilling precision.

"It is not beyond the realm of possibility," Gibson conceded. "Intellectual disagreements can, in some individuals, take on a deeply personal and even fanatical dimension. Professor Sterling is known for his rather... impassioned defenses of his academic positions. He has, on occasion, engaged in rather heated exchanges with colleagues he believes are misrepresenting or disrespecting the literary canon. Clara, with her sharp intellect and her provocative interpretations, was a frequent target of his criticism."

Gibson picked up another photograph, this one of Clara's apartment, meticulously tidy, almost sterile. "The absence of forced entry, the intimate nature of the scene... it suggests a killer who was known to Clara or at least had gained her trust. Someone who could move within her sphere without arousing suspicion."

"Someone who understood her world," Maria finished. "Her passion for literature, her academic pursuits, even her apartment décor."

"Indeed," Gibson said, his gaze sweeping across the images. "This is not the work of a stranger, Detective. This is the intimate violation of a world known and understood. The killer is not merely an outsider seeking to inflict pain; they are an insider, or at least someone who has intimately studied Clara's life, her intellectual landscape, her very being. They have dissected her, much like a scholar dissects a text, and then proceeded to enact their own interpretation of her story."

He looked directly at Maria, his eyes holding a flicker of something akin to shared dread. "The weight of knowledge, Detective, can be a terrible burden. For Clara, knowledge was a path to liberation, a means of understanding and transforming the world. For this killer, knowledge has become a weapon, a tool for control, for the perpetuation of a narrative they deem essential. They are not simply committing murder; they are performing an act of profound intellectual and philosophical arrogance, believing themselves to be the arbiter of tragic destiny."

Gibson paused, then continued, his voice low and deliberate. "The concept of the tragic heroine, the woman defined by her suffering and her eventual downfall, is a potent archetype. It speaks to a deep-seated cultural fascination with female vulnerability, with the ways in which women are often both idealized and victimized. The killer appears to be drawn to this archetype, not out of empathy, but out of a desire to embody it, to control it, to enact it. Clara, with her intellectual engagement with these figures, has become the first in what might be a series of performances. The killer is not just seeking justice or revenge; they are seeking to validate their own dark philosophy, to prove that these literary tragedies are not mere fictions, but immutable truths that can be brought to life, blood and bone."

He gestured to the sonnet again. "The killer wants an audience, Detective. They want to be understood, to have their intellectual edifice recognized. This isn't just about a single murder; it's about the creation of a grand, ghastly work of art. And Clara Bellweather is merely the first brushstroke on a canvas that is likely to be stained with further tragedy. The weight of this knowledge is indeed immense, not only for you, the investigator, but for all of us who believe in the power of literature to illuminate, rather than to destroy."

CHAPTER 3

THE SOCIETY OF SHADOWS

Maria sifted through Clara Bellweather's extensive personal files, a digital labyrinth of academic papers, lecture notes, and deeply personal journals. Clara's laptop, meticulously preserved by the forensics team, was a treasure trove of her intellectual life, a life that Maria was increasingly realizing, was far more complex and shadowed than a cursory glance would suggest. Amidst the dense academic discourse and the thoughtful, yet sometimes unsettling, reflections on mortality and the human condition, a recurring name began to emerge: the 'Aeon Society.'

The term itself conjured images of antiquity, of timeless knowledge and whispered secrets. Initially, Maria dismissed it as another one of Clara's academic tangents, perhaps a study group for a particularly esoteric branch of literature. But the more she delved, the more the Aeon Society appeared not as a casual academic affiliation, but as something far more clandestine, more... deliberate. Clara's entries alluded to it with a mixture of reverence and apprehension. Phrases like "the hidden sanctum," "the council of minds," and "the eternal dialogue" peppered her private writings, hinting at a group that operated far beyond the public face of Elmwood University.

The society, by all indications, was a creature of the shadows, a collective that prided itself on its intellectual exclusivity.

Membership, if it could even be called that, was seemingly by invitation only, reserved for those deemed to possess a certain intellectual acuity, a certain *je ne sais quoi* that set them apart from the common academic fray. Clara, a rising star in her field, clearly fit this description. Her writings suggested that the Aeon Society was a breeding ground for radical thought, a space where intellectual boundaries were not just pushed, but gleefully obliterated. They were a collective of the brightest, the most ambitious, the most intellectually restless souls within Elmwood, drawn together by an insatiable hunger for knowledge that transcended textbooks and lectures.

The University's ancient library, a gothic behemoth of worn stone and hushed reverence, seemed to be their favored haunt. Clara's journal entries spoke of clandestine meetings held in its forgotten corners – the disused Astronomy Tower, the sub-basement archives accessible only through a service tunnel, the seldom-used private reading rooms tucked away behind unassuming oak doors. These weren't the sterile, brightly lit lecture halls of modern academia. These were spaces steeped in history, in the silent contemplation of centuries of scholarship, places where the very air seemed to hum with the residue of intellectual pursuit. The Aeon Society, it seemed, had an aesthetic, a preference for environments that mirrored their own perceived profundity. They sought out the echoes of the past to amplify their own forward-thinking, even radical, ideas.

Maria found herself drawn into the mystique, an almost involuntary fascination taking hold. The Society's allure wasn't just intellectual; it was laced with a dark, almost romantic, undercurrent. Clara's descriptions painted a picture of intense philosophical debates that stretched into the early hours, fueled by strong coffee and perhaps something stronger, discussions that dissected the human psyche, the nature of reality, and the very fabric of existence. These were not students passively absorbing information; they were actively constructing their own intellectual realities, forging connections and insights that few outside their cloistered circle could comprehend. The atmosphere was one of intense intellectual camaraderie, but also of a subtle, pervasive competition, a silent jockeying for intellectual dominance.

The philosophical underpinnings of their discussions, as alluded to in Clara's notes, were not for the faint of heart. They delved into existentialism, nihilism, and even more esoteric branches of thought that flirted with the occult and the transcendent. It was a world where the boundaries between profound academic inquiry and something akin to intellectual mysticism blurred. Clara's fascination with the darker aspects of human nature, her reinterpretation of tragic figures, seemed to align perfectly with the rumored leanings of the Aeon Society. It was a place where embracing the shadow, where exploring the abyss, was not just tolerated, but actively encouraged.

Professor Gibson, when Maria cautiously broached the subject of the Aeon Society, became uncharacteristically still. His usual calm demeanor was replaced by a subtle tension, a flicker of recognition in his eyes that spoke volumes. "The Aeon Society," he mused, the words rolling off his tongue with a carefully measured cadence, as if tasting their import. "A rather... exclusive circle, from what I understand. Their reputation precedes them, even in more traditional academic circles. They are known for their intellectual rigor, of course, but also for their rather... unconventional approaches to literary and philosophical study."

He adjusted his spectacles, his gaze distant, as if conjuring images from a distant memory. "They are a testament to the enduring human desire for intellectual communion, for the forging of bonds based on shared ideas and a mutual pursuit of what they perceive as higher truths. Their members are often those who find the standard academic curriculum... limiting. They crave a deeper dive; a more radical exploration of concepts that mainstream institutions might shy away from."

Maria pressed, her detective's instinct sensing a crucial link. "Clara was a member, wasn't she? Her journals are filled with references to it."

Gibson nodded slowly. "Clara was... attracted to their brand of intellectual exploration. She found in their discussions a space where her own radical interpretations were not only accepted but celebrated. She thrived in an environment that encouraged the questioning of established norms, the subversion of traditional interpretations. The Aeon Society, in essence, provided her with a sanctuary for her more provocative intellectual pursuits."

He leaned back, a thoughtful expression on his face. "They are a group that believes in the transformative power of ideas, Detective. Not just to understand the world, but to fundamentally alter one's perception of it. This can be a powerful force, leading to genuine breakthroughs in thought. But, as with any potent force, it can also be wielded irresponsibly, or lead individuals down paths of increasingly radical, even dangerous, ideation."

Maria's mind raced. If Clara was part of this society, and if her death was as meticulously staged as it appeared, then the Aeon Society was no longer just a curious academic footnote. It was a potential crucible, a place where the seeds of such a macabre performance might have been sown. The intellectual fervor, the desire to transcend conventional morality, the embrace of dark themes – these were all elements that resonated with the chilling artistry of Clara's murder.

"What kind of ideas were they exploring, Professor?" Maria asked, her voice low and intense. "What were the 'radical interpretations' you mentioned?"

Gibson hesitated, his brow furrowing. "Their interests were broad, Detective. They engaged with the full spectrum of human thought, from the sublime to the depraved. There were certainly discussions on the nature of sacrifice, the catharsis of destruction, and the concept of intellectual 'ascension' – the idea that by shedding societal constraints and embracing forbidden knowledge, one could achieve a higher state of being." He paused, his gaze sharpening. "Some of their more extreme members, I believe, explored concepts that bordered on the transgressive, ideas that challenged the very foundations of morality and ethics. They were fascinated by the power of ritual, by the symbolic weight of actions, and by the notion that certain individuals were destined to fulfill specific, often archetypal, roles."

The words sent a shiver down Maria's spine. Sacrifice. Destruction. Ascension. Archetypal roles. It was all there, echoing in the sterile room, a chilling premonition of the darkness that lay beneath the surface of Elmwood University. The killer, with their meticulously crafted narrative, their symbolic staging, their chosen victim, was not just an isolated psychopath. They were, Maria suspected, a product of this intellectual hothouse, a twisted fruit of the Aeon Society's forbidden orchard.

"And Professor Sterling," Maria continued, her voice laced with suspicion, "was he part of this society?"

Gibson's expression shifted subtly. He seemed to weigh his words carefully. "Professor Sterling was... an admirer of their intellectual prowess, certainly. He held many of the core members in high regard for their sharp minds and their contributions to certain obscure fields. However, whether he was a formal member, actively participating in their clandestine gatherings, is less clear. His public persona was one of unwavering adherence to traditional scholarship. He often presented himself as a bulwark against the very kind of radical intellectualism that the Aeon Society espoused. Yet, I have always found it curious that someone so outwardly conservative would maintain such a... visible connection, however subtle, to such a reputedly heterodox group."

Maria felt a growing unease. Sterling, the ardent traditionalist, the vocal critic of Clara's "feminist interpretations," being connected to a society that reveled in intellectual transgression? It was a dissonance that screamed for further investigation. Perhaps Sterling's public stance was a carefully constructed facade, a deliberate misdirection. Perhaps he saw the Aeon Society not as a threat, but as a secret weapon, a source of ideas and justifications that he could leverage for his own purposes.

"Clara's journals mention a schism within the society," Maria probed, her gaze fixed on Gibson, searching for any crack in his controlled facade. "Something about a disagreement over their... direction."

Gibson's jaw tightened almost imperceptibly. "Indeed. There was a... divergence of opinion. A faction, I understand, began to advocate for a more active engagement with their theories. They believed that the abstract exploration of concepts like sacrifice and transcendence was no longer sufficient. They felt that these ideas needed to be tested, to be... embodied. To be brought into the tangible world."

The implication was stark and terrifying. The Aeon Society wasn't just a collection of academics indulging in intellectual fantasies. It was a group that, for some of its members at least, had crossed a dangerous threshold, moving from theoretical discussion to a desire for practical application. And Clara Bellweather, with her provocative interpretations and her willingness to challenge the status quo, had become a focal point of this dangerous ideological shift. Her murder, then, was not merely an act of personal animosity, but a horrifying manifestation of a philosophy that had taken root within this clandestine intellectual collective.

The society of shadows, Maria realized with a dawning dread, was far more than just a collection of books and debates. It was a breeding ground for a darkness that was now spilling out into the real world, staining the hallowed halls of Elmwood University with blood. The investigation had just taken a much more sinister turn, plunging into the heart of a secretive intellectual world where ideas, unchecked and untempered, could indeed become deadly weapons. The meticulous staging of Clara's death, the carefully chosen poem, the symbolic placement of her body – these were not the isolated acts of a lone deranged individual. They were, Maria was convinced, the deliberate performance of a doctrine, an enactment of theories discussed and refined within the hushed, shadowed confines of the Aeon Society. The professor's files had revealed not just the victim's life, but the chilling intellectual ecosystem that had, in all likelihood, nurtured her killer.

The cryptic note, tucked away within a seemingly innocuous academic paper on Renaissance lamentations, had been a desperate whisper from Clara, a breadcrumb for anyone willing to follow. "The root of all," it read, scrawled in Clara's familiar, elegant hand, "lies not in bloom, but in the earth from which it springs. Seek the soil, the undisturbed loam, beneath the grand edifice." Maria had pondered it for days, the phrase gnawing at her, a puzzle piece that refused to fit any obvious picture. Then, piecing together other fragmented references in Clara's digital footprint—mentions of "uncharted territories" within the library's physical structure, a peculiar fascination with historical cartography, and a fleeting, almost involuntary admission of a secret "repository"—the meaning had solidified with an unnerving clarity. The "grand edifice" was undoubtedly Elmwood University's main library, a sprawling Gothic monument to knowledge. And the "undisturbed loam"? That had to be the forgotten, undocumented sections of its archives.

With Gibson's reluctant, albeit carefully worded, approval—he'd spoken of "historical preservation" and the "importance of cataloging even the most obscure of holdings"—Maria secured a temporary researcher's pass, granting her access to areas usually off-limits. The pass felt less like a privilege and more like a key to a crypt. Her destination was not the well-lit, meticulously organized stacks, but the rumored sub-basement levels, a place whispered about by veteran librarians as a dumping ground for centuries of accumulated academic detritus. Armed with a powerful LED flashlight, a dust mask, and a gnawing sense of unease, Maria descended. The air grew cooler with each step, heavier, carrying the faint, metallic tang of ancient paper and something else, something indefinably... old. The polished oak and brass of the upper floors gave way to rough-hewn concrete and exposed pipework, a subterranean labyrinth of dimly lit corridors that seemed to stretch into infinity. The silence here was different, not the respectful hush of contemplation, but the profound stillness of abandonment, a silence that swallowed sound whole.

Her flashlight beam cut through the oppressive darkness, illuminating towering shelves that sagged under the weight of their burden. These were not the neatly cataloged volumes of the main library. Here, stacks of brittle, leather-bound tomes leaned precariously against cardboard boxes overflowing with loose manuscripts. Yellowed journals lay haphazardly, their pages fused by time and damp. The scent of decay was more pronounced, a melancholic perfume of forgotten intellects. Maria's heart hammered against her ribs, a mixture of trepidation and a desperate hope that Clara had left something, anything, that could illuminate the shadowy path her investigation had taken.

She moved slowly, her gloved fingers tracing the spines of books whose titles were faded beyond recognition, their subjects lost to the ages. Many were bound in materials that felt alien to modern touch – rough linen, coarse animal hide, even what appeared to be treated parchment. The sheer volume of forgotten knowledge was overwhelming. It felt like walking through a graveyard of ideas. Then, her flashlight beam caught a peculiar symbol etched into the spine of a thick, unassuming ledger. It was a stylized hourglass, its sand frozen mid-flow, flanked by two opposing crescents. It was a symbol Clara had sketched in the margins of several of her more esoteric notes, a symbol Maria had initially dismissed as a private doodle. Here, emblazoned on this forgotten tome, it felt like a beacon.

With trembling hands, she pulled the ledger from its resting place. Dust billowed, catching the light and swirling like specters in the air. The binding cracked as she opened it, revealing pages filled with meticulous, almost obsessive, handwriting. The ink was faded, the script archaic, but it was undeniably a record, a chronicle of sorts. The first entry, dated 1888, spoke of "the foundational discourse," of "communion for the ascendant mind." It was a membership ledger, Maria realized, a record of individuals who had, in some capacity, been part of the Aeon Society. The names that followed were a dizzying array of Elmwood University's historical intellectual elite—professors, scholars, and even a few prominent alumni whose contributions to academia were legendary, though often shrouded in academic obscurity.

As she turned the brittle pages, a disturbing pattern began to emerge. The early entries were filled with intellectual pursuits, discussions of philosophy, literature, and the nascent fields of psychology and anthropology. But as the ledger progressed through the decades, the tone shifted. The language became more intense, more focused on mortality, on the fleeting nature of existence, and on the perceived liberation that could be found in embracing the inevitable. There were notes on "the art of the final contemplation," "the aesthetics of dissolution," and "rituals of passage"—terms that sent a cold dread creeping up Maria's spine.

The Aeon Society, it seemed, had not merely been an intellectual discussion group; it had evolved into something far more somber, a collective obsession with death itself.

She found individual dossiers within the ledger, detailing the intellectual contributions and, disturbingly, the eventual fates of many members. One entry, from the early 1920s, described a Professor Samuel Croft, a renowned classicist. His entry spoke of his groundbreaking work on Greek funerary rites and his passionate belief that understanding death was the key to understanding life. The final annotation for Croft was stark: "Departed from this mortal coil, having achieved his final thesis." The accompanying note from the society's scribe was chillingly ambiguous: "His transition was a testament to his devotion. His final silence, the ultimate discourse." Maria cross-referenced the name with the university's mortality records. Samuel Croft had died under mysterious circumstances, his body discovered in his study, meticulously arranged in a posture resembling an ancient funerary effigy. The cause of death was officially recorded as a heart attack, but the details were scarce, the case swiftly closed.

Another file detailed the life of a Dr. Veronica Valentine, a pioneering botanist with an unusual fascination for poisonous flora. Her notes, transcribed by the Aeon Society's chronicler, spoke of the delicate balance between life and decay, of the potent energies released at the threshold of death. Her end was described as a "conscious shedding," a "return to the primal essence." Valentine had died from an accidental ingestion of a highly toxic plant from her own research collection. The accident, the official report stated, was due to a lapse in lab safety protocols. Yet, within the Aeon Society's records, her death was celebrated as a deliberate act of self-transformation, a deliberate merging with the very forces she studied.

The more Maria read, the more the chilling reality of the Aeon Society's intellectual trajectory became apparent. They weren't just contemplating death; they were actively seeking it, theorizing about it, even, it seemed, ritualizing it. The brittle pages whispered of forbidden texts, of ancient grimoires whispered to hold secrets of immortality, or conversely, of the perfect, artful demise. Clara's own research into mortality, her fascination with the morbid and the macabre, suddenly seemed less like an academic curiosity and more like an immersion into a deeply ingrained, and potentially dangerous, tradition.

Amidst the ledgers and dossiers, Maria discovered a collection of loose manuscripts, bound together with a brittle, faded ribbon. These were not official records, but personal accounts, journals and letters from members that had been deemed too... potent, too revealing, for the main archive. One journal, penned by a student named Thomas Ashton in the late 1950s, spoke of a growing unease within the society. Ashton described a schism, a faction that believed the society's explorations were becoming too abstract, too divorced from tangible experience. "Professor Armitage," the journal entry read, "advocates for a more visceral understanding. He speaks of the necessity of 'witnessing the transition,' of understanding the 'sacred silence' not through conjecture, but through direct observation. He believes the abstract contemplation has reached its limit. The next stage, he posits, demands a more... profound engagement."

Armitage. The name resonated. Professor Allen Armitage, the esteemed philosopher whose theories on existentialism had been a cornerstone of Elmwood's curriculum for decades. His public persona was one of rigorous intellectual discipline, of a steadfast commitment to empirical evidence and logical deduction. Yet, here, in this hidden archive, he was depicted as a proponent of something far more extreme, a belief that intellectual understanding of death required a more direct, a more potent, form of engagement. Ashton's journal grew increasingly desperate, detailing a growing fear of Armitage's influence and the unsettling experiments that were apparently being conducted in secret. The last entry was a hurried scrawl: "They are moving beyond words. The shadows lengthen. I fear what 'engagement' truly means." Ashton's fate, like Samuel Croft's, was recorded in the main ledger as a "transcendence," a "final shedding." His body was never recovered, presumed lost during a supposed solo archaeological expedition to a remote region.

Maria's flashlight beam fell upon a small, velvet-lined box tucked away in a recess of the shelving. Inside, resting on faded silk, was a single, tarnished silver locket. She opened it with a deep breath. On one side was a miniature portrait of a young woman with intelligent, haunted eyes—Clara, perhaps in her youth, before the shadows had fully claimed her. On the other side, however, was a different inscription, etched with a fine, almost surgical precision. It wasn't a name, but a date, and below it, a single, chilling word: "Unbound." The date was a week before Clara's murder. The word, "Unbound," echoed Ashton's fears of moving beyond words, of a profound engagement. It felt like a culmination, a designation, a chilling premonition of the macabre performance Maria had witnessed. The Aeon Society, it seemed, had not just documented death; they had begun to orchestrate it, to refine it, to imbue it with a perverse intellectual significance. Clara's meticulous murder was not an aberration; it was, Maria now feared, the horrifying culmination of a century-long intellectual obsession, a dark ritual brought to its terrifying conclusion within the hallowed, and now deeply corrupted, halls of Elmwood University. The hidden archive had revealed not just the society's past, but a chillingly clear trajectory towards the present, a path paved with the pursuit of forbidden knowledge and culminating, it seemed, in a desire to break the ultimate bonds of life itself.

The dusty ledger, now Maria's most incriminating piece of evidence, held more than just a roster of names and cryptic annotations. As she delved deeper into the brittle pages, a stark ritual began to unfold, a chilling testament to the Aeon Society's escalating descent into a macabre fascination with mortality. The entries detailing the induction of new members were particularly disturbing. These weren't mere formalities of academic collaboration; they were solemn oaths, sworn under the weight of secrecy and a shared, clandestine pursuit. Phrases like "the sacred bond of the silenced word" and "a vow to unearth the final narrative" peppered the early sections, suggesting an initiation that transcended intellectual curiosity and bordered on a quasi-religious devotion. The members pledged their absolute discretion, their very existence to be a vessel for the society's esoteric quest for "ultimate truth"—a truth, it became increasingly apparent, that was inextricably linked to the very concept of death.

One particular passage, penned in a spidery hand that spoke of age and fervent conviction, detailed the "Ritual of the Unspoken Covenant." It described a clandestine gathering, held under a new moon, where initiates were required to recite a series of verses, each more arcane than the last, culminating in a solemn pledge. The oath, as transcribed, was terrifying in its simplicity and its implications:

"I pledge my intellect, my spirit, and my very breath to the pursuit of the Final Revelation. I shall bear witness to the Silence, and in so doing, shall transcend the ephemeral. My secrets are the society's, my silence unbreakable, until the Grand Unraveling."

The act of taking such an oath, Maria imagined, must have been deeply unsettling, a step across a threshold from which there was no easy return. The society was not merely studying death; it was worshipping it, imbuing it with a profound, almost sacred significance as the ultimate narrative climax. The idea of death as a "Grand Unraveling," a "Final Revelation," was a perspective so alien, so chillingly detached from the human experience of grief and loss, that it made Maria's blood run cold. It suggested a collective delusion, a philosophical abyss into which these once-brilliant minds had willingly plunged.

The ledger's progression chronicled not just the society's intellectual evolution, but its gradual transformation into a cult of sorts, a brotherhood bound by a shared, morbid obsession. The names listed were not confined to the obscure or the fringe. Maria's eyes widened as she recognized several figures who had shaped, and in some cases, still shaped, Elmwood University's academic landscape. Professor Allen Armitage, whose name had surfaced in Ashton's journal as a proponent of a more "visceral understanding," was a prominent early member, his initial entries filled with philosophical discourse on existential dread. But as the years progressed, Armitage's contributions became more unsettling, focusing on "the aesthetic of surrender" and "the catharsis of cessation." He seemed to view death not as an end, but as a profound, perhaps even beautiful, act of self-definition.

Then, Maria's gaze fell upon a name that made her pause, a name she recognized with a jolt of surprise and growing unease: Dr. Aris Gibson. The Gibson, the very man who had reluctantly granted her access to these forbidden archives, the man whose reputation as a rigorous, albeit somewhat eccentric, historian of medieval texts was impeccable. His name appeared in a section dated from the late 1970s, a period when Gibson was a younger, ambitious academic. His contributions were noted as "prolific analyses of textual mortality," and there was a curious annotation from the society's scribe: "Gibson's keen eye for the veiled narrative promises much for our deeper investigations." He was listed as an active participant, his intellectual prowess apparently recognized and valued by the Aeon Society. This revelation was a dagger to Maria's already frayed nerves. Gibson, the man who had been her reluctant gatekeeper, her seemingly detached academic mentor, had himself been a part of this clandestine organization. Had his current reserved demeanor been a deliberate disguise? Was his caution born of a genuine academic skepticism, or was it the practiced wariness of someone with a hidden past, someone who knew the true depths of the rabbit hole she was so eagerly descending? The implications were staggering. If Gibson was involved, then the scope of the Aeon Society's influence, and its potential to impact present-day events, was far greater than she had dared to imagine. His knowledge of these archives, his understanding of their contents, was not merely academic; it was personal, lived.

The ledger continued, each page a descent into a more profound darkness. The society's interest in literature, initially framed as an exploration of human mortality through narrative, had warped into something far more sinister. They weren't just analyzing stories of death; they seemed to be actively seeking to replicate them, to understand the "ultimate narrative climax" not through fiction, but through direct, chilling experience. Maria found references to lost texts, to forbidden manuscripts whispered to contain the true secrets of life and death, texts that the society had allegedly sought to acquire, to decipher. The pursuit of knowledge had morphed into an obsessive quest for forbidden power, a desire to unlock the very mechanisms of existence and its cessation.

She discovered a section dedicated to "exemplars," members who had, in the society's warped lexicon, achieved a significant level of understanding, individuals whose deaths were not seen as tragedies but as triumphs of intellectual pursuit. Professor Samuel Croft was listed here, his "final discourse" a testament to his dedication. Dr. Victoria Valentine, the botanist, was lauded for her "conscious shedding." These weren't just euphemisms; they were celebratory accolades, marking the society's perverse triumph over what they perceived as the mundane finality of death. The language was consistent, a chillingly detached reverence for the act of dying, a conceptualization of death as a deliberate, almost artistic, choice. Maria felt a wave of nausea wash over her. This wasn't academia; it was something far older, far more dangerous, a perversion of intellectual curiosity into a life-and-death obsession.

The more she read, the more Clara's own research, her fascination with the macabre, her intense study of mortality, seemed less like a personal quirk and more like an immersion into a deeply ingrained, and profoundly disturbing, tradition. Clara had clearly been a part of this, a student, a disciple, perhaps even a convert. The locket she'd found, with its cryptic "Unbound" inscription and the date preceding her murder, now felt like a symbol of her own supposed transcendence, a mark of her completion of some dark rite. Maria shuddered, the cold of the sub-basement seeping into her bones, a chilling echo of the emotional void she sensed within the Aeon Society's members. They had, it seemed, successfully detached themselves from the very essence of what it meant to be human, replacing empathy and sorrow with a cold, intellectual fascination with the ultimate unknown. And Maria suspected, with a dread that tightened her chest, that this fascination was not confined to the past; it was a living, breathing force, lurking in the shadows of Elmwood University, and it had claimed Clara as its ultimate, tragic narrative. The question now was, who or what would be its next subject? The presence of Gibson in the ledger cast a long, dark shadow of suspicion, suggesting that the society's influence might extend far beyond the dusty archives, reaching into the very heart of the university, and perhaps, even into the investigation itself.

The air in Dr. Gibson's study, usually thick with the scent of aged paper and dry ink, now felt heavy with an unspoken tension. Maria, clutching the worn leather ledger like a shield, met his gaze, her own a mixture of accusation and a desperate plea for truth. The familiar shelves of books, once a comforting testament to his scholarly life, now seemed like silent witnesses to a hidden history. She had laid the ledger open on his polished mahogany desk, a stark contrast to the brittle, yellowed pages. The name, 'Aris Gibson,' circled in a faded, almost apologetic red ink, was a glaring indictment.

"I found this, Dr. Gibson," Maria began, her voice barely a whisper, yet it seemed to echo in the stillness. "In the sub-basement archives. It's... it's a record of the Aeon Society."

Dr. Gibson, usually so composed, a picture of professorial gravitas, visibly stiffened. His normally placid expression tightened, a flicker of something akin to apprehension crossing his eyes before he masked it with his characteristic scholarly detachment. He leaned back in his chair, his gaze drifting to the window, as if seeking an answer in the placid university grounds outside.

"The Aeon Society," he repeated, his voice carefully neutral, devoid of the surprise Maria might have expected. It was confirmation, delivered with a practiced ease that did little to quell her growing unease. "An archaic curiosity, Detective. A historical footnote. I believed all its records were long since secured and cataloged."

"Not all of them," Maria pressed, her fingers tracing the indentation of his name on the page. "And this one... it details your involvement. Your contributions. It says you were a 'prolific analyst of textual mortality'." She looked up at him, her eyes searching his face for any sign of remorse, any hint of the man who had so readily dismissed her earlier inquiries. "You were a member, Dr. Gibson. You were part of it."

He finally met her gaze, his eyes holding a depth of weariness that seemed to go beyond the simple confession of past affiliation. There was a melancholy resignation in his posture, as if the weight of years had finally found its voice. "Yes, Detective," he admitted, the words slow and deliberate. "I was a member. A long time ago. In my youth."

His admission, though expected, sent a fresh wave of disquiet through Maria. The way he spoke of it, as a youthful indiscretion, a phase he had outgrown, felt... incomplete. The ledger spoke of a fervent intellectual engagement, a "keen eye for the veiled narrative" that promised "deeper investigations." It painted a picture of an active participant, not a dilettante.

"Youthful intellectual pursuit?" Maria echoed, her voice tinged with skepticism. "The ledger describes it as a 'shared, clandestine pursuit' of 'ultimate truth.' It speaks of oaths, Doctor. Of a 'vow to unearth the final narrative.'" She gestured to the page, her hand trembling slightly. "Your name is here, among people like Professor Armitage, Professor Croft, Dr. Valentine... people who, according to this, saw death not as an end, but as a... revelation. A transcendence."

Gibson sighed, a sound that seemed to carry the dust of decades. He picked up a heavy, leather-bound volume from his desk, running his fingers over its embossed cover. "Maria," he began, his tone shifting, becoming more intimate, more reflective. "The Aeon Society was founded on principles of intellectual exploration, of pushing the boundaries of human understanding. We were scholars, students of history, literature, and philosophy. We were fascinated by the human condition, and what greater aspect of that condition is there than mortality?"

He paused, his gaze distant, as if replaying scenes from a lifelong past. "In my younger years," he continued, "I was drawn to the raw, unfiltered expressions of life's ephemeral nature. The medieval texts I studied, they were filled with a directness, a stark contemplation of death that is absent in much of modern thought. The Aeon Society offered a forum, a crucible, where such ideas could be explored without the constraints of societal norms or academic dogma. We sought to understand how humanity grappled with its inevitable end, not just through philosophical discourse, but through the very narratives that chronicled its passage."

"But it became more than just an academic pursuit, didn't it?" Maria challenged, her voice gaining an edge. "The entries... they speak of rituals. Of a 'Ritual of the Unspoken Covenant.' Of pledging one's 'very breath to the pursuit of the Final Revelation.' That sounds less like scholarly debate and more like... worship. A morbid obsession."

Gibson winced, as if the words had struck a nerve. He set the book down, his hands clasping in his lap. "You must understand, Detective, the nature of obsession. It is a subtle poison, insidious. What begins as a fascination can, over time, consume one entirely. The lines blur. The intellectual pursuit can morph into something... more fervent." He hesitated, his eyes clouding with a familiar melancholy. "There were members, of course, who embraced this fervor more readily than others. They saw in death not an end to discourse, but the ultimate discourse itself. The cessation of the body, the silencing of the individual voice, was to them a gateway to a profound, ineffable truth."

He looked directly at Maria, his gaze piercing. "There was one student, in particular. A young woman... brilliant, exceptionally so. Her intellect was sharp, incisive. But her preoccupation with death... it was extraordinary. Insatiable, one might say. She saw life as a prelude, a mere preamble to the grand narrative that only death could truly author. She was drawn to the darker texts, the more esoteric interpretations of mortality. She found... beauty, in the concept of annihilation."

The way Gibson spoke of this student, with a mixture of intellectual respect and profound concern, sent a chill down Maria's spine. It was not the detached, clinical observation of a historian, but the troubled recollection of someone who had witnessed a descent. "Who was she, Dr. Gibson?" Maria asked, her voice tight. "Who was this student?"

Gibson's jaw tightened, and he looked away, his gaze fixed on a point beyond Maria, beyond the room, as if looking into a chasm. "Her name is not important," he said, his voice low and strained. "What is important is that her path became a cautionary tale for me. Her insatiable hunger... it frightened me. It was a hunger that could not be satisfied by books or theories. It demanded... more."

Maria felt a surge of frustration. His reticence, his carefully chosen words, only served to deepen her suspicion. He was holding back, admitting only what he could no longer deny, but carefully curating the narrative. "More?" she prompted, leaning forward. "More of what? What did she demand?"

"She sought to understand the finality not through observation, but through... experience," Gibson said, his voice barely audible. "She believed that true enlightenment lay in shedding the burdens of existence, in embracing the void. Her pursuit became... reckless. Dangerous." He finally turned back to Maria, his eyes filled with a haunted weariness. "The Aeon Society, in its early days, was a sanctuary for the intellectually curious. But as its members delved deeper into the abyss, some became lost within it. The fascination with death, for some, ceased to be an exploration and became an obsession. And obsessions, Detective, can lead to ruin."

He clasped his hands together, his knuckles white. "I... I withdrew from the society shortly after that period. The direction it was taking, the increasingly morbid preoccupations of some members... it became too much. I realized that some doors, once opened, should perhaps remain firmly shut. The knowledge we sought, the 'ultimate truth'... it was not a revelation to be unearthed, but a profound mystery best left undisturbed."

Maria studied him, the admission of his withdrawal a small victory, but the underlying reluctance still palpable. He had been more than just a passive observer; he had been deeply immersed, had witnessed the rot set in. And his description of the insatiable student... it resonated with a chilling familiarity. It sounded like Clara. The same desperate pursuit of a final answer, the same intellectual intensity, the same apparent disregard for the conventional boundaries of life and death.

"You say you withdrew," Maria stated, her voice firm. "But did you truly disengage Dr. Gibson? Or did you merely retreat? This ledger... it suggests the society continued, evolved, and that its influence, its morbid fascination, didn't simply fade away with your departure. You said you knew all the records were 'secured and cataloged.' Yet here I am, holding one that was clearly not. Does that not raise questions about who else might have access, who else might still be... operating within its shadows?"

Gibson remained silent for a long moment, his gaze fixed on the ledger. The weight of his past, of his involvement with the Aeon Society seemed to press down on him. Maria could sense the struggle within him, the battle between the desire for quiet retirement and the lingering obligation to truth. His reticence was not just about his own past; it was about protecting something, or perhaps someone, from the dangerous currents that still swirled beneath the surface of Elmwood University. And that, Maria knew with a growing certainty, was the most unsettling revelation of all. He knew more. He knew far more than he was willing to share, and his silence was a testament to the enduring power and peril of this society of shadows. The implications of his past membership were far-reaching, casting a long, dark shadow over his present role, and over the very investigation Maria was undertaking. He wasn't just a gatekeeper to dusty archives; he was a living, breathing link to a dangerous legacy, a legacy that seemed to have claimed Clara and might yet have its eyes set on others.

Maria's mind reeled from the implications of Dr. Gibson's admission. The Aeon Society wasn't merely a collection of dusty historical documents; it was a living, breathing entity, or at least, its influence certainly seemed to persist. The hushed reverence with which Gibson had spoken of the "ultimate truth," the "final narrative," now took on a far more sinister hue. He had alluded to a fascination with death that became an obsession, a reckless pursuit of experience that led to ruin. And Clara... Clara, with her own burgeoning obsession with mortality, her desperate search for answers that seemed to mirror the very tenets of the society. The possibility that her death was not an isolated act of madness, but a deliberate consequence of her involvement, or perhaps even a macabre ritual enacted by another member, sent a cold dread coursing through her veins. The university, with its ivy-covered walls and ancient traditions, suddenly felt like a labyrinth of shadowed corridors, each one potentially leading to a deeper, darker secret.

The weight of this realization pressed down on her. The familiar faces of esteemed professors, the learned discussions in lecture halls, the very intellectual ecosystem of Elmwood, now seemed to harbor a hidden undercurrent of dangerous ideologies. If Dr. Gibson, a man of such apparent gravitas and intellect, could be so deeply entangled, what about others? Were there still active members within the faculty, students, or staff, people whose academic pursuits merely served as a sophisticated cover for the society's clandestine agenda? The thought was chilling. It painted a portrait of Elmwood not as a bastion of knowledge, but as a fertile ground for a dangerous cult, its members hidden in plain sight, bound by shared secrets and a morbid curiosity that could easily spill over into violence. The murders, once seemingly random acts of brutality, now felt connected, orchestrated by a shared understanding of the society's philosophy, perhaps even its rituals. The killer, Maria surmised, was not just a murderer; they were a disciple, a product of the Aeon Society's enduring influence, someone who saw death not as an end, but as a transition, a sacrifice, or even a testament to their twisted beliefs.

The idea of a clandestine network operating within the university's supposedly transparent academic structure was a terrifying prospect. Dr. Gibson's hesitant confession had confirmed her suspicions that the society was more than a historical footnote; it was a shadowy influence that had seeped into the very fabric of Elmwood. The names he had mentioned – Armitage, Croft, Valentine – were not relegated to obscure historical texts. They were names still spoken in hushed academic circles, some of them founders of current departments, their legacies woven into the university's proud history. Had their intellectual curiosity, their exploration of mortality, been a prelude to something more? Had they, like Gibson suggested, crossed a line from fascination to obsession, and then from obsession to something far more perilous? The ledger, with its cryptic entries and coded language, hinted at a progression, a deepening of their involvement that transcended mere intellectual debate.

Maria found herself replaying Gibson's words, searching for any overlooked detail, any subtle nuance that might shed more light on the society's activities. He had spoken of "textual mortality" and "analysis of veiled narratives." This suggested a methodology, a way of deciphering hidden meanings within texts related to death and dying. Perhaps the victims were chosen because of their connection to such texts, or perhaps their deaths were meant to be interpreted through a specific, Aeon-approved lens. The "Ritual of the Unspoken Covenant" was particularly unsettling. Covenants implied agreements, obligations. What had these members sworn to? What was the "Final Revelation" they sought? It sounded like a perversion of enlightenment, a twisted quest for ultimate knowledge achieved through forbidden means.

The mention of Gibson's youthful involvement and his subsequent withdrawal was significant, but also frustratingly vague. He had claimed to have left due to the society's increasingly morbid preoccupations. But the fact that he was so reluctant to discuss it, and the presence of this 'lost' ledger, suggested that his departure was not a clean break. Had he been privy to secrets he couldn't unburden himself of? Had the society's influence followed him, subtly shaping his career, his research, his entire life at Elmwood? His reticence felt less like the timidity of someone with a minor past indiscretion and more like the fear of someone who had glimpsed a profound and terrible truth and knew the danger of stirring it. He was a man haunted by his past, and that past, Maria now understood, was deeply entwined with the very institution she was investigating.

Her thoughts drifted back to Clara. Clara, who had been so consumed by her research into obscure mortality rituals, her relentless pursuit of answers that seemed to border on the obsessive. Had she, too, stumbled upon the Aeon Society? Had she been actively seeking them out, or had they found her? Gibson's description of the brilliant student whose "preoccupation with death was extraordinary" and "insatiable" echoed unnervingly. It was a chilling parallel, a potential link that made Clara's fate all the more tragic and terrifying. If Clara had indeed become involved, even peripherally, it would explain her desperate search for information, her secretive meetings, and her eventual demise. The society, with its promises of profound understanding of life's greatest mystery, could have been a siren call to someone like Clara, drawing her into a fatal embrace.

Maria realized that her investigation had just taken a sharp, dangerous turn. The killer was no longer just a suspect within the university's general population; they were likely connected to the Aeon Society, a member or a former member, someone who understood its doctrines, its secrets, and perhaps its methods. This meant the threat was not just personal; it was ideological. The murders could be interpreted, by the perpetrator, as acts of purification, of ritual, or as a means to silence those who threatened to expose the society's continued existence. The university's hallowed halls, the very spaces where knowledge was supposed to be freely exchanged and debated, now felt like a carefully constructed facade, hiding a dangerous, secretive underbelly.

She considered the implications for her own safety. If the society was still active, and if its members were capable of such violence, then she, by digging into its past, was now a direct threat. The society's influence, as Gibson had vaguely alluded to, might extend beyond mere intellectual circles. It could involve people in positions of power, people who could easily manipulate circumstances, silence witnesses, and cover up evidence. The notion of a "clandestine network" was no longer a theoretical concept; it was a palpable, immediate danger. The university, once a place of intellectual pursuit and personal growth for Maria, was transforming into a treacherous landscape, where every shadowed corner and every polite smile could conceal a hidden agenda.

The ledger felt heavier in her hands, not just with the weight of paper and ink, but with the burden of the knowledge it contained. Dr. Gibson's carefully guarded confession had opened a Pandora's Box, revealing a secret society that had potentially woven itself into the very fabric of Elmwood's academic and social structure. He had admitted his youthfully naive entanglement, his subsequent disillusionment, and his withdrawal. But the ledger, and Gibson's palpable unease, suggested that the story was far from over. The society's influence, its morbid fascinations and its potential for extreme actions, had not simply dissolved with Gibson's departure. It had persisted, lurking in the shadows, waiting.

Maria understood that the killer might not be acting out of personal malice in the conventional sense. Instead, they could be motivated by the society's core beliefs, their skewed understanding of death as a form of revelation or transcendence. The murders might be seen, by the perpetrator, as a necessary step in a larger, more significant endeavor – the continuation of the society's work, the pursuit of its "ultimate truth." This ideological framework made the killer all the more dangerous, as their actions would be driven by a conviction that their deeds were justified, even sacred.

The academic veneer of Elmwood University, with its esteemed faculty and its pursuit of higher learning, now seemed like a thin, fragile veil, barely concealing the darker, more ancient forces at play. The legacy of the Aeon Society, it appeared, was not confined to the archives; it was a living, breathing menace, its tendrils reaching into the present, its secrets buried deep within the very institution Maria had come to trust. The pursuit of knowledge, it seemed, could lead down very dark, and very deadly, paths. She had to consider that the individuals involved in this society, past or present, might possess a unique set of skills. Their intellectual background would likely lend them a degree of cunning and foresight. They would be adept at deciphering complex information, at constructing intricate plans, and at anticipating potential obstacles.

The "veiled narratives" Gibson mentioned could be literal – coded messages, hidden meanings within academic papers, or even symbolic interpretations of the murders themselves. This meant the killer might be leaving behind clues, not for the police, but for other members of the society, or as a testament to their own adherence to its doctrines. Maria would need to think like them, to try and understand the logic, however twisted, behind their actions.

The society's secretive nature also implied a capacity for manipulation and influence. If they had operated within the university for decades, it was plausible that members had risen to positions of authority, not just within academia, but perhaps even within administrative or security departments. This could explain the initial resistance Maria had encountered, the deliberate stonewalling, the misplaced files, and the general sense of being stonewalled. It wasn't just bureaucratic inefficiency; it was a coordinated effort to protect the society's secrets. Gibson's hesitancy to fully reveal what he knew could also stem from this very fear – the fear of retribution from a network that had proven its ability to operate with impunity for so long. The idea that the university itself, or at least significant parts of it, could be compromised, was a daunting realization. It meant that Maria couldn't rely on official channels for support, and that anyone she approached for help could potentially be part of the problem.

She thought about the victims again. Two years ago, Professor Albright, the historian specializing in ancient death cults and Dr. Anna Heart, a lecturer in comparative literature, known for her work on Gothic literature and themes of mortality. And now, Clara, a brilliant doctoral candidate whose thesis delved into the psychological impact of existential dread. Each one had a distinct connection to the study of death, of mortality, of the liminal spaces between life and the unknown. It was too much of a coincidence. These weren't random targets; they were likely chosen for their perceived proximity to the society's core interests, or perhaps because they had stumbled too close to its secrets. The murders could be viewed, by the perpetrator, as a form of selective pruning, eliminating those who posed a threat or those who, in the society's twisted view, were ready for their own "final revelation." The ledger, with its cryptic entries, might hold the key to understanding this selection process, perhaps detailing a hierarchy of knowledge or a prescribed path for members.

The concept of "textual mortality" was particularly intriguing. It suggested that the society might have a particular methodology for interpreting texts related to death. Perhaps they believed that certain texts held the secrets to unlocking the mysteries of mortality, and that the individuals who studied them were either candidates for initiation, or threats to be neutralized. This could explain why Albright, with his expertise in death cults, and Heart, with her focus on Gothic literature, were targeted. And Clara, in her own way, was also delving into the existential abyss. Maria wondered if the society believed that true understanding of death could only be achieved through a particular kind of scholarly or intellectual engagement, one that bordered on obsession. Gibson's own description of his youthful fascination, and how it had morphed into something more fervent for others, pointed to this dangerous progression.

The moral implications were also significant. If the Aeon Society was still active, and if its members were involved in murder, then the university had a moral obligation to expose them. But how could she do that when the evidence was so fragmented, and when the very institution she sought to protect might be complicit? Gibson's confession, while damning, was still couched in terms of his own youthful indiscretions and his subsequent withdrawal. He was a witness, yes, but perhaps also a reluctant protector of the society's legacy, unwilling to fully implicate himself or his former colleagues. His silence, while born of fear, was also a testament to the society's enduring power to cast a shadow over even the most learned minds. Maria knew she was treading on dangerous ground, a path that led away from academic inquiry and towards a very real, very present danger. The university's quiet mask of academic pursuit was a deceptive mask, and behind it lay a society that had transformed the study of death into something far more sinister, a pursuit that had claimed Clara's life and now threatened to engulf Maria in its chilling embrace.

CHAPTER 4

THE SECOND ACT OF VIOLENCE

The stale air of the library, usually a comforting balm to Maria's overstimulated senses, now felt suffocating. Dr. Gibson's hushed confession, the implications of the Aeon Society's pervasive influence, and the phantom whispers of Clara's involvement swirled in her mind like an academic tempest. She had retreated to the familiar sanctuary of her office, a space that had once represented order and intellectual rigor, now feeling like a fragile island in a sea of encroaching darkness. The ledger, a physical embodiment of Elmwood's hidden history, lay open on her desk, its cryptic entries, a maddening testament to a truth she was only beginning to grasp. The society wasn't a mere historical curiosity; it was a living, breathing entity, its tendrils woven into the very fabric of the university. Gibson's hesitant admission had confirmed her deepest fears: that the pursuit of knowledge, especially when it brushed against the macabre, could lead down a path of obsession, and ultimately, destruction. He had spoken of a fascination with death that had festered into an obsession, a reckless pursuit that had ultimately led to ruin, and Maria couldn't shake the chilling parallel to Clara's own descent into the abyss of mortality research. Had Clara, like Gibson himself in his youth, been lured in by the promise of forbidden knowledge? Had her relentless questioning, her desperate search for answers, inadvertently placed her on a collision course with a society that viewed death not as an ending, but as a macabre rite of passage?

The university, with its ivy-clad walls and venerable traditions, now seemed less like a bastion of learning and more like a carefully constructed labyrinth, its shadowed corridors concealing secrets that had proven fatal to its brightest minds. The very people she had once admired and respected – professors, scholars, mentors – now felt like potential players in a much larger, more sinister game. If Gibson, a man of such evident intellect and standing, could be so deeply entangled, who else might be involved? Were there others within the faculty, the student body, or the administrative staff, whose academic pursuits were merely a sophisticated facade for the society's clandestine agenda? The thought sent a shiver down her spine, painting a grim picture of Elmwood as fertile ground for a dangerous cult, its members hidden in plain sight, bound by shared secrets and a morbid curiosity that could easily spill over into violence.

The murder, once seemingly isolated acts of brutality, now appeared to be interconnected, orchestrated by a shared understanding of the society's philosophy, perhaps even its rituals. The killer, Maria surmised with a growing sense of dread, was not merely a murderer; they were a disciple, a product of the Aeon Society's enduring influence, someone who viewed death not as an end, but as a transition, a sacrifice, or a testament to their twisted beliefs. The idea of a clandestine network operating within the university's ostensibly transparent academic structure was a terrifying prospect. Gibson's carefully guarded confession had validated her suspicions that the society was more than a historical footnote; it was a shadowy influence that had infiltrated the very essence of Elmwood. The names he had mentioned – Armitage, Croft, Valentine – were not mere relics of the past. They were names still whispered in academic circles, some of them foundational figures in current departments, their legacies indelibly etched into the university's proud history. Had their intellectual curiosity, their deep dives into the nature of mortality, been a prelude to something more? Had they, as Gibson had hinted, crossed a perilous line from fascination to obsession, and then from obsession to something far more dangerous? The ledger, with its cryptic entries and coded language, provided a chilling glimpse into a progression, a deepening of their involvement that transcended mere intellectual debate.

Maria found herself replaying Gibson's words, dissecting each syllable, searching for any overlooked detail, any subtle nuance that might illuminate the society's activities. He had spoken of "textual mortality" and "analysis of veiled narratives," suggesting a methodical approach to deciphering hidden meanings within texts pertaining to death and dying. It was a methodology, she realized, that could explain the victims' selection. Perhaps they were chosen for their connection to such texts, or perhaps their deaths were intended to be interpreted through a specific, Aeon-approved lens.

The "Ritual of the Unspoken Covenant" sent a fresh wave of unease through her. Covenants implied agreements and obligations. What had these members sworn to? What was the "Final Revelation" they sought? It sounded like a perversion of enlightenment, a twisted quest for ultimate knowledge achieved through forbidden means. Gibson's own youthful involvement and subsequent withdrawal were significant, yet frustratingly vague. He claimed to have left due to the society's increasingly morbid preoccupations. But his evident reluctance to discuss it, coupled with the existence of this 'lost' ledger, hinted that his departure was far from a clean break. Had he been privy to secrets too profound, too terrible, to ever fully unburden himself of? Had the society's influence followed him, subtly shaping his career, his research, his entire existence at Elmwood? His reticence felt less like the timidity of someone with a minor past indiscretion and more like the palpable fear of someone who had glimpsed a profound and terrible truth and understood the danger of disturbing it. He was a man haunted by his past, a past that Maria now understood was inextricably entwined with the very institution she was investigating. Her thoughts inevitably drifted back to Clara. Clara, who had been so utterly consumed by her research into obscure mortality rituals, her relentless pursuit of answers that seemed to teeter on the edge of obsession. Had she, too, stumbled upon the Aeon Society? Had she actively sought them out, or had they found her?

Gibson's description of the brilliant student whose "preoccupation with death was extraordinary" and "insatiable" resonated with a chilling, almost visceral, familiarity. It was a potential link that made Clara's fate all the more tragic and terrifying. If Clara had indeed become involved, even peripherally, it would explain her desperate search for information, her secretive meetings, and ultimately, her demise. The society, with its seductive promises of profound understanding of life's greatest mystery, could have been a siren call to someone like Clara, drawing her into a fatal embrace. Maria recognized that her investigation had just taken a sharp, and undeniably dangerous, turn. The killer was no longer just an abstract suspect within the university's general population; they were likely connected to the Aeon Society, a member or a former member, someone who understood its doctrines, its secrets, and perhaps, its methods. This meant the threat was not merely personal; it was ideological. The murders, from the perpetrator's perspective, could be interpreted as acts of purification, of ritual, or as a means to silence those who threatened to expose the society's continued existence.

The university's hallowed halls, the very spaces where knowledge was supposed to be freely exchanged and debated, now seemed like a meticulously constructed face, concealing a dangerous, secretive underbelly. She considered the implications for her own safety. If the society was still active, and if its members were capable of such violence, then she, by her relentless pursuit of its past, was now a direct threat. The society's influence, as Gibson had vaguely alluded to, might extend far beyond mere intellectual circles. It could involve individuals in positions of power, people who could easily manipulate circumstances, silence witnesses, and meticulously cover up evidence. The notion of a "clandestine network" was no longer a theoretical concept; it was a palpable, immediate danger.

The university, once a place of intellectual pursuit and personal growth for Maria, was transforming into a treacherous landscape, where every shadowed corner and every polite smile could conceal a hidden agenda, a deadly secret. The ledger felt heavier in her hands, not just with the physical weight of paper and ink, but with the profound burden of the knowledge it contained. Dr. Gibson's carefully guarded confession had indeed opened a Pandora's Box, revealing a secret society that had potentially woven itself into the very fabric of Elmwood's academic and social structure. He had admitted his youthful, naive entanglement, his subsequent disillusionment, and his eventual withdrawal. But the ledger, and Gibson's palpable unease, strongly suggested that the story was far from over. The society's influence, its morbid fascinations, and its potential for extreme actions, had not simply dissolved with Gibson's departure. It had persisted, lurking in the shadows, waiting.

Maria understood that the killer might not be acting out of personal malice in the conventional sense. Instead, they could be driven by the society's core beliefs, their skewed understanding of death as a form of revelation or transcendence. The murders might be viewed, by the perpetrator, as a necessary step in a larger, more significant endeavor – the continuation of the society's work, the relentless pursuit of its "ultimate truth." This ideological framework made the killer all the more dangerous, as their actions would be driven by a profound conviction that their deeds were justified, even sacred.

The academic veneer of Elmwood University, with its esteemed faculty and its unwavering commitment to higher learning, now seemed like a thin, fragile veil, barely concealing the darker, more ancient forces at play. The legacy of the Aeon Society, it appeared, was not confined to the archives; it was a living, breathing menace, its tendrils reaching into the present, its secrets buried deep within the very institution Maria had come to trust. The pursuit of knowledge, it seemed, could indeed lead down very dark, and very deadly, paths. She had to consider that the individuals involved in this society, past or present, might possess a unique set of skills, honed by decades of intellectual rigor and secretive practice. Their academic background would undoubtedly lend them a degree of cunning and foresight. They would be adept at deciphering complex information, at constructing intricate plans, and at anticipating potential obstacles. The "veiled narratives" Gibson mentioned could be literal – coded messages, hidden meanings embedded within academic papers, or even symbolic interpretations of the murders themselves. This meant the killer might be leaving behind clues, not for the authorities, but for other members of the society, or as a testament to their own unwavering adherence to its doctrines. Maria knew she would need to think like them, to try and understand the logic, however twisted, behind their actions.

The society's inherent secrecy also implied a formidable capacity for manipulation and influence. If they had operated within the university's walls for decades, it was plausible that members had risen to positions of authority, not just within academia, but perhaps even within administrative or security departments. This could explain the initial resistance Maria had encountered, the deliberate stonewalling she had faced, the inexplicably misplaced files, and the pervasive sense of being systematically obstructed. It wasn't just bureaucratic inefficiency; it was a calculated, coordinated effort to protect the society's deeply buried secrets. Gibson's hesitancy to fully reveal what he knew could also stem from this very fear – the fear of retribution from a network that had demonstrably proven its ability to operate with impunity for so long.

The chilling idea that the university itself, or at least significant portions of its infrastructure, could be compromised, was a daunting realization. It meant that Maria couldn't rely on official channels for support, and that anyone she approached for help could potentially be part of the very problem she was trying to solve. She thought about the victims again, their lives extinguished, their stories abruptly silenced. Professor Albright, the esteemed historian specializing in ancient death cults. Dr. Anna Heart, a lecturer in comparative literature, renowned for her work on Gothic literature and its pervasive themes of mortality. And now, Clara, the brilliant doctoral candidate whose thesis delved into the profound psychological impact of existential dread. Each one possessed a distinct, undeniable connection to the study of death, of mortality, of the liminal spaces between life and the vast, unknown beyond.

It was far too much of a coincidence to be mere chance. These weren't random targets; they were likely chosen for their perceived proximity to the society's core interests, or perhaps because they had inadvertently stumbled too close to its deeply guarded secrets. The murders could be viewed, by the perpetrator, as a form of selective pruning, eliminating those who posed a threat or those who, in the society's twisted worldview, were ready for their own "final revelation." The ledger, with its cryptic entries, might hold the key to understanding this sinister selection process, perhaps detailing a hierarchy of knowledge or a prescribed path for members. The concept of "textual mortality" was particularly intriguing, sparking Maria's academic curiosity despite the surrounding dread. It suggested that the society might possess a particular methodology for interpreting texts related to death. Perhaps they believed that certain ancient texts held the secrets to unlocking the profound mysteries of mortality, and that the individuals who studied them were either potential candidates for initiation, or threats to be neutralized.

This could explain why Albright, with his expertise in death cults, and Heart, with her focus on Gothic literature, were targeted. And Clara, in her own unique way, was also delving into the existential abyss. Maria wondered if the society believed that true understanding of death could only be achieved through a particular kind of scholarly or intellectual engagement, one that bordered on, and perhaps even embraced, obsession.

Gibson's own description of his youthful fascination, and how it had demonstrably morphed into something far more fervent for others, pointed to this dangerous, insidious progression. The moral implications of her findings were also significant and deeply troubling. If the Aeon Society was still active, and if its members were involved in murder, then the university had a clear moral obligation to expose them. But how could she possibly achieve that when the evidence was so fragmented, and when the very institution she sought to protect might be complicit? Gibson's confession, while undeniably damning, was still couched in terms of his own youthful indiscretions and his subsequent withdrawal. He was a witness, yes, but perhaps also a reluctant protector of the society's legacy, unwilling to fully implicate himself or his former colleagues. His silence, while likely born of fear, was also a testament to the society's enduring power to cast a long, dark shadow over even the most learned and principled minds. Maria knew she was treading on exceptionally dangerous ground, a path that led away from detached academic inquiry and towards a very real, very present danger. The university's quiet facade of academic pursuit was a deceptive mask, and behind it lay a society that had transformed the study of death into something far more sinister, a pursuit that had already claimed Clara's life and now threatened to engulf Maria in its chilling, unforgiving embrace.

The discovery of Dr. Toby Bennett was a grim punctuation mark in the escalating narrative of fear gripping Elmwood. He was found slumped over his desk, a solitary figure lost amidst towering stacks of arcane texts and yellowed manuscripts. The scene was disturbingly reminiscent of historical accounts of scholars driven to madness by their obsessive research, their minds consumed by the very darkness they sought to illuminate. Bennett, a reclusive historian known for his deep dives into morbid folklore and ancient death rituals, had always existed on the fringes of the university's academic community. His office, tucked away in a rarely visited wing of the humanities building, was a place whispered about in hushed tones, a sanctuary for esoteric knowledge that few dared to explore. Now, it had become a tomb.

The sheer volume of material surrounding him was staggering – tomes on necromancy, treatises on funerary rites from forgotten civilizations, brittle folios detailing obscure curses and superstitions. It was a landscape of death, meticulously curated and intensely studied. Maria, standing at the periphery of the crime scene, felt a cold dread seep into her bones. The scene wasn't just a discovery; it was a statement. The meticulous staging, the deliberate arrangement of the texts, the almost theatrical presentation of Bennett's demise – it all spoke of a calculated act, not a spontaneous outburst of violence. And then she saw it, tucked beneath Bennett's outstretched hand, a small, intricately carved wooden bird. The same symbol, she realized with a sickening lurch, that had been found with Professor Albright and Dr. Heart.

The killer's signature, a morbid calling card, had returned, confirming her worst fears. This was not a copycat. This was the same perpetrator, their macabre dance continuing, their selection of victims seemingly dictated by an increasingly specific and terrifying criteria. Bennett's specialization in morbid folklore and ancient death rituals placed him squarely within the orbit of the Aeon Society's interests. He was not just a scholar; he was a custodian of the very knowledge the society seemed to covet, or perhaps, sought to control. His death, staged to mirror a historical account of a scholar consumed by his research, was a chillingly direct message. It suggested that Bennett, like Clara, had delved too deep, had perhaps unearthed a truth that the society deemed too dangerous to remain unearthed. The return of the wooden bird was a confirmation, a brutal handshake from a phantom presence. It solidified the connection between Bennett's death and the previous murders, weaving a tighter, more terrifying thread through the unfolding mystery.

Elmwood University, once a place of intellectual exploration and scholarly pursuit, was rapidly transforming into a hunting ground, its academic pursuits serving as a deadly lure for a predator operating with chilling precision and a profound understanding of its victims' obsessions. The meticulously staged scene in Bennett's office was more than just a gruesome tableau; it was a chilling testament to the killer's intimate knowledge of their victims' scholarly pursuits and their possible connection to the Aeon Society. It was a deliberate, almost artistic, display, designed to send a message, not just to the authorities, but to anyone who dared to peer too closely into the dark heart of Elmwood's hidden history. The sheer volume of arcane texts surrounding Bennett suggested a deep immersion in the very subjects that Maria now believed were central to the Aeon Society's philosophy. These weren't the casual interests of a historian; they were the obsessions of someone who sought to understand the profound mysteries of life and death, the very mysteries that Gibson had alluded to the society's pursuit of.

The specific historical account to which Bennett's death alluded—a scholar consumed by his research—was a particularly pointed reference. It served as a warning, a grim prophecy for anyone who dared to follow a similar path. It was a clear indication that the killer viewed their victims not as individuals, but as archetypes, embodying certain forbidden quests for knowledge. The carved wooden bird, a symbol of such macabre significance, was undeniably the killer's mark. Its reappearance was a chilling confirmation that the same entity responsible for the deaths of Albright and Heart was now responsible for Bennett's demise. This was not a series of unrelated tragedies; it was a deliberate, orchestrated campaign. The meticulous staging, the thematic resonance with historical accounts of obsessive scholarship, and the recurring symbol all pointed to a perpetrator with a deep understanding of obscure lore, a penchant for ritual, and an unwavering commitment to their terrifying agenda.

The air in Dr. Bennett's office, usually thick with the scent of aging paper and forgotten ink, now carried the metallic tang of something far more disturbing. It was a scent Maria had come to associate with death, a grim perfume that clung to the fabric of her investigation like a shroud. The scene itself was a tableau of scholarly obsession, a testament to a life dedicated to the forgotten narratives of humanity's darkest corners. Bennett, a man whose reclusive nature had often been the subject of hushed academic gossip, lay as if asleep, though the unnatural stillness and the subtle pallor of his skin betrayed the finality of his repose. The meticulously arranged books, the scattered notes, the faint impression of his head against the aged oak of his desk – it all spoke of a mind so engrossed in its own labyrinthine world that it had become oblivious to the intrusion of the outside, the mundane, the deadly.

But it wasn't just the disarray of a life tragically cut short that held Maria's attention. It was the deliberate artistry of the scene, the chilling precision with which the killer had curated Bennett's final moments. The carved wooden bird, a symbol that had now become a grim harbinger, lay nestled beneath Bennett's lifeless hand, its smooth, dark wood a stark contrast to the pallor of his skin. It was a signature, a boast, a testament to the killer's continued presence, their unwavering pursuit of a dark agenda. Maria knelt, her gloved fingers hovering over the object, a sense of profound unease prickling at her skin. The bird was more than just a marker; it was a carefully placed piece in a game she was only beginning to comprehend.

As her gaze swept across the desk, her eyes fell upon another item, almost hidden beneath a loose sheaf of papers. It was a vellum card, elegantly aged, bearing an inscription in a familiar, calligraphic hand. Maria's breath hitched. She recognized the script from the previous scene, a cruel signature that seemed to mock the very act of scholarly inquiry. Her fingers, steady despite the tremor running through her, carefully lifted the card. On it, a passage was penned, a lament from a world both ancient and achingly familiar:

Phaus, who had loved Aurora, had, by the cruel caprice of fate, been transformed into a bird of ill omen.

So too, Callisto, once proud nymph, now a constellation, forever bearing witness to Jupiter's deceit and Juno's wrath. Even Narcissus, his beauty a fatal snare, found his form eternally reflected, a prisoner of his own desire. Such are the metamorphoses, the transformations wrought by gods and by the cruel hands of destiny, where beauty curdles into sorrow, and existence becomes a perpetual echo of loss.

Maria read the words again, the Latinate cadence of the passage resonating with a chilling familiarity. It was a direct quote, she realized with a sickening jolt, from Ovid's Metamorphoses, a seminal work of classical literature, a tapestry of myths woven with themes of transformation, loss, and the often tragic consequences of divine intervention or mortal hubris. This wasn't just a random quote; it was a deliberate choice, a literary allusion that spoke volumes about the killer's mindset.

The passage detailed the sorrowful transformations of characters touched by divine decree or the brutal whims of fate. Phaus, the bird of ill omen, forever a harbinger of misfortune. Callisto, the nymph, eternally bound to the heavens, a celestial monument to betrayal. Narcissus, forever captivated by his own reflection, a prisoner of vanity. Each a story of beauty curdled into sorrow, of existence becoming a perpetual echo of loss. It spoke of a beautiful but doomed existence, a poignant reflection of Bennett's own reclusive life, dedicated to the morbid and the obscure. His scholarly pursuits, his immersion in the very folklore of death and transformation, had made him, in the killer's eyes, a kindred spirit to these doomed figures. He had sought to understand the ultimate transformation, death, and in doing so, had perhaps become a subject of it, a character in this grim Ovidian drama.

A profound sense of dread, heavier than any she had yet experienced, settled upon Maria. The killer wasn't merely choosing victims based on a shared interest in mortality. They were curating a narrative, a grotesque anthology of death, drawing inspiration from a literary canon that explored the very essence of transformation and despair. The wooden bird was their signature, but these literary excerpts were their commentary, their twisted interpretation of the lives they so callously extinguished. It was a chilling realization: the killer was not just a murderer, but a scholar of sorts, a twisted literary critic wielding a blade instead of a pen.

Maria felt a creeping unease that transcended the immediate horror of Bennett's death. The Ovidian lament wasn't just a poetic flourish; it was a blueprint. It suggested a methodical approach, a systematic working through of a literary canon, each victim a character plucked from the pages of myth, their lives mirroring the tragic fates depicted in the ancient texts. The selection process, once seemingly tied to obscure death rituals, now appeared to be guided by a more sophisticated, and more terrifying, logic. The killer was not simply eliminating individuals; they were enacting a macabre play, casting their victims in roles that resonated with their perceived obsessions, their perceived descent into the abyss of mortality research.

She recalled Professor Albright, his work on ancient death cults, the primal rites that sought to commune with the departed. Had he been Ovid's Numa, perhaps, seeking divine pronouncements on mortality? And Dr. Heart, her expertise in Gothic literature, the tales of spectral encounters and the haunting echoes of the past. Was she meant to embody the tragic figure of Eurydice, forever lost to the underworld, her beauty a cruel reminder of what could not be reclaimed? Each victim, now, seemed to be a character in a grand, tragic narrative, their deaths carefully orchestrated to resonate with specific mythological archetypes.

Bennett, with his fascination for morbid folklore and ancient death rituals, was a perfect fit for the Ovidian theme of transformation through sorrow. His life, spent delving into the very myths that spoke of characters forever altered by fate, had seemingly led him to his own cruel metamorphosis. The passage spoke of beauty curdled into sorrow, of existence becoming a perpetual echo of loss. It was a fitting epitaph for Bennett, a man whose life had been dedicated to the study of sorrow and transformation.

Maria's mind raced, piecing together the fragments of this horrifying mosaic. The Aeon Society, Gibson's confession, Clara's obsession, and now this – a killer meticulously selecting victims and leaving behind literary clues that spoke of Ovidian tragedy. It was a pattern of terrifying coherence, a progression that suggested a mind not only capable of brutal violence but also steeped in classical literature, using it to frame their actions, to imbue their killings with a perverse sense of purpose.

The killer was working through a literary canon, Maria realized, a chillingly intellectual killer who viewed their victims as characters in a preordained drama. They were not just extinguishing lives; they were casting them into roles, assigning them mythological fates that mirrored their academic pursuits. The Ovidian lament was a clear indication that the killer possessed a deep understanding of classical literature, and that they were using it to communicate something profound, something terrifying.

The "transformation" Ovid wrote of was no longer a poetic metaphor; it was a literal reality for the victims. They were transformed from scholars into cautionary tales, from seekers of knowledge into tragic figures forever etched into the grim annals of Elmwood University. Bennett's quiet, reclusive existence, dedicated to the study of death's myriad forms, had rendered him a prime candidate for such a grim metamorphosis. His life's work had become his epitaph, his office a stage set for his final, Ovidian act.

Maria felt a cold knot tighten in her stomach. The killer was not a random entity driven by primal rage. They were deliberate, calculated, and possessed a disturbing intellectual bent. They saw themselves, perhaps, as a facilitator of fate, an agent of transformation, ushering these scholars towards their destined, tragic ends. The "cruel caprice of fate" Ovid described was being enacted by a very human hand, a hand that meticulously chose its verses, its victims, its violent crescendos.

She looked back at Bennett, his face serene in death, a stark contrast to the turbulent depths he had explored in his research. Had he, too, felt the siren call of transformation, the allure of understanding the ultimate change? Had his pursuit of the morbid and the arcane led him to a place where the line between scholarship and personal peril had blurred into non-existence? The Ovidian passage suggested a fatal beauty, a doomed existence. Bennett's life, in its solitary dedication to the dark arts of academia, had possessed a certain somber beauty, a beauty now extinguished by a brutal reality.

The wooden bird, so small and unassuming, felt heavy with implication. It was the marker of a presence that understood the power of symbols, both ancient and literary. It was the mark of a killer who was not just taking lives, but composing a narrative, a horrifying opera of death, with classical literature as its libretto. The echoes of Ovid's myths now mingled with the stark reality of Bennett's demise, creating a dissonance that was both deeply unsettling and profoundly illuminating. Maria knew, with a chilling certainty, that the killer was weaving a complex tapestry of violence and allusion, and that she, too, was becoming a character in this unfolding Ovidian tragedy. The university, once a sanctuary of learning, had transformed into a macabre stage, its hallowed halls now echoing with the silent laments of its fallen scholars, each death a carefully chosen verse in a killer's terrifying poem.

The meticulous selection of the Ovidian quote was not arbitrary; it was a deliberate choice, a subtle declaration of intent. It indicated that the killer possessed a deep appreciation for narrative structure, for the power of storytelling, and for the enduring resonance of classical myths. This was not mere murder; it was a performance, a carefully crafted act designed to convey a specific message to a specific audience. And Maria, by her very presence at these crime scenes, was increasingly becoming that audience.

The parallels were too striking to ignore. Each victim, in their own way, had wrestled with the mysteries of mortality. Albright, the historian of death cults, seeking understanding in ancient rituals. Heart, the literary scholar, exploring the psychological landscapes of fear and the spectral. Bennett, the folklorist, delving into the very stories that sought to explain the inexplicable transformations of life and death. And Clara, her doctoral thesis a deep dive into the existential dread that death inspires. They were all, in essence, Ovidian figures, characters grappling with profound existential questions, their lives marked by a certain doomed beauty in their relentless pursuit of knowledge.

The killer's choice of Ovid was particularly apt. The Metamorphoses is a sprawling epic filled with tales of gods and mortals, of love and betrayal, of curses and transformations. It's a work that explores the fluidity of existence, the way in which form and identity can be irrevocably altered by powerful forces, be they divine or, in this case, human. The killer seemed to be enacting a modern-day Metamorphoses, transforming scholars into symbols of dread, their academic pursuits becoming the very catalysts for their tragic ends.

Maria's thoughts drifted to the specific figures mentioned in the passage. Phaus, transformed into a bird of ill omen, was perhaps a nod to the harbinger of death that the wooden bird represented. Callisto, the nymph cursed by Juno, her transformation a consequence of divine wrath, could be an allusion to the perceived transgressions of the victims, their academic curiosity perhaps seen as a form of hubris by their tormentor. And Narcissus, eternally trapped by his own reflection, spoke of obsession, of a self-absorption that could lead to one's downfall. This resonated deeply with Maria's understanding of Clara's own descent into her research, a potential self-imprisonment within the labyrinth of her thesis.

The passage was not merely descriptive; it was prescriptive. It suggested a worldview where transformation, especially in the face of fate, was inevitable and often sorrowful. The killer was not simply killing; they were orchestrating what they perceived as inevitable transformations, guiding their victims towards a final, dramatic metamorphosis. Bennett's death, staged to evoke a scholar consumed by his research, was a textbook example of this Ovidian interpretation. He had been transformed from a living scholar into a grim symbol of scholarly obsession, his life's work culminating in his own tragic end.

The implications for Maria were stark. If the killer was working through a literary canon, then the next victim would likely be chosen based on their resonance with another myth, another tragic figure. And the next quote would be another clue, another piece of the puzzle deliberately placed to guide, or perhaps to taunt, her investigation. The killer was not just a murderer; they were a curator of death, an artist whose medium was human lives, whose canvas was the ancient literature that spoke of life's deepest fears and transformations. The Ovidian lament was a testament to a mind that saw the world through the lens of myth, a mind that believed itself to be fulfilling a grand, albeit horrific, narrative. The ivory tower of Elmwood University had become a stage for a chillingly intellectual drama, and Maria was now an unwilling participant, forced to decipher the verses of death before she, too, became a character in its final, tragic act.

Dr. Bennett's office, a sanctuary of morbid curiosity, revealed a mind consumed by the very abyss it sought to understand. Maria sifted through the professor's meticulously organized chaos, the air still heavy with the spectral scent of his final moments. It wasn't just his untimely demise that was a testament to his obsessions; it was the nature of those obsessions themselves. His life's work, it seemed, had been a lifelong interrogation of death, not as an ending, but as a phenomenon, a subject of profound study and, disturbingly, artistic contemplation.

His research spanned continents and centuries, a breathtakingly comprehensive catalog of humanity's darkest engagements with mortality. Maria found files detailing ritualistic suicides, not as acts of desperation, but as meticulously planned farewells, echoing the self-immolations of ancient martyrs or the stoic suicides of Roman philosophers. There were studies on deaths that eerily mirrored mythical accounts – individuals who met their end in ways that seemed plucked directly from the annals of legend. He had compiled extensive bibliographies on figures who actively courted death, who saw it not as an enemy to be feared, but as a final, definitive masterpiece.

The sheer volume of his research was staggering. Beyond the academic papers and peer-reviewed journals, Bennett had amassed a collection of ephemera: newspaper clippings detailing bizarre deaths, translated ancient texts describing funeral rites, and even crude sketches and photographs of sites where unusual deaths had occurred. Each item was a breadcrumb, leading Maria deeper into the labyrinth of Bennett's psyche, and by extension, the mind of the killer who had curated his final tableau.

One particular section of his archives, however, sent a shiver down Maria's spine. It was a collection of Bennett's private journals, their worn leather covers hinting at countless hours of introspection. These were not the detached observations of an academic; these were raw, philosophical musings that bordered on a reverence for death. He wrote of death as the ultimate artistic expression, the final brushstroke on the canvas of existence. He spoke of the beauty in finality, the profound artistic statement inherent in a life deliberately extinguished, particularly when it resonated with a narrative, a myth, a predetermined fate.

The language was evocative, almost poetic. Bennett described the act of dying as a form of transcendence, a transformation into something eternal, an artwork frozen in time. He mused on the courage of those who faced their end with agency, who dictated the terms of their own dissolution. He theorized that the most profound works of art were not those created by the living, but by the dying – their final moments a testament to their essence, their life's narrative brought to its most impactful conclusion. He saw echoes of this in the stories of Sati, the ancient Indian practice of widow sacrifice, where a wife would immolate herself on her husband's funeral pyre, a deeply symbolic and, in his view, artistically significant act. He analyzed the suicides of figures like Seneca, who faced execution with philosophical composure, turning his final moments into a public discourse on mortality.

Maria felt a growing sense of dread. The themes Bennett explored – the artistic nature of death, the significance of transformation, the concept of life as a narrative culminating in a dramatic end – were chillingly familiar. They mirrored, with unsettling precision, the fragmented lore she had uncovered concerning the Aeon Society. The cult, in its esoteric writings, had also spoken of death as a form of liberation, an ultimate artistic act, a shedding of the mundane to embrace a higher, perhaps eternal, form. The Society's members weren't just seeking immortality; they were exploring the *aesthetics* of existence and its cessation. Bennett's journals were not just academic observations; they were a confession of a shared, dangerous fascination.

He had meticulously documented his study of various death cults and esoteric groups, his academic curiosity seemingly a thin veneer for a deeper, more personal engagement. He explored the ways in which different cultures and historical periods had mythologized death, creating narratives that gave meaning to the inexplicable. He was particularly drawn to stories of individuals who, through their deaths, achieved a form of apotheosis, becoming figures of legend or even deities. The Ovidian figures mentioned in the previous note—Phaus, Callisto, Narcissus—were not just characters in a book to Bennett; they were case studies in the power of transformation, the way a life could be irrevocably altered, its essence preserved or reimagined through its ending.

Bennett's fascination wasn't limited to the grand, mythical narratives. He delved into the more intimate, psychological aspects of mortality. He studied the phenomenology of dying, the sensory and emotional experiences reported by those who had near-death experiences. He collected accounts of people who claimed to have "seen the light," to have experienced a profound sense of peace or transcendence at the threshold of death. These were not just scientific curiosities for him; they were glimpses into the ultimate transformation, the subjective experience of moving from one state of being to another.

His journals also contained disturbing philosophical inquiries into the nature of consciousness and its relationship to the physical body. He wrote of the possibility of consciousness persisting beyond death, not in a spiritual or religious sense, but as an imprint, an energetic residue that lingered in the places where intense emotions, particularly those surrounding death, had been experienced. This was a theme that resonated with some of the more fringe theories within the Aeon Society, their talk of residual psychic energy and the ability of certain individuals to attune themselves to these lingering impressions.

The proximity of Bennett's death to these lines of inquiry was not coincidental, Maria felt. The killer was not simply picking random victims; they were selecting individuals whose obsessions intersected with their own, individuals who, in the killer's twisted logic, were ripe for a "transformation" that would align with a specific narrative. Allen, with his deep dive into the psychological and artistic dimensions of death, his exploration of its mythic resonance, and his almost reverential contemplation of its transformative power, was a prime candidate. He had, in a sense, been living within the very themes the killer was enacting.

The meticulous nature of Bennett's research suggested a mind that craved order, even in the face of chaos and death. His files were categorized with almost obsessive precision, his notes cross-referenced to an astonishing degree. Yet, within this framework of order, there was a clear trajectory towards the macabre. He wasn't just studying death; he was *immersing* himself in it, dissecting its every facet, from the primal fear it evoked to the transcendent peace it might offer.

Maria found a sub-section in Allen's archives labeled *The Art of Letting Go*, a collection of personal accounts and historical anecdotes of individuals who had approached their death with a sense of artistic purpose. There were stories of artists who completed their final masterpieces on their deathbeds, of musicians who composed their last symphonies in their final hours, of writers who penned their dying confessions with a clarity and focus that belied their physical state. Bennett viewed these individuals not as victims of fate, but as artists who seized control of their final act, transforming their demise into a profound statement.

He had even begun to formulate his own theories on the "aesthetic of mortality." He believed that a death, to be truly significant, had to possess a certain narrative coherence, a thematic resonance that elevated it beyond mere biological cessation. This was where his academic work began to blur into something far more dangerous, something that bordered on a glorification of death as the ultimate art form. His journals spoke of the "symphony of the void," the "sculpture of silence," and the "painting of oblivion." The language was highly metaphorical, but the underlying sentiment was clear: death, when approached with intention and understanding, could be the most profound artistic expression of all.

This philosophical bent, this reverence for death as an artistic culmination, was the most disturbing aspect of Bennett's obsessions. It was a viewpoint that, Maria now realized with chilling certainty, was shared by the killer. The Aeon Society's texts had spoken of "shedding the temporal shell" and embracing the "eternal canvas." Bennett's journals articulated a similar sentiment, albeit from a more scholarly and less cultish perspective. He was not a member of the Aeon Society in the traditional sense, but his research had led him to the very same philosophical precipice.

The carved wooden bird, placed beneath Allen's hand, now took on a new significance. It was not merely a signature; it was a symbol of this artistic transformation, a tangible representation of the "bird of ill omen" mentioned in the Ovidian passage. Phaus, transformed into a bird of ill omen, was not just a character in a myth; he was a representation of fate, of inevitable change, and perhaps, for the killer, a symbol of artistic influence. Allen, by his deep contemplation of death as art, had perhaps invited this transformation, this final, grim artistic interpretation of his own life.

Maria found herself tracing the lines of Bennett's handwriting, the ink a stark contrast to the aged paper. He had written extensively about the psychological allure of death, the morbid fascination that drew people to its edge. He theorized that this fascination was not necessarily a pathology, but a fundamental aspect of the human condition, a primal drive to understand the ultimate mystery. He believed that by exploring death in all its forms – its rituals, its myths, its psychological impact – one could gain a deeper understanding of life itself.

He had compiled case studies of individuals who, through their fascination with death, had achieved a unique form of enlightenment or artistic expression. These were often figures who lived on the fringes of society, ostracized for their morbid interests, yet who found a profound sense of purpose in their exploration of mortality. Bennett seemed to admire their dedication, their willingness to embrace the taboo, to stare into the void and find meaning there. He saw them as pioneers, charting unknown territories of human experience.

The Ovidian quote, Maria realized, was not just a reference to transformation; it was a commentary on the perceived destiny of those who delved too deeply into forbidden knowledge or pursued beauty with a dangerous intensity. Phaus, Callisto, Narcissus – these were figures whose lives were irrevocably altered by their desires, their actions, or the whims of fate. Bennett, in his relentless pursuit of understanding death's artistic potential, had become a figure of similar tragic resonance. He had, in the killer's eyes, transformed himself into a subject of his own morbid fascination.

The journals also revealed Bennett's interest in the concept of "pre-death experiences." He had gathered accounts from individuals who, before their actual demise, experienced vivid dreams or visions that seemed to foreshadow their end. He analyzed these experiences not as supernatural phenomena, but as psychological phenomena, the mind's way of preparing for the ultimate transition. He speculated that these pre-death visions often contained symbolic imagery, reflecting the individual's deepest fears, desires, and unresolved issues. This, too, resonated with the killer's apparent method of weaving symbolic and literary allusions into their crimes.

Maria's gaze fell upon a passage where Bennett mused on the nature of legacy. He wrote that true legacy was not measured by wealth or fame, but by the impact of one's final act, by the enduring resonance of one's departure. He believed that a death, when imbued with meaning and purpose, could become a timeless testament, a work of art that continued to speak to generations to come. It was a chillingly nihilistic perspective, one that saw the cessation of life as an opportunity for a profound artistic statement.

The professor's own office, with its carefully curated collection of macabre artifacts and scholarly tomes, was a reflection of his life's obsession. It was a space where the academic and the arcane converged, where the study of death was not a morbid curiosity, but a profound philosophical pursuit. The meticulously arranged books, the shelves lined with anatomical models and ancient funerary texts, the faint scent of dust and decay – it all spoke of a life dedicated to understanding the ultimate mystery. And now,

Bennett himself had become a part of that mystery, a subject in the very narrative he had so diligently studied. The killer had, in a sense, completed his final artistic commission.

The theme of transformation, so central to Ovid, was not merely a literary conceit for Bennett. He saw it as a fundamental aspect of existence, particularly in relation to death. He explored the ways in which death could transform individuals, not only in the eyes of others but also in their own self-perception, even if that perception was only achieved in the moments leading up to their end. He wrote of the potential for a death to be a catalyst for profound change, a shedding of the old self and an embrace of something new, something eternal, however one defined that eternity. This was a concept that the killer had clearly seized upon, using it as the philosophical undergirding for their brutal acts. Bennett's fascination with transformation, with death as the ultimate art form, had made him an ideal subject for the killer's twisted artistic vision. He had, by his own intellectual and philosophical pursuits, paved the way for his own dramatic, and tragic, metamorphosis. The killer was merely the agent of this perceived artistic destiny.

The realization dawned not as a thunderclap, but as a cold, creeping tide. Maria stood amidst the remnants of Professor Bennett's academic life, his meticulously cataloged obsessions now a chilling mirror to the present horror. It wasn't merely the morbid fascination with death that Bennett had documented, but the *way* he had documented it, with an almost religious reverence for its potential for transformation, for its status as the ultimate, immutable artwork. This was the missing piece, the interpretive key that unlocked the killer's macabre theater. The university, once a place of learning and quiet contemplation, had become the stage for a tragedy penned by a deranged auteur, its students and faculty unwitting players in a drama of death.

The killer wasn't simply extinguishing lives; they were composing them. Each victim, each scene, was a deliberate brushstroke on a canvas of terror. Bennett's research into ritualistic suicides, into deaths that eerily mirrored myth, into figures who courted their own demise as a final, definitive masterpiece – these weren't just academic curiosities to the killer. They were a handbook, a manifesto. The Aeon Society's pronouncements on death as liberation, as an artistic act, as a shedding of the mundane for a higher form, were not abstract theories for this murderer. They were executable principles. Maria saw it now: the killer was not just a murderer, but a curator of demise, a Composer of mortality, orchestrating a symphony of the void.

The professor's journals, filled with his musings on death as the ultimate artistic expression, on the beauty in finality, on the profound statement inherent in a deliberately extinguished life, were a terrifying confession of shared ideology. Bennett had spoken of death as the final brushstroke, the ultimate transformation. The killer had taken that philosophy and made it visceral, horrifyingly literal. The Ovidian echoes, the carefully selected literary allusions – these weren't random flourishes. They were signposts, guiding the audience, Maria included, through the killer's narrative. Phaus, Callisto, Narcissus – these weren't just characters from ancient texts; they were archetypes, roles to be cast, fates to be enacted. The killer was selecting victims who, in their eyes, embodied certain traits, destined to fulfill a specific, preordained role in this grand, horrific play.

Maria felt a phantom chill, imagining the killer selecting their next player. Who would it be? What scene would they inhabit? The university was a vast repository of potential, a veritable library of lives waiting to be cast. The meticulousness of Bennett's work, his obsessive categorization, his detailed cross-referencing – it all suggested a mind that craved order, even in its descent into madness. The killer possessed a similar, twisted order. They weren't acting on impulse; they were executing a script, each murder a carefully plotted act designed to advance the narrative, to deepen the thematic resonance.

Dr. Gibson sat across from Maria, his usual air of detached intellectualism replaced by a palpable unease. The fluorescent lights of the precinct interview room seemed to cast him in a harsh, unforgiving glow, highlighting the subtle tremor in his hands as he fiddled with a loose thread on his tweed jacket. Detective Richards had just laid out the grim facts of Professor Bennett's demise; the gruesome tableau Maria herself had so recently witnessed. The mention of the specific Ovidian quote, the one scrawled with chilling deliberation near the body, had been the final catalyst, shattering whatever fragile composure Gibson had managed to maintain.

"Bennet...Jacob Bennett?" Gibson's voice was a low murmur, laced with disbelief, as if the name itself were a foreign object he was struggling to recognize. He looked at Maria, his eyes wide and searching, seeking an anchor in the storm of dawning horror. "Are you certain? Jacob Bennett is...was...a colleague. We shared," he paused, struggling for the right word, "a certain intellectual kinship."

Maria watched him, her own gaze unwavering. She recognized the genuine shock in his expression, the flicker of distress that tightened the lines around his mouth. Yet, beneath that, she sensed something else, a carefully guarded reserve, a subtle withholding that pricked at her detective's intuition. Gibson was a scholar of human nature, of its darkest impulses and most profound mysteries. He understood the performance of grief, the nuances of confession, and the subtle art of omission. And he was, at this very moment, performing.

“A kinship?” Maria prompted, her tone neutral, but her eyes sharp. She’d seen enough to know that academic circles, particularly those dabbling in esoteric philosophy, could harbor their own peculiar rivalries and secrets.

Gibson cleared his throat, a dry, rasping sound. “Yes. Jacob and I...we spent many late nights, often fueled by too much coffee and not enough sleep, dissecting the grand pronouncements of literature, the philosophical underpinnings of mortality. We debated,” he sighed, a weary sound that seemed to carry the weight of years of intellectual sparring, “the nature of existence, the allure of the void. He was...he was profoundly interested in the intersections of art and death.”

Maria leaned forward slightly. "The Aeon Society. Did your discussions touch upon that?" The name had surfaced in Bennett's papers, a shadowy organization dedicated to exploring death as liberation, as the ultimate artistic act. It was a concept that seemed to permeate Bennett’s research, and by extension, the killer's macabre designs.

Gibson's composure faltered for a fraction of a second. His eyes flickered away, towards the grimy window of the interview room, as if seeking an escape route. "The Aeon Society?" he repeated, the name tasting unfamiliar on his tongue, yet he knew it intimately. "Jacob's interests were broad, Detective. He explored many philosophical currents. He was...eclectic. He believed that by understanding the boundaries of life; by confronting the ultimate unknown, one could unlock deeper truths about the human condition. He saw death not as an end, but as a transformation, a profound artistic statement. He often spoke of it in terms of the great artists, those who seemed to channel their final moments into a transcendent work. He felt it was the ultimate control, the ultimate expression."

His explanation was eloquent, carefully constructed, and entirely plausible. Gibson was an expert wordsmith, a weaver of eloquent narratives. But Maria felt the artifice, the deliberate shaping of his words to present a particular, palatable version of the truth. Bennett's obsession with death as art, the Aeon Society's pronouncements on mortality as liberation – these weren't just abstract intellectual curiosities for Gibson. They were shared battlegrounds, arenas of debate where he and Bennett had wrestled with the very concepts the killer was now enacting.

"And this quote," Maria pressed, tapping the folder containing the crime scene photos, the damning piece of evidence. " 'Mors ultima linea rerum est.' Death is the end of all things. Did Bennett quote Ovid often in your discussions?"

Gibson's breath hitched. The academic mask slipped entirely, revealing a man genuinely unnerved. His gaze darted from between Maria to the empty wall, a flicker of something akin to fear in their depths. "Ovid," he murmured, his voice barely audible. "Yes. Jacob was fascinated by Ovid's exploration of transformation. The metamorphoses...he saw them as powerful allegories for the human drive to change, to transcend, even in the face of inevitable endings. He believed that true art lay in embracing that transformation, in consciously orchestrating one's own becoming, even if that becoming led to oblivion." He paused, then added, his voice a little stronger, as if regaining some measure of his academic footing, "He felt that a life lived fully, with a profound understanding of its finitude, could culminate in a death that was itself a masterpiece. A final, indelible act of creation."

Maria's mind raced. Bennett's journals had painted a vivid picture of a man captivated by death as art. He'd documented cases of artists who completed their final works on their deathbeds, musicians who composed their last symphonies in their final hours. He saw it as an act of defiance, a reclaiming of agency in the face of oblivion. He'd spoken of the *aesthetic of mortality*, a concept that seemed to have been adopted, and terrifyingly amplified, by their killer.

"So, Professor Bennett believed that death could be a work of art?" Maria asked, her voice deceptively soft.

Gibson met her gaze, and for a fleeting moment, Maria saw a reflection of Bennett's own academic fervor, albeit tinged with a newfound disquiet. "He believed that the *perception* of death as art was a profound aspect of human psychology," Gibson corrected, his scholar's precision returning. "That by imbuing it with narrative, with symbolic meaning, with a sense of deliberate finality, one could elevate it beyond a mere biological event. He studied the rituals, the myths, the historical figures who courted death, who seemed to embrace it with a peculiar grace, transforming their final moments into something...legendary. He saw it as the ultimate expression of self, a final, definitive statement. He often mused on what he called the 'symphony of the void,' the 'sculpture of silence,' the 'painting of oblivion.' Poetic language, of course, but it spoke to his deep fascination with death's potential for profound, artistic meaning."

Maria felt a chill creep up her spine. Gibson's words, while cloaked in academic discourse, echoed the very language she'd found in Bennett's personal writings, the chilling pronouncements that seemed to prefigure the killer's methodology. It was as if Gibson, through his intellectual engagement with Bennett, had inadvertently become a conduit for the killer's twisted philosophy.

"Professor Gibson," Maria began, choosing her words carefully, "Bennett was found in his office. It was...arranged. Almost curated. Like a stage. And the quote..." she let the implication hang in the air, "it suggests a deliberate narrative. A message. Did Bennett ever discuss with you the possibility of... staging one's own death? Or perhaps, someone else's?"

Gibson visibly recoiled. His hand flew to his chest, as if to ward off an unseen blow. His eyes, previously filled with a controlled intellectual distress, now held a flicker of something raw, of genuine alarm. "Staging? My dear Detective, Jacob was an academic, a scholar of life and its most profound mysteries, not a perpetrator of violence. His interest in death was purely theoretical, an exploration of its philosophical and artistic dimensions. He sought to understand its power, its allure, not to wield it as a weapon." He swallowed hard, his gaze fixed on Maria, as if searching for any sign of accusation in her eyes. "He was a man who lived in his head, immersed in ancient texts and abstract concepts. The idea of...of physically enacting such violence...it's abhorrent to everything he stood for, everything I stand for."

But Maria saw the slight tremor in his voice, the almost imperceptible clenching of his jaw. He protested too much. His distress seemed genuine, yes, but beneath it, she sensed the carefully constructed edifice of academic detachment beginning to crack, revealing something far more complex, and perhaps, far more dangerous. He was hiding something. Not necessarily direct involvement, but a piece of knowledge, a truth he was unwilling to share, a truth that might illuminate the killer's path, and in doing so, perhaps expose Gibson himself to the chilling repercussions of his intellectual dalliances.

"Professor," Maria continued, her voice low and steady, "Bennett's work delved into the Aeon Society's pronouncements on death as liberation, as an ultimate artistic act. He explored their texts, their theories on shedding the 'temporal shell.' Did he ever speak to you about the society itself? Its members? Its activities?"

Gibson hesitated. The tremor in his hands returned, more pronounced this time. He looked down at the worn surface of the interview table, his knuckles white where he gripped its edge. "Jacob's research was...vast," he said, his voice strained. "He was drawn to the fringes of philosophical thought, to movements that pushed the boundaries of conventional understanding. The Aeon Society...it was a subject of his academic curiosity. He found their writings on death as a transformative, artistic experience...compelling. From an analytical standpoint, of course. He admired their...boldness. Their willingness to challenge societal norms regarding mortality. He saw them as an extreme manifestation of an idea he himself explored in his more theoretical writings." He finally met Maria's gaze, his eyes holding a mixture of academic honesty and profound unease. "We debated their philosophy. I cautioned him about the potential dangers of such abstract notions when they intersected with reality. I warned him about the allure of the esoteric, the way it could warp perception. I told him that the line between intellectual exploration and dangerous obsession was a fine one, and that he was dancing very close to the edge."

Maria detected the subtle shift in his narrative. He was moving from shared intellectual pursuits to cautionary tales, positioning himself as the voice of reason against Bennett's perceived descent into dangerous territory. It was a subtle self-preservation tactic, a way to distance himself from the grim reality that was unfolding.

"And did he listen?" Maria pressed, sensing she was close to a breakthrough, or at least, a clearer understanding of Gibson's complicity.

Gibson sighed, a sound heavy with unspoken words. "Jacob was...driven by his intellect. He believed that to truly understand something, one had to immerse oneself in it, to explore its deepest implications, no matter how unsettling. He saw the philosophical underpinnings of death as art as a field ripe for exploration, a way to understand the very essence of human existence. He believed that a life dedicated to such profound contemplation, a life lived on the precipice of ultimate understanding, was itself a form of masterpiece. He often spoke of 'pre-death experiences,' of how the mind, when confronted with its own mortality, could conjure symbolic imagery, visions that mirrored its deepest desires and fears. He analyzed these not as supernatural events, but as psychological preparations, the mind's way of composing its final narrative." Gibson paused, his gaze distant, lost in his own troubled thoughts. "He saw the killer's actions, if...if they are indeed driven by such a philosophy, as a tragic, albeit extreme, manifestation of these very ideas. He believed that a death imbued with meaning, with narrative coherence, with artistic intent, could become a legacy. A timeless testament. He was fascinated by the concept of legacy, you see. Not of one's own life, but of one's ultimate act. The final statement. The killer is certainly making a statement, isn't that right?"

Maria didn't answer. Gibson's words painted a chilling picture of a scholar so consumed by his own theories that he had, perhaps, inadvertently invited the very darkness he studied into his own life. He had explored the philosophical precipice, and now, standing beside Maria, he seemed to be realizing that the killer had taken that leap, dragging Bennett, and potentially others, with them into the abyss. The intellectual fascination Gibson described was a precarious tightrope, and it was clear he felt the ground shifting beneath his own feet. His unease was no longer just a performance; it was the dawning realization that the ivory tower of academia had crumbled, revealing a blood-soaked reality, and he, through his intellectual kinship with Bennett, might be too close to the fallout. He was a man who understood the language of death as art, and he was beginning to understand that the killer was fluent, and Bennett had been their first, tragic masterpiece.

Gibson's own intellectual journey had led him to the edge of this macabre theater, and now, he was a reluctant observer, his academic composure shattered by the horrifying realization that the theories he and Bennett had so passionately debated were now being enacted with lethal precision. He understood the motive, the philosophy, the chilling artistic intent, and that understanding was a burden heavier than any academic text. He was grappling with the uncomfortable truth that his own intellectual curiosity, and Bennett's, had created fertile ground for this monstrous artistry.

CHAPTER 5

A DETECTIVE'S OBSESSION

The fluorescent hum of the precinct office had become a constant companion to Detective Maria Richards, a dull counterpoint to the relentless rhythm of her thoughts. Sleep, once a refuge, had transformed into a battleground. Each night, spectral figures from classical tragedies—a vengeful Clytemnestra, a tormented Oedipus, a desolate Eurydice—paraded through her dreams, their woes echoing in fragmented lines of verse. The Ovidian quote scrawled at Bennett's scene, "Mors ultima linea rerum est," Death is the end of all things, now resonated with a deeper, more disquieting resonance. It wasn't just a clue; it was a thesis, a declaration of intent that gnawed at her waking hours and infiltrated her subconscious.

The Elmwood murders were more than just a case; they had become an obsession. The killer, with their meticulous planning and chillingly precise execution, had presented a puzzle that appealed to the deepest, most analytical parts of Maria's mind. It was a dangerous intellectual game of cat and mouse, where the stakes were not just justice, but the very preservation of Maria's own sanity. She found herself scrutinizing every detail, every nuance, not just as a detective seeking truth, but as an intellect challenged by a formidable, albeit depraved, opponent. The killer's choices were not random acts of violence; they were carefully orchestrated performances, each victim a canvas upon which a twisted artistic vision was being realized. Maria felt a strange, unsettling kinship with this anonymous perpetrator, a recognition of the same intellectual rigor, the same drive for perfection, albeit manifested in something so monstrous. This was not the brutish violence she had encountered in other cases; this was calculated, refined, and horrifyingly beautiful in its own macabre way.

The weight of the investigation began to press down on Maria, blurring the lines between her professional duty and a growing, unsettling fascination. She found herself sketching out not just crime scene layouts, but also the killer's potential aesthetic motivations. She poured over Bennett's collected works, tracing the threads of his research on mortality, art, and the 'aesthetic of the void.' The Aeon Society, once a spectral rumor, now loomed large in her mind. She imagined clandestine meetings in dimly lit chambers, hushed pronouncements on the transcendent power of death, and the intoxicating allure of embracing oblivion as the ultimate artistic act. She saw Bennett not just as a victim, but as a misguided acolyte, a scholar who had strayed too close to the intoxicating fire of his own morbid theories.

Her apartment, once a sanctuary of calm and order, began to reflect the chaos of her mind. Books lay open, dog-eared and annotated, their pages filled with cryptic marginalia. The faint scent of stale coffee, the constant companion of sleepless nights, permeated the air. She found herself sketching, not architectural plans for her next house, but grotesque anatomical studies, reminiscent of anatomical illustrations from ancient texts that Bennett had so admired. It was as if the killer's macabre artistic sensibilities were seeping into her own, a dark stain spreading across the pristine canvas of her professional life.

Dr. Gibson, her reluctant informant, had become a source of both frustration and intrigue. His academic detachment, while a shield, also served as a barrier, preventing her from fully grasping the depth of his knowledge. He spoke of Bennett's fascination with Ovid, with the transformative power of mythology, with the idea of death as a deliberate, artistic culmination. But Maria sensed that Gibson knew more, that his intellectual kinship with Bennett had been deeper, more perilous than he was willing to admit. He had danced on the precipice of these dark ideas, and now, he seemed terrified of the abyss that had swallowed his colleague. His unease, she believed, was not just fear of the killer, but a chilling recognition of how close he himself had come to the same intellectual and philosophical precipice. He understood the language of death as art, and he was beginning to understand that the killer was fluent, and Bennett had been their first, tragic masterpiece. Gibson's own intellectual journey had led him to the edge of this macabre theater, and now, he was a reluctant observer, his academic composure shattered by the horrifying realization that the theories he and Bennett had so passionately debated were now being enacted with lethal precision. He understood the motive, the philosophy, the chilling artistic intent, and that understanding was a burden heavier than any academic text.

She started to see parallels everywhere. The way the lamplight cast long, distorted shadows on her walls reminded her of Caravaggio's chiaroscuro. The rhythmic clicking of a her keyboard echoed the percussive beat of a symphonic movement Bennett might have admired. As she looked out, the city itself, with its hidden alleys and shadowed courtyards, seemed to pulse with a latent, artistic dread, a stage set for the killer's next act.

Her Lieutenant, Stanley Laramount, noticed the change. Her usual sharp focus was now accompanied by a certain weariness, a haunted look in her eyes that spoke of battles fought not just in the streets, but within the confines of her own mind. He'd found her slumped over her desk one evening, a crumpled paper on the floor beside her, a rough sketch of a laurel wreath entwined with a serpent. When he'd asked if she was alright, she'd simply murmured, "It's... beautiful, in a way. The symmetry of it all." The chilling admiration in her voice had sent a shiver down his spine. He knew Maria was brilliant, but this case was pushing her into uncharted, and potentially dangerous, intellectual territory.

The case consumed Richards not just professionally, but personally. The intellectual challenge was undeniable, a formidable opponent for her keen mind. The killer's methodical approach, their ability to weave literary allusions and philosophical concepts into their horrific acts, spoke of a profound, albeit twisted, intellect. It was this very intellect that captivated Maria, drawing her deeper into the labyrinth of the investigation. She found herself researching esoteric philosophical texts, deciphering the killer's cryptic messages with an almost obsessive zeal. The lines between Maria Richards, the detective, and Maria Richards, the scholar of the macabre, began to blur.

Her dreams became a vivid tapestry of death and art, populated by figures from Greek mythology and Renaissance painting. She saw the Fates spinning threads of blood, Persephone emerging from the underworld not in sorrow, but in triumph, adorned with poisonous flowers. She dreamt of Renaissance artists painstakingly rendering the contorted faces of the damned, their canvases dripping with an almost hallucinatory realism. It was as if her subconscious was trying to process the case, to find a framework, an artistic lens through which to understand the unfathomable.

One particular dream recurred with unsettling frequency. She stood before a vast, echoing hall, its walls adorned with macabre tableaux. In the center of the hall, a figure, cloaked and hooded, stood before an easel, painting with a brush dipped in what appeared to be... lifeblood. The air thrummed with a silent, intense creative energy, a palpable sense of profound, artistic purpose. As the figure turned, Maria saw not a face, but a swirling vortex of shadows, a void that seemed to pull at her very soul. The figure raised a hand, not in threat, but in invitation, and a single, perfectly formed Ovidian verse, “Ars longa, vita brevis,” Art is long, life is short, echoed through the hall. Maria would wake up with a gasp, her heart pounding, the scent of phantom oil paint and something metallic, like old blood, lingering in the air.

The obsession started to manifest in subtle ways during her waking hours. She found herself absently humming fragments of obscure Renaissance madrigals that Bennett had apparently been fond of. She’d catch herself analyzing the composition of everyday scenes, the play of light and shadow on the gritty streets, the geometric patterns of the fire escapes, as if searching for hidden artistic meaning. Her conversations with her Lieutenant became increasingly laden with literary references, much to his bewilderment.

"Richards, are you sure you're getting enough sleep?" Laramount asked one morning, watching her meticulously arrange the scattered case files on her desk into a near-perfect grid. "You've been a bit... intense lately."

Maria looked up, her eyes unfocused for a moment before snapping back to the present. "Intense, Stanley? Or inspired?" she countered, a faint, unsettling smile playing on her lips. "This killer isn't just a murderer; they're an artist. And I intend to understand their masterpiece, from inception to bloody conclusion."

Her obsession was a double-edged sword. It sharpened her intuition, allowing her to see connections others missed. She began to anticipate the killer's moves, to feel the rhythm of their twisted artistic cycle. But it also made her vulnerable, susceptible to the very darkness she was trying to expose. The intellectual game was no longer just a professional challenge; it was a personal descent, a journey into the heart of artistic madness. She was no longer just chasing a killer; she was chasing a philosophy, a dark artistic creed that threatened to consume her as surely as it had consumed Bennett. The weight of the Elmwood murders had become more than just a burden of responsibility; it was a crushing, all-encompassing presence, a shadow that stretched from the dimly lit offices of the precinct to the deepest, most disturbing corners of her own mind. She knew, with a chilling certainty, that this case would either make her a legend or break her entirely. The art was long, but her life, she feared, was proving to be quite short in the face of such all-consuming obsession. The carefully constructed walls of her professional detachment were crumbling, revealing a yearning, a morbid curiosity, that mirrored the very darkness she was tasked with eradicating. She was not just investigating a crime; she was becoming intimately acquainted with the aesthetic of oblivion, and the cost of that knowledge was becoming alarmingly clear.

The sterile, ordered world of Maria Richards's mind had been irrevocably infiltrated. The killer's modus operandi, so meticulously crafted and artistically executed, had forced her hand. It was no longer enough to simply follow the physical evidence; she had to dissect the intellectual architecture of the crimes, to understand the very language the perpetrator was using. This necessitated a dive into the arcane currents of literary theory, a realm she had previously approached with academic respect but not personal urgency. Now, it was a vital battleground. Her apartment, once a testament to her methodical nature – books precisely shelved, papers meticulously filed – was undergoing a metamorphosis. Stacks of texts on semiotics, narrative archetypes, and the philosophy of tragedy teetered precariously on every available surface. The air, once crisp and neutral, now held the faint, mingled scent of aging paper, stale coffee, and the persistent hum of her laptop, its screen an unblinking portal to endless digital archives.

She began with Ferdinand de Saussure, the foundational architect of semiotics. The concept of the sign, the arbitrary relationship between a signifier (the word or image) and the signified (the concept it represents), became a key to unlocking the killer's symbolic lexicon. The Ovidian quote, "Mors ultima linea rerum est," was not merely a Latin phrase; it was a signifier, a deliberate choice meant to evoke a specific signified: a nihilistic worldview, an embrace of death as the ultimate conclusion, a rejection of life's perceived futility. Maria traced the killer's deployment of these signs, noting how they were often presented in contexts that amplified their meaning, transforming mundane objects or locations into potent symbols. A victim's pose, the placement of a specific artifact, the very method of death – each was a carefully chosen signifier, designed to communicate a particular, chilling message to an audience that Maria was now acutely aware she was a part of. The killer was not just killing; they were constructing a narrative, a semiotic puzzle designed to be read, deciphered, and, perhaps, ultimately understood by those who possessed the requisite intellectual keys.

From semiotics, Maria ventured into the realm of narrative archetypes, drawing heavily on Carl Jung's theories of the collective unconscious and Northrop Frye's structural analysis of literature. She saw the killer's actions as not just individual acts of violence, but as echoes of recurring mythological patterns. The theme of sacrifice, of the scapegoat bearing the sins of the community, resonated deeply. Was Bennett, the victim, a willing sacrifice, a prophet of this macabre philosophy? Or was he simply the pawn in a larger, more devastating game? The archetypal figure of the trickster, the agent of chaos who disrupts established order, seemed to embody the killer's elusive nature. They moved through the city like a phantom, leaving behind a trail of disruption and fear, their identity as fluid and unknowable as a shifting shadow. Maria began to map the narrative arc of the killings, attempting to discern a pattern beyond the immediate victims. Was this a tragedy in the Aristotelian sense, with a flawed hero (or villain) meeting a predestined end? Or was it something more primal, a descent into the abyss that mirrored the ancient myths of Orpheus and Eurydice, of Hades and Persephone, where the boundary between life and death was a permeable membrane?

The philosophy of tragedy became her most consuming pursuit. She re-read Aeschylus, Sophocles, and Euripides, not as a literary scholar but as a detective seeking a blueprint for the killer's mindset. The concept of *hamartia*, the tragic flaw, haunted her.

What was the killer's flaw? Was it pride, an intellectual hubris that believed they could transcend the mortal coil through artistic expression? Was it a profound sense of disillusionment, a rejection of a world they deemed unworthy of existence? She debated with herself, scribbling notes in the margins of her battered copies of "The Bacchae" and "King Lear." The killer's meticulous planning, their apparent belief in the necessity and even beauty of their acts, pointed towards a fatalistic worldview, a belief that fate, or destiny, was an inexorable force. This philosophical underpinning, she suspected, was what differentiated this killer from the more common perpetrators of violence she encountered. This was not driven by simple rage or greed, but by a profound, albeit twisted, philosophical conviction.

Her apartment became a physical manifestation of this intellectual immersion. Books were no longer neatly contained; they spilled from shelves, lay open on the floor, their pages marked with a frantic scattering of sticky notes and highlighter ink. Diagrams, some sketched with the precision of an architect, others rendered with the frantic energy of a street artist, covered the walls, attempts to map not just crime scenes, but the killer's conceptual landscape. She'd tape newspaper clippings beside passages from Nietzsche, juxtapose anatomical drawings with quotes from Baudelaire, creating a visual cacophony that mirrored the storm raging within her mind. The scent of old paper was now overlaid with the sharp, metallic tang of ink from her pens, and the faint, unsettling aroma of the exotic incense she'd begun burning, a desperate attempt to create an atmosphere conducive to deep thought, or perhaps, a misguided attempt to mimic the clandestine spaces she imagined the killer might inhabit.

Maria found herself spending hours in the dimly lit archives of the university's rare book collection, poring over ancient texts on mortality and the macabre. She traced the lineage of the killer's aesthetic, seeking its roots in the Renaissance fascination with *memento mori*, the medieval obsession with the Danse Macabre, and the more recent Symbolist movement's embrace of the decadent and the morbid. The killer's artistic sensibilities were not entirely novel; they were a terrifyingly potent distillation of centuries of human contemplation on death and its aesthetic potential. She studied anatomical illustrations from Vesalius, marveling at their stark realism, and then, with a shudder, compared them to the disturbing artistry of the Elmwood murders. The killer possessed a profound understanding of the human form, not just its mechanics, but its fragility, its vulnerability, and, in their eyes, its potential for profound artistic transformation, even in death.

The psychological dimension of literary theory became equally crucial. Maria delved into psychoanalytic criticism, examining the killer's actions through the lens of repressed desires, unresolved traumas, and archetypal fears. The theme of the uncanny, of that which is simultaneously familiar and unsettlingly strange, permeated the killer's work. The use of everyday objects imbued with a sinister significance, the violation of domestic spaces, the transformation of the human body into a grotesque work of art – these were all elements designed to evoke a profound sense of unease, to strip away the comforting veneer of normalcy and expose the underlying anxieties of modern life. She wondered if the killer's obsession with art and death was a manifestation of a deep-seated fear of their own mortality, a desperate attempt to achieve a form of immortality through their horrific creations, or perhaps, a profound disconnect from the lived experience of humanity.

Dr. Gibson, despite his initial reticence, had become an invaluable, if exasperating, resource. His academic background, once a barrier, was now a bridge. Maria would call him at all hours, her voice a desperate torrent of theoretical jargon and intuitive leaps.

“Gibson, I’m looking at the symbolism of the broken lyre at the scene. Is it a direct reference to Orpheus losing Eurydice, or is it more broadly about the death of art itself, a commentary on the cultural void? And what about the specific type of knot used to bind the victim? It has a distinct nautical feel, almost like a sailor’s knot. Does that connect to any particular mythological sea voyage, or is it simply a practical choice meant to signify control?”

Gibson, often roused from his own academic pursuits, would respond with a weary patience, his voice tinged with a knowledge that went beyond mere academic curiosity. He spoke of the "aesthetic of despair," a concept Bennett had been deeply interested in, a belief that true artistic transcendence could only be found by embracing the emptiness, the void. He explained how certain philosophical schools saw death not as an end, but as a transition, a purification, a state of ultimate being. Maria absorbed these explanations, piecing together the killer's philosophical framework, understanding that their actions were not random acts of barbarism, but calculated, deliberate expressions of a deeply held, and terrifyingly coherent, worldview. He confirmed that Bennett had been exploring ideas of "artistic suicide" as a form of ultimate self-expression, a concept that Maria found both horrifying and intellectually compelling.

Her Lieutenant, Laramount, watched this transformation with a mixture of awe and apprehension. She saw the raw intelligence at play, the way Maria's mind, usually so sharp and incisive, was now delving into depths she couldn't fathom. she'd found her one night, surrounded by a veritable fortress of books, her face illuminated by the harsh glow of her laptop, muttering about the semiotics of blood spatter and the archetypal significance of labyrinthine narratives. "Maria," she'd said, his voice gentle, "you need to step back. This is... a lot." She'd simply waved a dismissive hand; her eyes fixed on a passage in a thick volume. "Stanley, you don't understand. This killer isn't just a criminal; they're a philosopher with a very sharp scalpel. To catch them, I have to think like them. I have to understand their language, their art." Her intensity was palpable, a force of nature that both inspired and unnerved him. He saw the exhaustion etched on her face, the dark circles under her eyes, the slight tremor in her hands when she reached for her coffee cup. She knew she was brilliant, a detective par excellence, but this case was pushing her into a dangerous intellectual abyss, and he feared she might not find her way back. Stanley worried about the erosion of her own self, the potential for the darkness she was studying to seep into her own psyche. He had seen it before when she was a Detective. The lines between investigator and subject were blurring, and for Laramount, it was a deeply unsettling development. He saw not just a detective at work, but a scholar on the precipice of a profound, and potentially destructive, immersion into the very heart of human darkness, a darkness that spoke in the elegant, terrifying language of death as the ultimate art form.

The sterile glow of her desk lamp had become a constant companion, a beacon in the self-imposed labyrinth of her apartment. Maria traced the worn spine of *The Poetics* by Aristotle, the familiar words blurring into an unfamiliar haze. Her mind, once a sharp instrument honed by logic and evidence, now felt like a frayed rope, each strand pulled taut by the relentless dissection of the killer's motives. The *hamartia*, the tragic flaw, she had been so diligently seeking in the perpetrator had, insidiously, begun to manifest within her own mental landscape. It wasn't just about understanding the killer's intellectual architecture anymore; it was about recognizing the terrifying symmetry between their philosophical leanings and the unacknowledged sorrows of her own past.

She remembered the accident, a blur of screeching tires and shattered glass that had stolen her younger brother, Larry, years ago. He had been a budding poet; his verses filled with a youthful exuberance that Maria had often gently chided. He'd been chasing a kite, a splash of vibrant red against a bruised sky, a foolish, impulsive act that had ended in a silence that still echoed. The memory, usually buried deep beneath layers of professional stoicism, now resurfaced with a visceral clarity, amplified by the killer's own fascination with mortality. Larry's death had been a sudden, brutal disruption, a violent severing of a narrative arc that promised so much more. It was a tragedy, pure and simple, devoid of the philosophical justifications the killer so readily embraced. But the raw, gaping wound of grief it had left behind felt strangely akin to the void the killer seemed so eager to fill.

The killer's fascination with the *memento mori*, the artistic reminders of death, had become a personal torment. Maria found herself increasingly drawn to the stark black-and-white photographs pinned to her corkboard, not just crime scene images, but old family snapshots. There was one of her and Larry, their faces bright with a joy that felt impossibly distant. He was holding a wilting daisy, a fragile symbol of ephemeral beauty, a gesture that now resonated with a profound, painful irony. The killer's staged deaths, the meticulously arranged bodies, the stark symbolism – they were a grotesque echo of the quiet, personal ways Maria had tried to hold onto Larry's memory, to immortalize his fleeting presence. The daisy, once a simple childhood memento, now felt like a miniature *memento mori*, a harbinger of the fragility she had always carried, a fragility she had desperately tried to compartmentalize.

The killer's exploration of nihilism, the belief that life is without objective meaning, purpose, or intrinsic value, struck a particularly discordant chord. Maria recalled long nights spent in the hospital waiting room, the sterile smell of disinfectant mingling with the acrid scent of despair, grappling with the utter meaninglessness of Larry's sudden departure. The doctors had spoken of statistics, of probabilities, of the cruel indifference of fate. They offered no grand narrative, no cosmic explanation, only the stark reality of a life extinguished before its time. Maria had railed against the void then, clinging to the fragmented pieces of her brother's unfinished poems, desperate to find some semblance of meaning in his lost potential. Now, the killer's art of death, their belief in the ultimate futility of life, felt like a direct assault on that hard-won, fragile peace. It was as if the killer were validating the very nihilism Maria had fought so fiercely to overcome.

Maria found herself rereading letters from Larry, his youthful handwriting a stark contrast to the grim pronouncements of the killer. His words spoke of chasing dreams, of the thrill of discovery, of the simple joys of existence. They were words so full of life, so utterly antithetical to the killer's morbid pronouncements. Yet, with each word, Maria felt a pang of guilt, a sharp reminder of the life she had allowed to dim after his death, the years she had spent building walls around her grief, fearing that to fully embrace life would be a betrayal of his memory. The killer's obsession with art and death had, inadvertently, cracked those walls, allowing the old sorrow to seep back in, raw and potent. The irony was not lost on her: the very investigation meant to bring a killer to justice was forcing her to confront the unresolved tragedies of her own past, transforming the pursuit of a murderer into a deeply personal excavation of her own buried grief.

The philosophical underpinnings of tragedy, once an intellectual curiosity, had become a source of profound discomfort. Maria began to see parallels between the killer's chosen narratives and her own life's unscripted dramas. The concept of fate, the inescapable hand that guides events, had always been something she had resisted. Larry's death had been, in her mind, an accident, a random act of cruelty, not a fated encounter. But the killer's unwavering belief in destiny, their assertion that their actions were preordained, began to sow seeds of doubt. Was there a larger narrative at play, a cosmic design that encompassed both the killer's depravity and her own personal loss? The thought was both terrifying and strangely seductive. It offered a morbid comfort, a way to contextualize the senselessness, to find a pattern in the chaos.

She found herself revisiting places she hadn't been in years, places steeped in memories of Larry. The park where they'd spent countless afternoons, the small bookstore where he'd discovered his love for poetry, the quiet bridge over the river where they'd shared secrets under the moonlight. These were places now tinged with a melancholic resonance, their familiar landscapes transformed by the shadow of loss. The killer's aesthetic, their ability to imbue ordinary spaces with an aura of dread, seemed to mirror Maria's own internal landscape, where everyday objects and familiar scenes were now haunted by the ghost of her brother. The vibrant colors of the park seemed muted, the gentle flow of the river a somber dirge.

The killer's use of symbolism, particularly symbols of brokenness and decay, began to feel deeply personal. A snapped violin string found at a crime scene; a wilting rose left on a victim's chest – these were not just artistic flourishes; they were potent signifiers that spoke directly to Maria's own sense of fragmentation. After Larry's death, a part of her had broken. She had meticulously pieced herself back together, but the cracks remained, a subtle reminder of her vulnerability. The killer, in their twisted artistry, was exposing those cracks, forcing her to acknowledge the fragility that lay beneath her professional veneer.

She started to experience a peculiar sort of déjà vu. A phrase overheard on the street, a particular shade of twilight sky, the scent of rain on dry earth – these mundane occurrences would trigger vivid, almost hallucinatory, memories of Larry. It was as if the killer's descent into the abyss of darkness had somehow dislodged the carefully sealed chambers of her own grief, allowing the past to flood into the present. The lines between the investigation and her personal life were blurring, not in a way that compromised her judgment, but in a way that made the pursuit of justice an intensely cathartic, and equally agonizing, ordeal.

The concept of the scapegoat, a central theme in many tragic narratives, began to haunt her thoughts. She wondered if the killer saw themselves as a necessary force, a cleansing agent for a decadent world, sacrificing others to uphold a twisted ideal. This mirrored, in a dark and distorted way, the guilt Maria sometimes felt – the lingering question of whether she could have done more to prevent Larry's death, whether her own survival was a form of silent accusation against his lost future. The killer's actions, their apparent conviction of their own righteousness, seemed to feed into Maria's own internal dialogues of responsibility and blame.

She found herself spending less time in the sterile order of the precinct and more time in the quiet solitude of her apartment, surrounded by the physical manifestations of her intellectual and emotional struggle. The books on semiotics and tragedy were no longer just tools of investigation; they were mirrors, reflecting back the disquieting truths about her own life. She would stare at the complex diagrams on her walls, no longer seeing just the killer's conceptual landscape, but her own, a maze of unresolved grief and buried anxieties. The scent of old paper, once a comforting aroma of intellectual pursuit, now carried the faint, unsettling undertones of mortality. The exotic incense she burned to foster concentration now seemed to imbue the air with a sense of foreboding, as if she were actively conjuring the very darkness she was trying to understand.

The killer's artistic ambition, their desire to create a lasting legacy through their horrific acts, also resonated on a deeper level.

Maria, too, had always strived for excellence, for a kind of immortality through her dedication to her work, her pursuit of truth. But the killer's definition of legacy was one of destruction, a testament to their profound despair. This contrast served as a stark reminder of the path she had chosen, the path of rebuilding, of seeking justice, a path that, while fraught with personal pain, offered a stark alternative to the killer's nihilistic embrace. The investigation had become not just a race against time to apprehend a murderer, but an internal battle for her own soul, a fight to ensure that the echoes of her own tragedy did not lead her into the same abyss as the one she was hunting.

The Elmwood University Library, a gothic edifice of imposing stone and stained glass, had always represented sanctuary. For Maria, it was now something far more potent: a sprawling, silent battleground. The hushed sanctity of its reading rooms, usually a balm to her over-stimulated senses, had transformed into a tangible manifestation of the killer's intricate mind. Each towering shelf, crammed with the accumulated knowledge of centuries, felt less like a repository of wisdom and more like a meticulously constructed wall, designed to obscure and misdirect. The air, thick with the comforting scent of aged paper, decaying binding glue, and a faint, persistent hint of lemon polish, had begun to feel cloying, almost suffocating. It was the perfume of obsession, a scent that clung to her now, a constant reminder of the hours she was dedicating to this increasingly perilous hunt.

She moved through the cavernous halls like a specter, her footsteps muffled by the worn Persian rugs. The grand reading room, with its soaring vaulted ceilings and the sunbeams that slanted through the massive windows, creating ethereal dust motes dancing in the still air, was her primary focus. It was here that the killer had, in all likelihood, drawn inspiration, their mind weaving through the same dense fabric of history, philosophy, and literature that Maria now found herself wading through. The silence here was not merely an absence of noise; it was a pregnant, expectant silence, capable of amplifying the slightest rustle of paper, the faintest sigh, into a sound of profound significance. Every shadow seemed to lengthen and deepen, coalescing into indistinct forms that played tricks on her tired eyes. Was that a figure lurking in the stacks, or merely the play of light and architecture? The line between her heightened senses, honed by weeks of intense investigation, and outright paranoia was becoming alarmingly blurred.

Her initial foray into the library had been driven by a desperate need for context. The killer's choice of victims, their ritualistic staging, and the cryptic literary allusions embedded within their macabre tableau pointed to a mind steeped in a specific, esoteric knowledge. Maria suspected that understanding this chosen intellectual landscape was the key to unlocking the killer's identity. The library, with its vast and diverse collection, was the most logical place to begin this excavation. She started with the sections that seemed most relevant to the killer's known proclivities: classical philosophy, Renaissance art, and obscure theological texts. Each book she pulled from the shelves was a gamble, a hopeful leap into the unknown. She would run her fingers over the embossed titles, the faded gilt lettering, feeling a strange connection to the anonymous hands that had curated these collections, the generations of scholars and dreamers who had sought solace and enlightenment within these walls.

The sheer scale of the undertaking was daunting. The Elmwood University Library was renowned for its extensive holdings, a veritable ocean of information. To attempt to navigate it without a clear map, without any definitive guideposts, felt like being cast adrift. Maria found herself drawn to the Dewey Decimal system instead of the online system, the precise, almost surgical organization of knowledge, and yet, within this order, she perceived a terrifyingly complex labyrinth. Each call number represented not just a subject, but a pathway, a potential thread that might lead her closer to the killer. She began to meticulously categorize her findings, cross-referencing quotes, symbols, and any mention of forgotten societies or cults that had appeared in the case files. Her notebook, once a neatly organized document of facts and observations, was rapidly transforming into a dense tapestry of interconnected ideas, a visual representation of the killer's intricate mental architecture.

She found herself spending hours poring over ancient philosophical treatises, searching for the seeds of the nihilistic despair that seemed to animate the killer. Plato's dialogues, with their emphasis on ideal forms, offered a stark contrast to the killer's embrace of decay and destruction. Aristotle's *Poetics*, which she had been so focused on in her apartment, was here in its original Greek, its pages brittle with age. She imagined the killer here, perhaps late at night, when the librarians had long since departed, their silhouette cast against the moonlight filtering through the arched windows, poring over these same texts, finding in them not wisdom, but justification. The sheer volume of philosophical inquiry into the nature of existence, suffering, and death was staggering. Could the killer have found solace, or even a perverse sense of purpose, in the works of Nietzsche, Schopenhauer, or even the more esoteric writings of medieval mystics? Maria felt a growing dread that the killer was not simply a madman, but a deeply intellectual one, someone who had meticulously constructed a philosophical framework for their horrific acts.

The literary connections were equally pervasive. The killer's quotes, drawn from a seemingly disparate range of authors – from Baudelaire's morbid romanticism to T.S. Eliot's existential angst – were now appearing in context, revealing the depth of their literary erudition. Maria found herself revisiting poems she hadn't thought about since her university days, their verses now imbued with a sinister new meaning. The library's extensive collection of first editions and rare manuscripts felt like a treasure trove, but one guarded by a dragon of ambiguity. She would trace the faded ink on a page, imagining the killer's hand doing the same, their mind twisting the author's original intent into something dark and destructive. The very act of reading, of engaging with the written word, was becoming a source of tension, a constant reminder of the mind that was so effectively using literature as a weapon.

Her focus soon shifted to the more obscure corners of the library. The killer's interest in forgotten societies and secret rituals, hinted at by the symbols found at the crime scenes, led her to the special collections. Here, behind locked doors and under the watchful eye of stern librarians, lay the real rarities: dusty tomes bound in leather, their pages filled with arcane symbols, astrological charts, and accounts of alchemical experiments. The smell in these rooms was even more potent, a musty, earthy scent that spoke of centuries of undisturbed dust and forgotten lore. Maria requested access to manuscripts detailing esoteric orders, clandestine meetings, and the historical persecution of groups deemed heretical. She felt a chill creep up her spine as she turned the fragile pages, each line of text a potential echo of the killer's hidden agenda. Were these symbols mere flourishes, or did they represent a genuine adherence to a forgotten doctrine? The possibility that the killer was part of a larger, organized group, a secret society that had survived the centuries, sent a fresh wave of unease through her.

She started to map out connections, not just between the victims and the literary quotes, but between the literary quotes themselves. Were there recurring themes? Did certain authors tend to appear together in the killer's apparent bibliography? She began to create elaborate mind maps, connecting authors, philosophical concepts, and historical periods with brightly colored markers. The corkboard in her apartment had been a physical manifestation of this process, but here, surrounded by the actual sources, the connections felt more tangible, more potent. The library became a physical extension of her own mind, its vastness mirroring the labyrinthine nature of the investigation.

One particular aisle, dedicated to medieval philosophy and theology, began to draw her in with an almost magnetic force. It was here, amidst dense Latin texts and early Christian writings, that she found the most compelling parallels. The killer's fascination with mortality, with the nature of sin and redemption, seemed to find a spiritual if twisted resonance in these ancient works. The concept of *memento mori*, which had so deeply unsettled Maria in her personal life, was a pervasive theme in medieval art and literature. She found treatises on the Dance of Death, illustrated manuscripts depicting the grim reaper leading all manner of people, from kings to peasants, to their final resting place. The killer's staged scenes, the macabre beauty of their death tableaux, began to seem less like spontaneous acts of madness and more like deliberate interpretations of these ancient artistic and philosophical traditions.

She discovered a rare, leather-bound volume titled *Ars Moriendi: The Art of Dying Well.* Its pages, filled with woodcut illustrations and homilies on preparing for death, seemed to pulse with a dark energy. The killer's victims, arranged in their final moments, often held symbolic objects – a wilting flower, a shattered mirror, a single black feather – that seemed to be morbid reflections of the themes discussed in this ancient text. The killer wasn't just quoting philosophy; they were living it, or rather, they were enacting a grotesque parody of it. Maria felt a wave of nausea, realizing that the killer might see themselves as an artist of death, a philosopher of the macabre, using their victims as their canvas. The library, in this moment, felt less like a sanctuary and more like a mausoleum, filled with the ghosts of ideas that had been twisted into instruments of terror.

The search for the elusive society mentioned in the case files also led her down a rabbit hole of forgotten histories and suppressed movements. She found references to alchemical guilds, mystical orders, and groups that sought forbidden knowledge in the fringes of established religion. These were not the grand, well-documented organizations of history, but clandestine fraternities, their existence hinted at in fragmented manuscripts and obscure scholarly footnotes. The library's archives, in their meticulous preservation of the obscure, were providing the killer's roadmap. Maria felt a growing sense of urgency, as if each hour spent within these hallowed halls was an hour the killer had gained, an hour they had used to refine their plans, to deepen their philosophical justifications.

The quiet hum of the library, the low murmur of other researchers, the occasional rustle of pages – these sounds, once familiar and comforting, now seemed to carry an undercurrent of menace. Every stranger's glance felt like a potential assessment, every lingering shadow a potential threat. Maria found herself constantly looking over her shoulder, her senses on high alert. She was a detective hunting a ghost, and the library, with its endless corridors and hidden alcoves, was the perfect hunting ground. It was a place where secrets could be kept, where knowledge could be obscured, and where a determined mind, armed with a twisted ideology, could craft a terrifying masterpiece. The scent of old paper, once a symbol of intellectual pursuit, now carried the faint, unsettling odor of decay, a constant reminder of the darkness she was trying to unearth. She was lost in the labyrinth, and the Minotaur, she feared, was waiting for her in the heart of it all. She closed her eyes, took a deep, shaky breath, and forced herself to focus, to peel back another layer of this intellectual onion, to find the core of the darkness that held her captive.

The sterile glow of the security monitors in the precinct's dimly lit surveillance room offered Maria no solace. Instead, it amplified the gnawing frustration that had become her constant companion. Weeks had bled into a relentless cycle of interviews, dead ends, and the chilling silence that followed each of the killer's meticulously crafted performances. Dr. Bennett's demise, while undeniably horrific, had offered a maddeningly sparse trail of breadcrumbs. His opulent, yet sterile, downtown office building, a monument to modern architecture's cold efficiency, had been the stage for his final act. The building's integrated security system, usually a fortress of digital eyes, had, in this instance, proven to be more of a sieve. Glitches, conveniently timed power fluctuations, and an almost supernatural ability to evade direct observation had characterized the killer's movements.

Maria, hunched over a bank of screens, her face etched with exhaustion, was replaying the footage from the night of Bennett's murder for what felt like the hundredth time. Each frame was scrutinized, each flicker of light, each shift in shadow analyzed with an intensity that bordered on the obsessive. Her fingers, calloused from countless hours spent poring over case files and meticulously sketching mind maps, danced across the console, rewinding, pausing, and zooming in on minuscule details. The victim's last known moments were a brutal, silent tableau, devoid of any obvious perpetrators. The medical examiner's report had detailed the cause of death with clinical detachment, yet it offered no clue as to the identity of the individual who had orchestrated such a violent end.

Then, in a grainy, low-resolution segment captured by a camera positioned in a rarely used service corridor on the building's exterior, she saw it. A flicker. A distortion in the already imperfect image. It was a fleeting anomaly, easily dismissed as a hardware malfunction or a stray animal darting through the frame. But Maria's trained eye, honed by years of spotting the subtle tells of deception and the almost imperceptible traces of a crime scene, caught the movement. It was too deliberate, too fluid to be accidental.

She isolated the segment, the pixels blurring and reforming with agonizing slowness. A figure, swathed in what appeared to be a dark, voluminous cloak, was moving with an unnerving grace. The fabric billowed around them, obscuring any distinct features, rendering them an almost spectral presence against the stark brickwork of the building. It wasn't the clumsy furtiveness of a common burglar or the panicked haste of someone fleeing the scene of a crime. This was different. There was an almost theatrical quality to the movement, a deliberate theatricality that suggested a performance rather than an escape. The way the cloak swirled, the precise angle of the head as it turned, the almost balletic glide of the feet – it all spoke of a practiced, almost artistic, sensibility.

Maria's breath hitched. This was it. The first tangible, albeit ephemeral, glimpse of the individual who had haunted her thoughts and dominated her waking hours. It wasn't a face, not a clear identifier, but it was a presence. A confirmed, physical entity moving within the perpetrator's orbit. The killer wasn't an incorporeal phantom, as their uncanny ability to evade detection might suggest. They were real, and they moved with a deliberate, almost choreographed, flourish.

Her heart hammered against her ribs, a frantic drumbeat against the monotonous hum of the surveillance equipment. This brief, shadowy apparition was more than just a lead; it was a jolt of adrenaline, a fresh surge of determination in the face of what had felt like an insurmountable wall of anonymity. The killer wasn't just intelligent; they were... artistic. The word resonated in her mind, a strange and unsettling echo. Artistry in murder. It was a concept that both repelled and fascinated her, a grim redefinition of creative expression.

She rewound the footage again, then played it forward, her eyes tracing the phantom's every subtle shift. The way the cloak draped, the implied musculature beneath the fabric, the economical precision of each movement. It wasn't the clumsy bulk of a large man, nor the delicate fragility of a small woman. The figure seemed to possess an androgynous fluidity, a deliberate ambiguity that further confounded any immediate profiling. This was a deliberate choice, a calculated effacement of identity.

"Show me that again," she commanded, her voice hoarse with a mixture of excitement and apprehension. The technician, a young man named Henry, whose perpetual state of mild bewilderment Maria had grown accustomed to, obliged. The cloaked figure reappeared, a transient ghost caught in the harsh glare of the security camera.

Maria leaned closer to the screen, her gaze locked onto the subtle nuances of the movement. There was a certain elegance to the way the figure held themselves, a controlled poise that spoke of rigorous training or an innate, profound understanding of physicality. It was the kind of grace that one might associate with a dancer, a swordsman, or perhaps... an actor preparing for a pivotal role. The killer was staging their crimes, yes, but they were also staging themselves.

"Look at the drape of the fabric," Maria murmured, more to herself than to Henry. "It's not just a cloak; it's a costume. And the way they move... it's not a hurried escape. It's a deliberate exit." She paused, a new thought taking root. "They're not just leaving the scene; they're *performing* their departure."

Henry shifted uncomfortably. "So, you think it's someone... theatrical?"

Maria's gaze remained fixed on the screen. "I think they see themselves as an artist, Henry. And their art is death." The implication hung in the air, heavy and chilling. The killer wasn't driven by primal rage or simple greed. This was a calculated, ideologically driven pursuit, expressed through a medium that was as horrifying as it was meticulously executed.

She continued to play the clip, trying to extract any further detail, any hint of a facial structure, a gait, a characteristic gesture. But the cloaked figure remained an enigma, a silhouette of pure intent. The camera angle was too high, the resolution too poor, and the figure's movements too fluidly evasive. They seemed to melt into the shadows as quickly as they appeared, leaving behind only the lingering impression of an artist making their final bow.

"It's not enough," Maria whispered, a sigh escaping her lips. The fleeting glimpse was a tantalizing tease, a hint of the enemy, but it provided no concrete identity. Yet, it was more than she had had before. It was proof that the killer was not an abstract concept, but a physical being, capable of intricate movements and deliberate actions. This figure, cloaked and elusive, was the tangible thread that Maria would now chase with renewed ferocity.

The obsession, which had threatened to consume her in the isolating silence of the library, now found a new, sharp focus. The killer wasn't just a mind to be deciphered, but a body to be tracked. The artistic sensibility, once a purely intellectual construct derived from their victims' macabre presentations, now had a physical manifestation. This was a performer, a director, a sculptor of death, leaving behind not just the finality of their victims, but the ephemeral signature of their own clandestine presence.

She remembered the initial crime scenes, the almost artistic arrangement of the bodies, the symbolic placement of objects. It had always struck her as performative, but now, seeing the cloaked figure move with such deliberate grace, the notion solidified. This wasn't just about sending a message; it was about the aesthetic of the message. The killer was not merely a murderer; they were a curator of carnage, and their greatest masterpiece was the act of disappearing after its completion.

Maria's mind began to race, conjuring images of theaters, studios, and performance spaces. Where would someone with such a pronounced artistic inclination, such a penchant for dramatic exits, seek inspiration or sanctuary? The university library had offered her the intellectual framework for the killer's motives, but this fleeting image suggested a physical dimension she had perhaps underestimated.

"Henry, pull up the security logs for the entire week leading up to Bennett's murder," Maria instructed, her voice regaining its authoritative edge. "Focus on any individuals seen entering or exiting the building late at night, particularly those who might be considered... out of the ordinary. Anyone with an unusual gait, anyone carrying large, concealing bags, anyone who seems to be... performing their movements."

Henry nodded, his fingers already flying across the keyboard. The task was daunting, sifting through hours of footage for a single, fleeting anomaly. But Maria knew, with a certainty that settled deep in her bones, that this cloaked figure was the key. It was the whisper of the artist in the darkness, the tangible echo of a presence that had previously been perceived only through the chilling artistry of their crimes. The chase had just become more personal, more visceral. The phantom was starting to take shape, and Maria was determined to strip away the cloak and reveal the face of the artist who wielded death as their ultimate medium.

She closed her eyes for a brief moment, picturing the figure again. The flowing fabric, the deliberate stride, the almost imperceptible inclination of the head as they glanced towards the camera, as if acknowledging its presence, daring it to see. It was a moment of profound arrogance, a subtle flaunting of their mastery of concealment. This wasn't just a killer; it was a provocateur, a shadow puppeteer pulling strings from behind an impenetrable curtain of darkness.

The library had provided the 'why,' the philosophical underpinnings of the killer's pathology. But this glimpse, this fleeting vision caught on a grainy security feed, provided the 'how' and, more importantly, hinted at the 'who.' It was the silhouette of a dancer, the pose of a sculptor, the calculated entrance and exit of a lead actor. The killer was an artist, and their studio was the city, their canvas the lives they extinguished. Maria felt a grim satisfaction; she was no longer chasing a ghost, but a flesh-and-blood individual, however artfully they obscured their form. The hunt had entered a new phase, one that demanded not just intellectual rigor, but a keen eye for the performative, for the deliberate choreography of a killer's existence. The shadows in Dr. Bennett's service corridor had just illuminated a path, however narrow and uncertain, leading her closer to the heart of the darkness. She would follow it, relentlessly, until the final curtain fell.

CHAPTER 6

THE MACABRE MASTERPIECE

The pre-dawn chill of the university campus was a palpable entity, seeping into the very marrow of Maria's bones. It wasn't just the lingering frost or the biting wind; it was the icy dread that had coiled itself around the heart of academia. The news had arrived with the brutal efficiency of a midnight telegram: a third victim. Another life extinguished, another performance orchestrated. The air, usually alive with the murmur of early risers and the rustle of academic ambition, was now thick with a suffocating silence, punctuated only by the hushed whispers of fear.

Maria had arrived at the scene, a modest, ivy-clad building that housed the university's theater department, with a knot of apprehension tightening in her stomach. The initial reports had been vague, hinting at a disturbing tableau, a scene that defied conventional understanding of violence. But as she stepped through the police tape, the full, horrifying reality slammed into her with the force of a physical blow.

The victim was a young woman, her name, she would later learn, was Mary Underwood. Mary had been a star of the drama department, a prodigy whose talent had been lauded from the moment she stepped onto the stage. Her charisma was legendary, her passion for her craft infectious. Now, she lay still, her youthful vitality extinguished, her body posed with a chillingly deliberate artistry.

She was situated in the center of a small, circular clearing, a stark contrast to the surrounding manicured lawns. Her limbs were arranged in a posture of agonizing indecision, her head tilted back, her eyes, wide and vacant, staring up at the indifferent sky. Around her, arranged with meticulous precision, were several large, smooth stones, each inscribed with a single, Greek letter. The letters, when pieced together, formed words: "Moirae," a chilling reference to the Fates, the goddesses who spun, measured, and cut the threads of human destiny. The scene was a macabre re-enactment, a grim interpretation of a classical tragedy, with Mary cast as the ill-fated protagonist.

Maria's gaze swept across the scene, taking in the deliberate placement of each element, the stark brutality of the act juxtaposed with the almost delicate aesthetic. The killer's signature was undeniable. This was not the frenzied violence of a crime of passion, nor the opportunistic savagery of a random attack. This was a meticulously crafted narrative, a chilling testament to the killer's profound understanding of literature, mythology, and the darker aspects of human psychology.

"Who found her?" Maria's voice, though quiet, cut through the hushed murmurs of the forensics team.

Detective Donny Bates, a man whose weary face bore the indelible marks of countless grim discoveries, gestured towards a young woman huddled under a police blanket, her face buried in her hands. "One of the early morning janitorial staff. Said she thought it was some kind of art installation at first. Didn't realize... until she got closer."

Maria nodded, her eyes still fixed on the staged victim. Mary's costume, a simple, flowing tunic, seemed to accentuate her vulnerability, her tragic stillness. The killer had not only chosen the victim and the method, but also the stage, the props, and the narrative. It was a complete artistic endeavor, executed with terrifying precision.

"Anything?" Maria asked, her voice barely a whisper, directed at the lead forensic technician.

The technician, a stoic woman named Lena Hanson, shook her head grimly. "Minimal external trauma, aside from the obvious cause of death. She's been posed post-mortem, that much is clear. The inscriptions on the stones... they're fresh. And the arrangement, it's too precise to have been done in haste. The killer was here for a while, ensuring everything was perfect."

"Perfect," Maria echoed, the word tasting like ash in her mouth. The killer's pursuit of perfection was what made them so terrifying. They weren't simply killing; they were creating, sculpting their horrific visions into reality.

She knelt beside Mary, her movements slow and respectful. The victim's face was peaceful, almost serene, a stark contrast to the violence that had clearly preceded her final stillness. It was as if the killer, in their quest for artistic fulfillment, had somehow managed to erase the struggle, leaving only the final, tragic composition. Maria noticed a small, intricate symbol etched onto the palm of Mary's left hand. It was a stylized owl; its wings spread in flight.

The same symbol had been found at the previous crime scenes, a subtle, yet unmistakable, calling card.

"The owl," Maria stated, more to herself than to Donny. "It's always the owl."

Bates grunted, his eyes scanning the perimeter for any overlooked evidence. "We've been over this, Maria. No prints, no fibers, no DNA that doesn't belong to the victim or the first responders. It's like they're a ghost. A ghost with a literary degree and a penchant for theatrical murders."

Maria rose, her mind racing. Clara Bellweather, doctoral student, found in the pond. Dr. Bennett, the esteemed historian, found in his office, surrounded by antique maps, his body arranged as if to illustrate a lost civilization. Two years ago, Professor Albright, the renowned philosopher, discovered in the university's ancient library, his position mirroring a classical statue, a specific philosophical text clutched in his hand. And now Mary Underwood, the vibrant drama student, cast as a pawn in a mythological drama.

The victims were seemingly disparate, yet connected by their intellectual pursuits, their deep immersion in the world of academia. The killer was targeting those who held knowledge, those who shaped minds, those who delved into the realms of history, philosophy, and the arts. This wasn't random. This was a deliberate, calculated selection, a twisted form of intellectual assassination.

"The owl," Maria repeated, her gaze drifting towards the towering oak trees that fringed the campus. "It represents wisdom, knowledge, foresight. But it's also associated with the night, with mystery, and with death. It's the perfect symbol for someone who operates in the shadows, who believes they possess a superior understanding of the world, and who sees themselves as dispensing a form of... enlightenment."

She turned to Donny, her eyes blazing with a renewed sense of urgency. "They're not just killing these people, Donny. They're making a statement. Each murder is a chapter in their own twisted manifesto. Bennett was the past, Clara Bellweather the present, and Mary... Mary represents the future. The potential, the artistic promise that is now being extinguished."

The implication hung heavy in the air. The killer was not only escalating their violence but also refining their message. From historical allegory to philosophical discourse to mythological tragedy. Each performance was more complex, more symbolic, and more terrifying than the last.

"We need to look at everyone in the drama department," Maria declared, her voice firm. "Anyone with an obsession with Greek mythology, classical theater, anyone who might see themselves as a director in this macabre play. And we need to cross-reference that with anyone who had any connection, however tangential, to Bennett or Bellweather. This isn't just about one department anymore; it's about the entire university."

The university administration, initially hesitant to acknowledge the full gravity of the situation, had been forced into a state of panicked lockdown. Security was heightened, lectures were cancelled, and a palpable atmosphere of fear descended upon the campus. Students walked in nervous groups, their eyes darting into every shadow, their imaginations conjuring the killer in every stranger. The once vibrant hub of intellectual discourse had transformed into a landscape of suspicion and dread.

Maria spent the next few days immersed in Mary Underwood's life. She spoke with Mary's distraught professors, her heartbroken friends, and her grieving family. She learned of Mary's boundless energy, her infectious laughter, and her deep-seated belief in the transformative power of theater. Mary had been working on a new interpretation of Euripides' "Medea," a play filled with themes of betrayal, revenge, and tragic fate. The parallels were undeniable, chillingly so.

"She was so passionate about it," Mary's closest friend, a young woman named Laura, choked out, tears streaming down her face. "She said she wanted to explore the duality of Medea, the powerful woman driven to monstrous acts by her circumstances. She was researching ancient rituals, the role of the Fates in Greek society... Oh God, Detective, she was researching the very things he's using!"

The revelation struck Maria with the force of a physical blow. Mary hadn't just been a victim; she had, in a way, been a contributor to the killer's script. Her academic research, her artistic exploration, had provided the very elements the killer had woven into her demise. It was a twisted form of artistic collaboration, a horrifying fusion of victim and perpetrator.

Maria returned to the surveillance footage, her focus sharpened by this new understanding. She re-examined the grainy images from Bennett's murder, the blurred movements of the cloaked figure. Could this individual have been present at the theater department, observing Mary, studying her movements, her passion, her research? The killer was a chameleon, blending into the academic landscape, a predator disguised as a scholar.

She requested all recent visitor logs for the theater department, cross-referencing them with staff and student IDs. The list was extensive, filled with names of academics, guest lecturers, alumni, and even curious members of the public. But Maria was looking for a name, a face, a thread that would connect this killer to the intricate tapestry of the university.

One name, however, kept resurfacing in Mary's research notes and in conversations with her colleagues: a visiting scholar who had been consulting on ancient Greek texts and their theatrical adaptations. Dr. Conrad Feather. Feather was an obscure figure, a recluse who had published a few critically acclaimed but little-read essays on the intersection of classical tragedy and existential philosophy. He had been on campus for a series of guest lectures, the last of which had been just days before Mary's murder.

Maria felt a flicker of recognition, a subtle resonance. She vaguely recalled seeing Feather's name attached to some of the theoretical frameworks she had encountered in her own research on the killer's motives. His work, while academic, had a certain dark intensity, a fascination with the primal forces that drove human behavior.

She pulled up Feather's file. His photograph showed a man in his late forties, with sharp, intelligent eyes and a perpetually thoughtful, almost melancholic, expression. He had a distinguished air, but there was a hint of something unsettling in his gaze, a depth that suggested a profound, perhaps even dangerous, introspection.

"Where is Feather now?" Maria asked Donny, her voice tense.

Bates frowned, already accessing the database. "His contract ended last week. He checked out of his campus accommodation two days ago. According to the records, he booked a flight out of the country... to Athens."

Athens. The birthplace of tragedy, the cradle of Greek mythology. The killer was returning to their source, to the very wellspring of their inspiration. Maria felt a surge of adrenaline mixed with a chilling sense of dread. They weren't just a murderer; they were a pilgrim, on a quest to complete their macabre masterpiece. The game of cat and mouse had just escalated, the stakes raised to an almost unbearable level. The killer was no longer just a shadow lurking in the university corridors; they were a tangible threat, a literary scholar on a deadly pilgrimage, and Maria knew she had to stop them before they could pen the final, fatal act of their horrifying performance. The owl, it seemed, was taking flight, and its destination was a land steeped in the very myths it now so brutally embodied.

The vellum card, nestled carefully beneath Mary's posed hand, was a stark white against the dark, unyielding earth. Maria's gloved fingers, almost hesitant, lifted it. The script was as precise as the Greek letters on the stones – an elegant, unsettling calligraphy that seemed to weep with the weight of its message. It wasn't the stark pronouncement of "Moirae" from the previous scene, nor the cryptic symbol of the owl. This was something softer, something that spoke of a pain deeper than mere intellectual pronouncement. It was an excerpt from Euripides.

The words, when Maria read them aloud, were a lament, a heart-wrenching cry from the depths of despair.

"Alas, woe is me! What suffering is this that has befallen me?

O, to be spared this youthful bloom, this brief and fragile hour.

For cruel is the hand of Fate, and swift its chilling touch,

To snatch away the light, and plunge the soul into endless night."

Maria reread the lines, the chill of the pre-dawn air suddenly irrelevant. This was different. The previous victims, Bennett and Bellweather, had been presented as figures of historical and philosophical significance, their deaths seemingly designed to punctuate arguments or illustrate points in the killer's twisted intellectual discourse. Mary, however, had been cast not as an abstract concept, but as a victim of circumstance, her life tragically intertwined with the very forces the killer seemed to embody. The excerpt from Euripides wasn't a declaration of power, but a lament, a sorrowful acknowledgement of the victim's plight, or perhaps, the killer's own perceived helplessness in the face of an inexorable destiny.

"Euripides," Maria murmured, the name a soft echo in the otherwise silent clearing. She turned to Detective Bates, who stood a respectful distance away, his usual gruff demeanor softened by the solemnity of the scene. "The killer is quoting Euripides. This passage... it's about the sorrow of youth, the unavoidable nature of fate. It's a plea, in a way."

Donnys' brow furrowed. "A plea? From a murderer?"

"Not a plea for mercy, perhaps," Maria clarified, her mind already sifting through the layers of meaning. "More of a lament. A recognition of the tragedy. Euripides often wrote of the suffering of women, of the helplessness of individuals caught in the machinations of gods and fate. This passage, in particular, speaks of the ephemeral nature of youth, of how easily it can be extinguished by forces beyond one's control. It's a stark contrast to the intellectual pronouncements of the previous murders. This feels... personal. More emotionally charged."

She looked back at Mary, her posed form a silent testament to the words on the card. Mary, the vibrant drama student, so full of life and potential, now a symbol of lost youth. The killer's choices were becoming increasingly complex, their literary selections deepening in psychological resonance. It wasn't just about showcasing knowledge anymore; it was about eliciting an emotional response, about conveying a profound sense of tragedy.

"They're digging deeper," Maria said, her voice growing more intense. "Bennett was history, the foundation. Bellweather was philosophy, the framework of thought. Mary was art, emotion, the expression of life. And now this quote... it's not just about the intellectual; it's about the human cost. It's about the pain of what's being lost. The killer is not just a curator of death; they're becoming a poet, a playwright, weaving narratives of profound sorrow."

She paused, considering the implications. If Bennett represented the past and Bellweather the present, then Mary, with her youthful promise and her passion for contemporary interpretations of classical works, represented the future. The killer was not just eradicating individuals; they were symbolically destroying different facets of human experience and knowledge.

The selection of Mary, a student of theater and a devotee of classical drama, made the Euripidean excerpt all the more poignant. She had been immersed in these stories, in these explorations of human suffering, and now she was a character within one.

"This isn't just about symbols and allusions anymore," Maria continued, her gaze sweeping over the carefully arranged stones, the precise placement of Anya's body. "The killer is becoming more sophisticated in their emotional manipulation. They're using literature not just to convey a message, but to evoke a specific feeling. This plea from Euripides... it's designed to make us feel sympathy, to understand the tragedy, to perhaps even question the justice of it all. They want us to see Mary not just as a victim, but as a symbol of innocence tragically destroyed."

The academic community, already reeling from the previous murders, was now plunged into a deeper, more unsettling fear. The calculated precision of Bennett's demise and Bellweather's philosophical staging had been terrifying. But the anguish woven into Mary's scene, the heartbreaking plea from the vellum card, felt like a chilling escalation. It suggested a killer who was not only intellectually brilliant but also deeply, disturbingly empathetic to the suffering they inflicted, or perhaps, deeply tormented by their own role in it.

"What specific play is this from?" Maria asked, turning to Donny again. "Do we know?"

Donny had already made a call. "Forensics is running it through their databases. They think it's from the 'Medea'."

"Medea," Maria breathed, the name resonating with a dark power. "Of course. A play about betrayal, vengeance, and the devastating consequences of extreme emotion. A powerful woman driven to monstrous acts by her suffering. Mary was researching it, wasn't she? Her focus on the duality of Medea... the powerful woman driven to monstrous acts by her circumstances." Maria felt a cold dread creep up her spine. The killer wasn't just referencing a play; they were enacting its themes, casting their victim in a role that mirrored the tragic protagonists of classical literature.

The selection of this particular Euripidean passage was a masterstroke of psychological manipulation. It transformed the act of murder into a performative lament. It forced Maria and her team to confront not just the brutality of the deed, but the pathos of it. The killer was inviting them into the narrative, not as investigators, but as an audience privy to a profound, albeit horrifying, emotional spectacle. The "Euripidean Plea" was not just about the victim; it was also about the killer's own internal landscape, a landscape seemingly as tempestuous and tragic as the dramas they emulated.

Maria imagined the killer, alone with Mary's body, carefully arranging the stones, inscribing the words, and then, with a meticulous hand, placing the vellum card. Was there a moment of hesitation? A flicker of remorse? Or was it all part of the calculated artistry, the final flourish of a performance designed to shock, to disturb, and to elicit a specific emotional response? The "Moirae" stones had spoken of destiny, a cold, impersonal force. But this Euripidean quote spoke of suffering, of pain, of a lament for a life lost. It was a subtle but significant shift, indicating a growing complexity in the killer's psyche. They were moving beyond mere intellectual exercises into the realm of raw, agonizing human emotion, albeit expressed through the chilling lens of murder.

"The killer is showing us their hand, in a way," Maria mused, her voice barely audible. "They're revealing a deeper understanding of tragedy, of the human condition. It's not just about power or ideology; it's about something far more elemental. They're demonstrating a profound awareness of suffering, a sensitivity to the ephemeral nature of life. And yet, they use this awareness to justify their own acts of immense cruelty. It's a terrifying paradox. They understand the value of life, the sorrow of its loss, and that's precisely why they feel compelled to end it."

She looked at the Greek letters carved into the stones surrounding Mary. "Moirae," the Fates. They represented an inescapable destiny. But this Euripidean plea spoke of a different kind of inevitability – the inevitability of sorrow, of youthful beauty succumbing to a cruel fate. It was as if the killer was acknowledging that, despite their own actions, some things were destined to be tragic. Mary's vibrant future, her promising career, her very life – all were, in the killer's distorted view, tragically predetermined.

"This goes beyond just literary knowledge," Maria stated, her gaze fixed on the distant, fog-shrouded silhouette of the university's oldest building, the one housing the Classics department. "This is about a deep, perhaps pathological, connection to these ancient narratives. They're not just studying them; they're internalizing them, living them. And now, they're forcing us to confront the emotional weight of these stories, the sorrow they contain, through the stark reality of murder."

The university administration was requesting more and more information, their initial panic now tinged with a desperate need for understanding. They wanted to know what kind of mind was at play, what warped ideology was driving these meticulously crafted horrors. Maria knew that the answer lay not just in the physical evidence, but in the increasingly eloquent, increasingly disturbing, literary choices the killer was making. Each scene, each quote, was a piece of a larger psychological puzzle, a puzzle that was slowly revealing a mind steeped in the tragic arts, a mind that saw life itself as a grand, sorrowful drama.

"The killer isn't just selecting victims; they're selecting roles," Maria reiterated, her voice firm. "Bennett was the sage, the keeper of forgotten lore. The murder of Bellweather was the thinker, the architect of reason. Mary was the aspiring artist, the embodiment of passionate expression. And now, with this Euripidean lament, they're casting Mary as the tragic heroine, a symbol of youth and potential irrevocably broken by forces beyond her control. The killer, in this scenario, isn't the villain; they are the narrator, the interpreter of fate, the one who understands the depth of the sorrow being inflicted."

This was no longer just an investigation; it was an excavation of a mind, a descent into a psyche that was both terrifyingly brilliant and deeply disturbed. The "Euripidean Plea" was a signal, a clear indication that the killer's artistry was evolving, becoming more nuanced, more emotionally charged, and ultimately, more dangerous. The academic thriller was unfolding with each meticulously staged scene, and Maria knew, with a chilling certainty, that the next act would be even more profound, even more devastating. The owl, a symbol of wisdom and death, was not just observing; it was orchestrating, its silent wings casting a long, sorrowful shadow over the hallowed halls of academia. The killer was not merely an assassin; they were a scholar of suffering, and their masterpiece was far from complete. The university, once a sanctuary of learning, had become a stage for a drama of death, played out with the chilling precision of a classical tragedy.

The oppressive silence of the Classics department, usually a hushed sanctuary of ancient wisdom, had been shattered. Now, a different kind of stillness pervades the air, heavy with the unspoken fear that clung to the university like the persistent autumn fog. Maria felt it prickle her skin as she stepped away from the stark tableau of Mary's death and turned her gaze towards the imposing edifice of the Drama building. Its gothic spires, usually evoking a sense of theatrical grandeur, now seemed to loom with a more ominous presence, a silent witness to the unraveling tragedy. If Mary, the bright young star, was a tragic heroine scripted by a mad playwright, then the very institution that nurtured such talent must surely hold the keys to understanding this macabre masterpiece.

The transition from the stoic solemnity of ancient texts to the vibrant, often volatile, world of contemporary theatre felt like traversing a chasm. The Drama department was a labyrinth of studios, rehearsal rooms, costume shops, and black box theaters, each space humming with a peculiar energy – a blend of creative fervor and palpable tension. Sunlight, filtering through the tall, arched windows, cast dramatic shafts of light and shadow, mirroring the very essence of the stagecraft practiced within these walls. Maria, accompanied by Detective Bates, felt like an intruder stepping into a meticulously crafted set, where every prop, every costume, every student milling about, might hold a clue to the killer's script.

Their initial inquiries were met with a carefully constructed wall of artistic affectation and a genuine, if somewhat theatrical, shock. The students, many still in various stages of costume or makeup, spoke in hushed, dramatic tones, their voices imbued with a practiced resonance. They described Mary not just as a classmate, but as a force of nature, an artist consumed by her craft. "She *lived* her roles," one young woman, a budding Ophelia with tear-streaked mascara, confided, her voice trembling as if reciting a soliloquy. "She didn't just act them; she *became* them. When she was researching Medea, she... she'd stay up for days, barely eating, just immersing herself in that rage, that despair. She said she needed to feel it, to understand the true depth of a mother's broken heart."

This intensity, this pursuit of emotional truth, was a common thread. The department prides itself on its commitment to method acting, a philosophy that encouraged performers to tap into their own emotions and experiences to create authentic portrayals. For Mary, this had translated into an almost obsessive dedication. She was known for her passionate, often unsettling, interpretations, pushing boundaries with a fearlessness that both impressed and occasionally unnerved her peers. Professor Norman Tiller, the department head and a renowned director, spoke of Mary with a mix of pride and apprehension.

"Mary possessed a rare gift," Tillman stated, his voice a deep baritone, accustomed to commanding attention. He gestured with a long, slender hand, his fingers adorned with several silver rings, each bearing an obscure theatrical symbol. "She had an uncanny ability to plumb the depths of human emotion. Some might call it extreme, her dedication. But that is the nature of true art, is it not? To confront the darkest aspects of the human psyche, to hold a mirror up to society's ugliness, and to make the audience *feel* it. Mary understood that on a visceral level."

He led Maria and Donny into his office, a space that felt like a shrine to theatrical history. Playbills, framed photographs of legendary performances, and meticulously crafted miniature stage sets adorned the walls and shelves. The air was thick with the scent of old paper, dust, and a faint, lingering hint of stage paint. Tillman settled behind his ornate mahogany desk, his eyes, sharp and intelligent, fixed on Maria.

"You mentioned the Euripides quote," Tillman began, his brow furrowed. "Specifically, *Medea*. Mary was deeply immersed in that text. She was cast in our upcoming production, a rather... challenging interpretation directed by Dr. Albright's wife, actually. Patricia Albright. She's a... unique artist. Very much into the psychological underpinnings of classical tragedy. Mary was to play Medea, of course. A role that demands immense emotional fortitude. She was preparing for it with her usual... intensity."

Patricia Albright. The name sent a subtle ripple of unease through Maria. Albright, the philosopher, the victim of homicide two years ago. His wife, now a director, working with Mary on a play about a woman driven to horrific acts by grief and betrayal. The parallels were becoming alarmingly stark, weaving a narrative that felt terrifyingly orchestrated.

"What kind of interpretation was Mrs. Albright pursuing?" Maria asked, her voice carefully neutral.

Tillman sighed, a sound like the rustle of ancient parchment. "Patricia believes Medea's actions, while undeniably horrific, are a product of systemic oppression and profound psychological trauma. She sees Medea not as a monster, but as a victim of circumstance, driven to the extreme by the patriarchal society that abandoned and betrayed her. Mary, with her profound empathy, resonated deeply with that perspective. She was exploring the duality of Medea – the once-devoted wife and mother, and the vengeful sorceress. It was a very raw, very emotionally charged exploration. Mary was pushing herself, perhaps too much."

The concept of sacrifice, of existential dread – themes inherent in *Medea* and central to the killer's emerging pattern – were being explored not just in the abstract through literary quotes, but within the very fabric of the university's academic pursuits. Mary's death, it seemed, was not an isolated incident, but an extension, a horrifying culmination, of the very themes she was striving to understand and portray.

Donny steered the conversation back to the practicalities of the investigation. "Were there any... conflicts within the department? Any rivalries? Particularly involving Mary?"

Tillman hesitated, his gaze drifting to a framed poster of a production of *The Bacchae*. "The theatre world, as you can imagine, Detective, is a fertile ground for both profound collaboration and intense rivalry. Mary was brilliant, yes, but brilliance can sometimes breed... resentment. There were whispers. Some students felt she was favored by certain faculty, especially Patricia. There were others who struggled to match her intensity, her dedication. Method acting, as I said, is demanding. It requires a certain emotional resilience. Not everyone possesses it, and those who don't can sometimes feel... intimidated, or perhaps, overlooked."

He spoke of artistic temperaments, of the delicate egos involved in performance. He mentioned a student named Julian Zeller, a fellow actor who had reportedly clashed with Mary over roles, and who was also known for his own brand of immersive, often dark, performance. Zeller, Tillman admitted, had a fascination with the darker aspects of human psychology, and had spoken at length about the philosophical underpinnings of certain extreme theatrical works. He was known for his almost monomaniacal focus on roles that explored the "abyss of the human soul."

"Julian," Tillman mused, "he's a talented young man, but... troubled. He saw Mary's success, her raw talent, perhaps as a threat. He's deeply invested in the idea of suffering as a catalyst for artistic truth. He's spoken of the necessity of pain in creating truly profound art. He'd often engage Mary in debates about the ethics of such immersion, about the fine line between embodying a character and succumbing to them."

Maria's mind cataloged the information. Zeller, the rival, the one fascinated by suffering. Patricia Albright, the director, whose interpretation of *Medea* mirrored the themes of sacrifice and betrayal. And Mary, the victim, the talented actress who lived her roles with an intensity that bordered on self-destruction. The Drama department was proving to be a stage teeming with complex characters and simmering subplots, a fertile ground for the kind of psychological drama the killer seemed to be orchestrating.

They visited the costume department, a riot of silks, velvets, and worn leather, where the scent of mothballs and aged fabric hung heavy in the air. Amidst the discarded scraps and half-finished projects, Maria found a discarded sketchpad. It was filled with Mary's rapid, energetic drawings. They depicted not just characters from plays, but abstract representations of emotions – fear, rage, despair, and a recurring motif of a bird trapped within a cage. Interspersed with these were meticulously detailed anatomical drawings of human faces contorted in agony, and chillingly accurate renditions of ancient Greek masks, their expressions frozen in eternal suffering.

"She was working on something else, too," a young costumer, nervously twisting a stray thread around her finger, volunteered. "A personal project. She called it... 'The Anatomy of Sacrifice.' She was obsessed with historical instances of ritualistic sacrifice, not just the religious aspect, but the psychological impact on the individuals chosen. She was looking into everything – ancient Greece, Aztec rituals, even more modern... cults. She felt there was a connection between the extremity of sacrifice and the artistic impulse to confront the limits of human experience."

This personal project, this morbid fascination with sacrifice, echoed the themes of the play Mary was cast in and the killer's increasingly ritualistic murders. The lines between performance and reality were blurring, and the university's own academic pursuits were providing the fertile ground for this terrifying confluence.

Further interviews revealed a department rife with artistic eccentricity and a shared, almost fanatical, devotion to exploring the darker recesses of the human psyche. Students spoke of late-night rehearsals that devolved into intense philosophical debates about the nature of evil, the limits of empathy, and the role of suffering in artistic expression. They spoke of intense rivalries, not just for roles, but for the very philosophical interpretations of plays.

One student, a brooding young man with ink-stained fingers who specialized in set design, spoke of a recent incident where a piece of Mary's research material – a rare, annotated edition of *Medea* – had gone missing. He claimed Mary had accused Julian Zeller of taking it, escalating into a heated argument that had been overheard by several faculty members. "Julian was furious," the student recounted, his voice low and intense. "He said Mary was trivializing the 'essence' of Medea, reducing her to a mere psychological case study. He believed it was about primal forces, not mere 'trauma.' He was shouting about... purification through destruction. It was pretty intense."

The notion of "purification through destruction" resonated deeply with Maria, echoing the killer's earlier actions. Bennett, the historian, a guardian of past knowledge, had been "purified" from the present. Bellweather, the philosopher, an architect of flawed reasoning, had been "purified" by her own intellectual hubris. And now Mary, the actress on the cusp of embodying ultimate destruction, had been "purified" by her own artistic immersion into the very act.

The "Macabre Masterpiece" was taking shape, not just in the killer's mind, but within the very institution that was meant to foster learning and growth. The Drama department, with its focus on intense emotional portrayal and its inherent rivalries had become a microcosm of the larger tragedy unfolding. It was a place where art and life, performance and reality were in constant, often dangerous, negotiation.

Maria felt a growing unease, a sense that she was not just investigating a series of murders, but a carefully curated performance. The victims, each chosen for their symbolic significance, were being cast into roles that mirrored their academic pursuits and their personal lives. Bennett, the historian, representing the past. Bellweather, the philosopher, the present of thought. And Mary, the actress, the embodiment of emotion and artistic expression, poised to play a character driven to extreme acts. The killer, it seemed, was not just an assassin, but a director, meticulously selecting their cast and crafting a narrative of profound, horrifying depth. The secrets of the theater department, simmering beneath the surface of artistic ambition and theatrical rivalry, were beginning to bleed into the grim reality of the investigation. The stage was set, the players were in place, and the ultimate act was yet to unfold.

The air in the Drama department office, thick with the scent of dust and forgotten performances, seemed to hum with a disquieting energy. Maria, the weight of Mary's fragmented life pressing down on her, found herself drawn to a small, framed print on Professor Tillman's desk. It depicted a scene from a Greek tragedy, the figures rendered in stark black and white, their faces etched with an almost unbearable despair. It was a subtle detail, easily overlooked amidst the clutter of theatrical memorabilia, yet it snagged at her attention, a whisper of the deeper currents at play. The killer, she was increasingly convinced, wasn't merely selecting victims at random, nor were their acts born solely of impulsive rage. There was a deliberation, a carefully constructed narrative, and an unsettling thematic coherence that bound each brutal act together.

The recent discovery of Mary's personal project, "The Anatomy of Sacrifice," had solidified this nascent theory. It wasn't just a morbid fascination with the macabre; it was a profound exploration of extreme human experience, a philosophical inquiry into the ultimate price of one's beliefs or choices. And woven through Mary's research, as it had been through the other victims' lives and deaths, was the undeniable thread of fate. The preordained, the unavoidable, the tragic inevitability that seemed to dictate the characters' destinies in the ancient plays Mary so fervently studied. Maria saw it now, a chilling pattern emerging not just in the choice of victims but in the very *way* they were chosen, as if each was a pawn moved by an unseen hand onto a predetermined stage.

Bennett, the historian, had represented the past, a repository of stories and warnings that had been violently silenced. His death, occurring in the shadowed stacks of books, felt like a physical manifestation of history being erased. Bellweather, the philosopher, had embodied the present, her intricate theories and intellectual debates ultimately leading her to a brutal confrontation with the limitations of her own logic. Her demise had defined her existence, was a grim commentary on the disconnect between abstract thought and tangible reality. And now Mary, the embodiment of dramatic arts, a student of intense emotional immersion, had met her end in a manner that mirrored the very characters she sought to understand and portray. She was to be Medea, a woman consumed by grief and vengeance, a figure destined for horrific acts. Her death, therefore, wasn't just the end of a life; it was the catastrophic fulfillment of a role, a chillingly literal interpretation of dramatic destiny.

Maria voiced her growing suspicion to Detective Bates, who was meticulously examining Mary's belongings for any overlooked evidence. "It's not just random selection, Donny," she stated, her voice low and intense. "It's like a curated tragedy. Bennett was the past, Bellweather was the present of thought, and Mary... she was the future, or rather, the *performance* of emotion, the conduit for these archetypal narratives. The killer is treating these murders like chapters in a play, and each victim is a character playing out their fated role."

Donny paused his meticulous search, his gaze meeting Maria's. "A play? So, you think this is about the narrative? About telling a story through the killings?"

"Exactly," Maria confirmed, a knot of dread tightening in her stomach. "The literary selections, the symbolic locations, the victims' academic focuses – they all point to a deliberate construction. Bennett was researching the inevitability of historical cycles. Clara Bellweather was dissecting the philosophical foundations of free will and determinism. And Mary was immersed in *Medea*, a play steeped in the concept of inescapable fate, of a woman driven to unimaginable acts by betrayal and destiny. The killer isn't just a murderer; they're a playwright, an architect of despair, and each victim is a carefully chosen player in their macabre production."

The idea of 'fate' as a weapon was a chilling one. It suggested a killer who felt not just empowered, but perhaps even *justified* by a perceived cosmic order. They weren't simply acting out of malice; they were enacting a script, fulfilling a predetermined prophecy. And Mary's connection to the Drama department, her very identity as an actress, only amplified the irony and the terror. She, who sought to *embody* characters, to explore their deepest motivations and their tragic arcs, had become a character herself, her life extinguished at the climax of a narrative she may have unwittingly helped to shape.

Maria recalled Mary's intense dedication, her "almost obsessive dedication" to method acting. Tillman had described her immersion in Medea, her desire to *feel* the character's rage and despair. It was this very intensity, this blurring of the lines between performer and performance, that the killer seemed to exploit. Mary hadn't just been acting out Medea's story; she had, in the killer's twisted perception, become Medea, and her death was the ultimate, irreversible act of the play.

"Look at this," Donny said, holding up a small, leather-bound notebook he'd found tucked beneath Mary's theatrical scripts. It was small enough to fit in a pocket, its cover worn smooth with handling. Maria recognized Mary's distinctive, almost frantic handwriting filling the pages. It wasn't a diary in the conventional sense, but a collection of fragmented thoughts, philosophical musings, and observations, all centered around the themes of sacrifice, destiny, and the performance of self.

One entry, dated just weeks before her death, stood out:

The veil between the actor and the character is thinnest when the character is wrestling with the very forces that define their existence. Medea is not merely a woman scorned; she is the embodiment of an ancient, unavoidable truth. The universe conspires. The threads of fate are woven before we are born, and our greatest struggle is not to change them, but to understand the pattern, to find meaning in the inevitable unraveling.

'The universe conspires,' " Maria murmured, a shiver tracing its way down her spine. " That's it, isn't it? The killer believes they are an agent of this conspiracy, an instrument of fate. Bennett, Bellweather, Mary... they weren't just victims; they were characters whose arcs had reached their predetermined conclusion. Bennett, the keeper of the past, his story ending as the killer re-wrote the present. Clara, the seeker of truth, her philosophical inquiries leading him to an inescapable, brutal end. And Mary... Mary, who sought to understand the depths of Medea's despair, her fate sealed by the very intensity of her artistic pursuit."

The deliberate choice of a drama student for this particular act was, Maria realized, a masterstroke of cruel irony. A theater student, someone who lived and breathed performance, who understood the power of a well-crafted narrative had been turned into a symbol of that narrative's ultimate, fatal conclusion. It was a meta-commentary on the nature of acting itself, on the thin line between embodying a role and becoming consumed by it. The killer was not just taking lives; they were staging a deeply personal, intensely symbolic drama, using the university as their theater and its inhabitants as their tragic players.

Donny continued to leaf through Mary's notebook. "There's more here about 'roles.' She writes, 'We are all playing roles assigned to us by society, by our upbringing, by our own limitations. But the true artist, the true seeker, must question these roles, must try to transcend them. Or perhaps, as Medea suggests, the greatest art is to fully embrace the role that is thrust upon you, to embody its truth even unto destruction.'"

" 'Unto destruction,' " Maria echoed, the words hanging heavy in the air. This was the killer's modus operandi, their signature. Not just the literary allusions, not just the symbolic nature of the victims, but the overarching theme of inescapable tragedy, of fated roles played out to their bitter, often violent, ends. The killer wasn't just reacting to the world; they were actively curating a narrative of doom; a philosophical statement delivered through cadavers.

The concept of 'fate' as a guiding principle for the killer was deeply disturbing. It implied a profound sense of detachment, a belief that their actions were not choices but necessities. This wasn't the chaotic violence of a madman; it was the chilling precision of someone who believed they were acting out a cosmic decree. Each victim, in their own academic pursuit, had touched upon themes that resonated with this killer's worldview. Bennett, delving into the cyclical nature of history, perhaps seen by the killer as an unchangeable destiny. Bellweather, wrestling with the very concept of free will, her intellectual prowess ultimately rendered impotent against a perceived fate. And Mary, the aspiring actress, who was on the verge of embodying a character consumed by vengeance and despair, a character whose fate was sealed by the gods and her own choices.

Maria leaned back, the weight of this realization settling upon her. The killer wasn't just killing people; they were constructing a philosophical argument, a chilling testament to the power of destiny. The choice of Mary, a student of the dramatic arts, was particularly poignant. She was someone who understood, perhaps better than most, the power of narrative and the allure of archetypal characters. Her own life, in the killer's eyes, had become an extension of the tragic roles she sought to portray, her final act a horrifyingly literal interpretation of her craft. The university, with its rich tapestry of academic disciplines and its inherent human drama, had become the perfect stage for this macabre masterpiece, a place where the abstract concepts of fate and tragedy could be made brutally, undeniably real. The killer's signature motif wasn't just violence; it was the terrifying elegance of an inescapable destiny, played out in the most brutal of ways, with each victim a pawn moved by an unseen, and seemingly unyielding, hand of fate.

The wail of sirens, a mournful counterpoint to the hushed reverence that had descended upon Mary's apartment, was the first sign that Dr. Gibson had arrived. Maria watched from a distance as he was ushered into the scene, his usual academic composure replaced by a stark, almost visceral dread. His eyes, usually alight with intellectual curiosity, were clouded with a profound distress that mirrored the somber atmosphere. He moved with a heavy deliberation, his gait suggesting the weight of a burden far heavier than mere professional obligation. He'd been summoned, not as a suspect, nor even as a consultant in the traditional sense, but as someone who might, perhaps, recognize the insidious patterns woven into this unfolding horror.

As Gibson's gaze swept over the tableau, his attention, much like Maria's had been, was immediately drawn to the carefully arranged literary elements that served as the killer's chilling calling card. His breath hitched, a sharp, involuntary sound that cut through the ambient silence. His long, slender fingers, usually so adept at turning the delicate pages of ancient texts, now trembled slightly as he pointed to a specific passage, its stark typography a stark contrast to the surrounding disarray. It was a fragment from Sophocles, Maria noted, the same playwright whose works Mary had so intensely studied, and it spoke of inescapable doom, of characters caught in a web spun by the gods themselves.

"The Electra," Gibson finally managed, his voice a low, strained whisper, barely audible above the distant sirens. "And this specific stanza... it speaks of the crushing weight of inherited curses, of destinies that cannot be outrun, no matter the struggle." He looked up, his eyes locking with Maria's, and in their depths, she saw not just grief, but a deep, abiding fear. "This is... it's escalating. The choice of text, the emphasis... it's no longer just symbolic. It speaks of a profound, and I fear, dangerous, identification with these tragic protagonists. The killer isn't merely choosing victims who fit a theme; they are choosing victims who embody certain facets of these ancient, destructive narratives, and they are becoming increasingly immersed in the very essence of these doomed characters."

Maria felt a cold dread solidify in her gut. Gibson's words confirmed her own burgeoning suspicions. This wasn't just about selecting literary figures; it was about a psychological obsession that was deepening with each act. The killer was moving beyond academic allusion and into a disturbing form of imitative ritual. Mary, with her fervent immersion in *Medea*, had become the latest pawn in this macabre game, her life tragically mirroring the despair and vengeance of the mythical sorceress. And Gibson's distress wasn't just the shock of a brutal murder; it was the recognition of a specific kind of intellectual and psychological descent.

"You mentioned their 'identification,' Doctor," Maria prompted, her voice deliberately calm, a counterpoint to the storm raging within her. "With the tragic protagonists. What does that mean, precisely? Do you believe the killer sees themselves as one of these characters?"

Gibson paced a small, worn circle on the floor, his brow furrowed in deep concentration. "It's a complex psychological phenomenon, Detective. When an individual becomes deeply engrossed in a particular narrative, especially one that resonates with their own perceived grievance or worldview, they can begin to internalize the characters' motivations, their struggles, their very identities. In the context of these murders, it suggests a killer who feels a profound, almost righteous, connection to the characters' plight, and sees their victims as analogous to the antagonists or obstacles within those narratives."

He stopped pacing, his gaze fixed on a point beyond the immediate scene, as if seeing something far more distant, far more disturbing. "There was a society, you see, a small, informal group that met years ago that had splintered off from the Aeon Society. They called themselves *The Infinite Discourse*. It was a gathering of academics, students, thinkers – individuals who were fascinated by the great philosophical questions. And a significant portion of the discussions revolved around literature, specifically the enduring power of tragedy. They debated the nature of fate, the illusion of free will, the archetypal forces that shape human existence."

Maria's ears pricked up. Gibson was venturing into territory that felt both relevant and deeply personal. This wasn't just abstract literary theory; it was a glimpse into a past that might hold the key to the present. "The Infinite Discourse," she repeated, letting the name hang in the air. "Your were part of it?" She asked.

Gibson nodded his head.

"And what kind of discussions did you have, Doctor? Particularly concerning fate and free will?" Maria pressed.

Gibson's expression darkened. He hesitated, his eyes scanning the room as if seeking an escape from the memories that were clearly resurfacing. "The debates were... intense. Sometimes, they veered into uncomfortable territory. We explored the philosophical underpinnings of determinism, the idea that all events are predetermined. Some members argued passionately that human agency was a myth, a comforting delusion. Others countered that even within a fated framework, individual choices, however seemingly insignificant, could resonate with profound consequence." He sighed, a sound of profound weariness. "The lines between academic exploration and personal conviction began to blur for some. There was one individual, in particular, whose fascination with the destructive potential of fate was... alarming."

Maria seized on the opening. "One individual? Who was it, Doctor? This is important."

Gibson's jaw tightened. He shook his head, a definitive, almost painful gesture. "I... I cannot reveal their name. It would be a disservice to their privacy, and frankly, their trajectory was such that I've long since tried to distance myself from those associations. Suffice it to say, their interpretation of these themes was deeply personal, and it manifested in ways that were... unsettling. They believed that certain individuals were inherently destined for destruction, and that any force that facilitated that destiny was, in their view, acting in accordance with a higher, albeit brutal, order."

Maria felt a surge of frustration mixed with a growing certainty. Gibson knew more than he was letting on. His reluctance to name this individual wasn't just about privacy; it was about fear. Fear of a past association, fear of a past that had now, horrifyingly, returned. "But if this person was so obsessed with fate and destruction, why hasn't there been any indication of their involvement until now? Why the focus on these specific victims? Bennett, Bellweather, Mary... they seem so disparate."

"Disparate on the surface, perhaps," Gibson mused, his gaze returning to the literary passage. "But to someone with a skewed philosophical lens, they might represent crucial nodes in a narrative. Bennett, the historian, representing the unchangeable past, perhaps a past the killer felt wronged by. Clara, the philosopher, wrestling with the very concepts of choice and consequence, her inability to reconcile them leading to her own predetermined end. And Mary," he gestured almost reverently towards the area where Mary's spent most of her time, "Mary, the embodiment of dramatic expression, the one who sought to understand and portray the depths of human suffering and sacrifice. She represented the *performance* of tragedy. Perhaps," Gibson continued, his voice barely a whisper, "the killer sees themselves as an agent of that predetermined narrative. Someone who is not *choosing* to kill, but rather *fulfilling* a destiny, clearing the path for a narrative to unfold as it should."

The idea of the killer as an "agent of destiny" was a chilling one. It removed any semblance of personal motive, replacing it with a terrifyingly detached sense of cosmic obligation. It suggested a mind so consumed by a philosophical construct that it had become a justification for unimaginable violence.

"The Infinite Discourse's discussions," Maria pressed, "Did they ever touch upon specific plays or characters? Did this unnamed individual have any particular favorites, any characters whose plight they seemed to empathize with more deeply?"

Gibson closed his eyes, a deep tremor running through him. "There were many discussions, Detective. We dissected Orestes, Oedipus, Antigone... figures who were trapped by lineage, by circumstance, by the wrath of the gods. But there was a particular fascination with those who acted out of extreme passion, out of a perceived betrayal that drove them to unforgivable acts. Medea, of course, was a frequent subject. Her descent into infanticide, fueled by a consuming rage and a sense of absolute injustice... it was a potent symbol for some of the more... radical interpretations of destiny. They argued that her actions, however horrific, were the inevitable consequence of her circumstances, a logical, if brutal, conclusion to her suffering."

Maria felt a shiver crawl down her spine. Mary, the aspiring actress, had been deeply immersed in *Medea*. The killer, potentially a former member of this Aeon Society, held a particular fascination with Medea. The pieces were slotting into place with a terrifying finality. The killer wasn't just referencing tragedy; they were reenacting it, using Mary as their ultimate embodiment of a fated protagonist.

"So," Maria said, her voice gaining a new edge of urgency, "this individual, this former member of The Infinite Discourse, they believed that certain people were destined for destruction, and that their own actions were merely facilitating that destiny? And their fascination with Medea suggests a particular admiration for extreme, vengeful acts born of perceived injustice?"

"That is a distinct possibility," Gibson conceded, his gaze still distant. "They saw themselves not as perpetrators of violence, but as instruments of a cosmic balancing act. If someone was destined for ruin, then their intervention was, in their mind, merely hastening the inevitable, or perhaps even enacting a form of brutal justice. The choice of victims might not be arbitrary at all, but rather the selection of individuals who, in the killer's distorted perception, represented something that needed to be expunged, or whose predetermined arcs had reached their tragic conclusion."

He finally turned to face Maria fully, his eyes filled with a profound sorrow. "This is not merely a matter of academic interest anymore, Detective. This is someone who has taken these abstract philosophical concepts and weaponized them. The escalation is undeniable. The killer is no longer content with symbolic gestures; they are actively engaging in the destruction of lives, and they are doing so with a terrifying conviction, believing they are fulfilling a script written by forces far beyond human comprehension. Mary's death... it signifies a dangerous new phase. The playwright has moved from the theoretical to the visceral, and the stage is now stained with the blood of their characters."

Gibson's deep distress was palpable. He wasn't just a witness; he was someone who recognized the terrifying echoes of a past philosophical extremism that had now manifested in the most horrific way imaginable. The Infinite Discourse, once a forum for intellectual debate, had apparently incubated a dark ideology, an ideology that was now playing itself out on the streets, using innocent lives as its tragic props. Maria understood now. Gibson wasn't just concerned about the killer's methods; he was deeply, profoundly disturbed by the intellectual and philosophical underpinnings of these atrocities, recognizing the chilling resonance of dangerous ideas he had once encountered, and perhaps even dismissed, in the closed circle of The Infinite Discourse. The refusal to name the individual was no longer a matter of etiquette; it was a confession of a past intellectual dalliance that had yielded a monstrous progeny.

CHAPTER 7

THE PROFESSOR'S RIDDLE

The air in Mary's apartment still carried the acrid scent of disinfectant, a stark counterpoint to the lingering perfume of faded lilies. Detective Maria Richards stood by the window, her gaze fixed on the rain-slicked street below, the city lights blurring into an impressionistic smear. Dr. Aris Gibson's pronouncements, though delivered with a scholar's measured cadence, had settled in her mind like a swarm of agitated bees. His knowledge was too precise, his distress too profound, to be that of a mere detached observer. He spoke of Sophocles and Medea with an intimacy that suggested more than academic study; it hinted at personal acquaintance, perhaps even a shared past with the killer's twisted worldview. And his deliberate vagueness about the individual within The Infinite Discourse whose radical interpretations of fate had so alarmed him... it was a gaping hole in his narrative, a deliberate omission that screamed louder than any confession.

Maria wasn't prone to hasty judgments, but Gibson's demeanor was a tapestry woven with threads of apprehension and something more elusive – guilt, perhaps? Or a deep-seated fear that extended beyond the immediate horror of Mary's death. He'd been summoned, yes, as an expert in the literary currents that flowed through the killer's gruesome artistry. But Maria had seen a flicker of recognition in his eyes when he'd spoken of the specific passages, a recognition that spoke of a shared intellectual landscape, a terrain where such dark philosophies might have once been explored, debated, and perhaps even nurtured. His reluctance to name names, his insistence on privacy for someone whose ideas had clearly festered into murder, felt like a protective shield, not for the killer, but for himself.

She turned from the window, her gaze falling upon a photograph on a side table. Mary, laughing, her eyes bright with an almost theatrical spark. The killer saw her as Medea, Gibson had said. A performer of tragedy. But what if Gibson himself saw Mary, or someone like her, through a similar lens? What if his connection to The Infinite Discourse wasn't merely as a passive observer, but as an active participant in the very discussions that had twisted minds towards destruction? His description of the society's debates – the fervent arguments about determinism, the unsettling discussions on predetermined destinies – echoed with a disquieting familiarity, as if he were describing a shared intellectual playground he had long since abandoned, but which had now, monstrously, come to life.

Maria decided then and there. Gibson was not just a witness; he was a potential repository of crucial information, perhaps even the architect of the killer's intellectual scaffolding. His knowledge was a double-edged sword, offering insight while simultaneously deflecting direct scrutiny. It was time to move beyond his carefully curated academic persona and delve into the man himself, into the shadows of The Infinite Discourse and his specific role within it. If the killer was a product of that society's fertile ground for dangerous ideas, Gibson's personal history within it was the most fertile soil to excavate.

She returned to her office, the sterile hum of the fluorescent lights a stark contrast to the somber atmosphere of Mary's apartment. The case files lay open on her desk, a chaotic testament to her mounting frustration. Bennett, the historian whose work might have been seen as a lament for a lost past; Clara, the philosopher who grappled with the illusion of choice; and Mary, the actress who embodied the raw emotion of tragedy. They were disparate figures, yet in the killer's eyes, they had been pieces on a board, characters in a predestined narrative. And Gibson, with his intimate understanding of these literary archetypes and his connection to The Infinite Discourse, was the only link that seemed to bind them all.

Her investigation into Gibson began subtly, an attempt to gather information without raising his already palpable alarm. She started with his academic history, a seemingly innocuous dive into his published works and lecture series. His early research had indeed focused on classical tragedy, delving into the very themes he'd discussed: fate, free will, the cyclical nature of suffering. His doctoral thesis, titled *The Serpent in the Garden: Determinism and Agency in Greek Tragedy*, was a dense exploration of the philosophical arguments that had formed the bedrock of the Aeon Society's and The Infinite Discourse discussions. Maria noted the emphasis on *determinism*, a concept that seemed to have a particularly potent grip on Gibson's intellect, and, by extension, on the killer's actions.

She then turned her attention to The Infinite Discourse itself. It was an enigma, existing in the academic ether with little concrete evidence of its formal structure or membership. Gibson had described it as an "informal gathering," a "small society" of thinkers.

But Maria suspected it was more than that; it was a crucible, a place where abstract philosophical ideas could be forged into dangerous ideologies. She ran background checks on individuals known to have been affiliated with Gibson during his academic career, cross-referencing them with any known members of obscure philosophical or literary societies. The names were few and far between, a testament to the society's deliberate obscurity.

One name, however, surfaced with a degree of persistence: a Dr. Owen Draycott. Draycott, like Gibson, had been a specialist in classical literature, but his later academic career had taken a sharp turn. He'd published several controversial articles on "existential necessity" and the "ethical imperative of consequence," texts that Maria found deeply unsettling. Draycott's writings seemed to advocate for a radical form of fatalism, arguing that individuals who were "destined" for destruction should not be interfered with, and that those who acted to prevent such fates were, in essence, defying a higher cosmic order. The language was academic, veiled in scholarly prose, but the underlying message was chillingly clear: a justification for inaction, and perhaps, even for active intervention, in the face of predetermined downfall.

Maria dug deeper into Draycott's life. He had abruptly left academia a decade ago, disappearing from public life. There were rumors of a personal tragedy, a profound disillusionment that had driven him into isolation. Gibson's evasiveness regarding the individual within The Infinite Discourse now seemed less about protecting a past acquaintance and more about distancing himself from a dangerous ideological influence, an influence that might have originated with Draycott and been amplified within the society's discussions. Gibson's own fascination with the "destructive potential of fate" could have easily been a reflection of Draycott's more extreme views, a fascination he now deeply regretted and feared.

She requested Gibson's personal file from his university. It was a meticulously kept record of his academic achievements, his research grants, his sabbatical leaves. Nothing out of the ordinary. But Maria was looking for the subtle cracks, the inconsistencies. She found a notation about a disciplinary hearing during his postgraduate studies; a minor infraction related to "unauthorized access to archival materials." The details were vague, but it suggested a restless curiosity, a willingness to push boundaries in pursuit of knowledge, a trait that could easily manifest in darker ways.

The Infinite Discourse, Gibson had implied, was where the lines between academic exploration and personal conviction began to blur. This blurring was precisely what Maria was trying to quantify. Had Gibson been a proponent of these extreme ideas, or had he been a witness to their dangerous evolution? His distress when discussing the killer's actions suggested a deep personal stake, an awareness of the potential consequences of these philosophical debates gone awry.

Maria decided a direct approach was necessary. She scheduled another meeting with Dr. Gibson, this time at his university office. The space was a sanctuary of old books, leather-bound volumes lining floor-to-ceiling shelves, the air thick with the comforting scent of aging paper. Gibson sat behind his imposing mahogany desk, his usual academic composure subtly frayed. The events of the past few days had clearly taken a toll.

"Dr. Gibson," Maria began, her tone measured, "I've been looking into The Infinite Discourse and some of its associated figures. Your name, and the name of Dr. Owen Draycott, keep appearing."

Gibson's composure wavered for a fraction of a second. His eyes, usually steady and intelligent, flickered with a subtle unease. "Draycott? Owen Draycott. Yes, I knew him years ago. He was... a brilliant mind, though his ideas became increasingly... unorthodox."

"Unorthodox how?" Maria pressed, leaning forward slightly. "His writings on existential necessity and the ethical imperative of consequence suggest a profound belief in predetermined outcomes. Did you share those beliefs, Doctor?"

Gibson sighed, a heavy, weary sound. He ran a hand through his thinning hair. "We all engaged with those ideas, Detective. That was the nature of the Discourse. We explored the fringes of philosophical thought. Draycott, however, took those explorations to a place that many of us found deeply troubling. He seemed to believe that fate was not just a concept to be debated, but a force to be reckoned with, a rigid structure that dictated every aspect of existence. He argued that any deviation from one's predetermined path was not only futile but perhaps even an affront to the natural order."

"And this individual you mentioned previously," Maria continued, her gaze fixed on Gibson's face, searching for any tell-tale signs of deception, "the one whose fascination with destructive destinies was alarming. Was it Draycott?"

Gibson hesitated. The silence stretched, thick with unspoken words. He looked down at his hands, the long fingers that had pointed to Sophocles now clasped tightly together. "Draycott's conviction was absolute," he finally admitted, his voice low. "He genuinely believed that certain individuals were born to suffer, to be broken. He saw himself not as an arbiter of justice, but as an observer, perhaps even a facilitator, of these inescapable destinies. He was convinced that his role was to... remove obstacles, to ensure that the 'natural' course of events unfolded unimpeded."

"Remove obstacles," Maria repeated, the phrase resonating with a chilling finality. "You mean, people who stood in the way of what he perceived as someone's inevitable downfall?"

"Precisely," Gibson confirmed, his voice barely a whisper. "He spoke of 'cleansing the path,' of 'correcting the narrative.' It was couched in philosophical terms, of course, but the implication was... disturbing. He believed that some lives were simply meant to be cut short, their narratives concluded prematurely by forces beyond their control. And he saw himself as an agent of those forces."

Maria felt a cold knot tighten in her stomach. Draycott. The brilliant mind that had become a chillingly detached observer of human suffering, a self-appointed facilitator of predetermined doom. Gibson's knowledge wasn't just academic; it was personal. He had known Draycott, had been privy to his dangerous philosophies, and had, it seemed, distanced himself from them. But the echo of those ideas, the very foundation of the killer's actions, had clearly resonated with Gibson to a degree that made him deeply, profoundly fearful. His reluctance to name Draycott wasn't just about academic privacy; it was about the terrifying realization that the dangerous seeds of thought he'd once encountered in the hallowed halls of The Infinite Discourse had now borne such horrific fruit. He knew the killer, or at least, the intellectual progenitor of the killer's twisted worldview. And that knowledge, Maria suspected, was a burden he was struggling to bear, perhaps even a secret he was desperate to keep buried. The question now was, was he trying to protect Draycott, or was he trying to protect himself from the implications of his own past associations?

Maria's investigation into Dr. Aris Gibson had taken a decidedly introspective turn. It was no longer solely about the killer and their motives, but about the intellectual soil from which those motives had sprung. Gibson, she was learning, had retreated. His colleagues at the university, when pressed by Maria's discreet inquiries, painted a picture of a man increasingly consumed by his work, or perhaps, by something far more personal. He was described as brilliant, undeniably so, a luminary in his field of classical literature and its philosophical underpinnings. But lately, a profound melancholy had settled over him, a shadow that seemed to deepen with each passing season. His once vibrant lectures were now imbued with a somber gravity, his pronouncements laced with an almost unnerving gravitas, as if he were not merely discussing ancient texts but reading the grim pronouncements of their inevitable future.

His office, once a hub of intellectual discourse and lively debate, had become a hermitage. Gibson, it was said, had begun spending increasingly long hours within its confines, a self-imposed exile amidst the hushed reverence of his scholarly pursuits. The university administration had granted him a certain latitude, recognizing his prodigious output and the respect he commanded, but whispers persisted about his reclusiveness. Some attributed it to the pressures of academia, others to a personal tragedy he kept fiercely guarded. Maria, however, suspected a more direct correlation with the unfolding investigation. The more she delved into the philosophical currents that had animated the Discourse and, by extension, the killer's actions, the more Gibson's personal disquiet seemed to mirror the intellectual darkness they explored.

Her informant network, a motley crew of disgruntled academics and gossipy administrative staff, spoke of Gibson's personal library with a mixture of awe and apprehension. It was not merely a collection of books; it was a curated universe, a meticulously assembled repository of thought that spanned centuries and disciplines. The rumors spoke of rare manuscripts, first editions of obscure treatises, and an almost obsessive focus on the intertwined subjects of death, ritual, and literary theory. Maria could almost visualize it: shelves groaning under the weight of ancient papyri, vellum-bound tomes detailing forgotten rites, and modern critical analyses that dissected the very essence of human suffering and its artistic representation. This wasn't the casual accumulation of a scholar; it was the deliberate amassing of evidence, a deeply personal exploration into the very themes that had captivated the killer.

Maria requested Gibson's office keys from the department head, citing the need to retrieve some case-related documents Gibson had mentioned. The request was met with a slight hesitation, but ultimately granted. The department head, a man whose own career had long since stagnated, seemed more relieved than concerned by Gibson's withdrawal, attributing it to the eccentricities of genius. He spoke of Gibson with a patronizing affection, like one might speak of a brilliant but unstable child. "Aris has always been... intense," he'd said, tapping a pen against his chin. "Deeply immersed. Sometimes, I think he forgets the outside world exists. His library... it's legendary. He treats those books like they're alive."

The journey to Gibson's office felt like a descent into a forgotten corner of the university, a place where time moved at a different pace. The corridors grew narrower, the lighting dimmer, and the air took on a musty, venerable quality. The door to Gibson's office, when she finally found it, was a heavy oak affair, bearing the discreet brass plate of his name and title. There was no sign of Gibson himself, no sound emanating from within. With a quiet click, she turned the lock and pushed the door open.

The scent that greeted her was intoxicating, a heady perfume of aged paper, leather, and something faintly floral, perhaps dried flowers pressed between the pages of some long-forgotten love sonnet. It was exactly as she'd imagined, and yet, infinitely more potent. Floor-to-ceiling bookshelves lined every available wall space, crammed with volumes of every size and description. Some were meticulously cataloged, others appeared to have been pulled haphazardly from their shelves, their contents splayed open on various surfaces. The sheer volume was staggering, a testament to Gibson's lifelong dedication to his craft.

But it was the nature of the collection that immediately seized Maria's attention. Interspersed with the expected classical literature and literary theory were books that spoke of a darker, more esoteric interest. Titles like *The Anthropology of Death Rituals*, *Symbolism in Pre-Christian Sacrifices*, *The Phenomenology of Grief*, and *Ancient Forms of Requiem* were visible, their spines worn and faded. There were also works on mythology, focusing on darker deities and underworld myths, and philosophical texts that grappled with the nature of suffering and predestination, but with a far more visceral and less abstract approach than she'd seen in Gibson's published works.

Maria moved deeper into the room, her footsteps muffled by a thick Persian rug. The desk was a vast expanse of polished mahogany, cluttered with academic papers, open books, and a few personal effects. A framed photograph, slightly askew, showed a younger Gibson, his face open and hopeful, standing beside a woman whose features were blurred by the passage of time and the poor quality of the print. He looked happier then, less burdened. She resisted the urge to linger, her focus sharpening on the immediate task at hand.

Her gaze swept across the shelves, looking for anything that might connect to Mary, to the killer, to The Infinite Discourse's specific brand of fatalism. She noticed several books dedicated to Sophocles, a particular favorite of Gibson's, but also to Euripides, whose Medea was the killer's apparent touchstone. These were not just academic editions; many were annotated, with Gibson's meticulous, spidery handwriting filling the margins with observations, cross-references, and sometimes, unsettlingly personal reflections. One passage in *Medea*, detailing Medea's descent into infanticide, was circled repeatedly, with notes like "the absolute logic of despair" and "fate's cruel necessity" scrawled beside it.

She carefully pulled out a volume titled *The Ars Moriendi: Medieval Treatises on the Art of Dying*. It was a weighty tome, bound in dark, cracked leather. The pages, brittle with age, were filled with woodcut illustrations of deathbed scenes, spiritual guidance, and the rituals surrounding the final moments of life. Gibson had clearly studied this extensively; his notes here were more extensive, delving into the philosophical implications of a "good death" and the societal role of confronting mortality. He seemed to be wrestling with the very idea of agency in the face of inevitable demise, a recurring theme in his work and, Maria now realized, a central tenet of the killer's ideology.

As she leafed through the pages, a small, folded piece of paper slipped out from between two leaves. It was not a bookmark but appeared to be a hastily jotted note. The handwriting was Gibson's, but more agitated, less controlled than his usual scholarly annotations.

"O. – The arguments are circular. The conclusion is predetermined. But the *method*... the artistic expression of that inevitability... that is where the true horror lies. It is not enough to *believe* in fate; one must *perform* it. The orchestration, the staging... that is the divine mandate. To guide the inevitable, to sculpt the destined tragedy."

Maria's breath hitched. "O." She immediately thought of Owen Draycott. Draycott, whose theories on existential necessity had bordered on the fanatical. Draycott, who Gibson had been so reluctant to name. The note was chillingly direct, a glimpse into the terrifying abyss of Gibson's thought process, or perhaps, the thought process he was observing in others. The emphasis on "performance," on "orchestration" and "staging," echoed Mary's profession as an actress and the killer's deliberate theatricality. The killer wasn't just enacting fate; they were staging it, crafting it, directing it with a macabre artistry that Gibson seemed to both understand and, disturbingly, admire on some intellectual level.

She continued to sift through the books, her senses on high alert. She found a collection of essays on Nietzsche, particularly his writings on eternal recurrence and the Übermensch, subjects that had also been reportedly discussed within the Discourse Society. Gibson's annotations here were extensive, grappling with the idea of embracing one's destiny, even a painful one, with a fierce affirmation of life. But there was also an undercurrent of concern, a recognition of how such concepts could be twisted into justification for suffering and destruction. He wrote, "The affirmation of life can become a perversion of it if it negates the inherent value of individual suffering. To embrace the cycle is one thing; to actively perpetuate its crueler manifestations is another."

A specific shelf caught her eye, tucked away in a dimly lit corner. It seemed to house a more personal collection, less academic and more... symbolic. There were volumes on ancient divination, books detailing the language of omens, and collections of folklore that spoke of cursed lineages and inescapable doom. One book, bound in what looked like rough-spun wool, was titled *The Weaver's Loom: Patterns of Fate in Global Mythology*. Maria opened it, and her blood ran cold. Tucked within its pages, pressed flat and preserved, was a single, dried black rose. It was identical to the ones found at the crime scenes, a signature of the killer that Gibson, in his scholarly sanctuary, seemed to be holding as a tangible relic.

Beneath the rose, Gibson had written a single, stark sentence in pencil: "The bloom of inevitable sorrow."

This was more than just scholarly interest; it was an obsession. Gibson wasn't just studying these ideas; he was living with them, perhaps even collecting their gruesome manifestations. His scholarly retreat was not an escape from the horror, but a deeper immersion into its philosophical and symbolic underpinnings. He was surrounded by the very texts and artifacts that could have informed, or even inspired, the killer's actions. The question gnawed at Maria: Was Gibson a horrified observer documenting the descent of a dangerous ideology, or was he a complicit participant, a curator of the dark arts that had led to murder? His meticulously ordered office, with its chaotic undercurrent of profound darkness, felt like a physical manifestation of his own internal struggle. He was a scholar who had wandered too far into the shadows, and now, he was trapped in the labyrinth of his own intellectual obsessions, surrounded by the very tools that had forged the killer's horrifying narrative. The black rose, a symbol of doom and despair, resting on the page detailing mythological patterns of fate, was not just a discovery; it was a confession of sorts, a silent acknowledgment of Gibson's deep, disturbing connection to the case. He was not merely an expert; he was a custodian of the killer's intellectual heritage, and the weight of that responsibility was crushing him.

Maria's investigation had led her down a path that felt increasingly like a descent into a forgotten mausoleum of thought. Gibson's office, a sanctuary of esoteric knowledge, had yielded fragments of a disturbing intellectual landscape, but the true architects of The Infinite Discourse's macabre philosophy remained elusive. The black rose, a silent, poignant testament to Gibson's entanglement, still lay heavy in her mind. It wasn't enough to know *what* Gibson had been studying; she needed to understand *who* had cultivated these dark seeds. Her inquiries, initially focused on Gibson as a potential suspect or a victim of circumstance, were now broadening to encompass the wider ecosystem of the Discourse Society, seeking the source of the ideology that had birthed a killer.

She shifted her focus, her attention moving away from the solitary scholar and towards the collective consciousness of the society. The university archives offered a sterile, factual account of The Infinite Discourse's inception – a formal registry, a list of founding members, a sterile overview of its stated aims: "the philosophical exploration of existential consciousness and its artistic manifestations." But the human element, the fervent belief, the insidious slide into extremism, was absent from these dry records. To understand that Maria knew she needed to speak to those who had breathed the society's peculiar air, those who had been seduced by its promises before the inevitable disillusionment, or worse.

Her contacts, a tapestry of disgruntled academics, bohemian artists, and disillusioned former students, proved more fruitful than the university's official channels. These were individuals who had orbited The Infinite Discourse, some peripherally, others deeply involved, before its eventual implosion, its descent from intellectual salon to whispered cult. The name "Aris Gibson" surfaced sporadically in these conversations, always with a qualifier – "brilliant, of course," or "intensely intellectual," but often tinged with an unspoken unease, a recognition of a darkness that Gibson, even then, seemed to embody. Yet, no single individual emerged as the clear architect of the society's fatalistic trajectory. Instead, the whispers coalesced around a different, more nebulous figure – a charismatic ideologue, an almost mythical presence within the society's inner circle, whose influence, even now, cast a long shadow.

One former member, a poet named Rowan Pierce, whose own work had once flirted with themes of nihilism before a sharp turn towards existential affirmation, spoke of this individual with a mixture of reverence and fear. Pierce, a man whose eyes still held the haunted intensity of someone who had stared into the abyss, met Maria in a dimly lit jazz club, the mournful cry of a saxophone a fitting soundtrack to their conversation. He nursed a whiskey, the ice clinking like small, brittle bones in the glass.

"The Discourse," Pierce began, his voice raspy, as if scraped raw by years of unshed grief, "it was a beacon for those of us who felt... unmoored. We were adrift in a sea of meaninglessness, and they offered a raft. A very peculiar raft, mind you, but a raft nonetheless." He took a slow sip of his drink. "And at the heart of it, there was *him*. He was... the visionary. Or so we thought."

Maria leaned forward, her pen poised. "His name?"

Pierce gave a short, bitter laugh. "Names are slippery things in that circle, Detective. They preferred titles and archetypes. He was known as 'The Composer.' Or sometimes, simply 'The Artiste.' He didn't preach; he *performed*. His arguments weren't logical constructs; they were dramatic pronouncements, delivered with the conviction of a prophet and the theatricality of a seasoned tragedian."

"And what was the core of his message?" Maria prompted, her mind already drawing parallels to Gibson's annotations, to the emphasis on performance and staging.

"Death," Pierce said, the single word hanging in the air like a death knell. "But not just death as an end. Death as the ultimate artistic statement. He argued that life was inherently messy, chaotic, mundane. True beauty, he believed, lay in the exquisite finality of death. It was the perfect canvas, the ultimate form of expression. He saw the act of dying, particularly a death that was consciously embraced, as the zenith of human experience. A masterpiece of inevitable sorrow."

Maria's gaze sharpened. "A masterpiece of inevitable sorrow." The phrase echoed Gibson's own chilling inscription beneath the black rose. It was too precise, too poetic, to be a mere coincidence. She remembered Gibson's intense focus on *Medea*, on the "absolute logic of despair" and "fate's cruel necessity." Had Gibson been reflecting the Composer's teachings, or had Gibson's own profound engagement with these texts led him to embody the very philosophy the Composer espoused?

"He spoke of the 'grace of finality,'" Pierce continued, oblivious to Maria's internal struggle. "He believed that the universe was a grand, cosmic play, and we were all merely actors playing out our predetermined roles. But some were destined to be the playwrights, the directors, the ones who could truly understand and manipulate the narrative arc. He saw himself, and he convinced many of us, that he was one of them. That he could... orchestrate the ultimate conclusion, not just for himself, but for others, as a testament to the beauty of fate."

"Did he speak of specific rituals? Of particular methods?" Maria pressed, the images from Gibson's office – the books on death rituals, on sacrifice – flashing through her mind.

Pierce's eyes clouded over. "He spoke in metaphors, mostly. Of 'cleansing finales,' of 'ascensions through cessation.' But the implication was clear. He believed that by embracing death; by actively seeking it and controlling its presentation, one transcended the limitations of mortal existence. He saw it as a form of ultimate creation. He would speak of great artists, great thinkers, who had met their end in a way that cemented their legacy, that made their life's work a perfect, tragic whole. He was obsessed with the *how* of death, not just the *why*."

"And Gibson? Dr. Gibson. Where did he fit into this?" Maria asked, her voice carefully neutral.

Pierce hesitated, his gaze drifting to the swirling amber liquid in his glass. "Aris was... brilliant. Terribly brilliant. He was drawn to the intellectual rigor of the Composer's philosophy. He could dissect its logic, understand its nuances, perhaps better than anyone. He saw the beauty in the abstract arguments, the elegance of the fatalistic worldview. But I think... I think he was also horrified by it. There was a melancholy about Aris, even then. A sadness that seemed to seep from him. He'd engage with the Composer's ideas with a feverish intensity, but afterward, he'd withdraw. He'd question. He'd doubt. He was wrestling with the implications, while the Composer seemed to revel in them."

"So, Gibson was a follower, but a conflicted one?"

"A deeply conflicted intellectual," Pierce corrected. "He was fascinated by the abyss, but he was terrified of falling in. The

Composer, on the other hand... he was already there, and he was inviting others to jump with him. He had this way of looking at you, as if he could see the inevitable end of your story, and he'd present it not as a tragedy, but as a beautiful, almost divine, resolution. He made death seem... desirable. Like the ultimate escape from the banality of existence."

Maria probed further, asking about specific individuals, about the hierarchy within The Infinite Discourse, about the transition from philosophical discussion to tangible action. Pierce's recollections painted a picture of a charismatic leader who cultivated an atmosphere of intellectual superiority, a sense of being privy to profound truths that the rest of the world could never comprehend. He fostered a sense of elitism, a belief that only a select few were capable of truly understanding the "art of dying." This exclusivity, Pierce explained, was a powerful lure, appealing to the innate human desire for significance, for a purpose beyond the ordinary.

"There were others," Pierce admitted, his voice dropping to a near whisper. "Those who were... more practical. More eager to translate the theory into practice. The Composer never explicitly ordered anyone to do anything, not directly. His influence was more subtle, more insidious. He would pose hypothetical scenarios, explore the philosophical justifications for extreme actions, and then watch, with a detached fascination, as his listeners grappled with the implications. He was a master manipulator of the intellect, a sculptor of dangerous ideas."

Maria sensed she was on the cusp of a significant revelation. The "Composer's" description – charismatic, intellectual, obsessed with death as art, with performance and staging – resonated deeply with the limited understanding she had of Gibson's mental state and his scholarly pursuits. Gibson's office hadn't just been a collection of books; it had been a shrine to these very ideas, a meticulously curated testament to the Composer's philosophy. The black rose wasn't just a symbol; it was a tangible link, a relic from the Composer's domain, preserved by Gibson.

She asked about the society's endgame, its ultimate aspirations. Pierce spoke of a desire to create a "permanent artistic moment," a singular event that would encapsulate their core beliefs and leave an indelible mark on the world. The specifics remained vague, shrouded in the metaphorical language of the Composer's teachings, but the intent was clear: a desire for a grand, symbolic act that would validate their philosophy and achieve a form of eternal significance.

"Did this 'Composer' have a name that was more mundane?" Maria pressed, the question hanging in the humid air of the club. "A surname, perhaps? Something that might appear in official records?"

Pierce traced the rim of his glass. "I... I don't know. He kept his personal life fiercely private. We knew him through the lens of his ideas, his pronouncements. He was an enigma, a disembodied voice of profound, terrifying wisdom. He didn't seem to have a life outside the Discourse, outside his philosophy. He *was* the philosophy. He embodied it."

Maria left the club with a gnawing sense of unease. The Composer, this shadowy figure, seemed to be the missing piece, the gravitational center around which The Infinite Discourse, and perhaps Gibson himself, had revolved. The descriptions were too consistent, too aligned with the evidence she had gathered in Gibson's office. The killer, with their theatrical flair and fatalistic pronouncements, was a living embodiment of the Composer's dangerous vision. Gibson, the conflicted scholar, was caught in the crossfire of this deadly ideology, a custodian of its dark beauty, a man paralyzed by his own intellectual fascination and moral revulsion. The black rose was no longer just Gibson's possession; it was a symbol of the Composer's influence, a bloom of inevitable sorrow cultivated by a mind that saw death as the ultimate art form, and that mind, Maria suspected with a chilling certainty, was intimately connected to the professor's profound, disturbing riddle. The investigation was no longer just about finding a killer; it was about unmasking a dangerous philosophy and the seductive voice that had given it life.

The air in Professor Gibson's study was thick with the scent of aging paper and a faint, almost imperceptible aroma of pipe tobacco, a ghost of his presence that clung to the heavy velvet curtains and the worn leather of the armchair. Maria had secured this access under the thinnest of pretenses, a borrowed academic curiosity about a rare edition of Sophocles she claimed Gibson had mentioned in passing. It was a flimsy ruse, but Gibson's housekeeper, a woman whose loyalty seemed to extend beyond the grave, had granted her entry with a sigh, her own eyes holding a perpetual weariness, as if burdened by the weight of the secrets the house contained.

Maria moved with practiced stealth, her senses on high alert. The study was less a place of academic pursuit and more a meticulously constructed sanctuary of a singular, morbid obsession. Books lined the walls from floor to ceiling, their spines a kaleidoscope of leather and gilt, whispering titles on mythology, philosophy, existentialism, and, most disturbingly, the aesthetics of death. Each volume seemed carefully chosen, a testament to a mind that had delved deeply into the darker currents of human thought. She ran a gloved finger along the spines, the titles themselves a chilling litany: *The Anatomy of Melancholy*, *On the Genealogy of Morality*, *The Myth of Sisyphus*, *The Sorrows of Young Werther*. Gibson's annotations, which she had studied extensively from the fragments recovered from his office, were legendary for their depth and disturbing philosophical bent. But the true treasures, she suspected, would not be found on the public shelves.

Her gaze swept across the room, searching for any anomaly, any misplaced object that might betray a hidden compartment or a secret cache. The desk was tidy, almost unnaturally so, as if Gibson had meticulously prepared his space before his final act. Nothing seemed out of place, yet the very order of it felt like a carefully constructed disguise. She approached the large mahogany desk, its surface polished to a high sheen, reflecting the dim light filtering through the window. A single, antique fountain pen lay beside an inkwell, as if Gibson had been interrupted mid-sentence, a narrative too cruel to be true.

Her attention was drawn to a large, ornate atlas, its pages splayed open to a map of ancient Greece. It seemed incongruous with the otherwise somber tone of the room. She approached it cautiously, her heart beginning to thrum with a heightened anticipation. As she leaned closer, her fingers brushed against a slightly raised section of the desk's edge, near the atlas. It felt... different. A subtle inconsistency in the wood grain, almost imperceptible to the casual observer, but to Maria's trained eye, it screamed of manipulation. She pressed gently, then with more force. A faint click echoed in the silence, and a narrow section of the desk's facade, no wider than her hand, sprang open.

Behind it, nestled in a velvet-lined recess, was a manuscript.

It was bound in dark, unadorned leather, its pages brittle with age and use. There was no title, no author's name, only the silent weight of its presence. Maria's breath hitched. This had to be it. The key. The missing piece that would bridge the gap between Gibson's obsession and the killer's chilling artistry. With trembling fingers, she lifted it from its hiding place. The weight felt significant, imbued with a gravity that transcended mere paper and ink.

She settled into Gibson's armchair, the worn leather groaning softly beneath her. The room seemed to hold its breath as she opened the manuscript. The first page was filled with dense, handwritten script, the ink a deep, rich black. It was Gibson's hand, unmistakably. But there was a ferocity to the strokes, a desperation that hadn't been evident in his academic notes. The handwriting itself was disturbingly similar to the samples she had of the killer's notes – the same slant, the same distinctive loops and flourishes, but imbued with a raw, untamed energy. It was as if she were holding a direct conduit to the killer's mind, a mind that had, at some point, been inextricably linked with Gibson's.

The opening passages were a philosophical discourse on the nature of tragedy. Gibson didn't write of tragedy as a literary device; he wrote of it as a fundamental aspect of existence, an inherent force that shaped human lives. He argued that life, in its very essence, was a prelude to a grand, inevitable tragedy. The mundane struggles, the fleeting joys, the persistent anxieties – they were all merely scaffolding for the ultimate, devastating climax.

"The universe," he had written, his script almost aggressive on the page, *"is a stage set for sorrow. We are born into a narrative already fraught with inherent conflict, destined to play out a script of inevitable loss. To deny this is to embrace a comforting lie, a Sisyphean delusion of control. True wisdom lies not in the futile attempt to escape the tragedy, but in its profound, unfettered embrace."*

Maria turned the page, her mind racing. This wasn't just academic theorizing; this was a blueprint. A justification. She remembered Pierce's words: "He believed that by embracing death, by actively seeking it and controlling its presentation, one transcended the limitations of mortal existence." Gibson's words echoed this sentiment with a terrifying precision.

The manuscript delved deeper into the concept Gibson termed "narrative suicide." It wasn't simply about ending one's life; it was about orchestrating one's demise as the ultimate act of self-definition. It was about seizing control of the narrative at its most critical juncture, transforming the final act from a passive surrender into an active, deliberate masterpiece.

"Why," Gibson had scrawled, the letters practically vibrating with intensity, *"should we allow the capricious hand of fate to pen our final chapter? Why surrender the narrative's crescendo to the random machinations of circumstance? Life is the prologue; death is the epilogue that defines the entire work. And if the epilogue is the sole element that grants the preceding narrative meaning, then its crafting becomes the paramount artistic endeavor. The greatest*

artists do not merely depict suffering; they embody it, they culminate in it, they become it. The 'narrative suicide' is not an end; it is the ultimate apotheosis, the definitive brushstroke on the canvas of existence."

Maria felt a chill crawl up her spine. This was the language of the killer, the chilling rhetoric that had accompanied the victims' final moments. The meticulous staging, the symbolic elements – they weren't random acts of violence; they were deliberate artistic choices, meticulously planned to achieve a desired narrative effect. The manuscript was revealing the killer's philosophy, the twisted ideology that fueled their macabre performances.

She continued to read, her eyes scanning the pages with a growing sense of dread. Gibson explored the idea of imposing this narrative onto others. If one could orchestrate their own perfect tragedy, why not bestow this gift – or curse – upon those deemed unworthy of such a profound conclusion? He framed it as a mercy, a liberation from the mundane, a tragic elevation for those trapped in lives of quiet desperation.

"There are souls," Gibson wrote, his script softening slightly, though the underlying darkness remained, *"adrift in a sea of banality, their existence a prolonged, unremarkable ache. They are unfinished symphonies, their potential for profound sorrow left unrealized. For such souls, is there not a form of grace in providing the cathartic conclusion they are incapable of achieving themselves? To grant them the sublime finality that eludes their grasp, to transform their meaningless existence into a stark, indelible tragedy. It is not murder; it is an act of profound, albeit terrible, artistic intervention. We are not destroyers; we are curators of existential finales, sculptors of the definitive sorrow."*

Maria's breath hitched. Curators of existential finales. Sculptors of the definitive sorrow. These phrases were chillingly familiar, echoes of the killer's carefully chosen words, their precise, almost poetic pronouncements. This manuscript was not just a confession; it was a manifesto. It laid bare the warped reasoning, the intellectual gymnastics that allowed the killer to justify their horrific actions.

Gibson's musings became increasingly abstract, blurring the lines between personal philosophy and a guide for action. He discussed the importance of symbolism, of narrative coherence, of ensuring that the "performance" of death resonated with the victim's life, or more accurately, with Gibson's perception of its lack of resonance. He analyzed historical figures who had met tragic ends, dissecting their deaths for their artistic merit, for their contribution to their overall narrative. He spoke of the "elegant surrender," the "symbolic self-immolation," the "final tableau."

"The victim," he wrote, *"must become a character in a larger drama, their demise a crucial plot point. Their life, however insignificant it may seem to the uninitiated, must be scrutinized for its thematic potential. Every detail, from their profession to their personal relationships, can be woven into the tapestry of their final act. The more profound the tragic resonance, the more complete the artistic statement. It is not enough to simply kill; one must stage. One must orchestrate. One must ensure that the final scene is a work of art, etched into the annals of human experience."*

Maria felt a surge of adrenaline. This was it. The link she had been searching for. Gibson, the conflicted intellectual, had been more than just a follower of the Composer; he had been an active participant, a co-conspirator in the creation of this horrifying philosophy. Or, perhaps, he had been the Composer himself, cloaked in academic respectability, his intellect a weapon used to craft the ultimate justification for murder. The similarity in handwriting between Gibson and the killer was no longer a mere observation; it was a damning indictment.

She continued to pore over the manuscript, her gloved fingers carefully turning the pages. Gibson discussed the ethical considerations of his "art," dismissing them with a chillingly detached logic. He argued that societal norms and moral codes were mere constructs, designed to suppress the inherent beauty of tragedy and the transformative power of death.

"Morality," he asserted, his script growing bolder, almost defiant, *"is the opiate of the uninspired. It is a shield wielded by the timid to protect themselves from the profound truths that lie at the heart of existence. We, who understand the inherent beauty of dissolution, who recognize death as the ultimate canvas, cannot be bound by such pedestrian limitations. We are the alchemists of sorrow, transforming the dross of mortal existence into the gold of eternal tragedy. Our actions, however they may be perceived by the ignorant masses, are acts of profound creation, of existential liberation."*

The sheer audacity of his pronouncements was breathtaking. Gibson wasn't merely theorizing; he was articulating a worldview that sanctioned murder, that elevated it to the status of an art form. Maria's mind flashed back to the crime scenes, to the deliberate placement of objects, the symbolic gestures, the carefully crafted narratives that the killer had left behind. Each detail, which had previously seemed like the work of a deranged individual, now clicked into place as part of a meticulously planned artistic endeavor.

She noticed, tucked away in a corner of one of the later pages, a small, almost insignificant sketch. It was a rough drawing of a black rose, its petals unfurling in a somber, elegant arc. Beneath it, Gibson had scrawled a single sentence: *"The bloom of inevitable sorrow."*

Maria's heart leaped. The black rose. The symbol she had found in Gibson's office, the one that had haunted her thoughts, was here, in his own hand, directly linked to his philosophical treatise. It wasn't just a personal memento; it was an emblem of his ideology, a tangible representation of his morbid aesthetic. Gibson hadn't just possessed the black rose; he had created its meaning within the context of his twisted philosophy.

She realized with a sickening certainty that this manuscript was not merely a reflection of Gibson's thoughts, but a direct precursor, or perhaps even the source, of the killer's actions. The killer wasn't just inspired by Gibson; they were likely a direct product of his teachings, a fervent disciple who had taken his abstract theories and translated them into brutal reality. The fragmented notes, the cryptic pronouncements, the unsettling theatricality – it all pointed back to this hidden document, to the dark, fertile ground from which such horrific acts had sprung.

The final pages of the manuscript were filled with a sense of escalating obsession, a desperate attempt to codify his theories into something actionable. There were notes on historical assassination methods, on the psychology of mass hysteria, and on the impact of ritualistic behavior. He explored the idea of the "perfect victim," one whose demise would have the most profound symbolic weight, one whose life was a stark contrast to the tragic beauty of their end.

"The greatest tragedies," Gibson wrote, *"are those that shock the conscience, that force a re-evaluation of the human condition. They are not confined to the realm of fiction; they are potential realities waiting to be actualized. The artist who dares to step beyond the canvas and into the world, who wields life and death as their mediums, is the true visionary. They do not merely tell stories; they create them, shaping the very fabric of our understanding of existence."*

Maria closed the manuscript, her hands still trembling. The silence of the study pressed in on her, no longer just the quiet of an empty room, but the heavy, suffocating silence of unspoken horrors. She had found what she was looking for. This hidden manuscript was Gibson's dark heart laid bare, a chilling testament to a mind that had embraced death not as an end, but as the ultimate artistic expression. It was a roadmap, a confession, and a terrifying justification for the murders she was investigating. The riddle of the professor had finally begun to unravel, revealing a truth far more disturbing than she could have ever imagined. The black rose, indeed, was the bloom of inevitable sorrow, cultivated by a mind that had found profound, terrible beauty in the act of ending. And the hand that had penned these words, she now knew with chilling certainty, was inextricably bound to the hand that had delivered the fatal blow.

The brittle pages of Gibson's manuscript, still warm from Maria's touch, seemed to hum with a dangerous energy. The air in the study, once merely heavy with the scent of old paper, now felt charged, vibrating with the echoes of the professor's most guarded thoughts. Maria, still seated in his worn leather armchair, the weight of the leather a palpable presence, felt a prickling sensation crawl across her skin. She had just navigated the labyrinthine corridors of Gibson's philosophical descent, a journey into a mind that had meticulously constructed a justification for murder, framing it as art, as liberation, as the ultimate expression of existence. The manuscript was more than a confession; it was a manifesto, a chilling testament to a worldview that saw death not as an ending, but as a canvas for the most profound of artistic statements. The black rose, once a haunting enigma, now bloomed with stark clarity, its petals unfurling as a symbol of Gibson's perverse aesthetic. But the true burden, she knew, was yet to be faced: the confrontation with the man himself.

A subtle shift in the atmosphere signaled Gibson's return. The soft creak of the study door, followed by the hesitant tread of his footsteps, drew Maria's attention away from the damning evidence clutched in her hands. She carefully placed the manuscript back into its hidden alcove, the click of the mechanism a soft punctuation to the tense silence. As the door swung open, Professor Aris Gibson entered, his frail frame seeming to shrink under the weight of the oppressive grandeur of his study. His eyes, once sharp and intellectual, now held a hunted look, a weariness that seemed etched not by age, but by a profound inner turmoil. He carried a small, leather-bound book, not a literary work, but something more personal, its cover worn smooth with countless passages.

"I hope you found the Sophocles edition... to your liking," Gibson began, his voice a raspy whisper, a stark contrast to the authoritative tone Maria had heard in recordings. He avoided direct eye contact, his gaze darting around the room, settling on the dust motes dancing in the slivers of light that pierced the heavy curtains. A tremor ran through his hands as he clutched the book, a nervous tic Maria had noted in archival footage of his public lectures.

Maria rose from the armchair, the worn leather groaning softly in protest. She met his gaze, her own steady, her resolve hardening. "The Sophocles was... informative, Professor. But I was more intrigued by your personal annotations. Your insights into the inherent tragedy of existence are... profound." She chose her words carefully, each syllable laced with a subtle accusation, a delicate probe designed to elicit a reaction.

Gibson flinched, a barely perceptible tightening of his jaw. He finally turned to face her fully, his eyes, a pale, washed-out blue, flickering with an unsettling mixture of defensiveness and a strange, almost melancholic understanding. "Tragedy, Detective," he said, his voice regaining a fraction of its former timbre, though still laced with a palpable fragility, "is not merely a literary device. It is the very fabric of the human condition. The universe... it orchestrates its own narratives, and we, as ephemeral beings, are but characters playing our predetermined roles."

He paused, his gaze drifting to the large atlas still open on his desk, the map of ancient Greece a stark reminder of the foundations of his philosophical edifice. "To deny the overarching tragedy of life is to embrace a delusion. To seek meaning in the fleeting pleasures, in the mundane struggles, is to miss the grand, inevitable crescendo."

Maria took a slow step forward, her voice soft but firm. "And what of the one who attempts to *direct* that crescendo, Professor? The one who believes they can elevate the narrative by... curating its conclusion?" She watched him closely, observing the almost imperceptible tension in his shoulders, the way his breath caught in his throat.

A shadow passed over Gibson's face, a flicker of something unreadable – recognition, perhaps, or a dark, internal acknowledgment. He shifted his weight, his grip on the book tightening until his knuckles turned white. "The allure of the grand finale," he murmured, his gaze now fixed on the dark wood of his desk, "is undeniable. To orchestrate one's own ending, to imbue it with meaning and purpose... that is a power that has long captivated the human imagination. It is the ultimate act of defiance against the caprice of fate."

His words hung in the air, heavy with unspoken implications. He wasn't confessing, not directly, but he was acknowledging the seductive logic, the twisted rationale that underpinned the Composer's horrific deeds. He spoke of it not with revulsion, but with a detached, almost academic curiosity, as if dissecting a particularly fascinating, albeit morbid, specimen.

"And when that 'defiance' extends to others?" Maria pressed, her voice barely above a whisper. "When the curator decides to bestow their 'artistry' upon those deemed... unworthy of such a profound conclusion?"

Gibson finally lifted his head, his eyes meeting Maria's. There was no outright guilt, no admission of direct involvement, but a profound, unsettling resonance in his gaze. It was the look of a man who understood the depths of the abyss, who had perhaps even peered into it with a dangerous fascination. "There are souls," he said, his voice dropping to a near inaudible level, "who drift through existence, their lives a series of unfulfilled melodies, their potential for profound sorrow left tragically unrealized. For such individuals, the mundane struggle becomes an unbearable weight, a constant ache of inconsequence."

He paused, a peculiar glint entering his eyes, a light that seemed to emanate from a place of profound, intellectual detachment, rather than human empathy. "To grant them... a final, resonant chord," he continued, his words measured, each syllable carefully chosen, "to transform their quiet desperation into a stark, indelible tragedy... is that not a form of liberation? A profound, if terrible, act of artistic intervention?"

Maria's blood ran cold. This was not mere philosophical musing; this was the precise language of the killer, the chilling rhetoric that had accompanied the victims. Gibson was not condemning the acts; he was, in his own oblique way, rationalizing them, framing them within the context of his own warped aesthetic. He was articulating a worldview that elevated murder to the status of a sacred, artistic endeavor.

"Liberation?" Maria echoed, the word tasting like ash in her mouth. "Or the ultimate assertion of control? The imposition of one's will, one's narrative, onto the lives of others?"

Gibson's gaze softened, a weary resignation settling upon his features. He finally released the book he had been clutching, setting it gently on a nearby side table. "Control," he conceded, a faint sigh escaping his lips. "There is, of course, the undeniable allure of control. To be the architect of one's own destiny, to script the final act with absolute precision... it is a profound temptation for any mind that grapples with the inherent chaos of existence."

He looked at Maria, a flicker of recognition in his eyes, as if he saw in her not an accuser, but a fellow traveler who had, by some miracle, avoided straying too far down the dark path. "We are all, in our own ways, storytellers, Detective. We weave narratives to make sense of the world, to impose order upon the formless void. Some of us... are more ambitious in our storytelling than others. We seek to create works of profound resonance, works that linger in the consciousness long after the final page has been turned."

He gestured vaguely towards the desk, towards the hidden compartment that had once concealed his manuscript. "Life," he mused, his voice gaining a strange, almost poetic cadence, "is but a prologue. It is the epilogue that grants the entire work its meaning. And if that epilogue is the sole element that defines the preceding narrative, then its crafting becomes the paramount artistic endeavor. The true artist does not merely depict tragedy; they embody it. They culminate in it. They *become* it."

Maria felt a shiver trace its way down her spine. This was it. The direct link she had been searching for. Gibson, the esteemed professor, the recluse, was not merely an observer of the 'Composer's' philosophy; he was, in essence, the blueprint. His theories, so meticulously laid out in the manuscript, were the very foundation upon which the killer's actions were built. The handwriting, the philosophical parallels, the disturbing justifications – it all converged on this one fragile, haunted man.

"And what of the victims, Professor?" Maria asked, her voice firm, cutting through the professor's philosophical reverie. "What narrative did they serve in this grand design? Were their lives merely insignificant threads to be woven into someone else's 'masterpiece'?"

Gibson's gaze flickered, a brief flash of something akin to pain, quickly masked by a profound weariness. He walked over to the window, his back to Maria, and peered out at the manicured, yet somehow somber, garden. "The victim," he began, his voice distant, as if speaking of a concept rather than a person, "must become a character in the larger drama. Their demise a crucial plot point. Their life, however insignificant it may appear to the uninitiated, must be scrutinized for its thematic potential. Every detail... can be woven into the tapestry of their final act."

He turned back, a faint, almost wistful smile gracing his lips. "The more profound the tragic resonance, the more complete the artistic statement. It is not enough to simply kill, Detective. One must *stage*. One must *orchestrate*. One must ensure that the final scene is a work of art, etched into the annals of human experience."

His words painted a chilling picture of meticulous planning, of a deliberate and calculated artistry that transformed human lives into mere props for a macabre performance. Maria's mind flashed back to the crime scenes, to the symbolic placement of objects, the carefully chosen motifs, the unsettling theatricality of each death. These were not random acts of violence; they were deliberate artistic choices, a direct manifestation of Gibson's twisted philosophy.

"The 'black rose'," Maria said, her voice a low, steady murmur, "the symbol of inevitable sorrow. It seems it found its bloom within your own philosophy, Professor."

Gibson's eyes widened almost imperceptibly. He glanced at the side table where he had placed his small, leather-bound book. His hand trembled as he reached for it, his fingers brushing against its worn cover. "A bloom," he repeated, his voice barely audible, "is the culmination of a process. It is the ephemeral beauty that signifies a life's purpose fulfilled. Some blooms are destined for vibrant display, while others... are fated to a more somber elegance."

He opened the book, revealing pages filled not with academic prose, but with delicate, almost ethereal sketches of flowers. His hand, surprisingly steady now, traced the outline of a black rose, its petals rendered with exquisite detail, its form exuding a profound, melancholic beauty. "The black rose," he whispered, his gaze fixed on the drawing, "is not merely a symbol of sorrow. It is a symbol of the profound, terrible beauty that can be found even in dissolution. It is the bloom of inevitable sorrow, yes, but also the bloom of... ultimate truth."

Maria watched him, a knot of conflicting emotions tightening in her chest. He hadn't confessed, not in the way she had hoped. But he had offered something more chilling: an indirect validation, a disturbing communion with the killer's mindset. He had revealed the source of the ideology, the fertile ground from which such horrific acts had sprung. The burden of his knowledge, his complicity, hung heavy in the air, a palpable weight that seemed to press down on them both. Gibson was not merely a passive observer of a dark philosophy; he was its progenitor, its reluctant, yet undeniable, champion. The riddle of the professor was unravelling, revealing not a simple confession, but a far more complex and terrifying truth: that the artist of death had found his muse, and his masterpiece, in the very heart of academia.

CHAPTER 8
THE GHOSTS OF LITERATURE

The air in Gibson's study, thick with the scent of aged paper and Gibson's peculiar blend of pipe tobacco, had taken on a new, unsettling dimension. Maria, still reeling from Gibson's oblique yet damning philosophical pronouncements, felt a tremor beneath the surface of his carefully constructed academic persona. He hadn't confessed, not in the explicit, black-and-white manner she had anticipated, but he had laid bare the twisted roots of his worldview, revealing the fertile ground from which the Architect's macabre art had sprung. His words, spoken with the quiet cadence of a man unburdening himself of a profound, if terrible, truth, had painted a chilling picture of life as a narrative, and death as the ultimate, deliberate act of authorship. The black rose, once a symbol of inscrutable menace, now bloomed with the somber elegance of a philosophical conviction, a testament to the terrible beauty found in dissolution, as Gibson had so chillingly articulated.

Yet, as Gibson retreated into his own quietude, his frail form hunched over the small, sketch-filled book, Maria's mind raced, not towards closure, but towards a deeper, more complex puzzle. Gibson's intellectual architecture was undeniably the foundation upon which the Composer had built his house of horrors, but the immediate, pressing threat remained. The Composer was still out there, his literary theatre still playing out on the hallowed grounds of the university. Gibson's pronouncements were the *why*, but the *who* and the *how* still eluded her. And the increasingly specific literary allusions that had marked the Composer's previous crimes were not merely philosophical pronouncements; they were pointed, personal, and seemed to be escalating in their specificity.

She recalled the details of the previous murders, each a meticulously staged tableau, each a twisted homage to a literary work. The first victim, found posed as a character from a forgotten Victorian melodrama, the second, a twisted re-enactment of a tragic moment from an obscure Elizabethan play. These were not random literary references; they were deeply embedded, almost personal. It was as if the Composer was not just drawing inspiration from literature, but was actively engaged in a dialogue with it, perhaps even a violent revision. And now, these allusions were becoming even more granular, more pointed, hinting at a deeper, more personal grievance.

Maria's gaze swept across Gibson's study; the walls lined with books that represented a lifetime of intellectual pursuit. These shelves, once symbols of academic prestige, now felt like a library of potential clues, a vast repository of the Composer's dark muse. Gibson had spoken of life as a narrative, of death as the ultimate act of authorship. But what if the Composer wasn't merely acting out pre-existing narratives? What if he was attempting to *rewrite* them, to correct perceived wrongs, to impose his own warped sense of justice onto the literary history of the university itself?

The thought sent a shiver down her spine. The university, a place she had always associated with the pursuit of knowledge and enlightenment, was slowly transforming into a literary battleground, each building, each quad, each shadowed alcove, imbued with the echoes of forgotten stories, waiting to be brought back to life by the Composer's bloody pen. She remembered the chilling observation from an earlier investigation: that the victims seemed to be connected, not just by their proximity to the university, but by a subtle, almost imperceptible thread woven through its literary fabric. It was a thread Maria was now convinced the Composer was deliberately pulling, unravelling a narrative that had been decades in the making.

She recalled the initial reports, the bewildered detectives poring over crime scene photographs. The second victim, a Classics scholar, had been found with a tattered copy of Euripides' *Medea* clutched in his hand, a single, black rose placed on the open page. It was an allusion, yes, but one that had seemed almost too direct, too personal. Gibson had spoken of Medea's fury, her tragic descent, but he had also spoken of the "curator" who sought to elevate the narrative. Could the Composer be seeking to re-enact or even *correct* these ancient tragedies, to impose his own resolution upon them?

Then there was the incident involving Professor Debrah Stevens, the renowned Shakespearean scholar. The details were still hazy, shrouded in academic gossip and official redactions, but Maria remembered a whisper of something about a rare folio, a heated debate, and a threat that had been dismissed as the ravings of a disgruntled academic. Stevens's research had focused on the lesser-known works, the apocryphal plays, the disputed authorship. Was it possible the Composer was targeting those who dared to question or tamper with the established canon, those who sought to unravel the authorship of literary giants?

Maria's mind began to draw connections, tenuous at first, then strengthening with each passing moment. Gibson's theories, their emphasis on the narrative arc, the profound tragedy of existence, the desire to orchestrate the final act – these were not abstract philosophical musings anymore. They were a direct influence, a chilling justification for the Composer's actions. The Composer was using Gibson's words as his script, his manifesto. But to what end? What was the overarching narrative he was trying to tell?

She thought back to the initial crime scene of the very first victim a few years ago that had been dismissed as a suicide, but now inextricably linked to these string of murders, since it was surrounded in melodrama. The victim was an unassuming archivist, someone who dealt with dusty manuscripts and forgotten histories. His death had been staged to mimic a scene from *The Sorrows of Young Werther*, a novel Maria knew Gibson held in particular disdain, viewing it as a sentimental indulgence rather than true tragedy. Gibson had subtly, almost dismissively, alluded to it as a work that "failed to grasp the profound implications of existential despair." Was the Composer targeting those who embodied what Gibson, and by extension the Composer, considered literary misinterpretations, or worse, literary transgressions?

The university, in the Composer's eyes, was not just a place of learning; it was a grand library, a repository of stories that he felt had been mishandled, misunderstood, or left incomplete. Each murder was an edit, a revision, a commentary on the literary works that defined the institution's intellectual heritage. The victims were not just individuals; they were characters in a grand, unfolding drama that the Composer was meticulously composing.

Maria stood up, the worn leather of Gibson's armchair groaning under her movement. She walked towards the window, gazing out at the manicured laws. The Gothic architecture, some structures had ivy-covered walls, most had venerable oak trees – they all seemed to whisper tales of generations past, of intellectual triumphs and quiet tragedies. The very stones of the Gibson's house seemed to hold their breath, waiting for the next act in this unfolding literary horror.

She remembered a conversation with a colleague, a literature professor specializing in early modern poetry. They had discussed the university's obscure literary societies, its forgotten endowments, and its hidden collections. The colleague had mentioned a peculiar incident from decades ago, a scandal involving a prestigious literary award that had been withdrawn under mysterious circumstances, a poet whose career had been abruptly derailed. The details were murky, lost in the mists of time, but the professor had hinted at a deep-seated resentment, a sense of injustice that had festered within certain academic circles.

Could the Composer's agenda be tied to such historical literary grievances? Was he not just re-enacting literary scenes, but also seeking to right perceived wrongs, to bring a bloody resolution to old academic feuds, to literary slights that had been left unaddressed for years? Gibson's philosophy of "curating the narrative" could easily extend to re-writing history, to imposing a definitive, albeit violent, conclusion to literary debates that had long been settled, or perhaps, in the Composer's eyes, had been wrongly settled.

Maria's mind flashed back to the meticulous detail of each crime scene. The symbolic placement of objects, the specific editions of books used, the chilling notes left behind, each a cryptic allusion to a literary text. These weren't just random acts of violence; they were carefully crafted statements, designed to be read and understood by those who possessed the requisite knowledge. And that knowledge, she was now certain, was rooted in the very literary heart of the university, a heart that Gibson's pronouncements had laid bare.

She thought of the university's archives, the dusty repositories of its past. If the Composer was indeed targeting specific literary legacies, then the archives would be his hunting ground, his source material for his gruesome productions. He was not just a killer; he was a literary critic with a scalpel, a historian with a penchant for enacting his critiques in blood.

The thought of the archives sent a fresh wave of unease through her. She recalled a recent conversation with Dr. Aris Gibson about the university's collection of rare manuscripts, his particular interest in the works of a forgotten poet named Sammy Blacksmith. Gibson had spoken of Blacksmith's tragic life, his unfulfilled potential, his reputation as a misunderstood genius. He had even alluded to Blacksmith's supposed "lost sonnets," a collection rumored to have been destroyed in a fire years ago. Gibson had spoken of it with a peculiar reverence, a sense of mourning for what could have been.

Could Sammy Blacksmith be more than just a literary obsession? Could the Composer's current campaign be a twisted attempt to "resurrect" or "complete" the legacy of this forgotten poet? The name itself – Sammy Blacksmith – held a resonance, a dark poetry that seemed to align with the Composer's aesthetic. And the black rose, Gibson's symbol of inevitable sorrow, might have a direct connection to this poet.

Maria turned away from the window, her gaze falling upon Gibson's open manuscript, its pages filled with a sprawling, academic dissection of existentialism and artistic expression. Beside it lay the small, leather-bound book of sketches, the black rose blooming on its delicate pages. Gibson's words, his philosophy, provided the theoretical framework for the Composer's madness. But the specific literary targets, the escalating personal allusions, pointed to something far more immediate and dangerous: a meticulously planned campaign rooted in the very literary history of the university.

She remembered the specific phrases used by the Composer in his taunting notes, phrases that had previously seemed cryptic, but now resonated with Gibson's pronouncements. "The grand crescendo," the Composer had written, echoing Gibson's description of life's ultimate culmination. And then, chillingly, "The epilogue that grants the entire work its meaning," a direct quote from Gibson's musings on narrative. The Composer was not just influenced by Gibson; he was actively using Gibson's most guarded thoughts as his own inspiration, his own justification.

But what if Gibson was more than just an unwitting muse? What if his philosophical descent had been a deliberate preparation, a conscious crafting of the intellectual ammunition for a killer? Maria's suspicion intensified. The more Gibson spoke, the more his academic detachment felt like a carefully constructed facade, a mask to hide a deeper, more complicit involvement. He had not confessed to murder, but he had confessed to the ideology, to the artistic impulse that drove it. And that, in Maria's mind, made him an accomplice, if not the mastermind himself.

She thought about the university's library, a vast labyrinth of knowledge, a place where forgotten stories and obscure texts lay dormant, waiting to be unearthed. The Composer was using it as his arsenal, his scriptorium. And the faculty, the scholars, the students – they were all potential characters in his increasingly dangerous play. The campus itself, with its gothic spires and shadowed cloisters, was becoming a living embodiment of these literary narratives, a stage upon which the Composer was staging his final, bloody act.

The specific literary allusions were no longer random acts of intellectual sadism. They were precise, targeted, and seemed to be leading Maria towards a particular nexus within the university's literary history. It was a trail of breadcrumbs, leading not just to the killer, but to the heart of a literary conspiracy, a historical grievance that was now being violently resolved. The ghosts of literature were not just lingering in the academic halls; they were actively being invoked, brought to terrifying life by a killer who saw himself as the ultimate author, and the university itself as his personal, blood-soaked manuscript. Maria knew she was on the cusp of something far larger than a series of murders. She was uncovering a dark, literary cult, a historical vendetta played out in the most horrific of ways. And Gibson, the esteemed professor, was at its chilling epicenter.

A subtle shift had occurred in the nature of the Composer's communication. The previous allusions, while intricate, had felt like pronouncements of a grand, philosophical nature, woven into the fabric of Gibson's bleak worldview. But the latest fragment, discovered clutched in the hand of the latest victim – a mild-mannered librarian specializing in ancient texts – was different. It wasn't a quote from a renowned dramatist or a celebrated novelist. It was starker, more primal, resonating with an ancient, inescapable dread. The words themselves, scrawled in the familiar, elegant hand, were simple yet devastating: "The curse of Laius, a prophecy etched in blood, shall bind his lineage to unending woe."

Maria's breath hitched. The reference was undeniable, a direct echo of Sophocles' *Oedipus Rex*. This wasn't merely about a literary theme; it was about a destiny, a lineage, a tragedy that was not chosen but imposed. The theme of fate, of a predetermined path from which one could not escape, was a stark contrast to Gibson's emphasis on free will and the authorial control over one's narrative. It suggested a different kind of motivation, one rooted not in the desire to create meaning, but in the grim acceptance of an inherited burden. The Composer was no longer just curating literature; he was acting out an ancient, familial curse.

The implication sent a chill colder than any winter wind through Maria's veins. Gibson's philosophy, while dark, was ultimately about choice, about the conscious decision to embrace or reject the existential void. But this new clue spoke of something far more ancient and terrifying: an inherited doom, a fate woven into the very fabric of blood and bone. Could the Composer be a victim of a past wrong, a profound injustice that had festered within their family for generations? Was this a quest for retribution, not for abstract literary sins, but for a personal, familial tragedy?

The carefully constructed intellectual puzzle was beginning to reveal hints of a deeply personal vendetta. The crimes, which had seemed like elaborate literary critiques, now began to resemble the tragic unfolding of an ancient Greek drama, where characters were often puppets of a destiny they could not comprehend, let alone escape. The choice of *Oedipus Rex* was not arbitrary. It was a story of unwitting parricide and incest, of a king's desperate attempts to escape a prophecy that ultimately sealed his doom. It spoke of the inescapable consequences of past actions, of the sins of the father being visited upon the son.

Maria found herself poring over the details of the victim's life, searching for any connection, any subtle thread that might link him to a larger narrative of familial strife. The librarian, Brandon Pendelton, was a man of quiet habits, his life seemingly devoid of the grand passions or bitter rivalries that characterized the academic world. Yet, the Composer had chosen him, had placed this damning quote in his lifeless hand. Why Pendelton? What was his role in this unfolding tragedy, this modern-day *Oedipus*?

The quote wasn't just a literary reference; it was an accusation, a declaration of intent. The "curse of Laius" implied that the Composer saw himself as the unfortunate inheritor of a terrible legacy, a legacy that had been passed down through generations. And the phrase "bind his lineage" suggested that the victims themselves were somehow part of this cursed lineage, or perhaps, that their deaths were a necessary step in breaking the curse.

Maria's mind grappled with the implications. If the Composer was driven by a familial curse, then the motive was not about correcting literary misinterpretations but about enacting a form of inherited justice, a bloody reckoning for wrongs committed long ago. Gibson's theories of narrative control, of the author's ultimate power, seemed to be morphing into something far more terrifying: the unravelling of a predetermined, tragic plot.

She revisited Gibson's cryptic pronouncements, searching for any resonance with this new theme. While Gibson had spoken of the inevitability of suffering, his focus had always been on the individual's response to it, their agency in confronting or succumbing to the existential abyss. He had never delved into the realm of inherited curses or inescapable prophecies. This new direction suggested an element of the Composer's psyche that Gibson, despite his profound insights into darkness, had either overlooked or deliberately excluded.

Was it possible that Gibson's philosophical explorations were a form of intellectual distraction, a meticulously crafted labyrinth designed to obscure a more primal, familial motive? Maria felt a knot of suspicion tightening in her gut. Gibson had spoken of the "unseen forces" that shaped human destiny, of the "narratives that transcend individual will." Had he been alluding to something like this, a deeper, more archaic narrative that held sway over the Composer's actions?

The black rose, Gibson's ubiquitous symbol, now took on a new significance. While it represented inevitable sorrow and the beauty of decay in Gibson's philosophy, it could also be seen as a symbol of a dark lineage, a bloom of tragedy that had sprung from a cursed root. The Composer wasn't just a reader of literature; he was a participant in an ancient, blood-soaked drama, one that had been unfolding for generations.

Maria's thoughts drifted to the university's own history, its long and often shadowed past. Were there any prominent families, any historical scandals that echoed the themes of *Oedipus Rex*? The university, with its centuries of academic intrigue and quiet power struggles, could easily be the stage for such a deeply personal, generational vendetta. The victims, carefully selected, were perhaps not mere literary archetypes but pieces on a chessboard, pawns in a game whose rules were dictated by an ancient, familial prophecy.

The quote was not just a clue; it was a window into the Composer's soul, a glimpse of a mind tormented by a past it could not escape. It spoke of a profound sense of injustice, a feeling of being trapped by the sins and mistakes of ancestors. Maria understood that the intellectual puzzle had just taken a chilling turn, moving from the realm of abstract philosophy to the deeply personal, the terrifyingly inescapable world of inherited tragedy. The Composer was not just a killer; he was a character in a play as old as time itself, a play written in the ink of blood and bound by the chains of fate. The hunt was no longer just for a killer, but for the origin of a curse, for the ghost of Laius that haunted the present.

Maria felt the weight of the university's history pressing down on her. Gibson's pronouncements had provided a chilling, philosophical framework, but the new clue, the quote from *Oedipus Rex*, had shifted the investigation into a more personal, more visceral realm. The concept of an inherited curse, a destiny etched in blood, spoke of a motive far removed from the intellectual debates on authorship and narrative control that had occupied Gibson. She needed to move beyond the theoretical and delve into the practical, the tangible connections that bound the victims, not to literary works, but to each other, and to the very fabric of the university itself. Her focus turned to the sprawling, often labyrinthine, records of the institution: the student files and alumni directories, a veritable archive of lives lived and paths taken within these hallowed, or in this case, haunted, halls.

She began with the most recent victim, Brandon Pendelton, the librarian. His academic record was impeccable, yet unremarkable. A dedicated scholar of ancient texts, his life had been one of quiet diligence, a stark contrast to the violent end he had met. Cross-referencing his tenure at the university with the other victims was Maria's first step. She requested access to the university's secure digital archives, a system as vast and interconnected as any modern-day Oedipal labyrinth. The initial search yielded little beyond the fact that all victims had, at some point, been affiliated with the university. This was a given, of course, but it was the nature of that affiliation, the subtle nuances of their time here, that Maria was desperate to uncover. She meticulously compiled lists, dates of enrollment, departments, academic achievements, and any disciplinary records. The second victim, the Classics scholar, had excelled in his field, a rising star whose promising career had been abruptly extinguished. The first victim, the archivist, had been a long-serving, if somewhat overlooked, member of staff, his world confined to the hushed silence of the Special Collections.

As Maria delved deeper into the records, a pattern began to emerge, subtle at first, like a whisper in a crowded hall. It wasn't a pattern of academic brilliance or significant achievement that linked them, but rather, a shared experience of being on the periphery. Pendelton, the librarian, had often been described as a quiet, almost invisible presence. The Classics scholar, while brilliant, had been known for his introverted nature, often preferring the company of ancient texts to his peers. And the archivist, the first victim, had spent his days cataloging the forgotten, his own professional existence a testament to his focus on the overlooked. They were not the luminaries, the celebrated figures of the university, but rather, the silent custodians, the diligent workers in the background. This was a crucial distinction. The Composer, if indeed driven by a sense of inherited injustice as the *Oedipus Rex* quote suggested, might not be targeting the perpetrators of past wrongs directly, but rather, those who benefited from or were complicit in the system that allowed those wrongs to occur, or perhaps, those who represented the academic establishment that had failed to rectify them.

Maria requested the complete alumni records for the Classics department over the past thirty years, a period that encompassed the potential timeframe for whatever past grievance the Composer was avenging. She cross-referenced these with the student records of the other victims, looking for any overlap, any shared classes, any academic advisors, or even any social circles. The sheer volume of data was daunting, a digital sea of names, dates, and course histories. She employed sophisticated search algorithms, looking for keywords, any mention of shared projects, or even any documented instances of collaboration, however minor. The goal was to find not just a connection, but a *shared experience* of the university, something that could have fostered resentment or a sense of being overlooked.

The process was painstaking. Hours blurred into days as Maria meticulously sifted through digital files, her eyes scanning lines of text, her mind piecing together fragments of academic lives. She looked for students who had been in the same cohort, who had shared the same professors, who had perhaps applied for the same scholarships or awards and been denied. The university, in its pursuit of excellence, had a notoriously competitive environment. It was a crucible that forged some into titans of their fields, but it could also break others, leaving them embittered and resentful. The Composer, Maria suspected, was one of those broken individuals, or perhaps someone deeply connected to one.

She focused on the years preceding the potential genesis of the Composer's grievance. If the curse was generational, as implied by the *Oedipus* reference, then the wrongs might have been committed decades ago, and the Composer was the one enacting the retribution. This meant she needed to look beyond the immediate careers of the victims and explore their student days. Were there any common threads in their undergraduate or graduate experiences? Any instances of academic rivalry, of plagiarism accusations, of disputes over research funding, or even personal conflicts that had been swept under the rug by the institution's administration?

Maria's search took a more specific turn when she began to cross-reference the victims' academic records with faculty lists from different eras. Gibson was an obvious point of interest, but he was too prominent, too established. The Composer's targets, so far, were not. They were the quiet ones, the ones who might have been directly affected by the actions of more influential figures within the university, figures who might have exploited them, dismissed them, or even stolen their work. She started by pulling the records of professors who had been active during the approximate periods the victims had been students. This was a vast undertaking, requiring access to faculty archives that were even more tightly guarded than student records.

She began to notice a recurring name in the faculty rosters from the late 1980s and early 1990s, a period that coincided with the early academic careers of several individuals who would later become significant figures at the university, and, perhaps, the original architects of the Composer's perceived injustice. There was a professor, a literary critic whose career had been marked by a certain ruthlessness and an insatiable ambition, had a reputation for both brilliant insights and a chillingly detached approach to his students. His name, unfortunately, was not yet linked to any of the victims in a way that screamed motive, but it was a thread, however thin, that Maria was determined to pull.

She expanded her search to include any disciplinary actions or official complaints filed against faculty members during that period. The university, like any large institution, had its share of scandals, but most were kept under wraps, buried deep within administrative files. Accessing these required navigating a complex web of confidentiality agreements and bureaucratic hurdles. Maria, however, was relentless. She leveraged her position, her contacts, and her growing reputation as a tenacious investigator to gain access to the restricted archives.

The digital archives, once a daunting expanse, began to yield their secrets. Maria discovered a series of anonymous complaints filed against the aforementioned ambitious professor. The complaints, originating from students in his seminars during the late 80s and early 90s, spoke of intellectual theft, of students' ideas being appropriated and presented as the professor's own, of talented individuals being deliberately sidelined or discredited. The language used in these complaints was impassioned, filled with a sense of betrayal and profound disappointment. One particular complaint, filed by a student whose name Missy recognized as a former peer of one of the victims, spoke of a stolen research paper that had been instrumental in securing a prestigious academic award for the professor.

This was it. This was the shift Maria had been searching for. The connection was no longer purely literary; it was personal, rooted in academic betrayal and the bitter aftermath of unacknowledged talent. The victims, or at least some of them, might have been directly wronged by this ambitious professor, or by individuals who were complicit in his rise to power. The *Oedipus Rex* quote about an inherited curse and lineage now made chilling sense. If the professor's actions had led to significant harm to a student, and that harm had been perpetuated across generations, perhaps through continued academic suppression or the systemic denial of opportunities, then the Composer could be seen as the inheritor of that wrong, seeking to break the curse by targeting those who embodied the system that had perpetuated it.

Maria meticulously cross-referenced the names of students who had filed these anonymous complaints with the university's alumni records. She was looking for any of them who might have later become victims, or who might have had close personal connections to the victims. The search was complex, as the complaints were anonymous, and the students' names were often only identified by student ID numbers or pseudonyms. However, with careful database cross-referencing and the use of advanced pattern recognition software, Maria managed to identify a few individuals who seemed to fit the profile.

One name, in particular, kept reappearing in connection with the complaints. A student named Victor Greer had been a promising literature scholar who had abruptly left the university under a cloud of academic dispute in the early 1990s. His academic record showed exceptional promise, but his graduate thesis was never completed. He had been a student in the very seminars where these complaints were filed, and there were whispers of a fierce intellectual rivalry between him and the ambitious professor. Victor Greer's name was not among the known victims, but his presence in the records, coupled with the accusations of intellectual theft and academic sabotage, painted a compelling picture. Could Victor Greer be the Composer? Or was he a victim whose legacy of grievance was now being carried forward by someone else, someone who felt themselves to be part of his "lineage" of injustice?

Maria found that Brandon Pendelton, the librarian, had been a fellow student of Victor Greer. They had been part of the same small cohort in the English department, and records indicated a friendship between them. The Classics scholar, while not directly linked to Victor Greer or the ambitious professor in the student records, had published a paper that critically analyzed the works of the very professor in question, a paper that had been met with significant backlash from certain academic circles, circles that had benefited from that professor's patronage. The archivist, the third victim, was harder to connect directly to Victor Greer or the professor. However, Maria discovered that the archivist had been responsible for cataloging a significant portion of the professor's early papers, including drafts and correspondence that might have contained evidence of intellectual appropriation. It was possible he had stumbled upon something incriminating, something that had marked him for death.

The pattern was becoming clearer, coalescing from the abstract realm of literary theory into the grim reality of academic politics and personal vendettas. The victims weren't just characters in a literary tragedy; they were individuals who, in some way, were either complicit in or beneficiaries of a system that had wronged a promising student, Victor Greer. The Composer, it seemed, was not merely enacting a philosophical argument; they were seeking to settle a score, to correct a historical injustice that had festered for decades within the university's hallowed walls. The university, with its vast network of alumni and its deep historical records, was not just the backdrop for these crimes, but the very source of the motive, the repository of the grievance that fueled the killer's deadly narrative. Maria's investigation was no longer solely about literary allusions; it was a hunt for a deeply aggrieved individual, someone who felt they were continuing a fight for justice, a fight that had begun with Victor Greer and was now being waged, bloodily, against those who represented the establishment that had seemingly crushed him. The ghosts of literature were indeed present, but they were also the ghosts of broken academic careers, of stolen potential, and of a profound, enduring resentment.

The weight of inherited curses, the whisper of predestined doom – these concepts, once confined to the dusty pages of ancient tragedies, now clung to Maria like the chill of a forgotten tomb. Victor Greer. The name resonated with a peculiar discord, a phantom limb of academic potential severed by the university's insatiable hunger for prestige. Maria had meticulously charted his brief, brilliant trajectory through the hallowed halls, a trajectory that ended not with graduation, but with an abrupt, unexplained departure. His academic record was a supernova – incandescent, powerful, and ultimately, self-destructive. The anonymous complaints, the hushed whispers of intellectual property theft, the alleged rivalry with the ambitious, now tenured, professor – it all pointed to a deep wound, a betrayal that had festered, turning a promising scholar into a ghost in the archives of his own potential.

Was Victor Greer the Composer? The question gnawed at Maria, a persistent irritant that refused to be soothed. The evidence, while compelling, remained circumstantial. He wasn't a victim, at least not directly in the sequence of murders. Yet, his narrative was inextricably woven into the fabric of the Composer's actions. If Greer was the architect of the Composer's grievance, then the current killings were a posthumous echo of his own academic undoing. The idea of an avenging angel, of someone driven by a moral imperative to right perceived wrongs, began to take root in Maria's mind. This wasn't just about revenge; it was about rectification, a skewed sense of justice enacted upon a stage the killer deemed complicit in the original sin. The university, with its inherent hierarchies, its competitive nature, and its penchant for preserving its reputation above all else, was the perfect, gilded cage for such a drama to unfold.

Maria found herself poring over Victor Greer's digitized thesis fragments, his scattered research notes, and the sparse remnants of his academic correspondence. It was like sifting through the ashes of a pyre, searching for the embers of truth. His early work was revolutionary, a daring deconstruction of established literary paradigms, a bold challenge to the very foundations upon which the ambitious professor had built his empire. The plagiarism accusations, if true, were not just acts of academic dishonesty; they were acts of intellectual assassination. Greer's ideas, his insights, his very intellectual legacy, had allegedly been co-opted, twisted, and re-presented as the product of another. This was more than a betrayal of trust; it was a violation of the scholar's soul.

The other victims, too, began to shift in Maria's perception. Pendelton, the librarian, had been Greer's friend, a confidante perhaps, someone who had witnessed the slow erosion of Greer's spirit. Had Pendelton known something? Had he been privy to Greer's pain, his desperation? The Classics scholar, whose paper had dared to critique the established professor, might have been seen by the Composer as a successor, an inheritor of Greer's intellectual defiance, or perhaps, a symbol of the academic establishment that had ostracized Greer. And the archivist, the quiet custodian of forgotten truths, had he stumbled upon something tangible in the professor's papers, a smoking gun of academic malfeasance that had sealed his fate? The connections were no longer random; they were a carefully orchestrated symphony of retribution, each victim a discordant note in a grand, tragic opera.

The concept of familial tragedy, of a curse passed down through generations, began to manifest not just as a literary device but as a potential psychological driver. Was the Composer a direct descendant of Victor Greer? Or was it someone who identified so profoundly with Greer's experience that they considered themselves part of his lineage of grievance? The *Oedipus Rex* parallel, initially dismissed as a purely intellectual flourish by the killer, now felt chillingly prescient. Oedipus was bound by fate, by an inescapable destiny woven by the gods. Could the Composer feel similarly ensnared, compelled to act by an invisible force, a historical injustice that demanded a bloody resolution? The privileged environment of the university, a sanctuary of learning and intellectual pursuit, had, in the Composer's eyes, become a den of thieves and betrayers. It was a place where brilliance was stifled, where integrity was sacrificed for ambition, and where the whispers of the wronged were silenced by the roar of success.

Maria imagined the Composer moving through the campus, a phantom fueled by decades of simmering rage. The hallowed lecture halls, the quiet libraries, the manicured quads – they were all witnesses to the original sin, and now, to the brutal expiation. The Composer wasn't just killing; they were performing a ritual of purification, cleansing the institution of the stain of betrayal. Each victim was a symbol, a representative of the system that had broken Victor Greer. The meticulous planning, the literary allusions, the calculated cruelty – it all spoke of a mind that saw the world through the lens of narrative, where every action had meaning, every death a symbolic resonance. The Composer wasn't just a killer; they were a storyteller, and the university was their stage, the victims their unwilling cast, and the pursuit of justice, however warped, their driving plot.

The ambiguity surrounding Victor Greer's departure from the university was a deliberate veil, a calculated obscuration. Maria's digital digging had unearthed a few oblique references in obscure academic forums, discussions that hinted at a severe fallout, a public humiliation, or perhaps a quiet, effective blackballing orchestrated by influential faculty members. It was the kind of event that could shatter a young academic's world, especially one as fiercely proud and intellectually driven as Greer seemed to be. The ambitious professor, now a respected, almost revered figure within the Classics department, had likely been the primary architect of Greer's downfall, directly or indirectly. He had a reputation for ruthlessness, for consolidating power, and for fostering an environment where sycophants thrived and dissent was systematically crushed.

Maria hypothesized that Greer, unable to fight back effectively within the existing academic structures, had either succumbed to despair or had found a way to channel his immense intellect and profound sense of injustice into a more...permanent form of protest. The *Oedipus Rex* quote, "He who cannot follow the path of the gods will be condemned," resonated with a chilling finality. It suggested a belief in a higher, perhaps a more brutal, form of justice than the university's flawed system could provide. The killer wasn't just seeking retribution; they were enacting a divine judgment, a cosmic rebalancing of scales that had been tipped too far by human greed and ambition.

The more Maria delved into Victor Greer's past, the more she felt the chilling presence of a broken man, someone whose life's work, whose very identity, had been stolen from him. It was a profound trauma, an intellectual violation that could easily fester into an all-consuming rage. This wasn't the detached, philosophical rage of a scholar debating abstract concepts. This was the visceral, personal fury of someone who had been robbed, not of possessions, but of their future, their reputation, their very reason for being. The Composer, then, was not just continuing a literary theme; they were living out the tragic legacy of Victor Greer, a legacy forged in the crucible of academic betrayal.

The university itself, with its sprawling grounds and labyrinthine corridors of power, had become the antagonist in this unfolding tragedy. It was a place of learning, yes, but also a place where ambition could curdle into corruption, where intellect could be weaponized, and where the pursuit of knowledge could be corrupted by the basest human desires. The privileged environment, designed to foster growth and innovation, had, in this instance, served as a fertile ground for resentment and a breeding pit for a killer driven by a profound, almost existential, sense of injustice. The ghosts of literature were not merely metaphorical; they were the spectral remnants of shattered dreams, of stolen futures, and of a betrayal that had echoed through the years, demanding a brutal, bloody resolution. Maria was no longer just investigating a series of murders; she was unearthing the deeply buried history of academic perfidy, a history that had finally, and fatally, come home to roost.

Maria laid out the printouts on Gibson's cluttered desk, the stark white paper a jarring contrast to the surrounding stacks of aged manuscripts and coffee-stained mugs. The printed passages, carefully highlighted, were from *Oedipus Rex*, the same chilling lines that had been left at the scenes of the murders. "He who cannot follow the path of the gods will be condemned." She watched Gibson's face as he read, his brows knitting together in a familiar, weary expression. He picked up one of the sheets, his fingers tracing the words as if seeking a hidden message within the ink.

"The gods," he murmured, the words barely audible above the hum of the ancient fluorescent lights. A profound sadness settled into his gaze, a palpable weight that seemed to emanate from him. He let out a long, slow sigh, the sound ragged, as if the very act of exhaling carried the burden of years. It wasn't the sigh of someone caught in a lie, but the heavy exhalation of someone confronting a painful, inescapable truth. He looked up at Maria, his eyes, usually sharp and analytical, now clouded with a deep melancholy. "This... this speaks of a certain kind of fate, doesn't it?" he said, his voice laced with a quiet resignation. "A belief that certain paths are chosen for us, and that straying from them invites retribution."

Maria leaned forward, her own resolve hardening. "This particular path, Professor Gibson," she began, her voice even, "seems to have been laid out by someone who felt deeply wronged. Someone who believed they were enacting a form of divine justice on those who had, in their eyes, deviated from a righteous course." She paused, letting the implication hang in the air. "The connection to Victor Greer, his academic downfall, the accusations of plagiarism against a respected faculty member... it all points to a profound sense of betrayal. A feeling of being condemned by the very system that was supposed to champion him."

Gibson's gaze drifted to a framed photograph on his desk – a younger man, perhaps a student, with an earnest, intelligent face. He picked it up, his thumb gently caressing the glass. Maria's mind flashed back to the fragmented records of Victor Greer, the brilliant but disgraced scholar. Was this him? The ghost in the archives, whose narrative had become so intertwined with the Composer's motive?

"Betrayal is a potent force, Detective," Gibson said, his voice now a low rumble, the academic equanimity he usually maintained fracturing. "It can twist even the noblest intentions. It can turn a scholar's pursuit of truth into a desperate, lonely war." He set the photograph down with a soft click. "There are... echoes. Whispers of such things within The Infinite Discourse."

Maria's heart leaped. The Infinite Discourse. Gibson had alluded to it before, a clandestine group of academics, intellectuals, and artists, bound by shared interests and, perhaps, shared secrets.

"Whispers of what, Professor?" she pressed, her tone urgent. "Were there members who felt wronged by the institution? Members who felt condemned?"

Gibson's expression became guarded, a subtle shift that Maria had come to recognize. The intellectual curiosity that usually shone in his eyes was replaced by a flicker of something akin to fear, or perhaps, a deep-seated loyalty. He ran a hand over his thinning hair, his gaze fixed on some unseen point beyond Maria's shoulder. "The Infinite Discourse," he began, his voice carefully modulated, "is a place where individuals seek solace, where they can explore ideas freely, away from the... pressures of the outside world. Sometimes, those pressures can be profound. They can lead to great disillusionment."

He picked up a well-worn leather-bound book from his desk, turning it over in his hands as if it offered some form of protection. "There was a time," he continued, choosing his words with deliberate care, "when a member of the society felt... profoundly wronged. A brilliant mind, ostracized, his work perhaps misunderstood or misappropriated. It caused a great deal of pain, not just to him, but to those who knew and respected him."

"Who was it, Professor?" Maria asked, her voice barely above a whisper. "Who was this member?"

Gibson's gaze met hers, and for a fleeting moment, she saw the same ghost she had glimpsed in the archived fragments of Victor Greer's life. But then, the moment passed, replaced by an impenetrable wall of academic reserve. "Names," he said, his voice hardening slightly, "are not easily spoken in such matters. There are old loyalties. A code of silence that predates even my own involvement." He tapped the leather-bound book. "We believe in protecting our own, and in respecting the privacy of those who have suffered. To name them would be to betray that trust, to reopen wounds that have, for some, never truly healed."

Maria felt a surge of frustration. Gibson was a puzzle, a keeper of secrets, and his evasiveness, far from deterring her, only fanned the flames of her determination. He knew something. He was hinting at a truth that lay buried beneath layers of academic politeness and institutional loyalty. His sadness, his heavy sighs, the way he clutched the book – these were not the actions of an innocent bystander. They were the subtle confessions of someone burdened by knowledge, someone caught between the desire to speak and the obligation to remain silent.

"But Professor," she argued, her voice tight with emotion, "these are not just old wounds. These are the reasons for the deaths we are investigating. The 'condemnation' you speak of isn't just a literary allusion anymore; it's a motive. A motive for murder. Victor Greer's story, whether he is the Composer or the inspiration, is clearly central to this. And if he was a member of The Infinite Discourse, then the society itself might hold the key to understanding why someone felt they had to enact such extreme measures."

Gibson's jaw tightened. He set the book down with a decisive thud. "Detective, you are treading on dangerous ground. The Discourse, as you call it, is not a conspiracy. It is a fellowship. Its members are scholars, artists, and thinkers. We share a common appreciation for the deeper currents of human experience, for the narratives that shape our lives. That Victor Greer may have felt himself a victim of the academic establishment, and that his story may have resonated with others, does not make him or us architects of violence."

"But his story *is* a narrative, isn't it?" Maria pressed. "A tragedy. And tragedies, as you well know, often have protagonists driven by a profound sense of injustice. The references to *Oedipus Rex* aren't random. They are deliberate. They are a commentary on fate, on destiny, on being condemned for actions taken, or for paths not followed. Someone is using Victor Greer's story, his perceived fate, to justify these killings."

Gibson looked away, his gaze fixed on the rain streaking down the windowpane. The silence stretched, thick with unspoken words. Maria watched him, acutely aware of the delicate dance they were engaged in. She was an outsider, an investigator, seeking to unravel a mystery that was deeply personal to him, and to the society he belonged to. He was a guardian of its secrets; a man caught in the crossfire of his own past and the unfolding present.

"The parallels you draw are... striking," Gibson conceded finally, his voice low. "The idea of a predetermined path, of a condemnation for straying. It's a powerful literary motif. And Victor... Victor was a man who felt he was fighting against the current. He saw his ideas, his potential, being stifled, perhaps even stolen. It's understandable that he might have felt a sense of profound injustice."

"And someone else felt that injustice too," Maria stated, not as a question, but as a fact. "Someone who identified with Greer, who perhaps felt that the academic establishment had wronged them as well, or had wronged Greer, and they needed to... correct it. To enact their own form of justice."

Gibson sighed again, a sound that seemed to drain the last vestiges of energy from him. "There are always those who feel the world is unfair, Detective. Who feel that the scales are tipped against them. The university, with all its prestige and power, can be a harsh environment for those who don't conform, for those whose brilliance is perhaps too... disruptive." He hesitated, then spoke with a renewed, though still melancholic, gravity. "The Infinite Discourse offered a refuge to many who felt marginalized or misunderstood. A place where they could find kinship, and perhaps, a shared understanding of their struggles. Victor Greer was... a very bright light, extinguished too soon. His story became a cautionary tale for some. A symbol of what could happen when ambition and integrity clashed, and integrity lost."

"And the victims?" Maria prompted, her gaze unwavering. "Pendelton, the librarian. The Classics scholar. The archivist. How do they fit into this narrative of injustice and condemnation?"

Gibson's expression shifted again, a flicker of pain crossing his features. "Pendelton," he said, his voice softening, "was a kind soul. He saw the brilliance in Victor. He understood the pressures of academia. He often tried to mediate, to offer counsel, but... some wounds are too deep to heal with words alone." He paused, as if reliving a painful memory. "The Classics scholar... her work, while commendable in its academic rigor, perhaps touched upon some sensitive nerves within the department. It challenged established narratives, much like Victor's early work did. There's a certain... resistance to disruption, within established institutions. A tendency to protect the status quo."

Maria's mind raced. Pendelton, the confidante. The Classics scholar, a potential inheritor of Greer's defiance. And the archivist... the custodian of records. "And the archivist?" She asked, her voice insistent. "Did he uncover something in Vitor Greer's papers? Something that confirmed the plagiarism, or revealed the extent of the betrayal?"

Gibson's sigh was heavy, laced with a weariness that seemed to transcend academic debate. "The past," he murmured, his eyes distant, "is rarely as tidy as we'd like it to be. It holds its own ghosts, its own unresolved narratives. And sometimes, those ghosts refuse to stay buried. They demand to be heard. They demand... a reckoning." He looked back at Maria, his gaze piercing. "Victor Greer's brilliance was undeniable. But his fall from grace was equally profound. It left a scar. A scar that some believed could only be healed through... drastic measures. Measures that would bring the perpetrators of his downfall to account. To be condemned, as the text suggests, is to be found guilty. And in the eyes of someone deeply wounded, the entire system that allowed that wounding to occur, and to go unpunished, could be deemed guilty as well."

He gestured vaguely towards the scattered papers on his desk. "You see the literary allusions, Detective. You see the echoes of tragedy. But understand this: those echoes are born from real pain. From real disillusionment. The Discourse was a haven for those who felt the sting of such pain. And yes, Victor Greer was one such soul. His story, his downfall, it became a symbol. A symbol of what can happen when the pursuit of knowledge is corrupted by ambition, and when the integrity of a scholar is sacrificed on the altar of personal gain."

Maria felt a cold certainty settle in her stomach. Gibson was not confessing, not directly. But he was confirming her suspicions. He was validating the narrative she had painstakingly constructed. The

Composer, whoever he or she were, was not acting out of mere malice. They were acting out of a profound, distorted sense of justice, fueled by the ghost of Victor Greer and the perceived sins of the academic establishment.

"Professor," Maria said, her voice firm, "you speak of a code of silence. Of old loyalties. But these are not abstract concepts anymore. They are the threads connecting a series of brutal murders. If Victor Greer was a victim, and if someone is seeking retribution in his name, then that retribution has already begun. And it will not stop until those responsible for his downfall, or those perceived as such, are brought to justice. Or perhaps," she added, her voice dropping to a near whisper, "until the cycle of condemnation is complete."

Gibson looked down at his hands, his knuckles white as he gripped the edge of the desk. The sadness in his eyes had deepened, tinged now with a profound sense of dread. "The paths we choose, Detective," he said, his voice barely audible, "have consequences. Some consequences are intellectual. Others... are far more grim. Victor Greer's story serves as a potent reminder of that. A reminder of what can happen when the gods of ambition and envy are worshipped above all else. And a reminder that sometimes, those who are condemned, are simply those who refuse to see the truth."

Maria knew then that Gibson's silence was not an absence of information, but a deliberate choice, born from a complex web of loyalty, pain, and perhaps, a fear of the truth he himself acknowledged. His resistance was a testament to the depth of his connection to Victor Greer's legacy, and to the enduring power of the Discourse's secrets. But it only solidified her resolve. The cryptic clues, the literary allusions, Gibson's own hushed references to past tragedies – they were all pieces of a larger, more dangerous puzzle. And she was determined to see it through, no matter how many ghosts she had to awaken, or how deeply buried the truths might be. The Composers carefully constructed narrative was beginning to unravel, and the ghosts of literature were about to demand a very real reckoning. The weight of Gibson's unspoken words, of the secrets he held close, pressed down on Maria, a tangible force urging her to dig deeper, to expose the darkness that festered beneath the veneer of academic respectability. The tragedy of Victor Greer was no longer just a historical footnote; it was a living, breathing motive, and its bloody tendrils were reaching out, ensnaring everyone caught in its path. Gibson's sorrow was an admission, a silent scream that echoed the Composer's own anguish. He knew the story, and in his knowing, he became inextricably linked to its tragic, violent conclusion.

CHAPTER 9

THE VICTIM'S TALE

The fluorescent lights of the Elmwood University library hummed with an almost accusatory intensity, casting a sterile glow upon the hushed aisles. It was a sanctuary for the intellectual, a fortress of knowledge, yet tonight, it had become a tomb. The discovery had been made by a frantic graduate student, Connie Englewood, searching for a rare translation of Seneca. Her screams, sharp and ragged, had sliced through the otherwise serene atmosphere, drawing the attention of a passing security guard, who in turn, alerted the authorities.

Detective Maria Richards arrived on the scene, the familiar knot of dread tightening in her stomach. The library, a labyrinth of towering bookshelves, offered a stark contrast to the gritty realities of murder. The air, usually thick with the scent of aged paper and binding glue, was now tainted with the metallic tang of blood and the faint, cloying sweetness of death. The carrel, tucked away in a secluded corner of the Humanities wing, was a tableau of academic despair. Books lay strewn about, pages splayed open as if in silent protest. And in the center of this disarray, slumped over a worn oak desk, was the victim.

Professor Edgar Nevel. His face, usually contorted in a sneer of intellectual disdain, was now slack, his eyes wide and unseeing, fixed on some unseen horror. A single, precisely placed wound marred his throat, a chilling echo of the previous murders. But it was the arrangement of the books, the peculiar details surrounding Nevel's demise, that drew Maria's attention. They weren't just scattered; they were curated. Arranged with a deliberate, almost theatrical, precision.

"What have we got, Donny?" Maria asked, her voice low, cutting through the hushed murmurs of the forensic team.

Detective Bates knelt beside the body, his expression unreadable. He gestured to the books. "Professor Nevel was found amidst his own literary critiques, Maria. It appears our killer has a penchant for narrative symbolism. Look at this." He pointed to a copy of *The Poetics* by Aristotle, open to a passage discussing catharsis, the purging of emotions through tragedy. "And this." He indicated a well-thumbed volume of literary theory; its pages heavily annotated with Nevel's famously vitriolic commentary. "The killer has staged this scene to represent a critical failure, a narrative's tragic denouement."

Maria followed his gaze, her mind already piecing together the fragments. Nevel, known for his withering critiques, his ability to dissect and destroy literary works with a few well-chosen, venomous words, had finally met his own critical failure. His recent review of his colleague, Professor Hannah George's, collection of avant-garde poetry, *Echoes in the Ether*, had been particularly brutal. It had been a public evisceration, a literary assassination that had sent shockwaves through the already fragile academic community. George, a quiet, introspective woman, had been utterly devastated, her artistic spirit seemingly crushed under the weight of Nevel's scorn.

"So, Hannah George is our primary suspect?" Maria mused, her gaze sweeping over the scene.

Donny shook his head slowly. "It's too convenient, Maria. Too obvious. Nevel's reviews were infamous. He'd alienated countless academics. There are probably a dozen people who would have relished seeing him meet a dramatic end." He picked up a small, leather-bound notebook from the desk, Nevel's personal journal. "But the killer's message is specific. It's not just about revenge; it's about a literary judgment."

He opened the journal, his gloved fingers carefully turning the pages. The handwriting, sharp and arrogant, mirrored the man himself. "Nevel was meticulous in his dissections. He treated literary analysis as a form of forensic science, dissecting flaws, identifying weaknesses, and ultimately, delivering a verdict. He saw himself as an arbiter of taste, a judge of artistic merit. And it seems our killer has decided to judge the judge."

Maria moved closer, peering at the journal. Nevel's entries were a litany of contempt, a catalog of artistic sins he believed he had eradicated. He railed against perceived pretentiousness, against sentimentality, against anything he deemed to be lacking in intellectual rigor. His critiques were not merely opinions; they were pronouncements, delivered with the certainty of divine revelation.

"He mentions George here," Donny said, pointing to an entry. "'George's latest offering is a testament to the bankruptcy of modern verse. A pretentious exercise in navel-gazing, devoid of genuine insight or emotional resonance. It is a critical failure of the highest order, a literary void masquerading as art.' Strong words, even for Nevel."

"And from what I know based upon the staff records I've reviewed, George is known for her... delicate sensibilities," Maria murmured. "Nevel's review could have been the final blow to her career, her passion."

"Indeed," Donny agreed. "But the killer's choice of location is also significant. A library carrel. A place of quiet contemplation, of solitary study. It suggests a desire for intimacy, a need to perform the act in a space that mirrors the very essence of literary engagement. The killer isn't just enacting revenge; they are performing a critique."

He gestured to a copy of *Hamlet*, placed prominently on the desk, open to the gravedigger scene. "The theme of mortality, of the finality of death, is here. And the specific text... it speaks of decomposition, of the body's return to dust. Nevel's own criticisms were often described as 'mordant,' meaning biting or corrosive. The killer has taken that metaphor literally."

Maria felt a chill crawl up her spine. The killer was not just intelligent; they were a scholar themselves, a twisted artist wielding literary theory as a weapon. The previous victims—the librarian who had inadvertently suppressed Victor Greer's crucial research, the classics professor whose work may have touched upon the sensitive history of The Infinite Discourse, the archivist who had been privy to sensitive departmental documents—all had been connected to the academic world, to the very institutions that Victor Greer had allegedly been wronged by. And now, Nevel, a figure who embodied the harsh, unforgiving nature of academic judgment.

"If the killer is delivering a critique, then they must have a particular philosophy of literary judgment," Maria mused. "Nevel's review of George was a judgment based on intellectual rigor and objective analysis, or so he claimed. But perhaps the killer believes in a different kind of judgment – one based on emotional truth, on authentic expression, or perhaps even on moral culpability."

Donny nodded, his eyes scanning the surrounding books. "The killer is showing us what he, because I'm leaning towards a male perpetrator, believes constitutes a 'fatal flaw' in a narrative. Nevel's perceived flaws were his arrogance, his cruelty, his intellectual dishonesty, and masquerading as objective critique. The killer is highlighting Nevel's own narrative downfall. It's a meta-critique, Maria. A critique of the critic."

He picked up another book, a collection of essays on literary ethics. "We've both read his critiques. Nevel believed in the power of criticism to purify literature, to elevate it above the mundane. But he was also notoriously uncompromising, often to the point of cruelty. He saw himself as a surgeon, excising diseased tissue from the body of literary work. But perhaps he was more of a butcher, leaving behind a mangled mess."

Maria's mind flashed back to Victor Greer, the brilliant scholar whose career had been destroyed by accusations of plagiarism. Greer's story was one of perceived injustice, of a brilliant mind undone by the very system that was supposed to nurture it. Had Nevel played a role in Greer's downfall? Was this murder an act of posthumous retribution for Victor Greer, delivered by someone who felt the sting of academic betrayal just as acutely?

"The references to *Oedipus Rex*," Maria said, her voice barely above a whisper. "'He who cannot follow the path of the gods will be condemned.' Nevel, with his rigid adherence to his own intellectual dogma, his unwavering belief in his own critical superiority, perhaps he believed he was on a divine path. And the killer is showing him just how wrong he was."

Donny's gaze met hers, a shared understanding passing between them. "The killer is not simply executing victims; they are constructing a narrative. Each murder is a chapter or an act, each victim a character whose flaws are exposed and judged. Nevel, the harsh critic, has been subjected to his own brand of critique. His death is the ultimate critical failure, a stark illustration of his own inability to perceive the true narrative of justice."

They continued their grim examination. The carrel itself became a canvas for the killer's message. A single, red rose lay on the desk, its petals wilting, a symbol of beauty corrupted, of potential unfulfilled. Beside it, a carefully placed bookmark marked a passage in a book of literary criticism that discussed the ethical responsibilities of critics. The passage detailed the devastating impact of overly harsh reviews on emerging artists.

"Nevel was proud of his ability to 'kill' bad books," Donny observed, his voice grim. "He reveled in it. He saw it as a necessary function. But he lacked empathy, Maria. He lacked the understanding that words, especially those delivered from a position of power, can have devastating consequences."

Maria's thoughts drifted to the Discourse, to the whispers of ostracized scholars and betrayed artists. Could Victor Greer himself have been a member? Or perhaps, his story had resonated so deeply within the society that one of its members felt compelled to act as his avenger, using Nevel's own methods of dissection and judgment against him.

"The audacity of this," Maria murmured, gesturing to the scene. "To commit murder in the university library, a place of supposed enlightenment and safety. It's a statement. A declaration that the pursuit of knowledge is not without its dangers, its dark undercurrents."

"It's a theatrical performance," Donny agreed. "The killer wants to be seen, to have their message understood. They are using the conventions of literary criticism to expose what they perceive as the moral failings of the academic elite. Nevel's review of George was a public humiliation. The killer is delivering a public judgment on Nevel himself."

He picked up a copy of *The Waste Land* by T.S. Eliot, another book that Nevel had relentlessly attacked. "Remember this critique?" Maria nodded. They had both thought it was an over-the-top rant. Detective Bates continued. "Nevel despised Eliot's work, calling it 'a fragmented mess reflecting a fragmented mind.' He saw no beauty in its despair, no truth in its disillusionment. But perhaps the killer sees a reflection of their own shattered world in such poetry. Perhaps they see Nevel's critiques as another layer of meaninglessness, another denial of genuine human suffering."

Maria felt a growing unease. The killer was not just targeting individuals; they were targeting the very foundations of academic discourse, the systems of judgment and validation that shaped the intellectual landscape. Victor Greer's story, the story of a promising scholar brought down by perceived betrayal, was clearly the central theme. The killer was acting as a self-appointed arbiter of justice, using literary theory as their moral compass.

"The previous victims were all connected to the Victor Greer case in some way," Maria stated, her voice firm. "Pendelton, the librarian, who may have held back crucial information. Clara Bellweather and Bennett, whose research might have been a threat. The archivist, who could have possessed damning evidence. And now Nevel, a critic whose harsh words may have contributed to Greer's ruin. It's a systematic dismantling of those involved, or perceived to be involved, in Greer's downfall."

Donny's gaze was fixed on a passage in the *Hamlet* edition, a monologue from Claudius that spoke of guilt and the inability to pray. "The killer is presenting his case, Maria. A prosecution. Each victim represents a charge. Nevel, the charge of cruelty and intellectual hubris. The librarian, the charge of obstruction. Clara and Bennett, the charge of complicity in the suppression of truth. And the archivist, the charge of guarding secrets that should have been revealed."

"So, the killer sees themselves as an instrument of a higher justice?" Maria asked, the chilling implication settling in her mind. "A form of literary divine intervention?"

"It would appear so," Donny replied, his voice tinged with a profound sadness. "They are enacting a narrative of judgment, using Victor Greer's story as their foundational text. Greer's perceived victimization has become the catalyst for this killer's mission. They are not just seeking revenge; they are seeking to correct the narrative, to re-establish a sense of cosmic balance that they believe has been irrevocably disrupted."

The carrel, once a place of quiet study, now felt like a morbid stage. The books, props in a deadly play, bore silent witness to the killer's chilling pronouncements. Maria knew this was not the end. The killer, whoever they were, was driven by a deeply held conviction, a warped sense of morality rooted in the tragic story of Victor Greer. And as long as that story resonated with the darkness within someone, the cycle of violence would continue. The Composer, as Gibson had termed the killer, was not just an individual; they were a manifestation of Victor Greer's enduring tragedy, a phantom haunting the hallowed halls of Elmwood University, demanding a reckoning for sins long past. The carefully crafted narrative was far from over; it was merely entering its most dangerous, and perhaps, most tragic, act. The air in the carrel grew colder, the silence heavier, as Maria and Donny stood amidst the fallen critic, acutely aware that the narrative of Victor Greer had found a deadly, terrifying continuation.

The vellum card, nestled precisely beside Professor Nevel's lifeless hand, was an artifact of chilling deliberation. It wasn't merely a calling card; it was a pronouncement, a literary indictment penned in elegant, looping script that spoke of an education far beyond the practicalities of law enforcement. Maria picked it up with a gloved hand, her gaze fixed on the embossed words that seemed to shimmer under the stark library lights. It was a quote, stark and unforgiving, plucked from the depths of Dante Alighieri's *Inferno*: "Lasciate ogne speranza, voi ch'intrate." *Abandon all hope, ye who enter here.*

Detective Bates, his brow furrowed, leaned closer. "Dante," he stated, his voice a low rumble. "The gateway to hell. Our killer is telling us they believe they are leading their victims into damnation."

Maria's eyes scanned the surrounding scene, the meticulously arranged books, the victim's final, horrifying tableau. Nevel, the arbiter of literary taste, the man who wielded his pen like a scalpel to dissect and destroy, was now himself dissected, his life's work reduced to a mere footnote in this grim narrative. The card wasn't just a quote; it was a theological judgment, a terrifying assertion that Nevel, and by extension, those who preceded him, were not merely being punished, but were being subjected to a divine sentence, a descent into a personal inferno orchestrated by their killer.

"It's not just about revenge anymore, Donny," Maria said, her voice tight. "This is about judgment. The killer believes they are enacting a form of justice, a retribution so profound that it warrants the ultimate condemnation. Dante's *Inferno* isn't just a literary work; it's a map of sin and its eternal consequences. Our killer is mapping their own path of retribution, and Nevel is being cast into a specific circle."

She flipped the card over. On the reverse, another verse, equally damning: "Giù per lo mondo sanza infamia e 'l danno." *Down through the world without fame and damage.* The words seemed to mock Nevel's own pursuit of academic notoriety, his relentless quest to leave his mark on the literary world. Now, his legacy was to be one of infamy, not acclaim, and his "damage" was absolute and irreversible.

"The killer is playing God," Donny murmured, his gaze sweeping over the scattered books, each one a silent witness to

Nevel's intellectual downfall. "They see themselves as an avenging angel, or perhaps, a demon of divine wrath. The choice of Dante is deliberate. It signifies a descent into a hell of their own creation, a place where the sins of the academic elite are purged through brutal, unforgiving punishment."

Maria felt a tremor of apprehension that went beyond the shock of another murder. The killer's intellectual prowess was undeniable, their understanding of literature profound. But this was no mere academic debate; it was a descent into a terrifyingly literal interpretation of literary themes. The Dantean quote wasn't just a stylistic flourish; it was a declaration of intent, a clear signal that the killer's vision of justice was escalating, becoming more severe, more damning with each subsequent victim.

"Think about the previous victims," Maria mused, her mind racing. "Pendelton, the librarian, who may have held back crucial information. Was his 'sin' the suppression of knowledge, a betrayal of his professional duty, thus deserving a place in a hell of ignorance? The doctoral student and Classics professor, whose research might have threatened to unearth a hidden truth about the Aeon Society. Was their punishment to be intellectually silenced, his knowledge rendered useless, trapped in a purgatory of forgotten texts? And the archivist, guarding secrets. Perhaps their 'damage' was the burden of hidden knowledge, a hell of buried truths."

Donny nodded, his eyes reflecting the cold, sterile light of the library. "And Nevel, the critic. The self-appointed judge of literary merit. His crime was his arrogance, his cruelty, his unyielding pronouncements that crushed artistic spirits. Perhaps the killer sees him as deserving of a circle where the tormentors are themselves eternally judged, where their own harsh criticisms are echoed back as their eternal damnation."

The sheer theatricality of the crime scene was staggering. It was a meticulously constructed stage, designed to convey a specific message, a chilling narrative of sin and retribution. The books weren't just scattered; they were positioned, their titles and passages speaking volumes about the killer's warped worldview. Nevel's own critical works lay open, pages marked with passages that spoke of intellectual hubris, of the dangers of unchecked power in the realm of criticism. The killer was holding Nevel accountable for his own literary pronouncements, forcing him to confront the destructive potential of his words in the most literal way imaginable.

"The phrase 'without fame and damage'," Maria repeated, tracing the words on the vellum card with her finger. "It's so ironic. Nevel craved academic fame, yet he inflicted damage on so many. The killer is flipping that script. They are ensuring Nevel is remembered, but not for his intellectual achievements. His fame will now be tied to his brutal end, and the damage he inflicted will be overshadowed by the ultimate damage done to him."

She felt a growing sense of unease, a cold dread that settled deep in her bones. The killer's intellectual journey was not linear; it was a descent. The initial murders, while brutal and calculated, had a degree of logic rooted in academic feuds and alleged complicity in Victor Greer's ruin. But this – this plunge into the hellish landscapes of Dante – suggested a more profound, more personal, and far more terrifying motivation. The killer was not just seeking to right perceived wrongs; they were seeking to condemn, to consign their victims to an eternity of suffering, a judgment far beyond the realm of human law.

"This isn't just about Victor Greer anymore, is it?" Maria asked, her voice barely a whisper. "This is about the killer's own internal torment; their own perception of a world steeped in sin and deserving of damnation. They are projecting their own internal hell onto their victims."

Donny looked at her, his expression grim. "The narrative is evolving, Maria. The killer is no longer just a prosecutor; they are becoming a judge, jury, and executioner, all rolled into one. And their courtroom is Dante's *Inferno*. Each victim is being assigned their particular torment, their specific circle of hell, based on the killer's interpretation of their sins."

He gestured to a copy of *The Divine Comedy* itself, lying open on a nearby lectern. It was a rare, leather-bound edition, the pages brittle with age. The killer had not just quoted Dante; they had brought his work into the heart of the crime scene, turning the library into a macabre extension of the poem. A specific passage was bookmarked, a vivid description of the punishments meted out to the avaricious in the fourth circle. Nevel, a man known for his avarice for intellectual superiority, for his insatiable desire for recognition and his ruthless acquisition of academic dominance, fit the profile disturbingly well.

"The avaricious," Donny said, his voice resonating with the gravity of the discovery. "Those who hoard, who grasp for more than their share. Nevel certainly embodied that in his pursuit of intellectual dominance. He never shared credit, never acknowledged the contributions of others, always seeking to be the sole authority. His 'sin' was his relentless accumulation of academic prestige, his refusal to distribute knowledge or recognition freely."

Maria knelt beside the body, her gaze not on the deceased professor, but on the carefully arranged books. Nevel's own scathing critiques of poets who dared to explore themes of suffering and despair lay open. He had dismissed them as maudlin, as self-indulgent. But now, he was in a position to experience that despair firsthand, amplified by the killer's twisted interpretation of divine retribution.

"The killer is showing us what he believes constitutes true 'sin' in the academic world," Maria stated, her voice hardening. "It's not just intellectual dishonesty or plagiarism. It's a deeper corruption – the corruption of spirit, the arrogance of intellect that leads to the dehumanization of others. Pendelton's sin was withholding knowledge, a form of intellectual stinginess. Bellweather and Bennett, perhaps their sin was in obscuring historical truths, a form of intellectual dishonesty that perpetuated a false narrative. And Nevel... his sin was the abuse of his critical power, the act of devaluing and destroying other's work with impunity."

The card, with its chilling Dantean pronouncement, felt like a brand, marking Nevel as irrevocably damned. Maria knew that the killer's descent was far from over. This was not a single act of retribution, but a meticulously planned series, each victim a step deeper into a hell of their own design. The academic world, with its intricate hierarchies, its intellectual rivalries, and its hidden histories, had provided the fertile ground for this twisted justice. And Victor Greer's story, the initial spark of perceived betrayal, had ignited a conflagration of vengeance that was now consuming those who had, in the killer's eyes, contributed to his downfall.

"The killer's interpretation of justice is becoming increasingly severe," Maria reiterated, her mind piecing together the fragmented clues. "They're not just seeking to punish; they are seeking to damn. The 'damage' they inflict is not just physical; it's eternal. Nevel's legacy will be this gruesome spectacle, his name forever linked to a descent into a literary hell. This is a chilling escalation, Donny. We're not just dealing with a murderer; we're dealing with a theologian of vengeance, a self-appointed architect of damnation."

Donny picked up a small, exquisitely carved ivory paperweight that had come from Nevel's desk, a subtle testament to the professor's refined, if arrogant, tastes. "The killer is not only judging them, Maria, but they are making a statement about the nature of judgment itself. Nevel believed his critiques were the ultimate arbiter of truth. The killer is demonstrating that all judgments, especially those delivered with such severity, can lead to a descent into a personal hell, for both the judged and the judge. They are showing us that even in the pursuit of what they perceive as justice, there is a danger of becoming the very thing they condemn."

The air in the library carrel grew heavy, thick with the scent of old paper, dried blood, and the chilling echo of Dante's infernal verses. Maria felt a profound sense of foreboding. The Composer was not simply killing; they were constructing a narrative of damnation, using literary genius as their weapon and academic injustice as their motive. Nevel's death was not an end, but a terrifying new chapter, a descent into a literary hell that promised only further horrors. The vellum card, a stark testament to the killer's descent, lay in Maria's hand, a chilling promise of what was yet to come. The gates to hell had been opened, and the killer held the keys.

The vellum card, a chilling artifact of the killer's escalating theatricality, remained in Maria's gloved hand. The Dantean pronouncement, "Lasciate ogne speranza, voi ch'intrate," echoed in her mind, not merely as a quote, but as a damning indictment. Nevel, the literary critic, had been cast into a hell of his own making, a personal inferno orchestrated by a mind that wielded words as weapons and justice as a divine, albeit twisted, mandate. The previous victims—Pendelton, the librarian who guarded knowledge like a dragon guards its hoard; the Classics professor, whose research threatened to unearth inconvenient truths; and the archivist, buried under a mountain of secrets—each had their perceived sins meticulously cataloged and punished. But Nevel , the arbiter of taste, the man who dissected and destroyed reputations with a flick of his pen, had been assigned a particularly cruel circle. The avaricious.

Maria traced the embossed words on the card, her thoughts shifting from the chilling pronouncements to the academic battlefield that was Nevel's domain: the literature department. His reputation preceded him, a double-edged sword of brilliant insight and brutal, often unforgiving, honesty. He was a titan, yes, but one whose pronouncements had left a trail of bruised egos and shattered careers in their wake. His recent targets, particularly those whose works he had savaged, now occupied a prominent position on Maria's mental suspect list. The killer wasn't merely executing a series of random acts of violence; they were systematically dismantling a perceived hierarchy of academic sin, each victim a carefully chosen sinner being purged by this self-appointed divine hand.

Maria had reached out to Dr. Aris Gibson to meet and discuss the latest victim. Maria and Donny had a series of questions that needed answers. Dr. Gibson could most likely provided them.

"His critiques," Maria mused, her voice low, directed more to herself than to Gibson, "were legendary. And not in a good way, for many. He had a way of cutting to the bone, of exposing not just flaws in writing, but perceived moral failings." She paused to watch his demeanor. Maria continued. "Donny and I have a theory and that theory is that Dr. Nevel saw himself as a guardian of literary integrity, but others saw him as a bully, a gatekeeper who delighted in crushing aspiring talent."

Gibson nodded, his gaze sweeping over Nevel's impeccably organized desk in the library, a stark contrast to the chaotic violence of his demise. "Gatekeepers often earn resentment. And Nevel was a particularly formidable one. His recent focus seems to have been on a rather contentious group of poets and novelists, those who explore... darker themes. He publicly denounced their work as self-indulgent, morbid, and lacking in any real artistic merit."

Maria's mind immediately went to the whispers she'd heard during her preliminary inquiries within the university. Nevel had recently penned a scathing review of a rising poet, a young woman whose work was characterized by raw emotion, themes of mental anguish, and a raw, unflinching exploration of personal trauma. The review had been so brutal, so dismissive, that it had sent shockwaves through the literary circles that championed her. Nevel had not merely critiqued her poetry; he had attacked her credibility as an artist, questioning her sanity and her right to even engage with such profound themes.

"The poet," Maria said, a flicker of recognition in her eyes. "Is her name Hannah George?"

Gibson's expression shifted, a subtle tightening around his jaw. "Hannah. Yes. Nevel's review was... particularly vicious. He called her work 'a testament to the diseased imagination of a broken mind, unfit for serious consideration.' It was widely seen as a career-ending attack. He painted her as a pathetic figure, exploiting her personal struggles for cheap literary gain."

The poet. Hannah George. Maria felt a jolt of something akin to professional instinct, a subtle hum of recognition that transcended the gruesome reality of murder. George's work, while undeniably dark, had also been praised for its cathartic power, its ability to articulate experiences that many found difficult to express. She had, in the past, been open about her struggles with anxiety and depression, and had even briefly been a member of The Infinite Discourse, the very organization whose secrets Victor Greer's downfall had begun to unravel. This detail, previously relegated to a footnote in George's biographical sketch, now loomed large.

"George," Donny repeated, the name hanging in the air. "She was involved with The Infinite Discourse, wasn't she? Briefly. A few years ago."

Gibson's eyes met his, a shared understanding passing between them. The Infinite Discourse. A clandestine group of academics, artists, and intellectuals, shrouded in mystery and rumored to engage in rituals and intellectual pursuits that bordered on the occult. Victor Greer, the man whose alleged betrayal had set this entire cascade of violence in motion, had been a prominent member. Pendelton, the librarian, had also been connected, as had the doctoral student and Classics professor, whose research had veered into the Discourse's ancient origins. Nevel, the critic, his sharp tongue having savaged many a Discourse member or their sympathizers, had been a vocal detractor, dismissing their esoteric interests as intellectual charades.

"The Infinite Discourse connection," Gibson murmured, his gaze drifting back to where Nevel's body had laid, then to the vellum card. "It's becoming an undeniable thread. If George was a member, even briefly, and Nevel publicly denounced her work and her perceived mental instability... it paints a rather compelling picture, doesn't it? The killer is targeting those who were perceived as Nevel's victims, or those who actively denigrated or ostracized individuals connected to the Discourse."

Maria nodded, her mind racing, weaving together the disparate threads of academic rivalry, personal vendetta, and the shadowy influence of the Discourse. Nevel's brutal critique of Hannah George was not just an isolated incident; it was another brick in the wall of perceived injustice that the killer was meticulously dismantling, one victim at a time. George, with her history of mental health struggles and her brief but significant connection to the Discourse, now stood at the precipice of Maria's suspicion. Had Nevel's vitriol pushed her over the edge? Or was she a pawn, a victim of Nevel's academic cruelty, whose fate was now intertwined with the broader narrative of revenge?

"Nevel's review of George," Maria continued, "was it just one in a series of attacks on artists exploring difficult themes? Or was it particularly egregious? What else did he say?"

Gibson retrieved a tablet from a nearby table, his fingers deftly navigating through Nevel's published works and online interviews. "I want to tell from the conversations that Nevel and I have had that he was particularly incensed by what he termed 'the cult of the suffering artist.' He was exasperated that artists were increasingly using personal trauma as a crutch, a way to gain sympathy and critical acclaim without the necessary artistic rigor. Nevel was one of the last 'old school critics,' where he argued that it was a dangerous trend, blurring the lines between genuine artistic expression and mere emotional exhibitionism. Nevel saw George as a prime example of this trend."

He scrolled through more articles. "Nevel also took aim at a philosopher who had written extensively on the nature of existential dread and its influence on artistic creation. Nevel dismissed this philosopher's work as 'nihilistic drivel designed to prey on the weak-minded.' The philosopher, ironically, was also a known associate of some of the more esoteric members of the Discourse, individuals who explored the darker aspects of human consciousness."

Maria felt a chill creep up her spine. The killer's meticulous selection of victims, their apparent motivation rooted in a perceived intellectual and moral corruption within the academic elite, was becoming chillingly clear. Nevel wasn't just a critic; he was a crusader against what he saw as the degradation of intellectual discourse, and his pronouncements had far-reaching consequences, impacting not just individual careers but entire philosophical and artistic movements. And his animosity extended to anyone he deemed a purveyor of this perceived intellectual decay, especially if they were connected to the shadowy Discourse.

"The pattern emerges," Maria stated, her voice firm. "Pendelton withheld knowledge. The doctoral student and Classics professor threatened to expose truths that might have damaged The Infinite Discourse's reputation. Nevel, in his own way, silenced and attacked those who explored themes he deemed dangerous or degenerate, often with ties, however tenuous, to the Discourse. He was effectively an antagonist to anyone who dared to delve into the very subjects the Discourse was rumored to explore. He saw them as a corrupting influence, a deviation from true intellectualism."

She paused, considering the implications. "If Hannah George was a target of Nevel's ire, and she has a history with the Discourse, then she's not just a potential suspect; she's a potential victim in this escalating narrative of retribution. The killer might be trying to silence Nevel's detractors, or perhaps, they're seeking to punish those who attacked or ostracized the Discourse's members. Or...," Maria's voice trailed off, a new, more disturbing possibility taking root. "Or perhaps George herself is the killer, driven to this extreme by Nevel's public humiliation and her own past association with the Discourse, which might have been further tarnished by Nevel's critiques."

The thought of Hannah George, the poet whose words bled with raw emotion and despair, orchestrating such brutal acts of violence was unsettling. Her poetry often explored themes of vengeance and the destructive nature of unchecked power, but it was always couched in metaphor, in the visceral language of the soul. Could that metaphor have bled into reality? Her documented history of mental instability, while often seen as a source of artistic inspiration, could also, in a twisted turn of events, have amplified her grievances, leading her down a path of radical, violent retribution.

"Her history with The Infinite Discourse," Dr. Gibson mused, his gaze fixed on the tablet. "How significant was it? The reports are vague. A brief membership, then a quiet departure. No scandals, no public pronouncements about their activities."

"That's often how it is with groups like the Discourse," Maria replied. "Members tend to be discreet. But a brief membership, especially for someone exploring themes of mental anguish and existential dread, could have been a crucial period for her. Perhaps she found solace, or perhaps she found something more... sinister. Something Nevel's intellectual purity couldn't comprehend."

She looked at the pristine vellum card again, the Dantean inscription a stark reminder of the killer's worldview. *Lasciate ogne speranza, voi ch'intrate.* Abandon all hope. It wasn't just a quote; it was a judgment. And Nevel, with his pronouncements of damnation on artistic merit, had become the target of a similar, albeit far more literal, judgment. The killer saw themselves as purging the academic world of those who, in their eyes, had corrupted it, betrayed its ideals, or attacked those who were unfairly persecuted. Nevel's critique of Hannah George might have been the final straw, the act that cemented his position as a target in the killer's infernal ledger.

"The poet's work," Donny interjected, his mind sifting through the nuances of literary criticism and psychological profiles. "Does it offer any clues? Any specific animosity towards Nevel, or towards the Discourse's critics?"

Gibson scrolled through reviews of George's poetry. "Many critics lauded her ability to capture the raw, unfiltered experience of suffering. Others found her work too bleak, too repetitive.

Nevel, of course, was among the latter. But there are also articles, interviews where Hannah herself speaks about the pressure to conform, the arbitrary judgments of the literary establishment, and the need for artists to explore uncomfortable truths, regardless of societal disapproval. She's spoken about how institutions and individuals often fear what they don't understand, and how they lash out at those who represent that unknown."

This sounded like a woman who had been deeply wounded by Nevel's public condemnation. The phrase "broken mind" wasn't just a professional insult; it was a deeply personal attack, especially for someone who had openly discussed their struggles with mental health. It was the kind of insult that could fester, that could fuel a desperate need for vindication, for a retribution that matched the scale of the perceived injustice.

"Her connection to the Discourse," Donny pressed, "even if brief, might have made her vulnerable. Perhaps Nevel's attack was not just about her poetry, but about her perceived association with something he deemed dangerous or deviant. He was known for his sweeping judgments, for lumping together anything he disliked under a broad umbrella of intellectual decadence."

Gibson nodded grimly. "And our killer, it seems, is systematically eliminating those who actively contributed to the marginalization or condemnation of individuals connected, however distantly, to the Discourse. Pendelton, the doctoral student and Classics professor, the actress, and now Nevel. They all, in their own ways, played a role in either concealing, attacking, or ostracizing those associated with the Discourse's inner circle or its sphere of influence."

Maria considered the implications. If Hannah George was indeed the killer, her motivation was complex. It wasn't just personal revenge for Nevel's review. It was likely tied to a broader sense of injustice, a feeling that individuals like herself, and perhaps others connected to the Discourse, had been unfairly judged and persecuted by figures like Nevel. The killer was not just avenging Victor Greer; they were avenging the perceived sins of the academic world against a fringe group that dared to explore forbidden knowledge and unconventional ideas.

"Her mental state," Maria said, her voice thoughtful, "coupled with Nevel's public humiliation of her, and her past association with the Discourse... she fits the profile of someone who might seek retribution. The question is, did she have the capacity for such calculated violence? Such elaborate staging?"

Gibson's gaze was distant, contemplating the deeper motivations. "Nevel's death, the Dantean quote... it suggests a mind that is not only enraged but also deeply philosophical, perhaps even theological in its outlook. The killer sees their actions as a form of divine judgment. It's a level of intellectualization that goes beyond simple revenge. It implies a carefully constructed worldview, a belief system that justifies these extreme measures. Hannah George, as a poet, delves into the darker aspects of human experience. It's not a stretch to imagine her grappling with concepts of sin, damnation, and retribution. Her art might be a reflection of a mind already predisposed to such darker contemplations."

Donny turned to Maria. "We need to investigate Hannah George. Her whereabouts at the time of Nevel's murder, her recent activities, any communication she might have had with Nevel or anyone connected to The Infinite Discourse. Her history of mental instability is a factor, but it shouldn't be the sole focus. We need to look at her actions, her motivations, and her potential capacity for orchestrating something of this magnitude."

Maria agreed , a knot of unease tightening in her stomach. The literary world, so often a realm of intellectual sparring and academic debate, had become the hunting ground for a killer who blurred the lines between critique and condemnation, between poetic expression and violent retribution. Hannah George, the poet savaged by Nevel, the former member of the enigmatic Discourse, was now a prime suspect, her art, her struggles, and her alleged connection to a shadowy organization all converging into a terrifying possibility. The gates to hell, it seemed, had been opened not just for Nevel, but for anyone who dared to challenge the killer's warped vision of justice. The poet, whose words spoke of inner turmoil, might be the very architect of this external inferno.

The killer's pronouncements, etched onto the vellum card with such deliberate calligraphy, were more than mere taunts; they were pronouncements of a deeply entrenched, albeit profoundly distorted, moral code. Maria turned the card over in her gloved fingers, the embossed Latin words, "Lasciate ogne speranza, voi ch'intrate," now seeming to emanate a tangible coldness. This wasn't the work of a madman driven by random impulse, but by an individual operating with a chillingly clear, albeit warped, sense of purpose. They saw themselves not as a murderer, but as a judge, an executioner, a dispenser of a grim, poetic justice.

"It's the self-righteousness that's most disturbing," Maria murmured, her gaze sweeping over the disarray of Nevel's study, a stark contrast to the meticulous order of the killer's apparent worldview. "They don't see themselves as a criminal. They see themselves as an arbiter of... literary sins. Each victim, a sinner deserving of damnation, not in some theological sense, but in a far more immediate, visceral way." She paused, picturing the scene from the crime photos, the calculated brutality that belied any suggestion of spontaneous rage. "Nevel, with his reputation for cutting down aspiring writers, for dissecting careers with a surgeon's precision and a cynic's glee, he's cast in the role of the avaricious. Perhaps the killer believes Nevel hoarded intellectual prestige, or perhaps he profited from the despair of those he crushed underfoot."

Donny, his brow furrowed in concentration as he reviewed Nevel's digital footprint, grunted in agreement. "The Dantean *Inferno* is a complex structure of punishment; each circle tailored to a specific sin. Our killer is clearly drawing from that wellspring. It suggests a mind that is not only intelligent but also one that views language and its misuse with a kind of zealous reverence. They believe they are correcting a profound imbalance, restoring some cosmic order by eliminating those who, in their eyes, have profaned the sacred art of writing." He gestured towards the scattered papers on Nevel's desk. "Pendelton, the librarian who guarded forbidden knowledge. The doctoral student and Classics professor, whose research threatened to expose uncomfortable truths, perhaps about the Discourse's own 'forbidden knowledge.' And Nevel, the critic who wielded his pen like a bludgeon, silencing voices he deemed unworthy. Each victim represents a different facet of what our killer perceives as a perversion of intellectual integrity or a betrayal of knowledge."

"But what defines that perversion for them?" Maria pressed, her mind sifting through the disparate elements of their current investigation. "Is it simply a difference in artistic opinion? Or is it something deeper? Nevel savaged Hannah George's work, calling it the product of a 'diseased imagination.' That's not just criticism; that's a declaration of war on her very being, on her right to express her pain through art. If the killer views Nevel as a punisher, then surely they see George's pain, her 'sin' of artistic expression, as something Nevel actively sought to extinguish. Perhaps the killer views Nevel's dismissal of George as an act of intellectual avarice, hoarding critical acclaim for himself by crushing those who dared to be different."

The idea of the killer as a purveyor of poetic justice, a self-appointed guardian of literary virtue, began to solidify. It wasn't just about eliminating perceived enemies; it was about rebalancing a cosmic scale of artistic merit and moral rectitude. The killer believed they were administering true justice, the kind that transcended human law. This elevated their actions from mere murder to something akin to a sacred duty, a righteous crusade against the perceived corruption of the intellectual world.

"Think about it," Donny added, his voice gaining a somber intensity. "Nevel's own critiques were often laced with moral judgment. He didn't just critique writing; he critiqued the perceived moral failings of the writers themselves. He positioned himself as a moral authority, a gatekeeper of not just good taste, but of intellectual and even moral purity. The killer is doing the same, but with far more lethal consequences. They've adopted Nevel's role but twisted it into a mechanism of death. They are, in essence, judging the judges. They are punishing the punishers."

Donny's gaze sharpened, a flicker of understanding igniting within his analytical mind. "So, if Nevel is the 'avaricious' in this scenario, it's because he 'hoarded' his critical authority, using it to stifle or silence others. And perhaps the killer sees themselves as liberating that stifled talent, or as avenging those who were similarly silenced. Hannah George's case becomes even more potent. Nevel didn't just critique her; he attacked her sanity, her very right to create art from her own lived experience. That's a profound act of intellectual violence. If the killer believes in poetic justice, then Nevel's annihilation might be seen as a poetic, albeit brutal, response to his own perceived literary and moral transgressions against George."

"Precisely," Maria confirmed, a shiver running down her spine at the sheer, cold logic of it all. "The killer is enacting a form of literary metempsychosis, perhaps. They are taking the sins Nevel attributed to others and reassigning them, or perhaps they are simply enacting a final, ultimate critique. Nevel condemned George's 'diseased imagination,' yet he himself has been rendered a grotesque spectacle. The irony is not lost on the killer; it's likely the very fuel for their grim satisfaction. They've shown Nevel what true damnation looks like, not in a literary review, but in a blood-soaked reality."

She walked over to a bookshelf, her fingers brushing against the spines of classic literature, the very domain Nevel so fiercely patrolled. "It's about the power of words, Donny. Nevel wielded them to tear down. This killer wields them to condemn and to kill. They're operating under a system where words have ultimate power, and those who misuse that power are subject to the ultimate penalty. Nevel's pronouncements, his literary judgments, were, in his mind, the absolute truth. The killer is now delivering their own absolute truth, carved in flesh and bone."

The concept of "poetic justice" took on a sinister new dimension. It wasn't about a neat resolution or a satisfying conclusion. It was about a violent, visceral mirroring of the perceived sin. Pendelton's secrecy was met with burial. The doctoral student and Classics professor's unearthed truths were met with a silencing that was far more permanent than any academic censure. The drama student as the future, and Nevel's brutal critiques were met with a condemnation so absolute that it obliterated him.

"This moral compass," Maria mused, her voice barely above a whisper, "it's not guided by empathy or conventional ethics. It's guided by a rigid, almost theological interpretation of intellectual conduct. The killer believes they are enacting a higher form of justice, one that cleanses the academic landscape of those who have corrupted it with their words, their actions, or their hoarding of knowledge. They see themselves as a necessary evil, a force of purification."

Donny nodded, his gaze distant, as if contemplating the vast, abstract landscape of the killer's psyche. "And that makes them incredibly dangerous. Someone who believes they are on a righteous mission is far more unyielding than someone driven by simple malice or personal gain. They are convinced of their own virtue, and that conviction can justify any atrocity. Nevel's death, the Dantean quote... it's a deliberate theatrical statement. The killer is sending a message: they are not just a murderer; they are a divine punisher, and their judgment is final."

Maria returned to the center of the room, her eyes now fixed on the vellum card lying on the desk, a stark, chilling testament to the killer's warped moral universe. "The killer sees themselves as a surgeon, excising a cancer from the body of academia. And Nevel, with his scalpel of critique, was perhaps seen as a purveyor of that very disease, or as someone who profited from it. The avarice isn't just about material wealth; it's about hoarding intellectual power, about exploiting the vulnerabilities of others for personal gain. Nevel, in the killer's eyes, was guilty of this on a grand scale. He wasn't just critiquing; he was consuming, diminishing, and ultimately, destroying."

The intricate layers of the killer's motivation were beginning to unravel, revealing a mind that was both brilliant and terrifyingly detached from conventional morality. They had crafted a personal inferno for Nevel, a hell of his own perceived sins, and the Dantean inscription was the burning decree at its gates. It was a chilling confirmation that this was not simply a series of murders; it was a carefully orchestrated campaign of retribution, guided by a twisted sense of divine justice, where words were the weapons, and death was the ultimate, unforgiving critique. The killer believed they were restoring balance, purging the literary world of its perceived corruption, one soul-destroying pronouncement at a time. And Nevel, the arbiter of literary fate, had finally met his own, fatal judgment.

The weight of the Dantean inscription, stark and undeniable, pressed down on Dr. Gibson. It wasn't just a quote; it was a confession of the killer's philosophy; a manifesto etched in Latin for all to see. Maria and Donny watched him, Maria's gaze unwavering, the silence in Nevel's study thick with unspoken dread. Gibson's usual composure, the carefully constructed intellectual detachment, was visibly fracturing. His hands, which had been meticulously sifting through Nevel's digital correspondence, now lay still on the polished mahogany desk, his knuckles white. His breath hitched, a faint, almost imperceptible sound in the oppressive quiet. The carefully maintained mask of academic detachment was peeling away, revealing a raw, terrified man beneath.

"Literary justice," Gibson finally choked out, the words tasting like ash in his mouth. He looked at Maria and Donny, his eyes wide with a dawning horror, not just at Nevel's death, but at something far older, far more deeply buried within The Infinite Discourse's hushed halls. "We... we talked about it. In the Discourse. Hypothetically, of course. Debates. Intellectual exercises." His voice, once a resonant baritone, was now a strained whisper, cracking under the immense pressure of his confession. "The idea of... of literary merit being judged not just by critics, but by a higher standard. A more *just* standard."

Maria's eyes narrowed, a chilling recognition dawning. "Hypothetically," she echoed, her voice laced with a dangerous calm. "And what did these hypothetical discussions entail, Gibson? Did they involve... consequences? For those who were deemed to have failed this 'higher standard'?" She gestured towards the vellum card, its elegant script mocking the brutality it represented. "Because this looks less like a hypothetical and more like a judgment delivered."

Gibson flinched as if struck. He ran a trembling hand over his thinning hair, his gaze darting around the room as if searching for an escape route, a hidden door, anything to pull him away from the precipice he now teetered on. "There was... a member," he admitted, his voice barely audible. "A poet. He was... passionate. Devoted to his craft. But he felt... wronged. Terribly wronged." He paused, struggling to articulate the nuanced, dangerous currents that flowed beneath the surface of their intellectual gatherings. "He believed Nevel, in particular, had deliberately destroyed promising careers with his reviews. He felt Nevel was not just critical, but malicious. That he hoarded power, stifling true artistry."

"And this poet," Maria pressed, leaning forward, the huntress sensing the scent of prey. "Did he have a particular affinity for... classical literature? For narratives of divine retribution?" She watched him closely, dissecting his every micro-expression, the involuntary tightening of his jaw, the tremor in his hand as he reached for a water glass, only to pull it back.

Gibson's eyes widened, a flicker of genuine fear – or was it guilt? – igniting within them. "He... he was obsessed with Dante," he confessed, the words tumbling out in a rush. "He saw parallels between the Purgatorio, the Inferno, and the struggles of artists in the modern world. He spoke of a 'literary purgatory' for those who were unfairly maligned, and a 'poetic hell' for those who inflicted such suffering. He believed in a form of... cosmic literary balance. That words themselves held a kind of karmic weight."

He swallowed hard, his gaze fixed on a point beyond Maria and Donny, lost in a memory that clearly haunted him. "He felt Nevel was a prime example of someone who abused that karmic weight. He saw Nevel's critiques as acts of intellectual avarice, hoarding his own prestige by crushing others. He would spend hours... poring over translations, discussing allegorical punishments. He saw himself, or at least he spoke of a certain kind of individual, as an agent of that balance. A dispenser of true, literary justice."

Maria remained silent, allowing the weight of his words to settle. The "struggling poet" was no longer an abstract concept. He was a potential perpetrator, his obsession with Dante now casting a terrifying shadow over the meticulous calculations of the killer. The Dantean quote wasn't just a thematic flourish; it was a direct echo of this individual's philosophy, a chilling testament to the depths of his conviction.

"And what was this poet's name, Gibson?" Maria asked, her voice dangerously soft. The question hung in the air, heavy with the unspoken threat of implications.

Gibson hesitated, his eyes clouding with a mixture of dread and an almost childlike fear. "I... I can't say. Not directly. I... I distanced myself from him. After Clara's death...and the professor's, then Pendelton's... I realized... this wasn't a hypothetical anymore." He wrung his hands, his academic detachment completely shattered, replaced by a raw, visceral fear. "He was always talking about... about correcting the imbalance. About ensuring that those who profited from the despair of others faced their own form of damnation. I heard him once, after a particularly brutal review by Nevel, mutter something about 'poetic justice being a dish best served cold, and eternal.' I... I tried to dissuade him, to reason with him. But he was... fervent. He saw himself as a righteous instrument."

"Dissuade him how, Gibson?" Maria's gaze was sharp, cutting through his evasion. "Did you offer him your assistance? Did you, perhaps, share information about the victims? Did you facilitate his... self-appointed crusade?" Maria paused and then began drawing legal lines. "Professor Gibson. You have information that is relevant to this case. You have a name." She stopped to let that resonate with Gibson. “Failure to provide the information is obstruction. Obstruction of a police investigation.” The accusation, spoken, hung palpably between them.

Gibson recoiled, his face paling further. "No! God, no. I would never... I mean, I *feared* this. When the first death occurred, I... I connected the dots. I recognized the language, the philosophy. It was *him*. But I convinced myself it was a coincidence. That he was just... mouthing off. The Dante references, the talk of justice... I thought it was just his artistic hyperbole. But when the second victim... and then the third... I started to truly panic. I tried to... to steer the society’s discussions away from such dangerous tangents. I thought if we stopped talking about 'literary justice,' it would die out. But it didn't. It festered."

He looked at Maria, his eyes pleading. "I knew he was capable of extreme actions. I saw the intensity of his conviction. He felt the world of literature was corrupt, and that he was one of the few who truly understood its sacred essence. He saw himself as a guardian, a punisher. Nevel was the ultimate target, the embodiment of everything he despised. But I never thought... I never imagined it would go this far. I never thought he would actually *do* it."

"So, you knew," Maria stated, her voice devoid of emotion, but carrying the weight of profound disappointment. "You knew who was being targeted, you knew the motivation, you understood the philosophy, and you suspected the perpetrator. And yet, you remained silent. You attended society meetings, you continued your work, all the while knowing that a murderer was operating within your midst, guided by a twisted sense of poetic justice that you yourself had, at least passively, contributed to."

Gibson's shoulders slumped. He looked like a man who had carried an unbearable burden for too long, a burden that had finally crushed him. "I was afraid," he whispered, the confession raw and honest. "Afraid of him. Afraid of what he might do if he knew I was aware. Afraid of the implications for the those in the Discourse. Afraid of... of being involved. I thought, if I didn't acknowledge it, if I didn't engage with it, it would simply fade away. It was... intellectual cowardice. I see that now. I saw the potential for danger, but I chose to believe it was just talk. I convinced myself that his obsessions were confined to his writing, to his mind."

He gestured vaguely towards the shelves of books surrounding them. "We, in The Infinite Discourse, we often explore the darker corners of human motivation, the philosophical underpinnings of morality, the nature of justice. It's a dangerous game, Detective. We dissect, we analyze, we debate. And sometimes, those discussions spill over into the real world. This poet... he took those abstract concepts and weaponized them. He saw Nevel, Pendelton, Bennett, Underwood, as characters in his own grand narrative of judgment. And he was determined to write their final act."

"You speak of 'intellectual cowardice,' Gibson," Maria said, her voice hardening. "But this goes beyond mere intellectual cowardice. This is complicity. By remaining silent, by choosing to believe it was merely 'talk,' you allowed this poet to continue his path of destruction unimpeded. You effectively provided him with a safe harbor, a place where his dangerous ideas could fester and grow without consequence."

Gibson didn't argue. He couldn't. He knew she was right. The guilt was a suffocating blanket, pressing down on him, making it hard to breathe. He had seen the danger signs, had heard the chilling pronouncements, had recognized the intellectual blueprint for murder, and he had done nothing. He had allowed his fear of confrontation, his desire to maintain his detached academic persona, to override his moral obligation.

"He was so convinced," Gibson continued, his voice thick with emotion. "He felt Nevel had personally wronged him, not just his poetry, but his very soul. He believed Nevel's critiques were designed to crush burgeoning talent, to maintain a literary oligarchy that stifled originality and rewarded mediocrity. He felt he was speaking for all the silenced voices. He saw Nevel's death as a necessary sacrifice to rebalance the scales. He even spoke of his next targets with a kind of grim anticipation, seeing them as individuals who also contributed to the 'corruption' of literature."

"And you allowed him to believe he was acting alone?" Maria probed. "Or did he have... collaborators? Was anyone else aware of his intentions?"

Gibson shook his head vehemently. "No. He was a solitary figure. His obsession was all-consuming. He operated in isolation, fueled by his resentment and his grand, twisted vision. The Discourse was his audience, his theoretical playground. He would discuss these ideas, test them, gauge reactions, but he never revealed any concrete plans. Not to me, not to anyone. His actions were his own, his crimes were his own. I merely... I merely failed to stop him when I had the chance. I failed to recognize the true depth of his conviction until it was too late."

He looked directly at Maria, his gaze filled with a profound regret. "I regret it every moment, Detectives. The weight of Nevel's death, of the others... it's crushing. I saw the warning signs, I understood the potential for violence, but I chose to look away. I chose to believe that abstract discussions could never lead to such tangible horror. I was wrong. Terribly, unforgivably wrong. He saw himself as a literary arbiter, a dispenser of Dantean judgment. And I, by my silence, became a silent witness to his descent into a very real inferno."

The confession hung in the air, a grim testament to the dangerous intersection of intellectual discourse and volatile human emotion. Gibson's fear was palpable, a raw, exposed nerve. He hadn't pulled the trigger, hadn't wielded the weapon, but he had borne witness to the build-up, had understood the destructive potential, and had chosen inaction. His confession, therefore, was not an absolution, but a deep dive into the complicity that could arise from intellectual detachment and fear. He was not the killer, but he was, undeniably, a man haunted by the knowledge of what was to come and the chilling realization that he could have, perhaps, prevented it. The poet, obsessed with Dante's *Inferno*, had found a willing audience in The Infinite Discourse, and Gibson, the intellectual coward, had become an unwilling spectator to the chilling realization of those deadly debates.

CHAPTER 10
THE ANONYMOUS POET

The weight of Gibson's confession settled over Maria like a shroud. The phantom poet, once a mere whisper in the labyrinthine corridors of The Infinite Discourse, now had a tangible, albeit still shadowy, form. His obsession with Dante, his twisted interpretation of literary justice, Gibson's agonizing admission of intellectual cowardice – it all coalesced into a chilling portrait of a man driven by a potent, dangerous ideology. Maria's gaze, sharp and unyielding, swept across the study, the meticulously organized bookshelves now seeming to hold not just knowledge, but the potential seeds of destruction. Gibson's fear was a tangible thing, a residue of the terror that had kept him silent, but for Maria, it was a testament to the reality of the threat. The 'poet' was no longer a theoretical construct; he was a flesh-and-blood individual capable of translating his literary grievances into brutal, deadly action.

Her mind, however, was already moving beyond Gibson's fractured admissions. The immediate task was to give this anonymous figure a name, a face, a history. Gibson's fear had painted a broad stroke, but Maria needed the fine details, the precise lines that would define the killer. The Discourse, with its coterie of intellectuals, artists, and critics, was a fertile ground for such resentments. Gibson had spoken of a poet "passionate," "devoted to his craft," and feeling "wronged, terribly wronged." This wasn't a dilettante dabbling in verse; this was someone who had poured their soul into their work, only to have it seemingly dismissed or, worse, actively undermined.

Maria pulled out a slim, leather-bound notebook, its pages filled with her precise, elegant script. This was her research bible, a repository of names, dates, and connections that had thus far eluded the official investigation. She began to flip through it, her fingers tracing the meticulously cataloged members of the Aeon Society and The Infinite Discourse, past and present. Gibson's description was a starting point, a beacon in the fog, but it was far too broad. The Society and Discourse, despite its exclusivity, had seen its fair share of aspiring artists, poets included, who had sought validation and found only criticism.

Her focus, Gibson had implied, needed to be on those who had experienced recent setbacks, public criticisms, or a perceived dismissal of their artistic merit. This wasn't about general literary ambition; it was about a festering wound, a deep-seated grievance that had festered to the point of violence. Nevel, Pendelton, Bennett, Bellweather, Underwood – each of them had occupied positions of influence within the literary world, positions that could have made them perceived gatekeepers, arbiters of success or failure for those who dared to present their work.

Maria began to cross-reference. She pulled up a mental index of known Aeon Society and Discourse members who were primarily poets, their names juxtaposed with articles detailing scathing reviews, literary award rejections, or academic dismissals that had made headlines – or at least, whispered controversies within artistic circles. The list was longer than she'd initially anticipated. The world of poetry, Maria knew, was a precarious one, fraught with ego, ambition, and the crushing weight of public opinion. Many poets, by their very nature, were sensitive souls, their work deeply intertwined with their identity. A harsh critique could feel like a personal assassination.

She recalled a recent, rather vitriolic review Nevel had penned of a debut collection by a young poet named Elias Baxter. Baxter, a fervent believer in the avant-garde, had been publicly lambasted by Nevel for what the critic had deemed "pretentious obscurantism masquerading as profundity." The review had been so brutal, so dismissive, that it had effectively derailed Baxter's burgeoning career before it had truly begun. Baxter had been a member of the Aeon Society and the Discourse for a brief period, though he had been expelled after a heated exchange with Nevel during a society debate on the merits of contemporary verse. Gibson had mentioned Nevel's "maliciousness," his tendency to "hoard power," and his habit of "deliberately destroying promising careers." Elias Baxter fit this description disturbingly well.

Then there was the case of Seraphina Bell. A poet of considerable talent, her work had been characterized by its raw emotional intensity and unflinching honesty. She had been considered a rising star until a plagiarism scandal, later proven to be a false accusation orchestrated by a rival, had tarnished her reputation. While she had been publicly cleared, the damage to her career was profound. Maria remembered Pendelton, the victim of murder, had been instrumental in initially championing the false accusation, a fact that had resurfaced in some of the hushed conversations surrounding The Infinite Discourse's internal politics. Seraphina had been a member, albeit briefly, and had resigned citing "untenable pressures." Her name, too, began to resonate with the "wronged" archetype Gibson had described.

Professor Bennett, another victim, had been a fledgling literary critic himself, known for his uncompromising standards. While his reviews were often insightful, they could also be devastatingly harsh. Maria tried to recall if he had any particularly notorious feuds, any individuals whose careers he might have inadvertently, or perhaps deliberately, stifled. It was harder to pinpoint a single, explosive incident with the professor, as his criticisms were often delivered with a more measured, academic tone. However, his influence was undeniable, and his pronouncements could shape the trajectory of a literary career with alarming finality. Gibson's description of the poet as an agent of "cosmic literary balance" suggested someone who wouldn't necessarily target just one critic, but rather those who embodied the perceived flaws of the literary establishment.

Maria's pen began to move with renewed urgency, sketching out a constellation of potential suspects. Elias Baxter and Seraphina Bell were clear frontrunners, their grievances against Nevel and Pendelton respectively being publicly known, or at least widely rumored. But the poet Gibson spoke of wasn't just angry; he was intellectual, philosophical, drawing parallels to Dante's *Inferno*. This suggested a more complex motivation than simple revenge. It implied a belief in a grand, overarching justice, a moral imperative that superseded conventional laws.

She considered the methodology. The Dantean inscription, the careful placement of the bodies, the thematic resonance of each crime scene – these were not the hallmarks of a haphazard killer. This was a meticulous planner, someone who saw their actions as part of a larger, symbolic narrative. The poet, if Gibson's account was accurate, saw himself as a righteous instrument, a dispenser of "true, literary justice." This wasn't just about settling scores; it was about rebalancing a perceived cosmic order.

Maria imagined the poet, perhaps late at night, surrounded by his work, poring over Dante, his mind consumed by a burning sense of injustice. He would have felt the weight of Nevel's dismissive critiques, Pendelton's complicity, the professor's pronouncements, as a personal assault. He would have seen them not merely as men, but as embodiments of a corrupt literary system. And in his twisted worldview, their removal was not murder, but a necessary act of purification, a purging of the literary world.

She returned to Gibson's words: "He felt Nevel was not just critical, but malicious. That he hoarded power, stifling true artistry." This was the core of the poet's perceived grievance. He saw himself as a champion of the downtrodden, the silenced voices, the artists whose potential had been crushed by the gatekeepers of literary power. Maria wondered if this poet had ever felt truly heard, truly validated. Had his own struggles, his own rejections, fueled his resentment and his grand, destructive vision?

The notion of "literary purgatory" and "poetic hell" Gibson mentioned was particularly chilling. It suggested a belief in a spiritual or karmic dimension to literary judgment, a realm where artists were held accountable not just by critics, but by some higher, unforgiving power. The poet, in this framework, saw himself as the earthly manifestation of that power, the one who administered the ultimate sentence.

Maria's thoughts drifted to another poet, a less prominent figure within the Aeon Society, but one who had always struck her as possessing a certain intensity, a simmering resentment beneath a veneer of intellectual detachment. His name was Julian Fox. Fox had published sparingly, but his published works often dealt with themes of betrayal, artistic integrity, and the ephemeral nature of recognition. Gibson hadn't mentioned him specifically, but Fox had been present at many of the Discourse's meetings where literary criticism and artistic merit were passionately debated. He had a reputation for being fiercely protective of his own work and highly critical of what he perceived as mediocrity in others.

Maria recalled reading a particular society meeting minutes, a few years prior, where Nevel had delivered a particularly brutal takedown of a poem that Fox had secretly admired. Fox had remained outwardly stoic, but Gibson had seen a flicker of something dangerous in his eyes – a cold, controlled anger that had unnerved her even then. He had a deep knowledge of classical literature, including Dante, and often quoted obscure passages on justice and retribution. Fox's quiet intensity, his intellectual leanings, and his apparent bitterness made him a compelling, if still unconfirmed, candidate.

The challenge, Maria knew, was to move beyond mere suspicion. Gibson's confession had provided a critical piece of the puzzle, a philosophical underpinning for the killer's actions. But to truly unmask this poet, she needed more than conjecture. She needed evidence, however circumstantial, that would tie him directly to the victims and their deaths.

She decided to delve deeper into the Discourse's archives, not just the membership roles, but also the records of their more informal gatherings, their private correspondences, any minutes or notes that might have been kept by members. Gibson had mentioned that the poet would "discuss these ideas, test them, gauge reactions." It was possible that in his fervent desire for validation, or perhaps in a moment of hubris, he had revealed more than he intended to someone within the society.

Her investigation would need to focus on those who had expressed a particular admiration for classical literature, especially Dante, and who had also suffered significant professional setbacks in the literary world. She would be looking for individuals whose grievances against Nevel, Pendelton, or the professor were deeply personal and who had displayed an almost evangelical zeal for their beliefs about literary justice.

The phantom poet was beginning to solidify. He was no longer just a concept, a philosophical construct. He was an individual, driven by a potent cocktail of artistic ambition, crushing disappointment, and a warped sense of morality. Maria felt a growing certainty that the answer lay not in the grand pronouncements of literary theory, but in the deeply personal wounds of an artist who felt the world had treated him unjustly.

She made a mental note to discreetly inquire about Julian Fox's current whereabouts and his recent activities. She also planned to revisit the details surrounding Elias Baxter and Seraphina Bell, looking for any subtle connections, any shared acquaintances or social circles that might have brought them into contact with the other victims, or with each other. The Discourse, with its insular nature, often fostered complex webs of relationships and rivalries. It was within these tangled threads that the truth, she suspected, was waiting to be found. The anonymity of the poet was a challenge, but not an insurmountable one. Every ghost eventually left a footprint, and Maria was determined to find hers.

She needed to revisit the crime scenes, not just with the eyes of a detective, but with the mind of a literary critic, searching for symbolic meanings, for echoes of the poetic manifestos Gibson had alluded to. The Dantean inscription was a clear starting point, but there might be other subtle clues, other literary references woven into the fabric of the murders themselves. The poet, Gibson had stated, saw the victims as "characters in his own grand narrative of judgment." Maria's task was to decipher that narrative, to understand the poet's personal mythology, and in doing so, to identify the author of this deadly literary critique. The weight of Gibson's confession was heavy, but it had also illuminated the path forward. The anonymous poet was no longer an enigma; he was a target.

Julian Baxter. The name surfaced in Maria's mind with a prickle of recognition, a faint echo from the periphery of her Aeon Society and The Infinite Discourse research. He wasn't a member who had commanded significant attention, a quiet presence rather than a vocal one, yet Gibson's description of a poet consumed by Dante and a burning sense of artistic injustice now coalesced around him with an unsettling clarity. Gibson's confession, particularly his insistence that the killer saw his victims as participants in a literary purgatory, a descent into a personal hell, resonated with Baxter's known preoccupations. Maria recalled his name appearing in the society's membership ledger, a footnote rather than a headline, associated with a small, intensely personal collection of poems that had circulated privately amongst a select few members years ago. His work, she remembered sensing even then, was steeped in a fervent, almost religious, devotion to his craft, interwoven with a palpable resentment towards those he perceived as holding the keys to artistic validation.

Baxter, as Gibson had indirectly alluded to, was not merely a poet; he was a disciple of damnation, a scholar of the infernal. His unpublished manuscripts, whispers of which had reached Maria through various channels within the society's notoriously gossipy circles, were reportedly dense with a dark, almost visceral, exploration of Dante's *Inferno*. The cantos of punishment, the layered circles of torment, were not just literary devices for Baxter; they were theological blueprints, divine architectures of retribution. He saw himself, it seemed, not as a mere wordsmith, but as an acolyte of cosmic justice, a divine arbiter tasked with administering a poetic, and now terrifyingly literal, form of literary purgatory. Maria remembered Gibson's words: "He believed in a true, literary justice. Not the kind dispensed by committees or academy awards, but the kind etched in stone, the kind that separated the divine from the damned." This wasn't the ranting of a failed artist; it was the manifesto of a zealot.

The particular sting for Baxter, Maria now understood, had come from a review. A single, devastating review, penned by one of the very figures now dead, had acted as the catalyst, the accelerant that had ignited his simmering grievances into a conflagration. Gibson had described the poet as being utterly incensed by a critic's dismissal of his work, a review so withering, so absolute, that it had been perceived by the poet as a literal "death sentence" for his literary aspirations. Maria's mind immediately flashed back to a particular incident. A few years prior, Ian Tolley a poet of a different, more boisterous ilk – had been the subject of a notoriously brutal critique penned by Nevel. Nevel, in his typical acid-tongued fashion, had declared Tolley's debut collection "a lamentable exercise in self-indulgent gibberish, utterly devoid of merit or artistic integrity." The review had been published in a prominent literary journal and had effectively shattered Ian Tolley's nascent career. Maria had dismissed it at the time as merely another instance of Nevel's destructive tendencies, a gratuitous act of intellectual sadism. But now, considering Julian Baxter, the description Gibson had provided for the poet's specific grievance – the "death sentence" review – made a chillingly precise connection. It was highly probable that Nevel, the architect of Ian Tolley's professional ruin, was also the author of Julian Baxter's own literary damnation.

Julian Baxter's obsession with Dante wasn't a mere academic interest; it was a framework through which he viewed the world, and more importantly, through which he judged others. His unpublished verses, as pieced together from fragmented accounts and rumors, painted a vivid tapestry of artistic damnation. He had written extensively, not of the gentle cleansing of Purgatory, but of the unyielding, eternal punishments of Hell. The circles of Dante's *Inferno*, for Baxter, were not merely metaphorical constructs; they were topographical maps of a moral universe, where artists who failed to achieve true artistic purity, or worse, those who actively corrupted it, were assigned their rightful, agonizing place. He saw himself as a Dante-like guide, not through the beauty of Paradise, but through the fiery depths of poetic perdition, leading the undeserving to their eternal literary torment.

The victimology, Maria mused, began to crystallize. Nevel, the relentless critic who seemed to revel in dismantling careers, was a clear embodiment of a malicious arbiter of literary fate. His dismissive review of Julian Baxter's work would have been a direct trigger, a profound personal insult that aligned perfectly with Baxter's infernal worldview. Nevel was not merely a critic; in Baxter's eyes, he was a tormentor, a figure who actively pushed artists into the fiery pits of obscurity. His death, Maria theorized, was the poet's first descent into his self-fashioned hell. The inscription on Nevel's body, the grim poetic justice meted out, would have served as Baxter's inaugural pronouncement, a public declaration of his grim creed.

And then there was Pendelton. Maria's prior investigations had revealed Pendelton's less-than-stellar role in the plagiarism accusation against Seraphina Bell. While Bell was eventually cleared, Pendelton had been one of the initial voices amplifying the false claims, adding his weight to the wave of public condemnation that had nearly destroyed her career. Baxter, with his fervent belief in artistic purity and his deep understanding of the devastating consequences of false accusations – how they could irrevocably taint an artist's legacy, casting them into a purgatorial limbo of suspicion – would have viewed Pendelton as a perpetrator of literary sin. Pendelton had actively participated in the destruction of an artist's reputation, a cardinal sin in Baxter's Dantesque cosmology. He was not merely a passive observer; he was an active tormentor, complicit in the 'damnation' of an artist. Maria recalled a particular passage from Baxter's rumored poetry: "The serpent's tongue, though veiled in learned guise, whispers lies that sear the soul, and damn the innocent to silent cries." Pendelton, in Baxter's eyes, was precisely such a serpent.

Professor Bennett, with his unyielding standards and his reputation for crafting devastatingly precise critiques, was a more complex figure in Baxter's infernal hierarchy. While his criticisms might have been intellectually sound, their impact on aspiring artists could have been equally soul-crushing. Baxter, however, seemed to operate on a different plane of judgment. He wasn't necessarily seeking to punish mere harshness; he was targeting those who, in his view, actively corrupted or obstructed the pursuit of true artistic merit. The professor, though his standards were high, was a respected figure, a guardian of literary integrity, albeit a stern one. Baxter might have perceived him not as a direct tormentor, but as a gatekeeper who, through his pronouncements and his influence, dictated who was allowed entry into the hallowed halls of artistic acclaim and who was cast out into the literary wilderness. Perhaps the professor had, at some point, publicly dismissed Baxter's work or denied him access to opportunities, marking him as an outsider, unfit for the esteemed circles Baxter so desperately wished to infiltrate. Gibson's statement that the poet saw his victims as embodying "the decay and corruption of the literary establishment" suggested a broader target than just those who had personally wronged him. The professor, as a prominent figure within that establishment, could have been seen as a symbol of its perceived failings, a figure whose influence contributed to the very decay Baxter so abhorred.

Maria's focus now sharpened on Julian Baxter. Gibson's confession, while providing the philosophical underpinning, had lacked a specific name. But Baxter's documented obsession with Dante, his rumored thematic preoccupations with damnation and retribution, and the chilling parallel between Nevel's review and the "death sentence" Gibson mentioned, all pointed to him with an almost irrefutable gravity. He fit the profile of an artist whose profound sense of grievance had curdled into a dangerous ideology. His unpublished works, if they indeed delved into the infernal punishments of Dante, provided the perfect blueprint for his subsequent actions. He wasn't just killing; he was enacting his own twisted interpretation of divine justice, assigning his victims their appropriate circles of literary hell.

She needed to delve deeper into Baxter's personal history, to unearth the specifics of his perceived slights. Where had Nevel's review been published? What was its precise wording? Had Pendelton's role in Seraphina Bell's ordeal been documented in any official capacity, or was it purely rumor? And the professor – what specific interactions, if any, had he had with Baxter? Maria's research bible, the slim leather-bound notebook, was opened again. She began to meticulously cross-reference Julian Baxter's name against Aeon Society and The Infinite Discourse records, looking for any mention of his presence at events where Nevel or Pendelton might have been speaking, any documented arguments or disagreements, any hint of a personal connection beyond their professional standing.

The Aeon Society and the Discourse, with their labyrinthine social circles and its often-intense intellectual rivalries, was the perfect breeding ground for such resentments. Baxter, a poet who felt his artistic soul had been unjustly condemned, would have perceived these dynamics through the lens of Dante's infernal circles. Nevel's scathing critiques were not mere opinions; they were pronouncements from a high circle of literary judgment, pushing artists into the lower depths. Pendelton's complicity in the plagiarism scandal was an act of betrayal, a descent into the circle of the fraudulent. And the professor, as an arbiter of taste and talent, held a position of immense power, a power that could grant access to heavenly acclaim or condemn one to eternal literary damnation.

Maria envisioned Baxter not as a frenzied killer, but as a methodical artist, meticulously crafting his deadly narrative. Each murder, each placement of the body, each inscription – these were not random acts of violence but carefully orchestrated performances, designed to mirror the punishments of the *Inferno*. He was not just a poet; he was a playwright, a director, and a gruesome executioner, all rolled into one. His unpublished works, filled with themes of artistic retribution and damnation, were more than just literary exercises; they were a chilling premonition, a detailed script of the horrors he intended to unleash. Gibson's confession about the "true, literary justice" and the idea of a "poetic hell" was the key, the Rosetta Stone to understanding Baxter's motivations. He saw himself as a divine instrument, an agent of cosmic literary balance, correcting the perceived injustices of the art world by ushering its offenders into their personal hells.

Her investigation would now pivot, focusing on extracting every scrap of information about Julian Baxter from the Aeon Society and Discourse's archives. She needed to find the specific review that had been the trigger. She needed to understand Pendelton's exact involvement in the Bell scandal. She needed to ascertain any direct or indirect connection between Baxter and the professor. The society's internal records, if they existed, might hold the key. Minutes from meetings, private correspondence, even anecdotal accounts from other members could shed light on Baxter's state of mind, his perceived grievances, and his growing disillusionment. Gibson had mentioned that the poet would "discuss these ideas, test them, gauge reactions." It was plausible that in his fervent, almost evangelistic desire to articulate his vision of literary justice, Baxter had confided in someone or at least revealed enough of his dangerous ideology to be noticed by the more perceptive members of the society.

The figure of Julian Baxter, the anonymous poet who had been lurking in the shadows of Maria's investigation, was rapidly solidifying into a tangible, terrifying presence. His obsession with Dante's *Inferno* was not a mere literary flourish; it was the guiding principle behind a series of brutal murders. His unpublished verses were not just poetry; they were a chilling testament to a mind twisted by perceived injustice, a mind that saw the world as a stage for divine literary retribution. The *Inferno* was no longer just a metaphor; it was a destination, and Julian Baxter was the self-appointed guide, leading his victims into its fiery embrace. The challenge now was to not only identify him but to understand the full scope of his infernal design before he could complete his ghastly descent into literary damnation. Maria felt a cold certainty settling in her gut: Julian Baxter was the poet Gibson had spoken of, and his inferno was just beginning to cast its shadow.

The weight of Julian Baxter's resentment, Maria realized, was far more complex than a simple artist's fury against a dismissive critic. It extended beyond Nevel's acid-laced pen, seeping into the very foundations of the academic institutions Baxter believed had become calcified, ossified, bastions of mediocrity that actively suppressed genuine, soul-stirring art. Gibson's cryptic pronouncements about the poet's perception of victims as embodiments of "decay and corruption of the literary establishment" began to resonate with a chilling clarity. Baxter wasn't just targeting individuals who had personally wronged him;

he was targeting the *system* that had perpetuated their perceived transgressions, the very edifice that had, in his eyes, denied him his rightful place.

The academic world, with its tenure tracks, its peer-review processes, its hallowed journals, and its esteemed professorships, was, to Baxter, a grand, impenetrable fortress, guarded by gatekeepers who prioritized dogma and tradition over true artistic innovation. He saw it not as a fertile ground for creativity, but as a stifling, anechoic chamber where true voices were muted, and mediocre ones were amplified by the very mechanisms designed to uphold quality. This resentment, Maria hypothesized, was not a sudden bloom but a slow, insidious growth, nurtured by years of perceived slights, ignored submissions, and the gnawing understanding that access to the highest echelons of literary validation were often determined by factors other than sheer talent or profound insight.

Clara Bellweather, the murdered student whose name had emerged earlier in Maria's research in connection with Seraphina Bell, now assumed a more prominent, albeit disturbing, role in this evolving narrative. Gibson had alluded to Pendelton's role in the plagiarism accusations against Seraphina, a scandal that had nearly destroyed her career. Maria had initially focused on Pendelton's malicious amplification of the false claims. But the summary provided suggested Clara, a promising doctoral student, might have been seen by Baxter not just as a student, but as a symbol of the academic establishment's favor. Perhaps Clara had been lauded for her work, work that Baxter deemed derivative, or perhaps her association with Seraphina, even tangentially, had placed her in his sights. It was possible Baxter viewed Clara's success, her potential within the academic sphere, as an unfair advantage, a testament to the system's tendency to elevate the connected and the compliant over the truly gifted. He might have seen her as a product of this corrupted order, a young artist groomed and promoted by the very same forces he despised. Gibson's words about the poet seeing his victims as "participants in a literary purgatory" took on a new dimension. Baxter, it seemed, wasn't merely punishing those who had actively harmed artists; he was also punishing those who represented the *status quo* that facilitated such harm. Clara, as a rising star within the academic firmament, could have been perceived by Baxter as one of its gilded ornaments, an emblem of its perceived decay.

The nature of academic validation itself became a focal point of Baxter's imagined inferno. He likely saw academic committees, tenure boards, and prestigious publishing houses not as arbiters of taste but as corrupt tribunals, dispensing their favor based on patronage and adherence to prescribed literary norms rather than on the incandescent spark of true genius. His own unpublished works, rumored to be steeped in Dante's *Inferno*, would have provided him with the perfect allegorical framework for his grievances. The circles of Hell were not merely descriptions of eternal damnation; they were a divine taxonomy of sin, and Baxter, in his warped perception, had identified the cardinal sins of the literary academy: the stifling of originality, the elevation of the mediocre, the silencing of true voices, and the perpetuation of a system that favored established reputations over burgeoning talent.

Dr. Nevel, the critic, remained a primary target, of course, but Maria now understood his role was amplified by his position within this very system. Nevel wasn't just a harsh reviewer; he was a gatekeeper, a judge, a vocal proponent of the established literary order that Baxter so vehemently opposed. His devastating review of Baxter's work was not merely a personal insult; it was a pronouncement from on high, a damning decree from one of the high priests of literary orthodoxy. Nevel's reputation for dissecting and dismissing works that deviated from his perceived standards meant he embodied the very intellectual rigidity Baxter railed against. Maria imagined Baxter poring over Nevel's reviews, seeing in them not just criticism, but a profound betrayal of the artistic spirit, a systematic dismantling of anything that dared to challenge the established canons. Nevel, in Baxter's mind, was actively pushing artists into the lower circles of obscurity, ensuring they were 'damned' by his pronouncements.

The summary's mention of Dr. Nevel as a "scholar of morbid folklore" added another layer of complexity. This suggested Nevel possessed an intimate knowledge of themes of death, damnation, and retribution – themes that Baxter himself had so deeply immersed himself in. It was possible Baxter saw Nevel's expertise not as a shared intellectual interest but as a perversion, a cynical exploitation of darkness for the purpose of literary critique, rather than for genuine artistic exploration. Baxter, who saw himself as a guide through a genuine inferno of artistic suffering, might have viewed Nevel as a charlatan, dissecting the very torments he himself was meant to embody, using his knowledge to inflict pain rather than to illuminate truth. This intellectual proximity, the shared interest in morbid themes, would have only intensified Baxter's resentment, transforming a professional disagreement into a deeply personal philosophical battle, a clash between genuine belief and intellectual opportunism.

The professor's role, while seemingly tangential, now began to coalesce with a disquieting logic. While his critiques might have been intellectually rigorous, his position within the Aeon Society and the Discourse and the broader academic world made him a significant figure. Gibson had described Baxter's victims as embodying "the decay and corruption of the literary establishment." The professor, as a respected elder statesman within that establishment, a figure whose pronouncements held weight, could have been perceived by Baxter as a primary architect of this decay. Perhaps Baxter had sought mentorship or guidance from the professor, only to be met with dismissal or a cold, academic indifference that Baxter interpreted as a deliberate act of exclusion. Or, more chillingly, perhaps the professor, in his pursuit of literary purity, had inadvertently — or perhaps, in Baxter's eyes, deliberately — shut doors that Baxter desperately sought to open. The professor, through his influence and his pronouncements, might have inadvertently positioned himself as a symbol of the academic system's failure to recognize and nurture true artistic merit. Baxter, in his infernal worldview, would have seen him as a key player in the damnation of genuine artists, a figure whose imprimatur, or lack thereof, determined one's fate in the literary afterlife.

Maria's investigation into the Aeon Society and Discourse's archives became a race against time, not just to find evidence but to understand the nuances of Baxter's perceived grievances. She needed to uncover any instances where Baxter might have interacted with the professor, any record of his submissions to journals the professor oversaw, any whispers of critique or dismissal. Gibson's mention of Baxter testing his ideas and gauging reactions became a crucial clue. Had Baxter, in his desperate need for validation, approached members of the Aeon Society and The Infinite Discourse, seeking an audience for his Dantesque visions of literary justice? It was entirely plausible that in his fervor, he had confided in someone or at least revealed enough of his disturbing ideology for discerning members to have taken notice, perhaps dismissing it as the ramblings of an eccentric artist. The society's notorious gossip network, usually a source of trivialities, might now hold the key to understanding the evolution of Baxter's dangerous obsession.

The idea that Baxter saw Clara Bellweather as a symbol of the stagnant academic order was particularly potent. He might have viewed her promising trajectory, her inherent talent, not as a cause for celebration but as evidence of the system's preferential treatment. If Clara's work was indeed lauded, and Baxter perceived it as derivative or lacking true depth, her success would have served as a stark indictment of the academic establishment's compromised judgment. He would have seen her as a pawn, or perhaps even a willing participant, in the perpetuation of a literary order that valued superficial polish over profound artistic truth. This resentment towards Clara, if it existed, would have been rooted not in personal animosity, but in a broader philosophical opposition to the structures that elevated individuals like her, individuals who, in Baxter's distorted view, represented the very corruption he sought to purge.

Maria considered the possibility that Baxter's resentment of the academic system was deeply personal. Perhaps his own artistic journey had been fraught with obstacles, with rejections that felt less like fair criticism and more like outright sabotage. The Aeon

Society and Discourse, with its intricate web of connections and its subtle hierarchies, would have been the perfect battleground for these perceived injustices. He might have witnessed firsthand how academic prestige, rather than artistic merit, opened doors, how established scholars like the professor could wield immense power, shaping careers with a word, a nod, or a dismissive gesture. Nevel, as a prominent critic, would have been the embodiment of this gatekeeping power, his reviews acting as pronouncements of artistic salvation or damnation.

The phrase "morbid folklore" applied to Nevel struck Maria. It suggested a fascination with the darker aspects of human experience, a subject matter Baxter himself had embraced with such intensity. Yet, if Nevel used this knowledge to dissect and dismiss, rather than to explore and understand, Baxter would have seen it as a profound betrayal. It was as if a priest of damnation had turned his sacred texts into tools for excommunication. Baxter, who saw his own Dantesque journey as a path to true understanding of literary justice, would have viewed Nevel's academic exploration of morbid themes as a cynical, self-serving endeavor, devoid of the genuine spiritual and artistic weight Baxter ascribed to it. This intellectual appropriation, this academic dissection of the very darkness Baxter inhabited, would have festered, turning a scholarly divergence into a personal war. Baxter's resentment wasn't just about being criticized; it was about the perceived hypocrisy of a scholar of darkness who wielded his knowledge as a weapon against those who truly lived and breathed its artistic essence. Baxter, in his twisted logic, was simply carrying out the divine retribution that Nevel, the scholar of morbid folklore, should have understood and respected.

The revelation of Julian Baxter's former membership in the Aeon Society and The Infinite Discourse sent a tremor through Maria's carefully constructed theories. It wasn't just a tangential connection; it was a foundational one. Gibson's cryptic hints, Baxter's obsession with literary judgment, his Dantesque framing of artistic damnation – it all began to coalesce around this enigmatic society. Maria imagined Baxter, years ago, perhaps a younger, more hopeful artist, seeking intellectual kinship within the Aeon Society and the Discourse's hallowed, or perhaps unhallowed, halls. He had likely found kindred spirits, individuals who shared his fascination with the darker, more profound aspects of existence, and critically, the narrative power of death. The societies, with its inherent focus on arcane knowledge and perhaps a certain intellectual indulgence in the macabre, would have been fertile ground for Baxter's burgeoning philosophical landscape.

Gibson, as a more established member, would have been a key figure in Baxter's early interactions. Maria could picture them engaged in late-night debates, the air thick with cigar smoke and the scent of aging paper, dissecting the very nature of finality. Baxter, with his youthful fire and his conviction that death was the ultimate authorial statement, would have found an eager, perhaps even an encouraging, audience in Gibson and others like him. They wouldn't have dismissed his morbid inclinations as the fevered dreams of an amateur; instead, they would have likely amplified them, fanning the flames of his intellectual obsessions, perhaps even validating his increasingly radical interpretations of art and its ultimate purpose. The societies, in its pursuit of intellectual depth, might have inadvertently provided Baxter with the very framework he needed to rationalize his later descent into vigilantism. They had, perhaps, given him the language, the philosophical scaffolding, to construct his inferno.

However, the synopsis also hinted at disillusionment. Baxter had left the Aeon Society and The Infinite Discourse, a departure that suggested a schism, a fundamental disagreement or a growing divergence in their shared morbid ideals. What could have caused such a break? Had Baxter's interpretations become too extreme, too literal, for even the self-proclaimed custodians of literary darkness? Or had he, upon leaving, felt betrayed by the very societies that had initially nurtured his dark muse? Perhaps the society, while reveling in the abstract contemplation of death as a narrative device, had balked at Baxter's increasingly concrete applications of this philosophy. They might have been content to discuss damnation in theory, but Baxter, it seemed, was intent on enacting it in practice. This separation, this severing of ties, would have undoubtedly fueled his resentment, transforming intellectual disagreement into a perceived betrayal of the highest order. He had likely felt that the societies, having taught him the power of the ending, had then abandoned him when he sought to truly wield that power.

Maria speculated that Baxter's departure from the societies wasn't a complete severing of his philosophical roots, but rather a redirection. He hadn't abandoned the societies darker tenets; he had internalized them, perhaps twisted them further, and made them his own. The members he left behind, the Gibson's and others, would have become, in his eyes, either complicit in his original disillusionment or, worse, outright hypocrites. They continued to philosophize about death's narrative climax while he was the one who had the courage, the conviction, to bring it to its ultimate conclusion for those he deemed worthy of poetic justice. The archives, Maria realized, were not just a repository of academic texts; they were a potential record of Baxter's intellectual genesis, the very crucible where his dark artistic philosophy had been forged. She needed to find records of his membership, his discussions, his departure, and critically, any evidence that he had continued to draw inspiration from the society's darker tenets even after his official estrangement. This connection to the Aeon Society and the Discourse was not merely a historical footnote; it was, Maria suspected, the very engine driving Baxter's meticulously orchestrated reign of terror.

The summary's mention of Gibson's role in fueling Baxter's philosophical discussions was particularly significant. Gibson, as a known figure within the Aeon Society and Discourse and now a subject of Maria's investigation, was no mere bystander. He had been a participant, perhaps even an instigator, in the creation of Baxter's artistic worldview. Maria envisioned Gibson as someone who thrived on intellectual provocation, a seasoned debater who found a certain intellectual thrill in exploring the boundaries of human experience, particularly its darker aspects. For Baxter, a younger artist grappling with profound existential questions and a burning desire for his work to possess ultimate meaning, Gibson's intellectual gravity would have been immensely appealing. Gibson, in turn, might have seen in Baxter a vessel for his own explorations, a willing student upon whom he could imprint his morbid ideals, perhaps without fully comprehending the trajectory Baxter's mind would ultimately take.

Their discussions, Maria inferred, were not mere academic exercises. They were likely passionate, deeply personal dialogues where the abstract concepts of death and narrative finality were imbued with a tangible, almost visceral, power. Baxter would have absorbed Gibson's pronouncements not as theoretical musings but as profound truths, as guiding principles for his own artistic and, as it turned out, his literal interpretations. Gibson's validation, however unintentional, would have provided Baxter with a crucial layer of intellectual reinforcement. It was one thing to hold such radical beliefs in isolation; it was quite another to have them echoed and amplified by a respected figure within a society dedicated to exploring such themes. This symbiotic relationship, born in the intellectual ferment of the Society's, had laid the groundwork for Baxter's later actions. Gibson's intellectual fire had, perhaps, ignited a spark that would eventually consume so many.

The fact that Baxter had left both society's years ago, "disillusioned but not entirely departed from its morbid ideals," spoke volumes. This wasn't a clean break; it was an acrimonious divorce where Baxter, still holding onto the shared beliefs, felt wronged by the very institution that had helped shape him. Maria pondered the nature of this disillusionment. Had the society's, in its academic detachment, failed to grasp the urgency Baxter felt in applying their shared philosophies? Had they remained content with theoretical debates while Baxter saw the world as ripe for a more dramatic, a more definitive, resolution? Perhaps Baxter had presented his more extreme ideas to the society, seeking their approval or endorsement, only to be met with polite dismissal or outright condemnation. Such a rejection, from a group he had once considered his intellectual kin, would have been a bitter pill to swallow, transforming his admiration into a deep-seated resentment. He likely saw their subsequent aversion to his more radical interpretations as a sign of their cowardice, their inability to follow their own logic to its inevitable conclusion.

His continued adherence to their "morbid ideals" suggested a stubbornness, a refusal to abandon the philosophical framework that had become so integral to his identity. Even after leaving, he would have continued to draw upon the society's tenets, reinterpreting them through the lens of his perceived injustices. The Aeon Society and The Discourse, in Baxter's mind, might have transformed from a source of intellectual inspiration to a symbol of betrayal. He could have viewed its members, including Gibson, as individuals who had preached about the beauty of the ultimate ending but had shied away from the messy, the dangerous, the truly artistic act of bringing it about. This perceived hypocrisy would have only solidified his resolve, cementing his belief that he, and he alone, was the true custodian of their shared dark legacy. Maria felt a cold certainty growing within her: the Societies were not merely a chapter in Baxter's past; it was a lingering, malignant influence, a ghost that continued to haunt his every act. The archives were her only hope of tracing the tendrils of that influence, of understanding how theoretical darkness had manifested into such brutal, tangible reality.

The chill in the air wasn't just the creeping October dampness; it was the bone-deep realization that had settled over Maria. Julian Baxter. The name echoed in the sterile quiet of Gibson's study, a phantom limb of their shared obsession now throbbing with a terrifying clarity. It wasn't just a theory anymore, not a loose thread; it was the knot at the center of the tapestry of murders. Baxter, the esteemed literary critic, the poet with a penchant for the macabre, the man whose intellect Gibson had so readily praised – he was the killer. The Societies, once a whisper of intellectual circles, now loomed large, not as a historical footnote but as the crucible that had forged this monstrous present. Baxter's departure, his "disillusionment but not entirely departed from its morbid ideals," was the key. He hadn't rejected their philosophy; he had weaponized it. He had taken the abstract contemplation of death as the ultimate narrative climax and, with chilling precision, begun to write his own bloody testament.

"He's not just quoting Dante; he's living him," Maria murmured, the words tasting like ash. She traced the rim of her teacup, the porcelain cool against her fingertips. The meticulously crafted poems left at each crime scene, the Dantesque allusions, the very framing of the victims as characters deserving of poetic justice – it all pointed to Baxter. His intellectual vanity, his conviction in his own superior understanding of literature, would have been precisely what Gibson had recognized, what the Aeon Society and The Infinite Discourse had nurtured. They had taught him to see the narrative power of death, and Baxter, in his warped vision, had decided to become the author.

Dr. Gibson, his face a mask of grim contemplation, nodded slowly. The realization had clearly dawned on him as well, a slow, agonizing dawning that mirrored Maria's own. "His ego. It's always been his Achilles' heel, and his greatest strength. He believes himself to be an arbiter of taste, a judge of literary merit, even when the 'work' is... life and death." He paused, his gaze distant, perhaps reliving past intellectual sparring matches with Baxter. "He saw their departure from the Aeon Society and Discourse not as a philosophical divergence, but as a betrayal. They preached the power of the final word, the ultimate ending, and then they recoiled when he chose to provide it, to enact it, for those he deemed unworthy of further prose."

Maria leaned forward, a spark of fierce determination igniting within her. "Then we use that. We use his ego against him. If he believes himself to be the ultimate literary authority, we challenge him. We force him to prove it." The idea began to take shape, a dangerous, intricate plan born from the ashes of their fear. They couldn't confront Baxter directly; he was too cunning, too dangerous. He would see it coming, anticipate their moves, and likely turn it back on them, another macabre plot twist in his unfolding tragedy. But a public intellectual challenge? That might be enough to draw him out of the shadows.

"A literary journal," Maria proposed, her voice gaining strength. "Something that caters to his world, his intellectual circles. The campus journal is too small, too insignificant. We need something with reach, something that would catch his eye, something that would make him feel... seen. And challenged."

Gibson considered it, stroking his chin. "The 'Literary Quarterly' is still highly regarded, though its readership has dwindled in recent years. Still, Baxter likely still scans its pages, looking for intellectual slights, for evidence of mediocrity he can dissect. If we were to publish something... something about Dante, about the very nature of literary judgment and damnation..."

"Precisely, a challenge per se." Donny interjected.

Maria nodded, her mind racing. "We write an analysis, not of his poetry, but of *our* interpretation of his 'work.' We dissect the killer's motifs, the literary allusions, but we frame it as a study of a hypothetical artist, an artist obsessed with Dante, with the concept of artistic damnation. We praise the *idea* of it, the boldness, the intellectual rigor, but we subtly critique the execution, the... amateurishness, perhaps, of applying such lofty ideals to such base acts. We imply that only a true master, someone with Baxter's intellect, could truly pull off such a grand, philosophical statement."

Gibson's eyes narrowed, a flicker of excitement mixing with the grim resolve. "We need to tread a fine line. We praise enough to pique his interest, to make him feel his brilliance is being recognized, but we critique enough to ignite his fury. He cannot tolerate perceived ignorance of his artistic vision. He'll feel compelled to correct us, to demonstrate his superior understanding."

"What do you think, we could frame it as a debate?" Donny offered.

Maria nodded. "Exactly." She continued, the plan solidifying. "A scholarly inquiry into the mind of a contemporary artist who employs classical themes. We'll highlight the Dantean parallels, the inferred moral judgments, the almost divine sense of justice he appears to wield. But then, we'll introduce a counter-argument. We'll suggest that perhaps this artist, in his zeal, is missing the deeper allegorical significance of Dante's journey. That true literary damnation isn't about punishment, but about the eternal, internal struggle. We can posit that the artist's current interpretation is... simplistic. Flawed. An insult to the very masters he purports to emulate."

The risk was immense. Publishing such an analysis, even under a pseudonym, could be seen as interfering with the police investigation. But the police were no closer to catching the killer than they had been months ago. The evidence was circumstantial, the motives buried deep within a killer's psyche. This was their only chance to flush Baxter out, to force his hand.

"We'll need a pseudonym," Gibson stated, his voice low and steady. "Something academic, yet unremarkable. Perhaps a 'Dr. Terance Stevens' or a 'Professor Lori Bart' – no, too close. A 'Dr. Lionel York.'"

Maria chuckled, a dry, humorless sound. "Lionel York. I like it. It sounds... pedantic. Perfect for someone who would dare to critique Julian Baxter." She pictured Baxter receiving the journal, his eyes scanning the pages, his brow furrowing as he encountered the article. She could almost see the spark of recognition, followed by the slow burn of indignation. He wouldn't be able to let it go. He would need to respond. He would need to show the world, and more importantly, show them, that he was the true interpreter of literary damnation.

They spent the next few days meticulously crafting the article. It was a delicate dance of intellectual flattery and subtle insult. They dissected Baxter's perceived methods, referencing specific elements of the crime scenes as if they were deliberate artistic choices. They spoke of the "poetic justice" as a brilliant, albeit crude, reinterpretation of Dante's infernal hierarchies. They even acknowledged the intellectual courage it must have taken for an artist to imbue their work with such profound thematic weight, especially in a world that had, in their fabricated analysis, largely forgotten the true meaning of artistic legacy.

"We are acknowledging his intellect," Maria explained as they debated a particular turn of phrase, "but we are questioning his depth. We are suggesting that he understands the *mechanics* of damnation, but not its *soul*. That he is a technician of terror, not a true artist of the abyss."

Gibson provided the scholarly framework, weaving in obscure Dantean commentaries and theories on literary criticism. Maria infused it with a sharp, incisive voice, a voice that dared to question the very foundations of Baxter's warped philosophy. They debated sentence structure, word choice, the precise nuance of every critique. Each word was a carefully placed stone, building not a bridge, but a carefully constructed trap.

“We need to make it undeniable that we are speaking *about* him, without ever naming him,” Gibson stressed, his brow furrowed in concentration. “The references must be too precise, too pointed, for him to ignore. The analysis of the victims' perceived transgressions, the poetic structure of the murders, the symbolism of the final gestures – it all has to scream Baxter without uttering his name.”

Maria nodded, her gaze fixed on the laptop screen. “And when he responds, when he inevitably publishes his own defense, or perhaps even sends us a private, furious missive, we will have him. He will have revealed his hand. He will have placed himself squarely within the narrative he created, a narrative we will then use to expose him.”

The concept of "artistic damnation" was central to their strategy. They would define it not as external punishment, but as an internal, eternal torment. They would argue that true literary damnation was the artist's inability to escape their own creations, the haunting realization of their own limitations, the inescapable shadow of their own darkness. This, they would posit, was the ultimate fate of an artist who wielded such power without true understanding. It was a critique designed to strike at the very core of Baxter's perceived superiority.

"He sees himself as a conductor of fates," Maria mused, tapping a pen against her chin. "He believes he is orchestrating the final acts of these individuals, bringing them to a divinely ordained conclusion. We need to suggest that the true Dantean hell is not a place of external torment, but the eternal awareness of one's own failure to achieve true artistic enlightenment. He is trapped not by divine judgment, but by his own limited understanding of it."

Gibson added, "We can frame it as a historical debate. How scholars have interpreted Dante's vision of hell. Some see it as literal punishment, others as metaphorical. We will champion the metaphorical interpretation, arguing that the true 'damnation' lies in the artist's eternal struggle with meaning, with the inability to transcend their own limitations. We will suggest that any artist who seeks to inflict 'justice' through literal death is, in fact, demonstrating their own profound failure to grasp the deeper artistic truths."

The plan was a gamble, a high-stakes intellectual duel where the lives of potential future victims hung in the balance. But the alternative was to wait, to let Baxter continue his deadly performance, to watch as he meticulously crafted each new tragedy. They had to act. They had to set the trap, baited with the very thing Baxter cherished most: the power of words, and the unassailable authority of his own perceived literary genius.

The final draft of the article was sent to the 'Literary Quarterly' under the pseudonym Dr. Lionel York, a professor of comparative literature at a small, obscure university in southern Virginia. Maria, Donny, and Gibson waited, the silence in Gibson's study now humming with a nervous anticipation. Every rustle of paper, every distant siren, sent a jolt through Maria. She knew, with a chilling certainty, that Julian Baxter would read it. And he would respond. The trap was set. The stage was, in a perverse way, being prepared for the final act. The anonymous poet was about to be drawn into a literary confrontation, one that, they hoped, would lead to his ultimate downfall. The ink on their article was barely dry, but it represented their most dangerous gambit yet, a desperate attempt to use Baxter's own weapon – his intellect, his ego, his twisted understanding of art and death – against him. They were playing his game, but with rules he would never anticipate, in an arena he believed was entirely his own.

CHAPTER 11

THE FINAL ACT'S OVERTURE

The glossy pages of the *Elmwood Literary Review* felt deceptively inert as Maria slid them from the padded envelope. Each crisp sheet was a potential spark; a carefully crafted ember tossed into the tinderbox of Julian Baxter's ego. The article, bearing the innocuous pseudonym Dr. Lionel York, was their meticulously constructed bait. It wasn't a direct accusation, no clumsy hand pointing fingers at a shadowed killer. Instead, it was a sophisticated intellectual probe, designed to dissect and re-interpret, to poke at the very philosophical underpinnings Baxter so proudly championed. Their target: his warped understanding of Dante's *Inferno* and the chilling notion of poetic justice he had so brutally enacted.

The review, chosen for its respectable, if somewhat provincial, academic standing, was Gibson's suggestion. It catered to the very intellectual circles Baxter frequented, a space where reputations were forged and broken with the sharpest of scalpels. The editors, blessedly oblivious to the deadly currents beneath the surface, had accepted their piece with surprising alacrity. "A bold, if somewhat contrarian, reading of the *Inferno*'s moral architecture," one of them had written in their acceptance email, a sentence that now sent a shiver of morbid amusement down Maria's spine. Contrarian indeed.

They had meticulously woven their argument, each sentence a tightrope walk between scholarly admiration and veiled criticism. The core of their critique centered on the very concept of *poetic justice*. Baxter, in his hubris, saw himself as an agent of a higher, literary form of retribution, doling out punishments that mirrored the perceived sins of his victims. He believed himself to be the ultimate arbiter, a modern-day Virgil guiding souls through a personal inferno of his own design. But Maria, Donny, and Gibson argued for a more nuanced, a more *human*, interpretation. They posited that Dante's vision wasn't about the external infliction of suffering, but about the internal, eternal torment of the sinner's own consciousness, their inability to escape the consequences of their choices, the gnawing regret that became their unending hell.

"We're not just questioning his application of Dante," Donny explained during one of their late-night drafting sessions, the glow of the laptop screen illuminating their grim determination. "We're challenging the very notion that an artist, any artist, has the right or the capacity to mete out literal judgment."

"The true power of art, we argue, lies not in imitation of divine or infernal justice, but more in its ability to illuminate the human condition, to explore the complexities of morality and consequence without pretending to be judge, jury, and executioner." Maria offered.

Gibson, his brow furrowed as he reread a particularly scathing paragraph, had nodded slowly. "We're framing it as a scholarly debate on the evolution of critical thought regarding Dante's hell. We acknowledge the historical interpretations that lean towards external punishment, but we firmly advocate for the psycho-philosophical reading. We suggest that any artist who attempts to impose their will as a form of cosmic retribution is, in fact, demonstrating a profound misunderstanding of the very masters they claim to emulate. It's an indictment of their own limitations, their own descent into a personal, self-imposed purgatory of their own making."

The article subtly referenced the "poetic structure" of the perceived crimes, the "thematic resonance" of the victimology, the "symbolic gestures" that accompanied each death. These were not direct allusions to Baxter, but they were specific enough, detailed enough, to resonate with someone intimately familiar with the inner workings of his twisted mind. They had described the killer as an "artist of damnation," a phrase designed to simultaneously flatter and condemn. They spoke of his "audacious ambition" to re-craft the *Inferno* for a modern audience, a feat that required not just intellect, but a profound understanding of the human soul – an understanding, they implied, that this hypothetical artist was still striving to achieve.

Maria found herself rereading the section that dissected the supposed "poetic justice" meted out to the disgraced financier. They had argued that the killer's choice to frame the victim's demise as a symbolic representation of greed, while intellectually stimulating, ultimately failed to capture the true essence of Dante's hell. "The financier's alleged transgressions, while undeniably reprehensible, are treated by this contemporary 'artist of damnation' with a crude, almost didactic literalism," the article read. "The true infernal torment, as envisioned by Dante, is not the outward manifestation of punishment, but the internal, inescapable awareness of one's own moral corruption, the eternal gnawing of guilt that corrodes the soul from within. To simply enact a symbolic death, however artfully conceived, is to miss the profound psychological and existential depth of Dante's vision. It is, in essence, an artistically superficial application of profound themes."

She imagined Baxter encountering this very passage. She pictured him pausing, his sharp eyes narrowing as he processed the words, the initial flicker of intellectual curiosity hardening into a slow-burning fury. They had deliberately avoided any mention of violence or specific murders, focusing solely on the literary and philosophical interpretations. This was crucial. A direct confrontation, or even an overt suggestion of their suspicions, would alert him, send him deeper into hiding. But an intellectual challenge? That was something he couldn't ignore. His ego, as Gibson had noted, was his greatest weakness. He craved recognition, validation, and above all, the undisputed authority of his literary pronouncements.

"We're not just attacking his interpretation; we're questioning his artistic merit," Gibson had observed, his voice resonating with a grim satisfaction. "We're suggesting that while his ideas might be bold, his execution is ultimately lacking. That he's a student who hasn't yet mastered the curriculum, a poet who has the vocabulary but not the soul. He'll feel compelled to defend his genius, to prove us wrong, to demonstrate that he is, in fact, the master interpreter of damnation he believes himself to be."

The *Elmwood Literary Review* was now a tangible symbol of their strategy. The campus, a hothouse of intellectual discourse and gossip, would be abuzz. Theories would circulate, discussions would ignite in hushed corners of the library and in the smoky haze of the student union. Baxter, accustomed to being lauded as a luminary, would inevitably seek out any critique, any discussion of his rarefied intellectual pursuits. And when he found Dr. Lionel York's article, Maria was certain he would see it for what it was: a carefully laid trap, baited with the very essence of his vanity.

The risk, of course, was immense. They were dabbling in the murky waters of police investigations, drawing undue attention to themselves by engaging in a public intellectual debate that so closely mirrored the ongoing case. But the official channels were yielding nothing. The killer remained a ghost; his motives shrouded in poetry and shadows. This was their gamble, their desperate attempt to lure him out of the darkness and into the harsh light of scrutiny. They were not merely seeking to catch a killer; they were seeking to expose the perverted artistry he championed, to dismantle the narrative he so meticulously constructed.

Maria traced the outline of the magazine's logo. The Elmwood. A quiet, unassuming name for a publication that now carried the weight of their most audacious plan. She imagined Baxter, perhaps in his elegantly appointed study, surrounded by first editions and leather-bound tomes, his brow furrowed as he read. She could almost hear the sharp intake of breath, the almost imperceptible clench of his jaw. They had not only challenged his intellect; they had challenged his very identity as a literary authority. They had dared to suggest that his understanding of Dante, the very bedrock of his twisted philosophy, was flawed, incomplete, even amateurish.

"The next step," Gibson had said, his voice barely a whisper, when they had finally agreed the article was ready, "is to wait. To let the seed of doubt, of indignation take root. He will want to respond. He will feel the need to correct the record, to reassert his dominance. And when he does, he will have placed himself directly into our narrative."

The waiting was the hardest part. It was a form of suspended animation, where every passing hour felt charged with an unspoken tension. The campus, once a familiar landscape, now seemed imbued with a new, unsettling significance. Every student, every professor, every passing stranger could potentially be a witness, an unwitting participant in their intricate drama. They had laid the bait, meticulously prepared and expertly disguised. Now, all they could do was watch, and wait for the predator to take the hook. The overture was complete. The stage was set, not for a play, but for a desperate, dangerous game of literary chess, with the very real stakes of life and death. The *Elmwood Literary Review*, in its quiet way, had become the overture to their final act, a prelude to the confrontation they both dreaded and desperately sought. Baxter, the architect of death cloaked in poetic grandeur, was about to be drawn into a debate he couldn't win, a debate where his own words, his own intellect, would be used as the instruments of his undoing. They had weaponized his ego, armed him with a righteous fury, and now they waited for him to draw his own sword. The silence that followed the article's publication was not empty; it was pregnant with anticipation, a coiled spring waiting for the inevitable release. Maria knew, with a certainty that chilled her to the bone, that Julian Baxter would read their words. And he would respond. The bait had been laid.

The silence that had enveloped the campus since the *Elmwood Literary Review* hit the newsstands was beginning to fray. Maria felt it most keenly in the hushed conversations that buzzed around her, the subtle glances that lingered a moment too long. The article,

The Infernal Mirror: A Reconsideration of Poetic Justice, penned under the moniker Dr. Lionel York, was doing its work. It wasn't a shouted accusation, but a precisely placed whisper, designed to echo in the chambers of a specific, arrogant mind. Gibson had been right; Baxter wouldn't ignore a perceived intellectual slight, not from an unknown entity in a publication he likely deemed beneath him, yet one that dared to question his interpretations of Dante.

The first missive arrived not by email, or through the usual academic channels, but as a crisp, cream-colored envelope hand-delivered to the *Review*'s editorial office. Maria, alerted by a nervous junior editor who recognized the unusual delivery method, intercepted it. The return address was a post office box, deliberately nondescript. Inside, the letter was a masterclass in controlled indignation, a scalpel disguised as a pen. The author, writing as a concerned reader, expressed "profound disappointment" with Dr. York's "simplistic and frankly pedestrian analysis" of Dante's *Inferno*.

"While Dr. York's attempt to engage with the profound moral architecture of Dante's vision is commendable in its youthful ambition," the letter began, the ink a deep, almost aggressive black, "his conclusions betray a fundamental misunderstanding of the punitive arts. To reduce the divine and infernal retribution to mere 'internal torment' is to strip it of its very essence: the visceral, tangible consequence of sin. Dante, a poet of unparalleled insight, did not merely observe the sinner's regret; he engineered a cosmic theater of pain, a meticulously crafted inferno where each torment was a perfect, damning reflection of the earthly failing."

Maria read the passage aloud to Gibson in the hushed sanctuary of his office, the only sound the rustle of the paper and the distant hum of the campus. “He’s defending it,” she murmured, a thrill of grim satisfaction coursing through her. “He’s not just defending it; he’s doubling down on his belief that he’s some kind of divine arbiter.”

Gibson leaned back, his expression unreadable for a moment. “It’s a beautifully crafted piece of misdirection, isn’t it? He’s so focused on proving York wrong that he’s oblivious to the fact that York’s arguments are *our* arguments. He’s arguing against himself, Maria, and he doesn’t even know it.”

The letter continued, weaving through labyrinthine discussions of Aquinas, of medieval allegorical traditions, of obscure Florentine commentaries on the *Commedia*. It was laced with references so recondite, so steeped in Baxter’s particular brand of esoteric scholarship, that they were virtually a signature. He didn’t name himself, of course. That would be too obvious, too crude for someone who saw himself as a Composer of subtle implication. Instead, he alluded to "certain scholars of discerning taste" who understood the "true artistry" of poetic justice, those who recognized that "the divine symphony of damnation requires not just thematic resonance, but a conductor who understands the score."

“A conductor,” Maria repeated, a faint smile touching her lips. “He sees himself as the conductor of hell.”

Another letter arrived a week later, this one addressed to the editor of the *Elmwood Literary Review* directly, again with a P.O. box for return. This one was more aggressive, the prose sharper, the tone more overtly dismissive of Dr. York’s “philosophical naivety.” Baxter, writing under a different, equally obscure pseudonym –

this time, "A Disappointed Classicist" – accused York of succumbing to a "modern, sentimentalist interpretation of eternal justice," one that prioritized psychological introspection over the stark, unvarnished truth of divine retribution.

"Dante's genius," the second letter asserted, "lies in his unflinching portrayal of a universe where actions have inescapable, eternal repercussions. His circles of hell are not mere metaphors for inner turmoil, but meticulously constructed realities of suffering, each perfectly calibrated to the transgression. To suggest otherwise is to demote Dante from cosmic architect to a mere moralizing poet, a dangerous oversimplification that robs the *Inferno* of its power and its terrifying truth. Dr. York's article, while perhaps well-intentioned, ultimately serves only to dilute the potency of Dante's masterwork, rendering it a quaint study in existential angst rather than the profound testament to divine judgment that it truly is."

Maria could almost feel Baxter's pulse quicken as he penned these words. He was a man who craved intellectual dominion, who felt a primal need to correct what he perceived as ignorance or misinterpretation. And here was Dr. Lionel York, an unknown quantity, presuming to lecture *him* on Dante. The injustice, in Baxter's mind, would have been palpable.

"He's using the language we used in the article against us," Gibson observed, a glint of admiration for Baxter's cunning in his eyes. "He's picking apart our arguments, twisting them back, making it seem as if York is the one who's misunderstanding Dante, when in fact, Baxter is demonstrating his own flawed understanding by his insistence on a literal, externalized punishment."

The letters continued to arrive, a steady stream of intellectual ammunition fired in defense of his deeply held, and deeply dangerous, ideology. Each one was a meticulous dissection of Dr. York's points, a public performance of Baxter's supposed superior intellect. He would quote passages of Dante, intersperse them with critiques of philosophical concepts, and pepper his arguments with the names of long-dead theologians and literary critics, all in an effort to establish his own unimpeachable authority. He never strayed into overt threats or personal insults, maintaining an air of academic detachment that only made his underlying fury more potent. This was his arena, his battlefield, and he fought with the precision of a seasoned scholar and the conviction of a zealot.

Maria meticulously cataloged each letter, noting the paper stock, the ink, the precise phrasing. She recognized the vocabulary, the intricate sentence structures, the subtle shifts in tone that hinted at a deeply ingrained sense of superiority. It was the same voice she'd encountered in Baxter's published lectures, in the footnotes of his obscure essays, the same intellectual arrogance that permeated his every public utterance. He was painting himself into a corner, a corner where his defense of his own interpretation of Dante was becoming a public spectacle.

"He's showing us exactly how he sees himself," Maria remarked, tapping a finger on a particularly verbose paragraph in the latest letter. "He's not just defending Dante; he's defending his own right to interpret and, by extension, his own actions. He believes he's enacting a form of superior justice, a literary retribution that transcends mundane morality. And he's so confident in his own intellectual prowess that he's willing to engage in this public debate, not realizing he's walking directly into our trap."

Gibson agreed. "His ego demands it. Dr. York has challenged his core beliefs, his very identity as a literary authority. Baxter cannot let that stand. He sees himself as the guardian of Dante's true meaning, and York has dared to trespass. His response is not just about defending his interpretation; it's about reasserting his dominance, about proving to himself, and to anyone who might be reading, that he is the true arbiter of infernal meaning."

The letters, while seemingly focused on literary exegesis, were filled with subtle nods to Baxter's perceived role. He spoke of the "artist of damnation" as a figure who understood the "necessary balance" between sin and suffering, a figure who possessed the "vision to orchestrate true justice." He lamented that critics like York lacked the "courage" to embrace the "unflinching realities of cosmic consequence," suggesting that such timidity was a symptom of a decaying moral compass.

Maria focused on a particular passage in a letter signed "A Scholar of the *Inferno*." It read: "The true measure of poetic justice is not its allegorical neatness, but its profound, terrifying efficacy. It is the mirror held up to the sinner's soul, reflecting not just their crime, but the eternal damnation they have irrevocably earned. Any less is a disservice to the gravity of sin and the perfection of divine retribution. The artist who understands this is not a judge, but a divine instrument, wielding truth with a steady, unwavering hand."

"A divine instrument," she whispered, her voice tight with a mixture of dread and exhilaration. "That's it. That's exactly how he sees himself. He truly believes he's divinely appointed to dispense this twisted form of justice."

The anonymity of the pseudonyms was a deliberate choice, a calculated move by Baxter to preserve his academic standing while still engaging in what he clearly felt was a vital intellectual battle. He likely assumed that by using such arcane and seemingly detached guises, he could engage in this debate without compromising his public persona. But for Maria and Gibson, these letters were more valuable than any direct confession. They were a detailed, albeit unintended, blueprint of Baxter's mind, revealing not only his obsession with Dante and poetic justice but also his profound self-delusion. He was so convinced of his own intellectual superiority that he couldn't conceive of being outmaneuvered, or that his carefully crafted arguments could be a reflection of his own guilt.

Maria and Donny began cross-referencing the obscure references in Baxter's letters with passages from his published works, searching for overlaps, for unique turns of phrase that could serve as a digital fingerprint. She was looking for the tell-tale signs, the linguistic DNA that would confirm their suspicions beyond a shadow of a doubt. The more he wrote, the more he exposed himself, the more he solidified their case, not just against his literary interpretations, but against him as a suspect.

The letters painted a picture of a man utterly consumed by his own twisted philosophy. He was not merely an academic; he was a proselytizer, eager to defend his doctrine of poetic justice against any perceived dissent. His arguments, while intellectually sophisticated, were devoid of genuine empathy, steeped in a cold, detached view of human suffering. He saw people not as individuals with complex lives and motivations, but as characters in a grand cosmic play, their fates predetermined by their sins and their punishments meticulously scripted by an unseen hand.

"He's trying to educate York, to bring him back into the fold of true understanding," Gibson mused, scanning a particularly lengthy missive. "He genuinely believes he's doing the world a service by correcting this 'misinterpretation.' The irony is, he's only digging his own grave, literarily speaking."

Maria found herself re-reading the article in the *Elmwood Literary Review* again, this time through Baxter's eyes. She imagined him poring over it, his initial annoyance escalating to a righteous fury. He saw Dr. Lionel York not as a fellow scholar, but as an adversary, an interloper who dared to question his mastery. The subtle criticisms, the veiled suggestions of artistic deficiency, had struck a nerve. He felt compelled to defend his genius, to prove that he was not merely a student of Dante, but a master interpreter, an artist of damnation in his own right.

The letters were not just a response; they were an escalation. They confirmed that Baxter was actively engaged with their trap, that he had taken the bait with an almost voracious hunger. He was so eager to defend his intellectual territory that he was willing to engage in a public debate, to lay bare his deepest beliefs, his most cherished interpretations. And in doing so, he was inadvertently providing them with the ammunition they needed to dismantle him, piece by intellectual piece. The architect of damnation was, in his own grand design, becoming the architect of his own downfall, constructing his refutation with every carefully chosen word.

The letters continued, the cream-colored envelopes a harbinger of Baxter's escalating obsession. Each new missive arrived with a palpable increase in intensity, the academic veneer thinning to reveal a raw, almost desperate need for validation. He was no longer merely defending his interpretation of Dante; he was subtly, insidiously, weaving a narrative of his own martyrdom, his own supposed victimhood within the labyrinthine corridors of academia.

"He's moving beyond literary critique," Maria murmured, tracing a particularly impassioned sentence in the latest letter, signed now as "A Vigilant Guardian of Classicism." "He's talking about 'correcting the narrative.' It's not about proving Dr. York wrong anymore; it's about proving *himself* right, in a grander, more existential sense."

Gibson nodded, his gaze fixed on the same paragraph. "He feels overlooked. The article in the *Review* wasn't just an intellectual slight; it was an affront to his perceived place in the literary firmament. He believes he's been denied the recognition he deserves, that others have usurped his rightful position as the preeminent voice on Dante, on poetic justice."

The language shifted, becoming more personal, laced with a chilling familiarity. Baxter began to allude to individuals, not by name, but through thinly veiled descriptions that Maria recognized with a sickening lurch. He spoke of "those who have been given prominence they have not earned," of "voices that drown out true understanding with their superficial pronouncements." There was a distinct bitterness in these passages, a resentful undertone that spoke of a deeply wounded ego.

"He's talking about people he feels have wronged him," Donny said, his voice barely above a whisper. "People who have achieved success or influence that he believes should have been his. He sees himself as a protagonist in a grand drama, and anyone who stands in his way, or overshadows him, is merely a character who has 'outlived their purpose.'"

The phrase hung in the air, heavy with unspoken threat. It was a chilling echo of the killer's internal monologue, the same twisted logic that had justified the brutal deaths of those whose only crime was to cross Baxter's path or, in his twisted view, to embody the very sins he sought to punish. He wasn't just a literary critic; he was a self-appointed arbiter of fate, someone who believed he had the right, indeed the *duty*, to prune the literary garden of those he deemed unworthy.

"'Outlived their purpose,'" Gibson repeated slowly, the words a dark incantation. "It's a terrifyingly detached way of viewing human beings, isn't it? Reducing people to mere plot devices, to characters in his own self-aggrandizing narrative. He doesn't see them as victims; he sees them as narrative obstacles that have been, or will be, removed."

The letters were becoming less about Dante and more about Baxter himself. He spoke of his own sacrifices, his dedication to scholarship, the years spent toiling in obscurity while others, less deserving, reaped the rewards. He hinted at betrayals, at professional jealousies, at a systematic effort by his peers to silence his "uncompromising vision." It was a lament, a public confession of perceived injustices, all carefully couched in the language of academic discourse.

"He wants us to see him as a martyr," Maria realized, the pieces clicking into place with horrifying clarity. "He's not just seeking to discredit Dr. York; he's seeking absolution for himself. He's painting himself as a victim of the very system he purports to uphold, a system that he believes has failed to recognize his genius."

The "Vigilant Guardian" penned another letter, this one even more personal, more revealing. It spoke of the "lonely burden of true insight," the "solitude of the enlightened mind." Baxter wrote of the "cacophony of mediocrity" that surrounded him, a constant barrage of "shallow interpretations" and "uninspired scholarship" that made his own profound understanding feel like a curse. He lamented the lack of "true disciples," those who could appreciate the "subtlety and artistry" of his worldview.

"He craves disciples," Gibson observed, a grim understanding dawning on his face. "He doesn't just want recognition; he wants followers. He wants people to embrace his ideology, to see the world through his eyes. And anyone who deviates from that path, anyone who challenges his dogma, is not just an opponent; they are an aberration, an enemy of truth."

The letters were a testament to his grandiose delusion. He saw himself as a prophet, a seer burdened with a truth too profound for the common academic mind. His pronouncements on poetic justice, once confined to academic papers and lectures, were now becoming a declaration of war against a perceived world of ignorance and compromise. He was convinced that he alone possessed the key to understanding the true nature of consequence, of divine retribution, and that it was his destiny to impose that understanding upon a recalcitrant world.

"The 'correction of the narrative' isn't just about his academic standing," Maria said, her voice taut. "It's about rewriting reality itself, as he sees it. He believes he's divinely authorized to deliver this 'poetic justice,' to enact the punishments he deems fitting. And the people who have died... they were just characters in his play who had served their purpose, or worse, who had actively resisted his narrative."

The word "character" resonated deeply. Baxter viewed the world, and the people in it, through the lens of literature. His victims weren't individuals with lives, families, and futures; they were flawed characters in a narrative he was actively constructing, and whose arcs he felt empowered to conclude. The perceived injustices he spoke of were not abstract slights; they were narrative inconsistencies, plot holes that he felt compelled to rectify with ruthless precision.

"He's projecting his own actions onto the world," Gibson concluded, his tone somber. "He sees himself as the author, the director, and the ultimate judge. Those who resist his vision, those who fail to conform to his prescribed narrative, are simply erased. They have become... irrelevant characters."

The carefully chosen words, the labyrinthine arguments, the subtle allusions to his own brilliance and the world's blindness – it all served a singular purpose: to justify his existence, to legitimize his actions, and to elevate him to a position of ultimate authority. The letters, intended as intellectual sparring matches, had become a desperate, public cry for the recognition he believed he deserved, a testament to the self-deception that had driven him to commit unspeakable acts. He was not just an academic with a dangerous ideology; he was a man lost in the labyrinth of his own creation, convinced that he held the thread of truth while walking willingly into the darkness. His monologues, poured onto paper, were not just a reflection of his mind; they were a chilling testament to the power of delusion, a narrative of self-deception so profound that it had become a weapon. The man who saw himself as the orchestrator of poetic justice was, in fact, a prisoner of his own twisted narrative, forever writing himself into a tragedy of his own making. The letters were his final act of defiance, his last desperate attempt to control the story, to ensure that history would remember him not as a killer, but as a misunderstood genius, a prophet of a more just, more perfectly ordered world. But in his pursuit of this grand narrative, he had only succeeded in etching his own damning indictment, a literary confession written in the ink of his own hubris. He was so consumed by his own perceived injustices that he failed to see the irony: the narrative he sought to control was the very one that would ultimately condemn him, a story of ambition, delusion, and destruction, penned by his own hand. He was the author of his own damnation, and the ink was still drying.

The weight of Baxter's words, meticulously penned and chillingly delivered, pressed down on Gibson, a physical manifestation of his growing dread. He sat in his study; the cream-colored envelopes spread before him like fallen leaves from a poisoned tree. Maria watched him, her gaze steady, her hand resting lightly on his arm, a silent anchor in the rising tide of his disquiet. The air in the room was thick with unspoken recriminations, with the ghost of conversations past that now echoed with a terrible new resonance.

"I... I think I understand why you're so disturbed, Gibson," Maria said, her voice soft, almost a murmur. "It's not just his descent into madness; it's the realization that... that perhaps we didn't see it coming. Or worse, that we might have, in some way, nudged him towards it."

Gibson's shoulders slumped, the controlled stoicism he usually maintained cracking under the immense pressure. He picked up one of the letters, his fingers tracing the elegant, yet frantic, script. "He talks about 'the crucible of true understanding'," Gibson murmured, his voice raspy. "He recalls our discussions in the Infinite Discourse, doesn't he? He frames them as... as revelations. As the shedding of light on a dark truth." He looked up at Maria, his eyes holding a profound sorrow. "And the worst part, Maria, is that he's not entirely wrong. We *did* discuss these concepts. We explored the theoretical frameworks of poetic justice, of consequence, of retribution. We debated the philosophical underpinnings of how actions ripple outwards, how certain deeds might invite a form of cosmic balance, however abstract."

He gestured to the letters, his hand trembling slightly. "But it was always intellectual. Always theoretical. A playground for the mind, not a blueprint for murder. I never... I never envisioned that any of it could be twisted into such a horrific justification for violence. To hear him use our debates as a foundation for his 'divine mandate,' his 'necessary corrections'... it's like watching a masterpiece of architecture being used to construct a torture chamber."

A wave of guilt washed over Gibson, cold and sharp. He remembered the fervent discussions, the late-night debates in the hushed, leather-bound confines of the Discourse. Baxter, with his sharp intellect and insatiable hunger for meaning, had always been a particularly engaged participant. He had absorbed every nuance, every philosophical labyrinth they'd navigated, with an unnerving intensity. Gibson, in his own intellectual curiosity, had relished the challenge of pushing those boundaries, of exploring the darker, more complex facets of human nature and their philosophical implications. He had seen Baxter's enthusiasm as a sign of a brilliant mind grappling with profound questions, not as the feverish obsession of a man teetering on the precipice of madness.

"We spoke of Dante's *Inferno*," Gibson continued, his voice heavy with self-recrimination. "Of the structured, proportional punishments. Of the idea that certain sins inherently carry their own retribution. Baxter latched onto that. He saw it not as a literary device, a metaphor for moral consequence, but as a literal, actionable principle. He wanted to *implement* it. And I... I didn't recognize the danger. I was so caught up in the intellectual sparring, the elegance of the philosophical argument, that I failed to see the rot festering beneath. I gave him the language, Detective. I provided the intellectual framework, the vocabulary of his madness. And now... now people are dead because of it."

He buried his face in his hands, the rough wool of his sweater a meager comfort against the raw ache in his chest. "It feels... it feels like a betrayal. Not just of Baxter, but of everything I believe in as a scholar, as a man. My pursuit of knowledge was meant to illuminate, to foster understanding, not to provide ammunition for a killer. How could I have been so blind? So utterly, tragically naive?"

Maria knelt beside him, her touch firm, yet gentle. "Aris, you couldn't have known. No one could have predicted this level of delusion, this terrifying leap from theory to atrocity. Baxter was brilliant, yes, but his brilliance was always tinged with a certain... fragility. A need for control, perhaps. You offered him intellectual stimulation, a space to explore his ideas. You didn't encourage him to commit murder."

"But did I do enough to steer him away?" Gibson countered, lifting his head, his gaze desperate. "Did I challenge his increasingly extreme interpretations with sufficient force? Or did I, in my own academic hubris, find his unique perspective... interesting? Did I, perhaps, tacitly encourage his darker musings by not shutting them down with the vehemence they deserved? The Discourse was meant to be a sanctuary for intellectual exploration, a place where challenging ideas could be debated freely. But the line between exploration and dangerous obsession is so terrifyingly thin. And Baxter, with his particular brand of... fervor, he crossed it. And I fear I stood by, too fascinated by the intellectual fireworks, to see the inferno he was about to unleash."

He recalled specific instances, fragments of conversations that now played on a loop in his mind with a sickening clarity. Baxter's pronouncements about the "decay of true virtue," his lament for a lost era of "unblemished artistic integrity," his growing disdain for any criticism that didn't align with his rigid, almost dogmatic, interpretation of classical literature. Gibson had dismissed these as the pronouncements of an academic deeply passionate about his field, perhaps a little too rigid in his views, but ultimately harmless. He had seen Baxter's isolation, his perceived lack of recognition, as the natural consequence of an unconventional mind operating within a sometimes-unappreciative academic landscape. He had offered solace, intellectual camaraderie, and a space for Baxter to voice his frustrations. He had offered the very things Baxter seemed to crave – validation and intellectual engagement.

"He used the term 'poetic justice' so frequently," Gibson said, his voice barely audible. "And we discussed it, of course. The concept of deserved consequences, of actions leading to inevitable outcomes. But he took it to an entirely new level. He saw it as a cosmic imperative, a force that he, Baxter, was chosen to enact. He believed he was not just interpreting it; he was *embodying* it. And every person who has died... they were, in his twisted perception, characters who had failed to live up to their predetermined roles in his grand narrative. They were figures who had, through their actions or their very existence, disrupted the divine order he felt compelled to restore."

Gibson's guilt was a suffocating blanket. He saw himself not as a perpetrator, but as an unwitting accomplice, a scholar whose intellectual curiosity had inadvertently provided the ammunition for a madman. He had prided himself on his intellectual rigor, his ability to dissect complex arguments, to engage with challenging ideas. But in Baxter's case, his analytical skills had failed him. He had been so focused on the *how* of Baxter's theories that he had missed the terrifying *why* that was festering beneath.

"I should have seen it," he insisted, his voice raw with emotion. "I should have recognized the signs. The way he would sometimes isolate himself, the intensity in his eyes when discussing certain... *imbalances* in the world. I attributed it to his dedication, his singular focus. I told myself he was simply a brilliant mind wrestling with the great questions. But it was more than that. It was a descent. And I, in my pursuit of understanding, may have inadvertently paved his way down."

He looked at Maria, his gaze pleading. "I feel... I feel responsible. Not for the acts themselves, but for the intellectual soil in which this monstrous ideology took root. I gave him the tools, Maria. The language. The philosophical justification. And that weighs on me more than I can express. I cannot stand by and let this continue. I will do whatever I can, whatever it takes, to help you stop him. To atone for my part in this unfolding tragedy."

He stood up, pacing the study, the contained energy of a man galvanized by a newfound and terrible purpose. "Tell me what you need. I'll retrace every conversation, every word I can remember from our time in The Infinite Discourse. We'll dissect his writings, his lectures, anything that might give us insight into his current state of mind, into his immediate plans. My guilt is a burden, yes, but it is also a powerful motivator. If my knowledge, my past interactions with Baxter, can be used to prevent further harm, then I will lay it all bare. This is not just about stopping a killer anymore; it's about trying to rectify a profound intellectual and moral failure. My failure."

He stopped and looked directly at Maria, his eyes clear, though still clouded with regret. "He sees himself as an agent of justice. He believes he's bringing balance. But all he's bringing is destruction. And if my intellect, my understanding of his twisted logic, can be a weapon against him, then I will wield it. I owe it to the victims. I owe it to myself. I will help you. Whatever it takes." The admission was a raw, painful tearing of the academic disguise, revealing the profound human anguish beneath. His guilt, once a silent specter, had become a driving force, a desperate plea for redemption in the face of unimaginable horror. He had provided the theoretical framework, the philosophical ammunition, and now he was bound by a terrifying imperative to help dismantle the very structure of madness he had, however unintentionally, helped to build.

The air in Gibson's study, still heavy with the scent of aged paper and unspoken anxieties, began to shift. The revelation of Baxter's letters, each a testament to a mind untethered by conventional morality, had been a seismic event, but it was the dawning realization of what it implied that truly sent a chill through Gibson. Maria's quiet observation, "He's building towards something, Aris. This isn't just a series of killings; it's a narrative arc," resonated with a terrifying clarity. Baxter, the frustrated academic, the overlooked literary scholar, was no longer content with mere recognition. He craved apotheosis.

"His 'crucible of true understanding'," Gibson mused, the phrase still tasting like ash in his mouth, "it's not a metaphor for intellectual awakening anymore. It's a stage. And the victims... they are the sacrifices required to complete the tableau." He picked up another letter, not from Baxter, but a hastily scribbled note from a colleague, a hushed whisper of unease about Baxter's increasingly erratic behavior in the library archives. The note spoke of Baxter's obsessive re-reading of obscure tragic plays, his fervent pronouncements on the 'necessary catharsis' of art, and his peculiar interest in the university's historic observatory. "The observatory," Gibson repeated, a flicker of alarm in his eyes. "Why the observatory?"

Maria's brow furrowed. "It's the highest point on campus, isn't it? A place where one can survey everything, where one's actions can be seen... or perhaps, feel closer to the heavens he believes he's serving." The thought hung between them, a somber premonition. Baxter, in his warped perception, saw himself as a cosmic playwright, and the university, with its hallowed halls and esteemed faculty, was his grand theatre. The preceding acts – the poisoned chalice at the faculty mixer, the staged 'accident' in the rare books section, the 'misplaced' chemical in the advanced chemistry lab – were merely preludes to the crescendo.

"He's been seeking validation for his literary theories for years," Gibson continued, his voice a low rumble of self-recrimination. "He felt ignored, dismissed. These killings, in his deranged mind, are not just acts of violence; they are his magnum opus, a living embodiment of literary principles he felt no one truly appreciated. He's using his victims as props, as thematic elements, to illustrate his warped interpretation of poetic justice. Each death is a carefully chosen word, a perfectly placed comma in his perverse prose." He paced the study, the polished floorboards creaking under his restless feet. "And the attention he's received, the fear he's sown... it's fed his delusion. He feels seen, finally. He feels *important*."

The campus, once a vibrant hub of intellectual discourse and youthful energy, now vibrated with an undercurrent of palpable dread. Whispers, once confined to hushed tones in faculty lounges, now slithered through lecture halls and across manicured quadrangles. Students moved in tighter groups, their eyes darting nervously towards shadows, each unexplained noise amplified into a potential threat. The academic year, which had begun with such promise, was slowly being consumed by a chilling narrative that Baxter had meticulously constructed. The university's reputation, its very soul, was under siege, not by external forces, but by one of its own.

"He's written about the 'perfect ending'," Maria stated, her voice devoid of emotion, the clinical precision of a seasoned investigator. "He's obsessed with closure, with a finality that leaves no room for ambiguity. He wants his work to be undeniable, to be etched into history. And if the previous acts were meant to establish his premise, then the final act must be the undeniable, irrefutable conclusion." She met Gibson's gaze, her eyes mirroring his own dawning horror. "He's preparing for his grand finale, Aris. The one that will make his 'masterpiece' complete."

The nature of that finale was the unspoken terror that tightened Gibson's chest. Was it a public spectacle? A symbolic act of destruction? Or something more personal, more devastating? The letters, with their labyrinthine prose and chilling pronouncements, offered glimpses into Baxter's psyche, but they remained maddeningly elusive regarding his ultimate objective. He spoke of 'cosmic alignment,' of 'restoring equilibrium,' of leaving a legacy that would 'transcend mortal understanding.' These were not the words of a man seeking simple revenge; they were the pronouncements of a self-appointed deity orchestrating his final, earth-shattering performance.

"Think about his obsession with classical tragedy," Gibson said, his voice distant, lost in the grim re-evaluation of past conversations. "The inevitability of fate, the downfall of the proud, the moral reckoning. He saw himself as an instrument of that reckoning. He believed he was correcting the narrative, imbuing it with the weight of consequence it had supposedly lost. His victims weren't just individuals; they were characters who had strayed from their assigned roles in his grand play. The professor who had dismissed his early work, the student who had plagiarized his research, the administrator who had denied him funding for his obscure monograph – they were all villains in his private theatre, deserving of their dramatic exits."

The university, a place Gibson had dedicated his life to, now felt like a tinderbox, and Baxter held the match. The intellectual sanctuary he had cherished was now a battleground for a twisted ideology, a space where scholarly debate had devolved into deadly pronouncements. He recalled Baxter's fervent discussions on the limitations of academic criticism, his lament that true artistry was lost on an unappreciative world, his growing conviction that only through extreme measures could genuine understanding be achieved. Gibson had, in his academic detachment, seen these as the pronouncements of a brilliant but frustrated mind. Now, he saw them as the chilling blueprints of a murderer.

"He feels he's been overlooked for too long," Maria said, her voice soft but firm. "He craves recognition, not just as a scholar, but as an artist. And what greater art form is there than a perfectly orchestrated tragedy? He's been meticulously crafting this narrative, ensuring that every element, every victim, serves his ultimate purpose. The fear, the chaos, the intellectual speculation – it's all part of the performance. He's relishing it, Aris. He's relishing the attention, the power."

The thought of Baxter, the man Gibson had once considered a protégé, now the architect of such widespread terror, was a bitter pill to swallow. His guilt, once a dull ache, now intensified, a burning ember in his gut. He had provided Baxter with the intellectual scaffolding, the philosophical vocabulary that the madman had so readily weaponized. He had engaged with Baxter's theories, debated his interpretations, never once imagining that such intellectual discourse could lead to such horrific ends. He had been so captivated by the elegance of Baxter's mind, by the sheer audacity of his arguments, that he had failed to recognize the abyss into which Baxter was spiraling.

"We need to anticipate his final move," Gibson stated, his voice regaining a measure of its academic authority, albeit now tinged with urgency. "What does he consider the ultimate expression of his thesis? What would solidify his reputation as a literary genius, in his own mind, and leave an indelible mark on this institution?" He looked at Maria, his gaze sharp and focused. "He's always spoken of the ephemeral nature of academic acclaim, the way discoveries and theories are quickly superseded. He wants something permanent. Something that cannot be erased by time or changing perspectives. He wants a legacy."

The campus atmosphere was thick with unspoken fear. Every rustle of leaves, every distant siren, every unaccounted-for face, fueled the growing anxiety. The narrative was undeniably building towards a tragic climax, and the question on everyone's mind, though few dared to voice it, was whether they would be spectators or unwilling participants in Baxter's final, terrifying act. Gibson knew, with a certainty that chilled him to the bone, that Baxter's carefully constructed narrative was nearing its denouement, and that the university was poised to become the backdrop for its devastating conclusion. The intellectual games had ended. The performance was about to reach its terrifying crescendo. The anticipation of the climax was, in itself, a form of psychological torture, a slow, agonizing build-up to an inevitable, tragic release.

CHAPTER 12

THE LIBRARY'S FINAL CHAPTER

The air in the library, usually a sanctuary of hushed contemplation, now felt charged with an almost palpable dread. It was more than just the lingering unease that had settled over Elmwood University like a shroud; it was a specific, chilling premonition that had coalesced in Maria's mind, sharp and inescapable. Baxter, in his elaborate, self-fashioned tragedy, would not choose a public spectacle or a remote, symbolic location for his grand finale. His pièce de résistance, the ultimate articulation of his warped literary philosophy, would unfold within the very edifice that represented the pinnacle of his perceived betrayal: the university library.

This was not a random guess, but a deduction drawn from the very essence of Baxter's delusion. He saw himself as a master of narrative, a purveyor of true literary understanding, yet he felt profoundly misunderstood, even scorned, by the very institution that housed the accumulated knowledge of centuries. The library, with its towering shelves groaning under the weight of countless volumes, its silent, echoing halls, and its air thick with the scent of aged paper and forgotten ink, was the physical embodiment of the academic establishment he both revered and despised. It was the temple of the knowledge he claimed to champion, and simultaneously, the altar upon which he intended to perform his ultimate act of desecration.

Donny, leaning over the collection of Baxter's annotated texts spread across his study table, felt a cold dread creep up his spine as Maria articulated her theory. "The library," he echoed, the word tasting brittle. "Of course. It's the perfect stage. Every book a potential character, every aisle a narrative path, every reader a potential... audience." His eyes scanned the room, as if the answer lay hidden within the familiar surroundings, but the image of Baxter, once alight with intellectual curiosity, now contorted with a terrifying conviction, superimposed itself onto his vision. Donny now saw Baxter not as a disgruntled academic, but as a macabre architect, meticulously planning the final scene of his morbid masterpiece.

"He's spoken of the 'enduring power of the written word'," Maria continued, her voice low and steady, the perfect counterpoint to Donny's claim. "This makes sense. He's always been fascinated by how stories shape our reality, how they can endure long after their creators are gone. What better place to make his own indelible mark than amongst the collected stories of humanity? The library is where knowledge is curated, preserved, and passed down. Baxter sees himself as a curator of a different sort, a rectifier of perceived literary injustices, and this is where he'll ensure his own narrative is immortalized."

The university library, a Gothic masterpiece of soaring arches, stained-glass windows depicting scenes of academic triumph, and vast, oak-paneled reading rooms, was more than just a repository of books. It was the intellectual heart of Elmwood, a place where generations of scholars had sought solace, inspiration, and enlightenment. For Baxter, however, it had become a symbol of everything he felt was wrong with academia: the rigid hierarchies, the stifling orthodoxies, the superficial pursuit of tenure and recognition over genuine intellectual pursuit. He had spent countless hours within its hallowed walls, poring over obscure texts, his frustration growing with each perceived dismissal of his radical theories. Now, he would turn that frustration into a devastatingly literal statement.

Donny remembered Baxter's passionate pronouncements on the "imprint of the author," the idea that a writer's essence, their very soul, was infused into their work, leaving a trace that could be felt by sensitive readers. Baxter had claimed that some spaces, saturated with intellectual energy and profound human thought, could amplify these imprints. The library, in his warped view, was the ultimate amplifier, a place where the very air was thick with the echoes of genius and the weight of human experience. It was the perfect canvas for his final, bloody pronouncement.

"He's been obsessed with the concept of the 'library of Alexandria'," Maria recalled Gibson asserting. Gibson had discussed that Baxter had often spoken of that mythical repository of knowledge, lamenting its destruction as the greatest intellectual tragedy in history. He'd romanticized the idea of a single, vast collection that contained all the wisdom of the ancient world, and he'd often lamented that modern academia, despite its vastness, lacked a central, unifying locus of true, unadulterated knowledge. "He saw it as the ultimate testament to human intellect, and its loss as the ultimate symbol of humanity's self-destructive tendencies. He believed that by preserving and interpreting these great works, we were attempting to stave off our own inevitable decline. Now, he's going to finish the job himself, in a way." Donny expressed.

Maria nodded, her gaze fixed on a point beyond Donny, as if she could already see the spectral outlines of Baxter's plan unfolding within the library's grand architecture. "This makes sense now. He's spoken of the library as a 'crucible of collective consciousness'," she stated, retrieving a phrase Baxter had used in one of his more esoteric essays. "He believes that within its walls, the very essence of human thought is distilled. He wants to add his own contribution to that distillation, not through scholarship, but through a visceral, unforgettable act. He's not just killing people; he's curating a final exhibition, and the library is his gallery."

The scent of old paper and leather, usually a comforting aroma for Maria, now seemed to carry a darker undertone, a subtle hint of decay and foreboding. She imagined Baxter, moving through the hushed aisles, his footsteps unnaturally loud in the silence, his mind a tempest of literary allusions and violent intent. The vastness of the library, once a symbol of boundless intellectual exploration, now felt like a trap, a labyrinth designed to disorient and overwhelm. Baxter, with his intimate knowledge of its nooks and crannies, would be the master of this domain, navigating its shadows with a predator's instinct.

"Think about the symbolism," Donny urged, his voice gaining a frantic edge. "The order of the Dewey Decimal System, the classification of knowledge... he'll see it as an attempt to impose artificial structure on the chaos of human experience. He'll want to shatter that illusion, to prove that true understanding lies not in categorization, but in the raw, untamed expression of emotion, even if that expression is through violence."

Maria's lips thinned. "And the students. The quiet researchers, the late-night crammers. They are the keepers of the flame, the inheritors of this knowledge. But to Baxter, they are also the complacent symbols of an academic system that has failed him. They represent the generation that will never truly appreciate the depths of his intellect, the nuance of his theories. They are the living embodiment of the intellectual mediocrity he despises." She paused, the weight of her words settling in the air. "He won't be targeting random individuals. He'll be selecting them, carefully, as characters in his final act. Perhaps a symbol of academic apathy, another representing the superficiality of modern learning, another who embodies the very elitism he feels has ostracized him."

The library's grand reading room, with its long, polished tables and high-backed chairs, would become a tableau of horror. Donny and Maria pictured Baxter, standing at the head of one of these tables, perhaps bathed in the ethereal light filtering through the stained-glass windows, delivering a final, chilling monologue. The silence of the space, usually a source of profound peace, would be shattered by the screams of his chosen victims, the desperate pleas swallowed by the vastness of the hall. The carefully cataloged knowledge surrounding them would become a silent, impotent witness to their demise, a stark contrast to the primal act of violence unfolding amongst the tomes of human civilization.

"He's mentioned 'the ultimate bibliographical error'," Donny said, recalling a particularly cryptic passage from Baxter's writings. "Gibson was illuding to Baxter railing against the perceived errors of historical interpretation, the misattribution of texts, the deliberate obfuscation of truth by those in power. He saw himself as the ultimate editor, the one who would correct the record, not with footnotes, but with decisive action. And what greater error could there be than to erase the very lives of those who perpetuate these perceived falsehoods?"

Maria's mind raced, piecing together Baxter's obsessions with his current actions. His fascination with the tragic heroes of antiquity, their inevitable downfalls brought about by hubris and fate, resonated deeply with his current trajectory. He saw himself as both the tragic figure and the avenging force, a dual role he was now intent on playing out to its terrifying conclusion. The library, as the repository of these ancient tragedies, would serve as both his muse and his bloody stage.

"He might even see it as a form of censorship," Donny mused, the intellectual gears in his mind turning at a frantic pace. "By eliminating those he deems unworthy, those who have corrupted or misinterpreted the true spirit of scholarship, he's performing an act of purification. He's removing the dissenting voices, the false narratives, to make way for his own unassailable truth. The library, where all voices are supposedly heard, will become the site where only his voice will ultimately matter."

The implications of Donny's deduction were terrifying. The library was not just a building; it was a symbol, and Baxter's choice of it as his final venue amplified the psychological impact of his actions immeasurably. He was not merely committing murder; he was making a profound, albeit deranged, statement about knowledge, truth, and the human condition. He was using the very foundations of intellectual pursuit as the backdrop for his descent into primal violence.

"The sheer audacity of it," Donny breathed, a mixture of awe and horror washing over him. "To take the place that represents the collective memory of humanity and transform it into the site of his ultimate act of barbarism. It's a perversion of everything a library stands for. He's turning knowledge into a weapon, and the silence of its halls into an instrument of terror."

Maria remained focused, her gaze sharp and unwavering. "We need to consider the specific areas. The rare books section, perhaps? Where the most precious and vulnerable texts are housed? Or the main reading room, where the symbolic act could be most visible? He might even target the archives, the very heart of the library's historical record, as a way of asserting his control over the narrative of the past."

The grandeur of Elmwood's library, with its intricate woodwork, its vast collections, and its profound sense of history, was about to be defiled. The hushed reverence that typically permeated its halls would be replaced by screams and terror. The scent of aging paper would mingle with the coppery tang of blood. Baxter, the disgruntled scholar, the frustrated artist, was about to deliver his final, devastating critique of the world, and his chosen venue ensured that his message, however horrific, would be undeniably heard. The library, a monument to the pursuit of understanding, was about to become the scene of its ultimate, tragic perversion. The grand finale was not just approaching; it had found its stage, and the curtain was about to rise on a tragedy of unimaginable proportions, etched not in ink, but in blood, within the silent, hallowed halls of knowledge.

The frantic urgency of Baxter's final letters had been a chilling crescendo, each word a tighter knot in the stomach. Maria had reread the latest one a dozen times, the ink blurring and reforming into a desperate plea for understanding that twisted into something far more sinister. "The opus is nearing completion," it had read, the phrase echoing the grand, self-important pronouncements Baxter was so fond of. "The final act demands the perfect stage, the definitive crescendo. Soon, the world will understand the true power of the unfinished sentence." Beside it, Gibson had scrawled his own terse note: "He's losing it. You have to go. Now."

Now, standing on the precipice of Elmwood University's hallowed library, the air was thick with an unnatural stillness. The cavernous space, usually alive with the rustle of pages and the low murmur of studious concentration, was eerily deserted. The only illumination came from the utilitarian desk lamps strategically placed on scattered tables, their harsh, focused beams cutting through the gloom and casting elongated, dancing shadows that seemed to writhe with a life of their own. It was a silence that didn't speak of peace, but of anticipation, a breathless pause before a storm.

Maria's heart hammered against her ribs, a frantic drumbeat against the oppressive quiet. She scanned the vast expanse of the main reading room, her gaze sweeping over the long, polished oak tables that stretched out like dark rivers in the dim light. This was it. This was Baxter's chosen arena, the sanctuary of knowledge he had come to desecrate. The very air seemed to hum with a suppressed energy, a tension that prickled at the skin.

Donny moved beside her, his breath catching in his throat. "My God," he whispered, the sound barely audible in the immense space. "He wasn't exaggerating."

The scene that unfolded before them was not merely a disruption; it was a deliberate, terrifying reinterpretation of the space. Baxter, with his theatrical flair and his profound, twisted understanding of narrative, had transformed the tranquil reading room into a stage. It was a macabre tableau; a meticulously crafted set designed to shock and awe; to make a statement so profound it would echo through eternity.

Scattered across the central tables, where students usually bent their heads in study, were carefully arranged props. Books, Baxter's beloved companions, were not merely placed; they were positioned with artistic intent. Some were splayed open, their pages dramatically illuminated by portable spotlights that had been jury-rigged to cast intense, theatrical pools of light. These lights, positioned at odd angles, created stark contrasts, plunging sections of the room into deep shadow while searing others with an almost blinding intensity. It was a deliberate manipulation of light and dark, a visual representation of Baxter's fractured worldview.

Certain volumes were propped open to pages bearing particularly graphic illustrations or passages of extreme emotional resonance. Maria recognized some of Baxter's annotations, his frantic scribbles in the margins now serving as a grim commentary on the unfolding horror. A volume of Poe, its pages turned to *The Raven*, sat beside a well-worn copy of *Macbeth*, its tragic pronouncements on ambition and consequence thrown into stark relief by the surrounding scene. Scattered amongst the books were elements that spoke of a deeply personal, almost ritualistic, preparation. Black velvet cloth, the kind used to drape stages or cover sensitive artifacts, was draped over sections of the tables, lending an air of solemnity to the desecration.

Candles, thick and unburned, stood in candelabra placed at deliberate intervals, their wicks untouched, suggesting a planned illumination that had either been superseded by the more modern spotlights or was yet to come. The scent of burnt wax, however, was absent, replaced by the dry, papery aroma of the library itself, now tinged with something else – a faint, metallic tang that Maria couldn't quite place, but which sent a shiver of dread down her spine.

Donny moved cautiously towards one of the tables, his eyes darting around the room as if expecting Baxter to materialize from the shadows. "Look at this," he murmured, gesturing towards a collection of dried roses, their petals brittle and brown, arranged in a wilting bouquet. They lay beside a tarnished silver locket, its clasp open to reveal... nothing. It was an empty space where a photograph should have been, a symbol of absence, of loss, of a narrative that had been deliberately erased. This was not just a scene of violence; it was a carefully constructed narrative of emotional desolation, a visual poem of grief and madness.

Maria followed his gaze, her mind racing to connect these disparate elements to Baxter's known obsessions. He had always spoken of the "eloquence of the void," the profound meaning that could be found in absence, in what was left unsaid, in the emptiness that remained after a story had ended. The empty locket, the unlit candles, the dried roses – they were all symbols of decay, of finality, of a beauty that had faded into oblivion.

"He's staging a tragedy," Maria breathed, the words catching in her throat. "He's not just going to commit the act; he's going to present it. He wants us to witness his final performance, to understand the narrative he's been building." She gestured towards the spotlights, their harsh beams carving out stark islands of illumination within the cavernous darkness. "These aren't just lights; they're spotlights, focusing our attention, directing our gaze. He's the director, the playwright, and the star of his own morbid production."

Donny pointed to a specific book, a large, leather-bound tome that lay open at the center of the largest table. Its pages were filled with dense, archaic script, and Baxter had placed a single, blood-red feather atop the text, a stark and brutal punctuation mark. "That's a first edition of *De Profundis*," Donny said, his voice tight with apprehension. "Oscar Wilde. Gibson had said that Baxter always claimed that book was the ultimate testament to the power of suffering, the way one could find beauty and meaning even in the depths of despair. He's using it as a centerpiece, a declaration of his own suffering, and the 'meaning' he's found in his descent."

Maria nodded, her gaze sweeping over the meticulously arranged scene. She noticed small, almost imperceptible details that amplified the unsettling nature of the display. A single, perfectly preserved autumn leaf rested on the cover of a book of poetry. A delicate, antique quill pen lay beside an inkwell that, unlike the candles, did contain ink – a deep, viscous black, not quite red, but suggestive enough. It was as if Baxter had meticulously planned every element, every symbolic gesture, to contribute to the overarching narrative of his final, catastrophic act.

"He's treating this like a museum exhibit," Maria said, her voice barely a whisper. "Each element is a curated piece, meant to convey a specific emotion, a particular aspect of his fractured psyche. The dried roses for lost love, the empty locket for an erased past, the feather for... what? A fallen angel? A broken muse?" She looked at

Donny, her eyes wide with a dawning horror. "He's not just planning to kill. He's planning to *perform* the act of killing; with all the dramatic flair and symbolic weight he can muster."

The silence of the library was no longer just an absence of sound; it was a canvas. A canvas upon which Baxter had painted his madness, his despair, his ultimate, terrible resolution. The shadows, cast by the strategically placed lights, seemed to deepen, to coil and writhe, as if they too were part of Baxter's grand design. The towering shelves of books, usually a comfort, now seemed to loom like silent, judgmental witnesses, their countless stories rendered mute by the impending tragedy.

Donny took another step forward, his hand instinctively reaching for the pocket where he kept his phone, though he knew there was no signal here, deep within the library's stone walls. "He wants us to see this," Donny said, his voice strained. "He wants us to understand the logic behind his madness. He's laid it all out, Maria. He's showing us the culmination of his intellectual journey, the 'opus' he's been so obsessed with."

Maria's gaze settled on a particular spot, an alcove carved into the far wall, usually a quiet nook for solitary study. Now, it was the focal point of Baxter's macabre theatre. A single, upright chair stood in the center of the alcove, bathed in an intense beam of white light. Beside it, Baxter had placed a small, antique music box, its intricate carvings hinting at a time of delicate artistry and perhaps, lost innocence. The box was closed, its melody silenced, another symbol of something beautiful that had been brought to an abrupt and irreversible halt.

"He's creating a narrative arc," Maria mused, her mind working at a feverish pace. "The props, the lighting, the chosen texts – they all serve to build towards a climax. The question is, who or what is the climax? Who is the intended audience for this twisted performance?" The implication hung heavy in the air: they were not just observers; they were, perhaps, the intended audience, and worse, the intended participants.

"He mentioned 'the unfinished sentence'," Donny recalled, his brow furrowed. "In his last letter. 'The true tragedy,' he wrote, 'lies not in the ending, but in the abrupt cessation of meaning. My opus will be the ultimate unfinished sentence; a question posed for eternity.'" He gestured around the room. "This whole setup... it's all about posing that question, isn't it? It's a visual representation of what he believes is the fundamental flaw in human existence – the inability to truly complete, to truly find closure."

Maria felt a prickle of fear, colder than any she had experienced before. Baxter's academic theories had always been abstract, intellectual exercises. But here, in the silent heart of the university, they had taken on a terrifyingly tangible form. He had translated his philosophical despair into a physical manifestation of horror. The library, the repository of reasoned thought and structured knowledge, had become the backdrop for a primal, irrational act.

"He sees us as characters in his play," Maria stated, her voice gaining a chilling certainty. "He's cast us. He's set the stage. And now, we have to figure out our roles before he begins the final act." The spotlights, harsh and unforgiving, seemed to mock her pronouncement, bathing the carefully arranged scene in an almost clinical light, as if dissecting the very essence of madness for the world to see. The silence, so profound moments before, now felt alive with the unspoken dread of what was to come. The library's final chapter was not to be written in ink, but in the stark, terrifying language of Baxter's ultimate, devastating narrative.

The air in the library was a suffocating tapestry of dread and the cloying scent of decaying flowers. Maria’s eyes, wide and disbelieving, swept across the meticulously arranged scene Baxter had orchestrated. The spotlights, stark and unforgiving, carved out illuminated pools, each a stage for Baxter’s twisted narrative. The book of *De Profundis*, the crimson feather, the empty locket, the dried roses – they were all elements of a prelude, building to a climax that Maria desperately hoped they had arrived at just in time to avert. But the space between the central table and the shadowed alcove, where a single chair waited under a stark white beam, remained empty of the final, terrible actor.

Then, a flicker of movement caught her eye. A shape, unnaturally still, coalesced from the deeper shadows at the periphery of the main reading room, just beyond the reach of the harsh, academic lighting. Donny moved towards it, his steps faltering as the truth dawned with the sickening, inexorable certainty of a descent into an abyss. His hand, which had been reaching for his useless phone, froze midway.

"No," Donny whispered, the sound choked and raw. "No, it can't be."

Baxter, the architect of this intellectual and emotional ruin, was not the figure Maria had braced herself to confront. Instead, it was Professor Gibson himself. Bound. Gagged. His usually sharp, intelligent eyes, now wide with terror and a profound, gut-wrenching betrayal, were fixed on Maria, pleading, demanding, *knowing*. He was seated in a heavy, ornate chair, not the one in the alcove, but another, placed strategically in the center of the main reading room, positioned as if to be the very heart of Baxter's morbid tableau. The rope binding his wrists and ankles was thick, industrial-grade, biting into his skin with brutal efficiency. A strip of dark cloth, rough and smelling faintly of old leather, was cinched tightly around his mouth, muffling any sound, any desperate cry.

Baxter had not merely invited them to witness his final act; he had cast them. Maria was the horrified observer, the one forced to confront the chilling logic of his descent. And Gibson... Gibson was the star. The protagonist of Baxter's final, devastating critique of academia, of mentorship, of a perceived betrayal that had festered into a monstrous obsession. She turned to Donny and whispered. "What ever happens, do not shoot Baxter. We need to take him alive." She paused looking at Gibson. "Donny, I need you to stay back and cover me. I think I know where Baxter is going with this."

Donny looked at Maria, "No problem, Maria. I've got your back."

Maria's breath hitched, a ragged sound in the oppressive silence. Baxter's words, from that last, frantic letter, echoed in her mind: "The opus is nearing completion... The final act demands the perfect stage, the definitive crescendo." This was the crescendo. This was the stage. And Gibson, the esteemed professor, the man who had tried to guide Baxter, was now the centerpiece of his protégé's ruin.

"He... he's making me watch," Gibson managed to articulate, his voice a distorted, muffled rasp against the gag. His eyes, locked onto Maria's, pleaded for understanding, for action, for an escape that seemed impossibly distant. "He thinks... he thinks I betrayed him. He thinks I abandoned... the Discourse. Our ideals."

Baxter's voice, when it finally echoed through the vast space, was not the frantic, unhinged tone they had come to expect. It was measured, almost serene, imbued with a chilling sense of vindication. He emerged from the deeper shadows near the circulation desk, a figure of stark, almost anachronistic elegance in his tailored tweed jacket, a stark contrast to the chaos he had wrought. In his hand, he carried a slender, ivory-handled letter opener, its tip glinting under the harsh academic light.

"Professor Gibson," Baxter began, his voice resonating with a deep, self-satisfied irony. "The esteemed educator. The guiding light. And yet, a man who chose to dim his own brilliance, to distance himself from the very principles he once espoused. You abandoned the salon, Professor. You recoiled from our discussions, from the pursuit of pure, unadulterated intellectual truth. You chose... compromise. You chose the comfortable, the mundane. You chose to silence the very voices that dared to question the established order."

Baxter walked slowly around Gibson, his gaze lingering on the bound professor with a mixture of triumph and a strange, almost paternalistic disappointment. "You, Professor, represent the academic establishment at its most cowardly. The man who, when faced with true intellectual rebellion, with a vision that threatened to shatter the comfortable illusions of your ivory tower, chose to retreat. To sanitize. To distance himself. You, sir, are the ultimate symbol of intellectual capitulation."

He gestured to the scattered books, the spotlights, the carefully arranged symbolism. "This, Professor, is not mere vandalism. This is a pedagogical demonstration. A final lecture, if you will, on the consequences of intellectual cowardice. You taught me the power of the written word, the profound impact of narrative. And now, I shall use that power to dissect your own story, to reveal its fundamental flaw."

Maria felt a cold dread seep into her bones. Baxter was not merely intending to inflict pain; he was intending to inflict a profound, intellectual punishment. He saw Gibson not as a victim, but as a character in his final, grand play, a character who had failed to live up to his role.

"You believed in the power of the unfinished sentence, didn't you, Professor?" Baxter continued, his voice a low, sibilant hiss. "You spoke of the beauty of ambiguity, the potential for meaning in what is left unsaid. But you misunderstood. True meaning, true *impact*, is not found in the void. It is found in the forceful, undeniable assertion of truth. It is found in the definitive, irrefutable statement that leaves no room for doubt, no space for compromise."

He circled Gibson again, his shadow falling over the bound professor like a shroud. "You distanced yourself from our society, Professor, because you feared the implications of our work. You feared the questions we asked, the boundaries we pushed. You feared the truth. And so, you relegated me to the periphery, hoping I would fade away, a minor footnote in your illustrious career. But I am not a footnote, Professor. I am the bold, undeniable thesis statement of a new era. And you, sir, are about to witness its definitive conclusion."

Gibson struggled against his bonds, his muffled protests laced with a desperate urgency. His eyes, pleading, shifted from Baxter to Maria, a silent, desperate plea for her to understand, to act, to break free from the paralysis of shock and horror.

"And you, Detective," Baxter's voice shifted, a more personal, almost intimate tone entering his speech as he turned his gaze towards her. "You, who understood my theories, who saw the brilliance in my early work. You, who stood by me when others faltered. You are here to bear witness. To see the culmination of my intellectual journey, the price of intellectual heresy. You are the audience, the validation for my final, irrefutable argument."

He moved towards the elaborate setup on the central table, picking up the ivory letter opener. "You both believed that knowledge was a passive pursuit, a matter of contemplation and debate. But knowledge, Professor, is power. And power, when wielded correctly, can reshape the world. My 'opus,' as I've called it, is not merely a collection of theories. It is a demonstration of that power. A testament to the fact that some sentences, once written, cannot be erased. They become eternal."

Baxter's gaze drifted towards a particular section of the library, one that Maria hadn't fully registered in her initial shock. Tucked away between towering shelves of historical texts and philosophical treatises, Baxter had created a smaller, more intimate stage. Here, a single, bare lightbulb dangled from a frayed cord, casting a harsh, sterile glow. Beneath it, resting on a small, antique wooden stool, was a collection of unbound pages, meticulously typed. They were not part of Baxter's earlier, symbolic arrangements. These were raw, unfiltered words, a manuscript, perhaps.

"You see, Professor," Baxter continued, his voice softening, almost wistfully, "you taught me the importance of a well-crafted narrative. You showed me how to build tension, how to develop characters, how to create a compelling arc. But you never taught me how to *finish.* You always cautioned against premature conclusions, against the arrogance of definitive pronouncements. You believed in the ongoing dialogue, the endless exploration. And in doing so, you crippled me. You left me perpetually searching for the perfect ending, the ultimate statement."

He gestured towards the manuscript. "This is my attempt to break free from that paralysis. These pages represent the 'unfinished sentence' made manifest. But it will not remain unfinished. Not after tonight. Tonight, the sentence will be completed. And its completion will be... definitive."

Maria's eyes darted between Gibson and Baxter. Then back to Donny who had taken up a defensive position. Gibson's struggles had intensified, a desperate, silent plea in his eyes. He was trying to communicate something, something beyond the immediate terror of his situation. Maria strained to understand, her mind racing, trying to decipher the frantic movements of his bound hands, the desperate expression on his face.

"He's... he's trying to tell me something," Maria whispered, her voice barely audible. "He knows... he knows the weakness. The key."

Baxter's head tilted, a flicker of something akin to annoyance crossing his features. "Your fascination with Professor Gibson's silent suffering is commendable, Detective, but ultimately futile. He is a character who has played his part. And now, his role is to observe. To witness the undeniable truth of my final argument. He will understand, in the agonizing silence that follows, the profound error of his judgment."

He took a step towards Gibson; the letter opener held with a chilling deliberation. "You always spoke of the beauty of the void, Professor. Of the profound implications of absence. Well, tonight, we shall explore the void together. We shall see what profound truths lie in the silence that follows the ultimate negation."

Maria's gaze snapped back to Gibson. His eyes were wide, fixed on something beyond Baxter, something in the shadowed alcove where the single spotlight awaited its occupant. A chill that had nothing to do with the library's temperature traced a path down Maria's spine. Baxter had spoken of the final act, of the definitive crescendo. He had the captive audience, the stage, the dramatic props. But who was meant to be the final victim? Who was the definitive statement?

The fear, which had been a cold knot in her stomach, began to bloom into a suffocating panic. Baxter was the architect of this destruction, but he was also, undeniably, its victim. His madness was a testament to his own intellectual and emotional ruin. And Gibson, the man he had once revered, was now to be the unwilling audience to that final, terrible self-immolation. But as Baxter's gaze drifted, not to Gibson, but towards Maria, a new, chilling realization dawned. Baxter saw himself as the ultimate intellectual martyr. Gibson was the embodiment of the system that had ostracized him. But Maria... Maria was the one who had chosen to walk away, to align herself with Gibson. And Baxter, in his twisted logic, saw her choice as another betrayal.

"You, Detective," Baxter paused. "Well, let's dispense of the formalities...Maria," Baxter's voice was soft, almost sorrowful, "you were the closest to understanding. You saw the potential, the brilliance. And yet... you chose the comfortable path. You chose convention. You chose to let the narrative die with the editor's red pen, rather than embrace the glorious, chaotic freedom of the unbound sentence."

He gestured with the letter opener towards the alcove. "Professor Gibson will witness my grand pronouncement. He will understand the gravity of his intellectual sins. But you, Maria, you will understand the true cost of silence. The cost of not speaking out, not fighting for the truth, even when it is uncomfortable, even when it is dangerous."

Maria's heart hammered against her ribs, a frantic counterpoint to the oppressive silence. Gibson's struggle intensified, a silent symphony of desperation. He was trying to convey a message, a warning, a desperate plea. Baxter was orchestrating a tragedy, and Maria was no longer just an observer. She was a potential participant, a character thrust onto Baxter's macabre stage, her role yet to be fully defined, but the threat of her own personal narrative being irrevocably altered, or even extinguished, hung heavy in the air. A fleeting thought crossed her mind. Baxter is addressing her in the singular. He is not aware that Donny is present and that could work out to their advantage. Maria motioned to Donny to find a blind spot.

The library, once a sanctuary of knowledge, had become a tomb, and Baxter, its mad conductor, was about to unleash his final, devastating symphony. Gibson's bound form was the stark, horrifying centerpiece, but Maria now understood with a chilling certainty: the performance was far from over, and the true intended climax remained terrifyingly, dangerously, uncertain. The fifth victim, it seemed, was not just Gibson, but potentially any one of them, caught in the crosshairs of Baxter's unraveling reality.

"Consider Jacob Bennett," Baxter mused out loud, his voice taking on a didactic tone. "A man who embodied the ossification of thought. His work, once groundbreaking, had become a shrine to past glories, a monument to his own unyielding dogma. He represented the intellectual dead end, the stubborn refusal to evolve. His narrative, therefore, had to be... concluded. Swiftly and decisively. His story served as a stark warning against the perils of intellectual rigidity."

He gestured vaguely towards the shelves laden with ancient tomes. "And then there was Professor Nevel. A man so consumed by his own perceived genius, so blinded by academic vanity, that he actively suppressed any dissenting voices. He was the gatekeeper, the silencer of progress. His demise was a necessary act of liberation, a symbolic breaking of the chains that bound true inquiry. His narrative was a tragedy of pride, a cautionary tale of how self-importance can suffocate intellectual curiosity."

Baxter's eyes, wide and intense, swept over Maria, and she felt a fresh wave of cold terror. He was not finished with his dissection. He was continuing his critique, drawing her into the vortex of his madness.

"And you, Maria," he continued, his voice dropping to a near whisper, laced with a chilling sincerity. "You, who once understood. You, who saw the spark of true innovation in my early work. You, who shared my yearning for something more, something beyond the sterile confines of academic convention. You represent the ultimate tragedy: the individual who glimpses the truth, who recognizes the potential for greatness, and then retreats. You chose safety over significance. You chose the predictable path over the exhilarating precipice of discovery. Your narrative, Maria, is the story of potential unrealized, of a spirit that could have soared but chose to remain earthbound. And that, I submit, is a tragedy far greater than any that has preceded it."

He stepped closer to Gibson, the letter opener now held at an unnerving angle, its tip dancing in the stark light. "Professor Gibson, you are here to bear witness to this final act of narrative purification. You will see how true artistry transcends the conventional boundaries of morality. You will understand that sometimes, to create something truly new, something that will shake the foundations of this complacent world, one must be willing to dismantle the old. To tear down the established structures, brick by symbolic brick. And if that dismantling involves the removal of certain... characters... then so be it. It is the necessary sacrifice for the sake of the greater narrative, for the ultimate artistic statement."

Baxter paused, a faint smile playing on his lips, a smile that held no warmth, only the cold satisfaction of a craftsman admiring his masterpiece. "You see, Professor, I am not merely an actor in this drama; I am its author. Its director. And its final, definitive editor. I am the force that compels the story forward, the hand that guides the plot to its inevitable conclusion. And this library, this hallowed ground of stagnant thought, will become the canvas upon which my magnum opus is finally completed."

The terror that had been a cold knot in her stomach began to bloom into a suffocating panic. Baxter was the architect of this destruction, but he was also, undeniably, its victim. His madness was a testament to his own intellectual and emotional ruin. And Gibson, the man he had once revered, was now to be the unwilling audience to that final, terrible self-immolation. But as Baxter's gaze drifted, not to Gibson, but towards Maria, a new, chilling realization dawned. Baxter saw himself as the ultimate intellectual martyr. Gibson was the embodiment of the system that had ostracized him. But Maria... Maria was the one who had chosen to walk away, to align herself with Gibson. And Baxter, in his twisted logic, saw her choice as another betrayal. The library, once a sanctuary of knowledge, had become a tomb, and Baxter, its mad conductor, was about to unleash his final, devastating symphony. Gibson's bound form was the stark, horrifying centerpiece, but Maria now understood with a chilling certainty: the performance was far from over, and the true intended climax remained terrifyingly, dangerously, uncertain. The fifth victim, it seemed, was not just Gibson, but potentially any one of them, caught in the crosshairs of Baxter's unraveling reality.

The air in the library was thick with a suffocating tension, a palpable weight that pressed down on Maria's chest, threatening to steal her breath. Julian Baxter, the self-proclaimed prophet of intellectual revolution, stood before her, his eyes gleaming with a manic fervor that was both terrifying and, in a warped way, pitiable. Gibson, bound and gagged, remained a silent, helpless figure in the periphery, his struggles a muted testament to the grim reality of their situation. Maria, despite the primal scream of fear clawing at her throat, forced herself to meet Baxter's gaze. Shock, though a potent adversary, could not be allowed to win. Not now. Not when the very fabric of their reality, and perhaps their lives, hung precariously in the balance. She drew upon the years spent dissecting narratives, analyzing character motivations, and understanding the subtle art of argumentation. If Baxter saw himself as the author of this grim tableau, then she would become the most incisive critic he had ever encountered.

"You speak of definitive conclusions, Julian," Maria began, her voice remarkably steady, though a slight tremor betrayed the sheer force of will required to produce it. "Of the 'unfinished sentence' made whole. But is a sentence truly complete when it is punctuated by violence? Is your 'truth' forged in the crucible of fear and coercion?" She gestured subtly to the scattered books, the carefully placed symbols of intellectual transgression. "You accuse Professor Gibson of intellectual cowardice, of a failure to embrace the bold assertion. Yet, what is more cowardly than to silence dissent through brute force, to silence the very voices you claim to champion with the blunt instrument of death?"

Baxter's lips curled into a smile that didn't reach his eyes. "Ah, Maria. Always the astute reader. But you misunderstand. This is not brute force; this is *narrative consequence*. Professor Gibson chose to distance himself from the very intellectual discourse that birthed me. He retreated into the safe harbor of the established canon, shunning the potential of the new, the transgressive. His silence was a choice, a betrayal of the very principles he preached. My actions are merely the logical, *literary* extension of that choice. The plot demands a resolution, and he, the character who shirked his responsibilities, must face the denouement."

"A denouement?" Maria scoffed, a flicker of defiance igniting within her. She watched as Donny, who remained undetected, moved in closer. "Or a cheap melodrama? You claim to be an artist, Julian, a visionary. But true artistry elevates, it illuminates. It does not debase itself by resorting to the basest of tactics. You speak of the power of the written word, of narrative impact. Yet, your current narrative is riddled with inconsistencies. You condemn compromise, yet you compromise your own ideals by engaging in these theatrics. You champion intellectual freedom, yet you seek to imprison Gibson, both physically and intellectually, in your twisted vision."

Her words seemed to strike a nerve. Baxter's head tilted, a spark of genuine irritation replacing the gleam of fanatical conviction. "Theatricals? Maria, this is a *performance* of ultimate truth! A didactic demonstration for a world too anesthetized by comfortable illusions to perceive the rot beneath. The 'compromise' you speak of is the very rot I aim to excise. Professor Gibson's refusal to engage with my ideas, his deliberate ostracization of me and my peers, that was the ultimate compromise. He chose to protect his reputation, his legacy, over the pursuit of raw, unadulterated intellectual honesty. And such a narrative deserves to be brought to a stark, unyielding conclusion."

"But what of your own narrative, Julian?" Maria pressed on, sensing a vulnerability beneath his bluster. "You claim to be a prophet, a man driven by an unassailable truth. Yet, your actions reveal a deep-seated insecurity, a desperate need for validation. You seek to silence the critics, to erase those who do not conform to your worldview. Is that the act of a prophet, or the tantrum of a failed academic? You lament the 'unfinished sentence,' the ambiguity that plagues literature, but isn't your own life an unfinished sentence? A life consumed by resentment, by a desperate quest for recognition, by a warped interpretation of the very texts you profess to revere?"

Baxter took a step closer, his hand tightening around the letter opener. The ivory gleamed menacingly. "Insecurity? You mistake the clarity of vision for insecurity, Maria. I am not seeking validation; I am seeking *vindication*. I am not a failed academic; I am an academic who has transcended the petty confines of the professorial ranks. The texts you hold so dear, the literary masterpieces that adorn these shelves, they are not mere entertainment; they are blueprints. Blueprints for understanding human nature, for dissecting power, for shaping reality. And I, unlike Gibson, have learned to wield them not as passive observers, but as active architects."

He gestured to the manuscript lying on the stool. "These pages, Maria, are the culmination of that understanding. They are not the ramblings of a madman, as Gibson would have it, but the distilled essence of a thousand narratives, a thousand characters, a thousand intellectual struggles. They are the definitive statement that the academic world, in its timidity, refuses to make. Professor Gibson, in his intellectual cowardice, chose to shy away from the very precipice of profound revelation. He preferred the comforting certainty of the known to the exhilarating, terrifying expanse of the unknown."

Maria's mind raced. Baxter was clearly operating on a deeply flawed premise, a delusion woven from his own interpretation of literary theory. He saw himself as a tragic hero, a misunderstood genius whose radical ideas were being suppressed by a stagnant establishment. Gibson was merely a symbol of that establishment, a convenient antagonist in Baxter's self-penned drama. "But Julian," she countered, her voice softening, an attempt to appeal to a shred of his former self, if such a thing still existed. "You speak of the 'unknown' as if it is a void to be conquered, a darkness to be banished. The beauty of literature, of human thought, lies not in the definitive statement, but in the enduring question. The power of a great novel is not in its conclusion, but in its ability to linger in the reader's mind, to provoke thought, to inspire further inquiry. Your manuscript, as you call it, may be 'definitive' in your eyes, but true understanding requires a continuous dialogue, not a monologue of destruction."

"Dialogue?" Baxter's laugh was a harsh, grating sound. "We have had years of dialogue, Maria! Years of Gibson's patronizing lectures, of Albright's dismissive pronouncements, of Ainsworth's rigid dogma. And what did it yield? Stagnation. Complacency. A suffocating adherence to the status quo. My 'monologue,' as you call it, is a necessary correction. It is a thunderclap that will shatter the illusion of intellectual peace and force a re-evaluation. Gibson represents the academic world's aversion to true intellectual risk. He teaches caution, not courage. He preaches interpretation, not revolution. And the world, drowning in its own ambiguity, needs a decisive hand to guide it towards clarity, towards *his* clarity."

He paced a short distance, his movements agitated, yet still retaining a sense of controlled menace. "You, Maria, you were once a beacon of that potential. You understood the power of subversion, the elegance of intellectual defiance. You saw beyond the gilded cages of academia. And yet, you chose to return. You chose the comfort of familiarity, the safety of the established order, over the exhilarating uncertainty of true discovery. You became complicit in Gibson's intellectual betrayal."

Maria felt a pang of guilt, swiftly overridden by a surge of anger. Baxter was twisting her choices, her life, into a narrative that served his warped agenda. "My choices, Julian, were not betrayals. They were decisions based on what I believed to be the most ethical and constructive path. I sought to engage with the system, to push for change from within, not to tear it down in a destructive frenzy. You speak of narrative arcs, but yours has become a descent into madness, a tragic deviation from the path of intellectual exploration. You have become the very thing you claim to fight against – a dogma, a rigid interpretation that allows for no deviation, no dissent."

Baxter stopped, his gaze fixed on Gibson. A strange, almost tender expression flickered across his face, a fleeting echo of the man Gibson might have once inspired. "Professor Gibson, you taught me the power of the unfinished sentence, the allure of the untold story. You showed me how a carefully crafted ambiguity can leave a reader breathless, yearning for resolution. But you failed to teach me the importance of the definitive stroke, the courage to commit to a narrative, to imbue it with an absolute, unshakeable truth. You taught me to question everything, but you never taught me how to *know* anything. And in that omission, you rendered my entire education incomplete. You left me adrift in a sea of possibilities, unable to anchor myself to any definitive shore. Tonight, I correct that deficiency. Tonight, the sentence is not merely finished; it is *defined*."

He turned back to Maria, his eyes now alight with a chilling conviction. "You see, Maria, the world does not thrive on endless debate. It thrives on pronouncements. On declarations. On the unshakeable conviction of a single, powerful voice. Gibson's approach, while perhaps intellectually palatable in a detached academic setting, is fundamentally incapable of enacting change in the real world. It is a whisper in a hurricane. My approach, though it may seem... extreme... is the only means by which to be heard above the din. It is the only way to force the world to confront the truths it so desperately tries to ignore."

Maria remained silent, her mind working furiously. Baxter was lost in his own literary labyrinth, a prisoner of his own creation. But within that labyrinth, she sensed a thread, a weakness in his carefully constructed facade. He craved recognition, but more than that, he craved understanding. He wanted his grand narrative to be perceived, not just enacted. "Your narrative, Julian," she said, her voice barely a whisper, yet carrying the weight of her conviction, "is a brilliant, albeit terrifying, piece of fiction. You have crafted a compelling villain in Professor Gibson, a damsel in distress in me, and yourself as the tragic hero. The symbolism, the imagery, it's all there. But what about the underlying theme? What is the ultimate message you hope to convey beyond the shock of your actions? Is it simply that those who fail to embrace your ideas deserve to be silenced? Or is there something more profound, something that speaks to the very essence of what it means to pursue knowledge, to engage with ideas, to live a life of meaning?"

Baxter paused, his brow furrowed. He seemed to be genuinely considering her question, the first crack in his manic certainty. "The theme," he intoned, his voice deepening, taking on a almost professorial cadence, "is the inherent danger of intellectual complacency. The catastrophic consequences of failing to evolve, to question, to adapt. Professor Gibson represents the apex of that complacency. He became so enamored with the edifice of established knowledge that he forgot its purpose: to be a tool for progress, not a monument to the past. My work, this... act... it is a testament to the fact that the pursuit of knowledge is not a passive endeavor. It is an active, often violent, struggle against the forces of stagnation. And the greatest force of stagnation, I have learned, is not ignorance, but the comfortable, self-satisfied ignorance of those who believe they already possess the truth."

He gestured around the library, his gaze sweeping over the silent shelves. "This place, Maria, is a monument to that comfortable ignorance. Filled with the pronouncements of men long dead, their words preserved, revered, but rarely truly interrogated. They are relics, not living entities. And Gibson, in his role as custodian, became a relic himself. He stopped *living* the pursuit of knowledge and began merely preserving its artifacts. A fatal error. A narrative dead end."

Maria seized on this. "But Julian, even relics can serve a purpose. They can remind us of where we came from, of the foundations upon which we build. To simply discard them, to destroy them in your pursuit of the new, is to risk losing the context, the understanding of *why* we build. Your manuscript, your 'definitive statement,' it seeks to erase the past, to replace it with your singular vision. But is that true intellectual progress, or is it intellectual arrogance? To claim that only your perspective holds value, that all that came before is mere dross, that is the ultimate intellectual sin. That is the kind of closed-mindedness you claim to abhor."

"Arrogance?" Baxter's voice hardened, the brief flicker of introspection extinguished. "It is *clarity*, Maria. It is the courage to recognize that not all paths lead to enlightenment. Some paths lead to intellectual dead ends, to the preservation of outdated paradigms. Gibson's path led to intellectual decay. He became a curator of the past, not a harbinger of the future. My path, however, leads to a new understanding. A more potent, more relevant engagement with the fundamental truths of existence. And that, my dear Maria, requires a severing of ties with the irrelevant, with the stagnant."

He took another step towards Gibson, the letter opener now held with a deliberate, menacing calm. "Professor Gibson, you taught me to dissect narrative, to find the hidden meanings, the author's intent. And now, I will demonstrate the ultimate act of dissection. I will reveal the author's intent behind the narrative of your intellectual cowardice. You will bear witness to the fact that sometimes, to illuminate the truth, one must first purge the falsehood. And the greatest falsehood, in your case, was your refusal to embrace the radical. Your insistence on maintaining a comfortable, predictable narrative when a bolder, more profound one was begging to be written. Tonight, we rewrite the ending of that narrative. We give it the conclusion it so richly deserves." The chilling finality in his tone left no room for further argument, only the grim anticipation of the climax he so meticulously orchestrated. The library, a sanctuary of thought, had transformed into a stage for intellectual theatre, where the lines between literature and life had become terrifyingly blurred.

CHAPTER 13

THE NARRATOR'S DOWNFALL

The meticulously crafted facade of Julian Baxter's grand narrative began to crumble under the relentless pressure of Maria's intellectual assault. She saw the subtle shifts in his posture, the tightening of his jaw, the almost imperceptible flicker of unease in his eyes, signs that her carefully aimed barbs were finding their mark. He, who had positioned himself as the ultimate arbiter of literary truth, was now on trial, his own logic dissected with a precision that mirrored his supposed mastery of textual analysis.

"You speak of 'narrative consequence,' Julian," Maria continued, her voice resonating with a newfound authority, amplified by the tangible unraveling of his carefully constructed persona. "But what consequence is there in barbarity? You elevate your actions to the level of literary necessity, a plot point demanded by the 'author' of this grim reality. Yet, the masters you claim to emulate – the Shakespeare, the Dostoevsky – their power stemmed not from the shock of gratuitous violence, but from the profound exploration of the human condition. They revealed the darkness within us, yes, but they did so with nuance, with empathy, with a deep understanding of the motivations that drive even the most monstrous acts. Your 'resolution' for Professor Gibson is not a denouement; it is a crude, gratuitous act of vandalism, a desecration of intellect."

She gestured to the scattered books, their spines cracked and pages dog-eared, a stark contrast to the pristine order Baxter clearly craved. "You condemn Professor Gibson for his 'intellectual cowardice,' for retreating into the 'safe harbor of the established canon.' But is there not a profound irony in that accusation? You, who claim to be a revolutionary, a prophet of a new intellectual age, are now resorting to the oldest trick in the authoritarian playbook: silencing dissent through brute force. You accuse him of betraying the principles he preached, yet in this moment, you have utterly betrayed your own. Where is the intellectual honesty in holding a man at knifepoint? Where is the pursuit of truth in the threat of physical annihilation?"

Baxter visibly bristled at the accusation of 'vandalism' and 'desecration.' His carefully cultivated image of the enlightened revolutionary was being chipped away, replaced by the stark reality of his actions. He had envisioned himself as a tragic figure, a misunderstood genius forced into extreme measures by an unappreciative world. Maria's words stripped away that illusion, reducing his elaborate drama to a cheap, violent spectacle.

"You speak of nuance and empathy, Maria," Baxter retorted, his voice strained, the confident cadence beginning to falter. "But these are luxuries afforded by a world that has the leisure for such introspection. The world I inhabit, the world I am trying to awaken, is a world drowning in the comfortable lies of complacency. Professor Gibson's 'nuance' is a shield for inaction. His 'empathy' is a tool for maintaining the status quo. He is a physician who diagnoses a terminal illness but refuses to administer the painful, curative treatment, preferring to let the patient languish in a state of blissful ignorance until death claims them. My actions are not vandalism; they are surgery. Painful, yes, but ultimately life-saving."

"Surgery?" Maria echoed, her voice laced with incredulity. "You call this surgery? This is a dismemberment. You speak of 'awakening' the world, but a true awakening is not forced; it is inspired. It is born of enlightenment, not terror. You claim to be a physician, but you wield a surgeon's scalpel with the reckless abandonment of a butcher. You dissect Gibson's 'intellectual cowardice,' but you fail to see the profound hypocrisy in your own methodology. You condemn the established canon, yet you are so utterly beholden to its dramatic tropes, to the archetypes of the tragic villain and the desperate hero. Your narrative is not revolutionary; it is derivative, a hollow echo of the very literary traditions you profess to transcend."

She took a step closer, her gaze unwavering, forcing Baxter to confront the man behind the prophet. "You dismiss my concerns as 'luxuries,' Julian. But what is more luxurious than the unchecked ego that believes its own pronouncements are the only ones of value? What is more comfortable than the delusion that one's own interpretation is the absolute, immutable truth? You accuse Gibson of becoming a 'relic,' a preserver of the past, but you are rapidly becoming one yourself – a relic of a misguided ambition, a monument to the dangers of unchecked intellectual fervor. Your 'awakening' is nothing more than a descent into a personal hell, dragging anyone unfortunate enough to cross your path into its depths with you."

Baxter's composure was fraying. He had anticipated intellectual debate, perhaps even defiance, but he had not prepared for Maria's sharp, surgical dissection of his motivations and his methods. He saw himself as a man of profound insight, misunderstood and maligned. Her words painted him as a deluded egomaniac, a dangerous lunatic playing out a twisted literary fantasy. The adulation he had craved for years, the recognition he believed he deserved, was replaced by the sting of her indictment.

"You call it delusion," Baxter spat, his voice losing its earlier measured tone, a raw anger surfacing. "I call it clarity. I call it the courage to confront the rot at the heart of our intellectual institutions. Gibson's legacy is one of compromise, of watered-down truths, of academic politeness that shields an underlying intellectual cowardice. He is a symptom of the disease, Maria, and I am the cure. Your accusations of hypocrisy are born of your own complicity, your own unwillingness to acknowledge the fundamental flaws that plague the very system you claim to uphold. You are so deeply embedded in the comfortable lies that you cannot bear to see them exposed."

"My 'complicity,' as you call it, is a commitment to ethical engagement," Maria countered, her voice sharp and unwavering. "It is the belief that genuine progress is forged through reasoned discourse and constructive criticism, not through coercion and violence. You speak of 'exposing flaws,' but in your zeal to purge the 'rot,' you have become the rot yourself. You have allowed your resentment, your perceived injustices, to consume your intellect, to twist your pursuit of knowledge into a quest for vengeance. The masters you admire would weep to see their legacies warped into a justification for such barbarity."

She pointed to the manuscript on the stool, its pages filled with Baxter's furious scrawl. "Your 'definitive statement,' Julian, is not a testament to intellectual evolution; it is a confession of intellectual failure. You have not transcended the 'petty confines of academia'; you have succumbed to its basest impulses. You have traded the rigors of scholarship for the theatrics of a madman. You condemn Gibson for intellectual cowardice, yet you yourself have not had the courage to confront the true source of your bitterness – your own unfulfilled ambitions, your own crippling insecurities. Instead, you externalize your demons, projecting them onto Gibson and using him as a scapegoat for your own profound disappointment."

The words struck Baxter like a physical blow. The accusation of insecurity, of unfulfilled ambitions, was a raw nerve he had long guarded. He had built his entire persona around the idea of being a visionary, a man beyond such petty human frailties. Maria's direct assault on his ego, on the very foundations of his self-perception, left him momentarily stunned. He had expected to be the architect of this scene, the masterful narrator controlling every word, every reaction. Now, he felt himself being unmade, his narrative stripped bare, his motives exposed as petty and desperate.

"Insecurity?" Baxter finally managed, his voice a low growl, the manic gleam in his eyes replaced by a simmering rage. "You mistake the clarity of a man who has seen the truth for insecurity, Maria. I am not driven by petty grievances. I am driven by a profound understanding of the way the world truly works. Gibson, in his intellectual naivety, believed in the power of incremental change, of gentle persuasion. He was wrong. The world does not respond to whispers. It responds to earthquakes. And I, Maria, am about to create an earthquake."

He gestured wildly towards Gibson, his grip on the letter opener tightening to a white-knuckle clench. "You champion your 'reasoned discourse,' your 'constructive criticism.' But what has it achieved? It has achieved stagnation. It has achieved complacency. It has achieved a world where the loudest, most assertive voices, not the most intellectually sound, dictate the narrative. Professor Gibson is a symbol of that failed discourse. He is the embodiment of an academic establishment that has become too comfortable, too complacent, too afraid to confront the uncomfortable truths that lie just beneath the surface. Tonight, I shatter that complacency. Tonight, I force the world to look."

Maria watched him, a chilling realization dawning. Baxter was not just playing a role; he was deeply immersed in his own delusion, a prisoner of the narrative he had so painstakingly constructed. His intellectual brilliance had been perverted, twisted into a tool for his own destruction, and tragically, for the potential destruction of others. His current actions were not a sign of intellectual superiority, but of a profound intellectual and emotional bankruptcy. The carefully honed arguments, the literary allusions, all served to mask a desperate, almost pathetic, need to be seen, to be heard, to finally claim the validation he felt had been denied him.

"You speak of earthquakes, Julian," Maria said, her voice calm, yet carrying a profound sadness. "But earthquakes often cause devastation, not enlightenment. They destroy; they do not build. You believe that by tearing down Gibson, by silencing him, you will somehow elevate yourself, your ideas. But true intellectual legacy is not built on the destruction of others. It is built on the foundation of rigorous thought, of open debate, of the willingness to engage with opposing viewpoints, even when they are uncomfortable. Your manuscript, your grand pronouncements, they will be meaningless if they are born from a place of pure destruction, devoid of any genuine contribution to human understanding. You are not creating a new narrative; you are merely adding another chapter to the long, tragic history of intellectual hubris."

The intensity of Baxter's gaze wavered for a fraction of a second, as if Maria's words had pierced through the layers of his delusion. He had crafted his entire world around the idea that his was the *only* voice that mattered, the only perspective that held true intellectual weight. Maria's assertion that his narrative was merely another instance of hubris, a destructive rather than a creative act, seemed to momentarily disorient him. He had expected her to argue about literary theory, about the merits of his philosophical underpinnings. He had not anticipated her dismantling of his fundamental premise – that destruction was a prerequisite for creation, that silencing dissent was a valid intellectual pursuit.

"Hubris?" Baxter scoffed, the word tasting like ash in his mouth. He attempted to regain his footing, to reassert the authority he felt slipping away. "This is not hubris, Maria. This is clarity. This is the necessary purging of intellectual dross. Gibson represents the comfort of stagnation. He is the academic who has become so enamored with the preservation of knowledge that he has forgotten its purpose: to propel us forward. My work, my actions, they are not about destruction for its own sake. They are about clearing the ground, about making space for a truly radical, truly transformative understanding. Gibson's academic complacency is not a minor flaw; it is a catastrophic impediment to progress. And impediments, Maria, must be removed."

He gestured to the surrounding shelves, his voice rising with a feverish pitch. "These books, these pronouncements of long-dead scholars, they are monuments to a past that no longer serves us.

They are relics that have become idols. And Gibson, in his role as their guardian, has become an idolater. He worships the past, rather than learning from it to shape the future. He has become stagnant, a symbol of an academic world that clings to its traditions out of fear, not out of wisdom. My manuscript, my work, is not an attempt to erase that past, but to transcend it. To build upon it with a clarity and a conviction that Gibson and his ilk could never comprehend."

Maria met his escalating fervor with a quiet resolve. "But Julian," she implored, her voice laced with a genuine concern that seemed to baffle him, "transcendence is not achieved through obliteration. It is achieved through integration, through understanding the context from which we emerge. To dismiss the past entirely, to declare it 'dross,' is not transcendence; it is intellectual amnesia. You risk repeating the very mistakes you claim to abhor, for without understanding the foundations, how can you build something truly stable, something truly meaningful? Your manuscript may be a 'definitive statement' to you, but in its attempt to erase the intellectual lineage that preceded it, it risks becoming a footnote, rather than a chapter, in the grand narrative of human thought. True intellectual progress requires acknowledging the continuum, not severing it with a violent stroke."

Baxter flinched at the word "severing." It struck a chord, echoing his own desperate desire to break free from the constraints of the past, from the perceived failures of his academic predecessors. But Maria's gentle redirection, her framing of his actions not as progress but as intellectual amnesia, began to plant a seed of doubt. He had seen himself as a liberator, a revolutionary who would usher in a new era of intellectual honesty. Now, she was presenting him as a destroyer, a purveyor of ignorance who had mistaken recklessness for revelation. The carefully constructed edifice of his self-importance was beginning to show hairline fractures, his ego bruised by an intellectual onslaught it had never anticipated. He was accustomed to being the acclaimed intellect, the visionary whose pronouncements were met with awe, not with incisive critique that exposed the flimsy foundations of his perceived genius. The narrative he had so meticulously crafted was not just unraveling; it was imploding.

The cacophony of Baxter's spiraling rhetoric, the venomous pronouncements aimed at Maria and the increasingly desperate pronouncements about his own perceived intellectual destiny, had formed a deafening shield around Professor Gibson. For what felt like an eternity, he had been a captive audience to his own dismantling, a passive observer of his narrative being rewritten by a deranged hand. The sharp edge of the letter opener, a constant, gnawing presence against his throat, had been a physical manifestation of the intellectual violence he was enduring. He had seen himself as a defender of a noble tradition, a guardian of literary nuance, yet Baxter's words, however twisted, had managed to burrow under his skin, whispering insidious doubts. Had he, in his pursuit of academic rigor, become complacent? Had his dedication to the established canon inadvertently fostered an environment where such fanaticism could fester, unchallenged? The chilling echo of Maria's earlier accusations – "intellectual cowardice," "safe harbor of the established canon" – returned, now amplified by the terrifying reality of Baxter's deranged logic.

But as Maria's impassioned defense continued, as she deftly dissected Baxter's self-aggrandizing narrative, something shifted within Gibson. It wasn't just Maria's words that began to chip away at Baxter's carefully constructed facade; it was the palpable desperation in his voice, the widening chasm between the prophet he claimed to be and the frightened, cornered man he was revealing himself to be. Baxter's fixation on his own perceived genius, his utter conviction that he alone possessed the keys to unlocking some grand intellectual truth, was not a sign of strength, but of profound isolation. Gibson saw, with a clarity that was both agonizing and liberating, that Baxter's twisted interpretation of literature was not a revolutionary act, but a desperate attempt to impose order on a reality that had disappointed him. And in that moment, Gibson understood that his silence, his initial shock and awe, had been a form of complicity. He had allowed Baxter to define him, to cast him as the symbol of an outdated, stagnant intellectualism, without offering a counter-narrative, without reclaiming the very principles Baxter sought to corrupt.

A flicker of movement, a subtle shift in Baxter's hyper-focused gaze as Maria's words about "intellectual amnesia" landed their subtle blow, presented Gibson with an infinitesimal window. It was a risk, a monumental one, but the alternative – to remain a silent pawn in Baxter's deranged drama – was no longer an option. The shame of his own perceived inaction, the horror of what Baxter was proposing in the name of literary interpretation, coalesced into a surge of defiant energy. Gibson drew a deep, steadying breath, the cold steel of the letter opener a stark reminder of his precarious situation, yet it no longer felt like an insurmountable threat. Instead, it became a focal point, a catalyst.

"Julian," Gibson's voice, though strained, cut through the charged atmosphere with an unexpected resonance. It was not the meek, academic tone Baxter had come to expect, nor the intellectual sparring he had anticipated from Maria. It was something different, something grounded in a deep, visceral conviction. "You speak of purging 'dross,' of 'clearing the ground.' But what you are proposing is not purification; it is desecration. These words, these ideas, the very essence of what we strive to understand, they are not instruments of violence. They are tools for empathy, for introspection, for building bridges of understanding, not for burning them down."

Baxter's head snapped towards Gibson, his eyes wide with a mixture of surprise and nascent fury. The unexpected defiance, the direct challenge from the man he had so meticulously dehumanized, had clearly caught him off guard. The carefully orchestrated narrative in Baxter's mind, the one where Gibson was a passive victim, a symbol of intellectual decay, was suddenly disrupted. Gibson, the supposed embodiment of everything Baxter despised, was not only speaking, but he was speaking with an authority that Gibson himself hadn't realized he possessed until this very moment.

"You interpret poetry, Julian, not reality," Gibson continued, his voice gaining strength, fueled by the growing unease he saw on Baxter's face. "You see metaphors where there is only human suffering. You speak of 'radical transformation,' but true transformation, the kind that endures, that elevates, is born from contemplation, not from coercion. The very masters you claim to revere, the Dostoevsky, the Shakespeare, they understood that true insight comes from grappling with the complexities of the human heart, with its capacity for both light and shadow, not from imposing a brutal, singular vision. Your 'earthquake,' Julian, would shatter not just complacency, but the very foundations of reasoned discourse, leaving behind only rubble and the echoes of your own despair."

Gibson's words, a direct refutation of Baxter's entire premise, landed with the force of a physical blow. Baxter had anticipated Maria's intellectual challenge, her reasoned arguments against his methodology. But Gibson's direct condemnation, his rejection of Baxter's extremist interpretations as antithetical to the spirit of literary study itself, struck at the very core of Baxter's self-proclaimed intellectual superiority. It wasn't just about disagreeing with Baxter; it was about disavowing his entire framework, his warped understanding of the artistic and intellectual endeavor. Baxter, who had positioned himself as the ultimate interpreter, the arbiter of literary truth, found his authority undermined not by a peer, but by the very symbol of the tradition he claimed to transcend.

The stunned silence that followed Gibson's pronouncement was electric. Baxter, momentarily paralyzed by the unexpected defiance, his grip on the letter opener faltering almost imperceptibly, was caught in a vortex of his own creation. He had expected Gibson to break, to plead, to be the passive recipient of his intellectual grandiosity. Instead, Gibson had risen, not physically, but intellectually, to meet him, stripping away the veneer of Baxter's supposed enlightenment and exposing the raw, destructive impulse beneath.

It was in this precisely calibrated moment of Baxter's disarray, this infinitesimal pause in his manic monologue, that Maria seized her opportunity. She had been observing Gibson's internal struggle, recognizing the nascent spark of defiance. She had seen how Baxter's increasingly unhinged pronouncements had begun to chip away not only at Gibson's composure but at the very foundation of Baxter's own conviction. Gibson's unexpected articulation of his own principles, his direct repudiation of Baxter's violent interpretations, had created a ripple in the carefully constructed psychological battlefield Baxter had established. The unwavering certainty in Baxter's eyes, that messianic glow that had made him so terrifying, had flickered, replaced by a raw confusion, a vulnerability that Gibson's words had unearthed.

Maria moved with a speed born of adrenaline and a desperate hope. She didn't hesitate, didn't overthink. Her gaze, locked onto Baxter's momentary lapse, saw the precise instant when his focus shifted, however infinitesimally, from his internal narrative of grand purpose to the unexpected voice of his intended victim. The letter opener, still held against Gibson's throat, was a tangible threat, but Baxter's mind, for that fleeting second, was no longer solely on Gibson. It was reeling from the implications of Gibson's words, from the unexpected challenge to his own intellectual legitimacy.

"Julian," Maria's voice was a sharp, clear counterpoint to Baxter's preceding monologues, cutting through the charged air with an urgent practicality. She didn't waste time with further philosophical debate. Her focus was singular: to disrupt Baxter's hold, to exploit the sliver of opportunity Gibson's defiance had created. "Your manuscript. You speak of it as a revelation, a grand unveiling. But what does it truly reveal, Julian? It reveals a profound misunderstanding of the very texts you claim to champion. It reveals a mind so consumed by its own perceived grievances that it has lost sight of the beauty and complexity it purports to admire."

She took a measured step forward, her movements deliberate, designed to draw Baxter's attention away from Gibson and towards her. She knew that Baxter craved an audience, that his delusion was fueled by the desire to be seen and acknowledged. By positioning herself as the primary interlocutor, the one engaging with his 'masterpiece,' she aimed to redirect his predatory focus. "You condemn Professor Gibson for his 'passivity'," she continued, her voice carefully modulated, projecting an almost academic interest that belied the perilous situation. "But in this moment, Julian, who is truly passive? Professor Gibson has found his voice, has he not? He has articulated his belief in the power of words to build, to connect, to enlighten. And what are you doing? You are silencing him. You are demonstrating the very stagnation you claim to abhor by resorting to the most primitive form of censorship: physical threat. That, Julian, is not the action of a revolutionary intellect. It is the act of a man who has run out of ideas, and resorts to intimidation when his arguments fail."

The direct accusation, delivered with such calm certainty, landed squarely in the nascent confusion Baxter was experiencing. Gibson's words had planted a seed of doubt; Maria's now aimed to cultivate it into a full-blown crisis of confidence. She was not attacking his intellect, not directly. She was attacking the *efficacy* of his actions, suggesting that his methods were not only morally reprehensible but also, more importantly to Baxter, intellectually bankrupt. She was framing his grand, violent act not as a necessary purging but as a pathetic admission of intellectual failure.

Baxter's grip tightened on the letter opener, his knuckles white. He was torn, his focus fractured. Gibson's unexpected words had dislodged him from his self-assured perch, and Maria was now expertly fanning the flames of his insecurity, her every word designed to expose the hollowness at the core of his grand pronouncements. He had envisioned a confrontation, a dramatic crescendo where he would emerge as the victor, the prophet validated. Instead, he found himself on the defensive, his carefully constructed narrative unraveling under the combined pressure of Gibson's quiet defiance and Maria's incisive critique. The sheer audacity of Gibson's intellectual stand, delivered in the face of imminent physical danger, had unnerved him. It was a level of conviction Baxter had never anticipated, a testament to the very principles he was so determined to obliterate. And Maria, sensing this internal turmoil, pressed her advantage, her voice unwavering, her gaze fixed on him with an unnerving intensity. She was not just talking; she was dismantling him, piece by painstaking piece, using his own words, his own ambitions, as the tools of his undoing.

The calculated silence that had descended upon the room, a fragile peace Gibson and Maria had meticulously carved from Baxter's frenzied pronouncements, shattered like glass. Baxter, stripped bare of his intellectual armor, exposed not as a prophet but as a hollow man, recoiled from their combined assault. Gibson's unwavering refutation, his embodiment of the very principles Baxter sought to extinguish, had not merely wounded his pride; it had fractured his delusion. Maria's sharp dissection of his failed arguments, her eloquent accusation of intellectual bankruptcy, had delivered the coup de grâce to his carefully constructed facade. He was no longer the messianic figure dictating literary destiny; he was a cornered animal, his eyes blazing with a primal, terrifying fury.

The letter opener, held loosely in his trembling hand, now became the sole focus of his unraveling reality. The meticulously planned tableau, the academic duel he had envisioned culminating in his vindication, had imploded. Instead of a captive audience to his genius, he faced two adversaries who saw through his grand delusions to the desperate fear beneath. Gibson's quiet strength, the unyielding conviction in his gaze, mirrored Maria's sharp intellect, their combined presence a stark testament to the very values Baxter had sought to obliterate. He had anticipated intellectual challenges, he had even braced himself for the possibility of being dismissed, but this... this was an annihilation of his narrative, a complete dismantling of his perceived reality. His own words, flung back at him with devastating accuracy, had trapped him, leaving him with only the raw, unadulterated rage that festered in the vacuum where his grand ideas once resided.

"You... you *cowards*," Baxter spat, the words thick with a venom that dripped from his contorted features. His voice, once a resonant instrument of perceived authority, now cracked with a desperate, guttural sound. His eyes, wide and unfocused, darted between Gibson and Maria, searching for an escape, a reprieve, anything to reignite the crumbling embers of his self-importance. The letter opener, a pathetic substitute for the intellectual weapons he had so arrogantly wielded, felt heavy and alien in his grip. It was no longer a symbol of his intellectual prowess, nor a tool of intellectual persuasion; it was a desperate, pathetic last resort, a testament to his utter failure.

"This is not how it was meant to be," he hissed, his voice rising to a frantic pitch. "This was meant to be a cleansing! A revelation! And you... you stand in the way of progress, of truth!" His gaze, wild and unfettered by any semblance of reason, fixated on Gibson. The professor, who had been the unwilling center of Baxter's deranged narrative, now became the immediate target of his unleashed fury. "You, Gibson! You, who have grown fat on the stale crumbs of tradition! You, who have stifled innovation, who have buried true genius under mountains of pedantic footnotes! You represent everything that is rotten, everything that must be purged!"

As Baxter's voice escalated, so did the tremor in his hand. The letter opener, its silver glinting dully in the dim light, seemed to vibrate with his agitated energy. He took a jerky step forward, his gaze locked onto Gibson, a predator assessing its cornered prey. The air crackled with an unbearable tension, the scent of old paper and dust suddenly thick with the metallic tang of impending violence. The towering shelves of books, once silent witnesses to intellectual discourse, now seemed to loom like ominous sentinels, their spines a blur of forgotten narratives that had, in this moment, been brutally interrupted.

Gibson, though outwardly calm, felt a cold knot tighten in his stomach. He had seen the shift in Baxter, the precipice of madness he had teetered on, and now he was plunging headlong into the abyss. He knew Baxter's words were a desperate attempt to reassert control, to reclaim the narrative that had so spectacularly slipped from his grasp. But Gibson also recognized the terrifying authenticity of Baxter's rage. It was not just academic frustration; it was the visceral desperation of a man whose entire world had been deconstructed, leaving him with nothing but the raw, exposed nerves of his own profound disillusionment.

"Julian, you're not thinking clearly," Gibson said, his voice steady, a deliberate counterpoint to Baxter's frenzied outburst. He kept his own hands visible, open, a silent plea for reason, a clear signal that he posed no immediate physical threat. He knew that any sudden movement, any perceived act of aggression, could be the spark that ignited the powder keg. "This isn't about purging. It's about understanding. It's about engaging with ideas, not destroying them." He spoke with a measured cadence, attempting to weave a thread of logic through the chaotic storm of Baxter's emotions. He was trying to offer Baxter an alternative, a path back from the edge, without conceding any ground on the principles he held dear.

Baxter scoffed, a harsh, grating sound. "Understanding? Engagement? You speak of these things as if they are benevolent acts! But they are the tools of stagnation, Professor! The endless debate, the committees, the conferences... they are all designed to dilute, to neuter, to maintain the status quo! My work... my work is a catalyst! An earthquake! It is meant to shatter the complacency, to force a confrontation with the raw, undeniable truths that your precious canon has conveniently ignored!" He gestured wildly with the letter opener, its tip now dangerously close to Gibson's face. The sharp metallic scent seemed to fill Gibson's nostrils, a primal warning.

Maria, positioned slightly behind Gibson, her eyes never leaving Baxter, saw the moment of terrifying clarity in his madness. The letter opener wasn't just a prop; it was a genuine threat. Baxter's eyes, once alight with intellectual fervor, now held a desperate glint, a feverish determination that spoke of profound despair. He had reached his breaking point, and the carefully constructed façade of intellectual superiority had crumbled, revealing the raw, unadulterated panic of a man who had lost everything. The culmination of his life's work, his magnum opus, had been exposed as a delusion, and the weight of that realization was crushing him.

"Julian," Maria's voice was a low, controlled hum, cutting through the rising hysteria. She moved with an almost imperceptible fluidity, her focus entirely on Baxter and the weapon he held. She had seen Gibson's calm resolve, but she also recognized the immense danger Baxter represented. Her initial strategy had been to dismantle his intellectual arguments, to expose the flaws in his reasoning. But that strategy had clearly failed to contain his escalating desperation. The intellectual duel had devolved into something far more primal, far more dangerous. "Your 'earthquake'," she continued, her words carefully chosen to resonate with Baxter's own rhetoric, but subtly twisted to highlight his current state, "is not a force of nature, Julian. It is the frantic flailing of a drowning man. You claim to be a revolutionary, but what you are demonstrating is simply a desperate attempt to cling to relevance, to force recognition when your ideas have failed to ignite on their own."

Baxter's head whipped towards Maria, his eyes narrowing with a renewed intensity. He had dismissed her as a secondary player, an obstructionist academic. But her words, delivered with such unnerving calm, pricked at the raw wound of his failure. She was not merely disagreeing with him; she was diagnosing him, dissecting his motivations with an accuracy that bordered on cruel.

"You understand nothing," Baxter snarled, his voice tight with suppressed rage. "You are as blind as he is, clinging to your comfortable illusions." He took another step, closing the distance between himself and Gibson. The letter opener was now inches from Gibson's throat, the polished steel reflecting the panic that flickered in Baxter's eyes. Gibson remained still, his breathing shallow, his mind racing. He knew Maria was strategizing, looking for an opening, but the immediacy of the threat was overwhelming. He could feel the coolness of the metal against his skin, a chilling testament to the fragility of his existence.

It was in this precise, agonizing moment, with Baxter's desperate gaze locked on Gibson, his body tensed for a decisive, violent action, that Maria made her move. It was a gamble, a desperate, uncalculated lunge born of pure instinct and the urgent need to protect Gibson. She didn't shout, she didn't warn. She simply acted. With a sudden, explosive burst of energy, she surged forward, not towards Baxter's face, but towards his hand, the hand that held the letter opener.

Her movement was a blur, a desperate act of physical intervention against a man consumed by intellectual and emotional turmoil. She knew she couldn't outfight him, but she might be able to disrupt him, to break his focus just long enough. Her fingers, honed by years of meticulous research and delicate handling of rare manuscripts, now reached for the slender blade and the hand that gripped it. The air filled with the sound of rustling fabric and a sharp, surprised intake of breath from Baxter.

Baxter, utterly consumed by his fixation on Gibson, was caught completely off guard. Maria's sudden, aggressive lunge was an unexpected variable, a physical intrusion into his carefully orchestrated, albeit chaotic, endgame. His grip on the letter opener, already strained by his agitation, faltered as Maria's hand clamped down on his wrist. The sharp edge of the metal, moments away from inflicting irreparable damage, was suddenly wrenched violently to the side.

A yelp of surprise and pain escaped Baxter as Maria's focused strength, amplified by adrenaline, took hold. The letter opener clattered onto the polished wooden floor with a sharp, metallic ring, skittering away into the shadows of the bookshelves. The immediate physical threat to Gibson vanished, replaced by the immediate, volatile chaos of a physical struggle. Baxter, his intended action thwarted, erupted in a guttural roar of pure, unadulterated fury. He lunged at Maria; his face contorted with a rage that had finally broken free of its intellectual pretenses.

"You interfering bitch!" He screamed, his voice raw and hoarse, the carefully cultivated veneer of intellectualism utterly stripped away. He shoved Maria with brutal force, sending her stumbling backward. The neatly arranged books on a nearby shelf swayed precariously, a cascade of paper and binding threatening to rain down on them. The academic sanctuary had devolved into a raw, desperate fight for survival, the quiet dignity of scholarship replaced by the primal instinct to protect and to lash out.

Gibson, momentarily frozen by the sudden escalation, snapped back to the grim reality of their situation. The letter opener was gone, but Baxter was far from neutralized. He saw Maria reeling, her breath coming in ragged gasps, and a wave of protective fury surged through him. The professor who had prided himself on intellectual detachment was now wholly, viscerally present in the terrifying immediacy of the physical confrontation. He had been a captive audience to Baxter's descent into madness, and now he was forced to confront its violent, physical manifestation. The narrative Gibson had so carefully defended, the integrity of knowledge itself, was under direct, brutal assault, and he would not stand idly by. His academic life, his reputation, everything he stood for, was on the line, not just in the abstract realm of ideas, but in this raw, desperate struggle amidst the hallowed halls of learning. He took a step towards Baxter, his fists clenching, the quiet scholar ready to defend more than just his reputation – he was ready to defend Maria, and the very principles Baxter sought to destroy. The academic thriller had just taken a terrifying, physical turn. The intellectual duel had ended, and a desperate struggle for survival had begun.

The vellum card, brittle with age and the residual tremor of Baxter's desperate grip, slipped from his grasp as Maria's counter-move disarmed him. It fluttered, a pale, silent moth, against the dark mahogany of the floorboards, unnoticed amidst the frantic scramble for equilibrium. Gibson, his senses still sharp, his focus narrowed to the immediate threat Baxter now posed to Maria, registered the slight disruption in the air, the subtle shift of mass, but his attention was anchored to the enraged man before him. Maria, her breath ragged but her resolve steely, maintained her defensive posture, her eyes scanning Baxter for any further signs of aggression, her mind already calculating the next calculated risk.

It was Gibson, as Baxter stumbled back, momentarily disoriented by the unexpected physical resistance, who saw it. The vellum card lay stark against the rich grain of the wood, a stark white interruption in the sepia tones of the study. His gaze, trained to spot the subtlest anomaly, the faintest deviation from the expected, was drawn to it. It was not merely a piece of paper; it was an object with intent, dropped in the heat of conflict, its presence a deliberate act, even in its unintended expulsion. He knew, with a certainty that chilled him, that Baxter, in his final, unhinged moments, had intended this card for an audience. An audience that, in Baxter's warped perception, was always present, always watching, always waiting to bear witness to his tragic brilliance.

"The card," Gibson managed to get out, his voice a low growl, barely audible over the ragged breathing of Baxter and the thumping of his own heart. He gestured subtly with his chin towards the floor, his eyes never leaving Baxter, creating a fragile, almost imperceptible divide between the immediate danger and the artifact of Baxter's undoing. Maria, following his gaze, saw it then. The small, rectangular piece of aged parchment, lying innocuously near Baxter's erratically twitching feet.

Baxter, his chest heaving, his eyes still burning with a wild, untamed fury, seemed to register Gibson's words, or perhaps just the shift in Gibson's posture. He glanced down, a flicker of something – alarm? recognition? – crossing his contorted features. The card was a fragment of his grand narrative, a carefully prepared epilogue to his staged drama. Its discovery, its retrieval by his adversaries, was an unwelcome intrusion, a theft of his final pronouncement.

"It's nothing," Baxter rasped, a pathetic attempt to dismiss the tangible evidence of his carefully constructed world crumbling around him. "A discarded note. An errant thought." But the tremor in his voice betrayed him, the desperate denial a transparent attempt to reclaim a sliver of control.

Maria, however, was already moving. Gibson held Baxter's attention, a human shield against any further violent impulse, while Maria, her movements economical and deliberate, glided towards the card. She knelt, her body a low profile, her eyes scanning Baxter's reaction. He tensed, his breath catching in his throat, his gaze darting from Gibson to Maria, a trapped animal considering its options. But the physical exertion of the struggle, the sheer force of his unraveling, had sapped his immediate strength. He was too consumed by his rage, too lost in the labyrinth of his own delusion, to react effectively to this new, albeit minor, affront.

Maria's fingers, long and slender, delicate yet firm, closed around the vellum. It felt strangely cool, almost unnaturally preserved, a stark contrast to the humid tension of the room. As she lifted it, her eyes scanned the surface. There was writing on it, in Baxter's distinctive, flamboyant hand. Not a manifesto, not a declaration, but something far more personal, far more revealing. It was a poem.

She held it up, turning it so the dim light of the study lamp caught the ink. Gibson, still maintaining his wary vigil, managed a quick, sidelong glance. Baxter, his focus momentarily broken by the sight of the card in Maria's possession, let out a strangled cry, a sound of pure, unadulterated anguish. It was the cry of a child whose treasured possession had been taken, the sound of a soul laid bare, exposed to the harsh glare of an indifferent world.

"Give that back!" Baxter bellowed, his voice cracking with a desperate, raw emotion that was far more chilling than his earlier pronouncements of intellectual superiority. He made a lunge, a desperate, clumsy movement, but Gibson was there, a solid, unyielding presence, blocking his path. Baxter recoiled, his chest heaving, his eyes blazing with a fresh wave of despair. The poem, the final testament to his perceived genius, was now in their hands.

Donny, realizing what Maria was about to do, revealed himself. His service weapon trained on Baxter. Baxter looked puzzled and it was clear to Donny that Baxter had not anticipated his involvement.

Maria's lips moved silently as she read, her brow furrowed in concentration. The academic analysis, the intellectual dissection that had been her primary weapon, now gave way to a different kind of understanding, a profound empathy for the tragic figure before them, even as she recognized the danger he represented. She began to read aloud, her voice low and steady, a somber counterpoint to Baxter's ragged breaths.

"They call it madness, this fire in my soul,
This vision that burns, beyond their dull control.
A symphony unheard, a canvas unperceived,
A truth they cannot grasp, a destiny bereaved.
They see the artist's hand, the fevered, frantic art,
But miss the cosmic dance, the breaking of the heart.
This world, a cage of clay, so drab, so dim, so small,
Cannot contain the light, the spirit's mighty call.
They judge the edifice, the towering, grand design,
And see but foolish dreams, no touch of the divine.
They whisper of descent, of reason's fragile hold,
When I am merely reaching for stories yet untold.
My masterpiece, I know, though shrouded in their doubt,

A whispered prophecy, that time will shout about.

But in this shadowed age, where shadows hold their sway,

The prophet is undone, by those who look away.

A hero's tragic fall, not by a noble foe,

But by the common touch, the seeds that cannot grow.

And so I fade, unseen, my legacy undone,

A star extinguished, ere its race was truly run."

As Maria's voice echoed in the sudden, heavy silence, a profound shift occurred in Baxter. The raging storm within him seemed to ebb, replaced by a deep, despondent weariness. The poem, his final, desperate cry into the void, had been heard, but not in the way he had intended. It was not a pronouncement of his impending apotheosis, but a lament for his own perceived failure, a confession of his artistic isolation, a poignant, heartbreaking admission that he, the architect of his own grand narrative, had ultimately failed to truly understand his own creation.

He sank to his knees, the fight draining out of him, leaving only the hollow shell of a man who had chased a phantom and found only emptiness. His hands, no longer wielding a weapon or gesticulating wildly, fell limply to his sides. His gaze, once piercing and accusatory, was now distant, unfocused, lost in the internal landscape of his own profound disillusionment. The grandiosity that had fueled his earlier tirade had evaporated, leaving behind the raw, vulnerable core of a deeply wounded ego.

Gibson and Maria exchanged a look. Donny moved in closer still brandishing his service weapon. The academic battle had concluded, the intellectual duel had been won, but the cost was etched in the defeated slump of Baxter's shoulders, the vacant stare in his eyes. The man who had sought to impose his singular vision upon the world had, in the end, been undone by it, and by his own inability to reconcile it with reality. The poem, a distillation of his perceived persecution, his intellectual alienation, was not a testament to his genius, but a tragic epitaph to his delusion. It was a masterpiece of self-deception, a work of art whose creator had become its first and final victim.

The poem, in its brevity, contained the essence of Baxter's downfall. It was a lament, yes, but also a subtle, almost unconscious confession. He spoke of a "symphony unheard," a "canvas unperceived," a "truth they cannot grasp." These were not the objective failings of his audience, but the subjective limitations of his own perspective. He saw himself as a prophet, a seer, blinded by his own vision, yet unwilling to acknowledge that perhaps the "cosmic dance" was merely a chaotic swirling of his own anxieties, and the "breaking of the heart" was the inevitable consequence of his own self-inflicted isolation.

His masterpiece, he claimed, was a "whispered prophecy." But what if the prophecy was merely a reflection of his own desperate need for validation? What if the "divine touch" he spoke of was simply the intoxicating allure of his own ego, amplified by the echo chamber of his own making? The poem revealed a profound disconnect between his perception of himself and the reality of his impact. He believed he was reaching for "stories yet untold," but in truth, he was merely retelling his own familiar narrative of the misunderstood genius, a trope as old as time, and as transparent as Baxter's own carefully constructed persona.

The "hero's tragic fall, not by a noble foe, but by the common touch, the seeds that cannot grow." This was the core of his self-pity. He cast Gibson and Maria not as intellectual equals who had challenged his work, but as representatives of the mundane, the ordinary, the forces that stifled true innovation. He couldn't conceive that his ideas, so potent in his own mind, simply failed to resonate, to take root, to grow in the fertile ground of intellectual discourse. The "common touch" was not a destructive force; it was simply the necessary element of shared understanding, the foundation upon which any true intellectual edifice must be built.

And then, the devastating finality of "And so I fade, unseen, my legacy undone, a star extinguished, ere its race was truly run." It was a plea for recognition, a desperate yearning for immortality that his work, in its profound isolation, could never grant him. He saw himself as a supernova, destined for cosmic significance, but ultimately snuffed out by the limitations of the universe, or rather, by the limitations of those who were not enlightened enough to witness his brilliance.

The words hung in the air, heavy with a tragic irony. Baxter, the man who had so confidently declared his intention to rewrite literary history, to reshape the very foundations of academic understanding, was reduced to this: a heartbroken poet, mourning the unacknowledged genius of a masterpiece that, in its conception and its execution, had ultimately failed to transcend the solitary confines of his own fractured psyche. The final poem was not a testament to his power, but a poignant elegy to his profound and tragic isolation. It was the echo of a genius that never truly existed, a lament for a masterpiece that was, perhaps, never truly understood, even by its creator, in its fundamental disconnect from the world it sought to influence. He had chased an ideal, a platonic form of literary perfection, and in his relentless pursuit, had lost sight of the human element, the collaborative spirit, the very essence of what makes art truly endure. The vellum card, clutched now in Maria's hand, was not merely a piece of paper, but a Rosetta Stone to Baxter's unraveling, a final, heartbreaking confession of a dream deferred, a genius stillborn, a tragedy of his own making. The academic thriller had reached its denouement, not with a bang of intellectual triumph, but with the quiet, mournful whisper of a poet's broken heart. The downfall was complete, and the poem, unintended witness to his ruin, served as the final, somber punctuation mark.

The library, once a hallowed sanctuary of whispered knowledge and the hushed rustle of turning pages, now bore the stark, undeniable imprint of a crime scene. The air, moments before thick with the acrid scent of Baxter's unraveling mind and the faint, papery dust of forgotten lore, was now tainted with a new, metallic tang – the sharp, sterile scent of impending officialdom. Scattered across the richly patterned Persian rug were not just the debris of Baxter's final, desperate performance – overturned chairs, pages torn from priceless tomes, a fallen bust of some long-forgotten philosopher staring blankly at the ceiling – but also the subtle, yet unmistakable, indicators of a struggle that had pushed intellectualism to its brutal, physical extreme.

Maria, her breath still uneven but her posture radiating a quiet, steely resolve, knelt beside Baxter. The vellum card, that final, poignant testament to his fractured genius, lay clutched in her hand, its brittle surface a stark contrast to the rough wool of Baxter's disheveled tweed jacket. Baxter himself was a study in utter collapse. The fire that had blazed in his eyes, the feverish intensity that had animated his every gesture, had been extinguished, leaving behind a hollow shell of a man, defeated not by an external force, but by the crushing weight of his own meticulously constructed delusion. He offered no resistance as Donny gently, but firmly, secured his wrists with a pair of zip ties. The soft hiss of the plastic tightening was a brutal counterpoint to the grandiose pronouncements that had echoed through these halls just minutes before. His grand artistic vision, the intricate tapestry of narrative he had woven with such obsessive care, was dissolving like mist in the harsh glare of reality. The applause he had so desperately craved had been replaced by the stark, unforgiving click of plastic fasteners.

Gibson stood a silent sentinel nearby, his gaze sweeping over the room, cataloging the chaos with the practiced eye of someone who had seen such wreckage before. He noted the specific damage to the bookshelves, the careless disregard for the very artifacts Baxter claimed to revere. It was a desecration, not of knowledge itself, but of the *idea* of knowledge, twisted and warped to serve Baxter's increasingly unstable narrative. He watched as Baxter, his head bowed, his shoulders slumped in a posture of utter, abject defeat, was guided to his feet. There was no defiance left, no last-ditch attempt to reclaim his narrative. The mask of the tortured artist, the misunderstood genius, had finally shattered, revealing the broken man beneath.

The silence that followed was profound, broken only by the distant, but steadily approaching, wail of sirens. It was a sound that seemed to punctuate the finality of Baxter's downfall, a soundtrack to the abrupt cessation of his reign. Maria rose, her movements economical, her face etched with a weariness that went beyond the physical exertion. She had faced down not just an opponent, but an entire philosophy, a twisted ideology that had sought to redefine reality through the lens of a single, incandescent ego.

As the first uniformed officers entered the library, their heavy boots echoing on the polished wood, the scene transformed. The intimate, almost suffocating atmosphere of Baxter's private intellectual arena was invaded by the impersonal efficiency of the law. The flickering lamplight, which had cast dramatic shadows on Baxter's face during his final, desperate monologues, now seemed harsh and unforgiving, exposing every detail of the disarray. The officers, their faces grim and professional, moved with a practiced haste, their commands clear and authoritative, cutting through the remnants of Baxter's dramatic pronouncements.

Baxter offered no resistance, no last-ditch attempt to escape or to reassert his control. He was a puppet whose strings had been definitively cut, his grand theatrical performance abruptly concluded not with a thunderous ovation, but with the mundane, yet devastating, clang of handcuffs. He was led away, his gaze fixed on the floor, his once vibrant eyes now dull and vacant. The elaborate edifice of his intellect, the carefully constructed theories, the grand pronouncements about the nature of art and reality – all of it had crumbled, leaving him exposed and utterly vulnerable. The library, which had served as both his stage and his fortress, now stood as the silent witness to his undoing. The books, once his cherished companions and tools, were now mere props in the grim tableau of his arrest.

Maria and Donny watched him go, a complex mix of emotions swirling within them. There was relief, undeniably, the satisfaction of having navigated a treacherous intellectual and emotional landscape and emerged victorious. But there was also a profound sense of melancholy. Baxter was a tragic figure, a man consumed by his own brilliance, a mind so potent that it had ultimately become his prison. He had chased a phantom of perfection, a Platonic ideal of artistic expression, and in doing so, had become lost to the very world he sought to influence. The poem, clutched in her hand, was a stark reminder of his profound isolation, a lament for a genius that had never truly found its audience, or perhaps, had never truly found itself. The curtain had fallen on Baxter's self-made tragedy, and the silence that followed was not one of triumph, but of profound, somber reflection. The grand narrative had reached its inevitable, devastating conclusion. The academy, and indeed the world, would breathe a collective sigh of relief, but the echoes of Baxter's descent would linger, a cautionary tale whispered in the hushed halls of intellectual pursuit.

The vellum card felt strangely fragile in Maria's hand, a stark reminder of the distance she had traversed. It had begun as an academic puzzle, a theoretical debate that had spiraled into a dangerous obsession. Now, it was tangible proof of a mind unraveled, a life irrevocably altered. The library, once a place of quiet contemplation and scholarly pursuit, had become the arena for a battle of wills, a clash of ideologies that had nearly cost lives. The silence that now permeated the room was heavy, not with the anticipation of new discoveries, but with the somber weight of consequences.

Baxter's captors were efficient, their movements practiced and devoid of any discernible emotion. They treated him not as the intellectual titan he believed himself to be, but as a disturbed individual who had committed a series of grave offenses. The uniform, the clipped tones of command, the metallic glint of the handcuffs – all served to strip away the last vestiges of his carefully cultivated persona. He was no longer the visionary artist, the architect of a new paradigm, but simply a man apprehended, his grand illusions shattered against the unyielding bedrock of reality.

Gibson approached Maria, his gaze still scanning the room, his senses alert for any residual threats, any lingering echoes of Baxter's volatile presence. He recognized the weariness in her posture, the subtle slump of her shoulders that spoke of an immense burden lifted, but also of the deep emotional toll it had taken. The intellectual sparring, the intricate dance of argument and counter-argument, had been brutal, and its aftermath was palpable.

"It's over," Gibson said, his voice low, a quiet affirmation in the echoing space. He gestured vaguely towards the officers escorting Baxter out of the library, their figures receding down the grand corridor. The rhythmic tread of their boots on the marble floor was a stark contrast to the soaring, often nonsensical, rhetoric Baxter had employed.

Maria nodded, her eyes still fixed on the vellum card. "He really believed it, didn't he?" she murmured, her voice barely audible. "The whole narrative. The misunderstood genius, the world too dull to comprehend his vision."

Gibson's gaze softened as he looked at her. He understood the complexity of her reaction. It wasn't just about solving a case; it was about witnessing the profound, and often tragic, consequences of intellectual hubris and profound psychological disturbance. "He constructed a reality where he was always the hero, always the victim of a world that couldn't appreciate him. And when that reality began to fray, he couldn't cope."

The library, as the uniformed officers continued their methodical sweep, began to feel less like a stage and more like a crime scene, stripped bare of its pretense. The books remained, silent witnesses, their pages filled with the wisdom and folly of centuries, indifferent to the human drama that had unfolded among them. Baxter's attempt to usurp that legacy, to rewrite it through the warped lens of his own ambition, had ultimately led to his own undoing.

Maria carefully placed the vellum card into a sterile evidence bag that one of the forensic technicians offered her. The poetry, so potent in its expression of Baxter's isolation, was now a piece of evidence, a clue to the labyrinthine workings of his mind. It was a testament to a brilliance that had, tragically, been self-destructive. The grand pronouncements, the elaborate theories, the carefully curated persona – all of it had been a facade, a magnificent illusion designed to mask a deep-seated insecurity and a profound alienation.

As the last of the uniformed officers filed out, leaving behind only Gibson, Maria, and Donny along with the lingering scent of disinfectant, the silence of the library returned, but it was a different kind of silence. It was no longer charged with the imminent threat of violence or the electric tension of intellectual debate. It was a quiet, heavy silence, filled with the unspoken acknowledgment of a chapter closed, a narrative concluded. Baxter's reign of intellectual terror was over. The curtain had fallen on his tragic play, and the applause he had so desperately sought would never come. Instead, there was only the stark, unvarnished reality of his crimes, and the quiet, undeniable truth of his downfall. The academic thriller had reached its final, somber act, not with a bang of intellectual triumph, but with the quiet, mournful whisper of a broken spirit and the cold, hard clang of justice.

CHAPTER 14

AFTERMATH AND RECKONING

The silence that descended upon Elmwood University in the days following Julian Baxter's arrest was not the peaceful quiet of academic contemplation, but a heavy, suffocating shroud. It clung to the ornate gothic architecture, seeped into the lecture halls where syllabi were dissected with newfound, morbid intensity, and settled like a fine, grey dust over the manicured lawns. The shockwaves from the events in the library, the shattering of a carefully constructed reality and the brutal unveiling of a mind teetering on the precipice of madness, had rippled outwards, leaving the academic community adrift in a sea of disbelief and unease. The hallowed halls, once symbols of intellectual pursuit and the pursuit of truth, now felt tainted, scared by the darkness that had been exposed.

Students, their youthful exuberance muted, moved through the campus with a subdued reverence. Conversations that had once buzzed with the usual academic anxieties – upcoming exams, dissertation deadlines, the latest faculty gossip – were now hushed, punctuated by stolen glances and whispered questions. The vibrant tapestry of campus life, usually a symphony of diverse voices and eager minds, had been muted, replaced by a pervasive sense of shared, unspoken trauma. The specter of Baxter, not as the brilliant but eccentric academic he had presented himself to be, but as a cold-blooded murderer and architect of delusion, haunted every quadrangle, every common room. The very air seemed to hold its breath, as if afraid to disturb the fragile peace that had been so violently disrupted.

Faculty members, too, found themselves navigating a new and deeply unsettling terrain. The collegial camaraderie, the shared pursuit of knowledge that had always been the bedrock of their professional lives, was now tinged with suspicion and a profound sense of vulnerability. Baxter had been one of their own, a colleague, a member of the intellectual ecosystem. His descent into such extreme violence forced a reckoning, a painful introspection into the pressures and potential pitfalls that lay hidden beneath the veneer of academic respectability. Questions, once theoretical, now carried the weight of chilling consequence: How had they missed the signs? What unspoken burdens had he carried? And, more disturbingly, could such darkness fester within their own ranks again? The intellectual rigor they so prided themselves on felt suddenly insufficient, a mere paper-thin defense against the chaotic forces of the human psyche.

Dr. Aris Gibson, his usual stoic demeanor underscored by a new layer of weariness, found himself increasingly sought after, not for his groundbreaking research in ancient history, but for his quiet, steady presence and his perceived understanding of Baxter's unraveling. He moved through the campus like a shadow, observing the subtle shifts in atmosphere, the nervous energy that pulsed beneath the surface of everyday life. He saw the unease in the eyes of his colleagues, the furtive glances exchanged during faculty meetings, the palpable relief that warred with the lingering shock. Elmwood was a community built on trust and intellectual exchange, and Baxter's actions had fractured that foundation, leaving behind a landscape littered with broken assumptions.

Maria Richards, her own resilience tested by the ordeal, found herself grappling with a different kind of aftermath. The vellum card, now safely cataloged as evidence, remained a potent symbol of Baxter's intricate, self-destructive narrative. She had faced him in the crucible of his own creation, armed with logic and an unwavering commitment to truth, and had emerged not unscathed, but victorious. Yet, the victory felt hollow, devoid of the celebratory fanfare she might have once imagined. Instead, there was the quiet, persistent hum of responsibility, the knowledge that she had been instrumental in bringing a dangerous man to justice, but also in witnessing the devastating implosion of a brilliant mind. Her days were now filled with debriefings, with meticulous reviews of case files, and with the quiet, internal process of disentangling herself from the emotional grip of Baxter's saga. The library, once her sanctuary, now held a somber resonance, a place where the ghosts of intellectual ambition and profound delusion still seemed to whisper.

The university administration, led by a visibly shaken President Holloway, found themselves facing a public relations crisis of monumental proportions. The narrative of Elmwood as an idyllic bastion of learning had been irrevocably tarnished. News vans, their satellite dishes like predatory eyes, circled the campus perimeter, eager to feast on the sensational details of the murders and Baxter's subsequent breakdown. The carefully cultivated image of academic excellence was now juxtaposed with headlines screaming of madness, obsession, and violence. Holloway's public statements were measured, carefully worded pronouncements of shock, grief, and an unwavering commitment to ensuring the safety and security of the Elmwood community. But beneath the practiced calm, there was a palpable desperation to restore order, to quell the rising tide of anxiety, and to somehow mend the fractured reputation of the institution.

The police investigation, meanwhile, continued its methodical work, meticulously piecing together the fragments of Baxter's disturbed life. The physical evidence was extensive, each item a testament to the chilling progression of his psychosis. Baxter's apartment, once a meticulously curated shrine to his intellectual obsessions, was now a sterile, impersonal scene, its secrets laid bare under the harsh glare of forensic lights. Every book, every note, every seemingly innocuous object was scrutinized, a desperate attempt to understand the genesis of his violence, to trace the labyrinthine pathways of his descent. The police, accustomed to the grittier realities of crime, found themselves drawn into a world of abstract theories and tortured artistic expression, a world far removed from their usual beat. They grappled with the nuances of Baxter's motivations, the blurred lines between intellectual pursuit and pathological obsession, a task that required not just investigative skill, but a certain degree of psychological acumen.

The vellum card, clutched tightly in Maria's hand in the immediate aftermath, had been more than just a piece of parchment; it was a window into Baxter's soul, a final, desperate plea, or perhaps a chilling testament to his warped perception of reality. Now, it resided in a climate-controlled evidence locker, a silent witness to the unraveling of a man. Its journey from a poignant piece of poetry to a crucial piece of evidence mirrored the trajectory of Baxter's own life, from revered academic to convicted criminal. The words, once intended to evoke a sense of profound artistic insight, now served as a stark reminder of the destructive power of unchecked ego and the terrifying capacity for human beings to construct realities that ultimately consume them.

Beneath the surface of campus quietude, a subtle but significant shift was occurring. The events had acted as a catalyst, forcing a re-evaluation of the very nature of intellectual inquiry and the potential dangers inherent in unchecked ambition. The ivory tower, once perceived as a realm of pure thought, had been exposed as a place susceptible to the same human frailties, the same darkness that afflicted the world beyond its manicured borders. The dust, both literal and metaphorical, was beginning to settle, but what it revealed was a landscape irrevocably altered, a community grappling with the profound and unsettling aftermath of a tragedy that had reached into the very heart of its identity. The reckoning was far from over; it had, in many ways, just begun. The quiet was not an end, but a pause, a moment of profound reflection before the necessary work of rebuilding and understanding could commence. The collective breath held by Elmwood was starting to release, but the air was still thick with unspoken questions and the lingering specter of what had been. The memory of Baxter's grand pronouncements, now rendered hollow and pathetic by his actions, served as a constant, chilling reminder of the fragility of intellect when divorced from empathy and grounded in delusion. The once vibrant academic discourse had been irrevocably altered, now carrying a subtle undertone of caution, a newfound awareness of the precipice upon which intellectual pursuits could sometimes tread. The very definition of "genius" was being interrogated, not in the abstract terms of philosophical debate, but in the brutal, lived reality of its destructive potential. The world had seen Baxter's art, and it was horrifying.

The library, its grand windows now reflecting a muted autumn sky, stood as a silent testament to the chaos that had erupted within its hallowed walls. The scent of disinfectant, an unwelcome but necessary intruder, still lingered faintly, a stark contrast to the familiar, comforting aroma of old paper and leather that had once defined the space. Every overturned chair, every displaced book, every subtle scuff mark on the antique mahogany tables, served as a quiet, persistent reminder of the terrifying clash that had transpired. The meticulous efforts to restore order – the careful re-shelving of volumes, the painstaking repair of damaged bindings, the deep cleaning of the Persian rug where so much had transpired – could not entirely erase the memory of that night. A subtle tension remained, a faint tremor in the otherwise tranquil atmosphere, as if the very structure of the building held its breath, remembering the violence it had witnessed. Students who now ventured into its depths did so with a newfound wariness, their hushed whispers taking on a more somber tone, their eyes scanning the shelves with a mixture of awe and trepidation. The sanctuary of knowledge had, for a time, been a stage for madness.

Gibson found himself spending more time than usual in his office, the familiar clutter of research papers and historical artifacts offering a small measure of comfort amidst the pervasive unease. He would often find himself staring out of his window, watching the students move across the campus, their faces etched with a mixture of shock and a dawning, unsettling understanding. They were the inheritors of this legacy, the ones who would have to navigate the consequences of Baxter's actions, who would have to rebuild trust and reaffirm the values that Elmwood stood for. He spoke with colleagues, the conversations often circling back to the same difficult questions: Where did intellectual passion curdle into obsession? At what point does a pursuit of artistic truth become a dangerous detachment from reality? These were not abstract academic debates; they were urgent, lived questions born from the wreckage of Baxter's life.

Maria, too, found solace in routine, the structure of her days a welcome anchor in the emotional maelstrom. She meticulously cataloged the remaining evidence from Baxter's apartment, each item a piece of a puzzle that explained, rather than excused, his actions. The scientific rigor of her work, the systematic approach to evidence collection and analysis, provided a necessary counterpoint to the deeply human tragedy that had unfolded. She found herself rereading Baxter's published works, his essays on art, his theoretical frameworks for understanding creativity, but now with a chillingly different perspective. The brilliance was undeniable, the intellect sharp and incisive, but it was now inextricably intertwined with a profound, and ultimately destructive, disconnection. It was like dissecting a beautiful, intricate clockwork mechanism, only to discover that the gears were powered by a dark, unstable energy. The beauty of the design could not mask the inherent danger of its core.

The university's response was a delicate balancing act. On one hand, they had to acknowledge the severity of the crimes and reassure the public of their commitment to safety. On the other, they had to protect the institution's reputation and avoid succumbing to a narrative of pervasive corruption or negligence.

President Holloway, guided by a team of crisis management experts, initiated several measures. Security protocols were reviewed and tightened, counseling services were enhanced to provide support for students and staff grappling with the trauma, and a series of public forums were scheduled to address concerns and foster open dialogue. These forums, however, were often fraught with tension, with parents and students alike seeking answers that were not always readily available. The administration found themselves fielding difficult questions about Baxter's mental state, the university's role in his life, and the potential for future incidents.

One such forum, held in the cavernous auditorium that had once hosted commencement ceremonies and visiting dignitaries, was particularly poignant. Parents, their faces a mixture of anger and fear, questioned the university's oversight, their voices echoing with concern for their children's safety. Students, their usual deference replaced by a raw vulnerability, spoke of the unsettling atmosphere, the fear that lingered in the quiet corners of the campus. Gibson, standing at the podium alongside Holloway and the Dean of Students, offered a measured, yet empathetic response. He spoke of the inherent complexities of the human mind, the challenges of identifying and addressing mental illness, and the university's unwavering commitment to creating a supportive and safe environment. He emphasized that while Elmwood was a community of scholars, it was also a community of human beings, susceptible to the same struggles and challenges that affected society at large. His words, delivered with a quiet sincerity, seemed to offer a measure of reassurance, a steady hand in the turbulent waters.

Maria, observing the proceedings from the back of the auditorium, felt a profound sense of melancholy. She had witnessed Baxter's descent firsthand, had seen the raw, unvarnished reality of his unraveling. The public discussions, while necessary, felt a world away from the intimate, terrifying encounter she had experienced. She understood the need for reassurance, for a return to normalcy, but she also knew that the scars left by Baxter's actions would take time to heal, if they ever truly did. The academic thriller had played out, not on a fictional stage, but within the very real corridors of Elmwood University, and its consequences were far-reaching and deeply personal. The dust was settling, yes, but the landscape it revealed was one of profound introspection and a sober re-evaluation of what it truly meant to pursue knowledge and create art in a world that was both beautiful and terrifyingly complex. The quiet that had settled over Elmwood was not an absence of sound, but a profound, contemplative stillness, a community holding its breath, and waiting for the dawn of a new understanding, a more resilient future. The aftermath was an ongoing process, a slow, deliberate excavation of truth, and a cautious rebuilding of faith in the enduring power of reason and empathy.

The silence that had descended upon Elmwood felt less like peace and more like a collective holding of breath. Dr. Aris Gibson found himself at the epicenter of this hushed unease, not as a perpetrator, but as a man whose past had become unexpectedly, and uncomfortably, relevant. The investigation, while ultimately clearing him of any direct complicity in Julian Baxter's horrific acts, had unearthed a history that now cast a long, unsettling shadow over his esteemed academic career. His association with the Aeon

Society and The Infinite Discourse, once a subject of quiet curiosity among his peers, now loomed large, re-examined with a critical and suspicious eye. Whispers, once mere academic gossip, now carried the weight of accusation, dissecting his every interaction with Baxter, scrutinizing their shared intellectual interests for any hint of the darkness that had consumed their former colleague.

Gibson felt the weight of this scrutiny with every step he took across the quadrangle. The once familiar nods of recognition from students and colleagues now often held a hesitant, questioning quality. He understood. In the wake of such profound tragedy, the human instinct was to find fault, to assign blame, to identify a lineage of complicity, however indirect. His name, his reputation, had been linked to Baxter's descent, and that linkage, regardless of the factual findings of the investigation, was a stain that could not be easily scrubbed away. He had been a mentor, a fellow scholar, a man who, by all outward appearances, had shared Baxter's passion for the intricate tapestry of human thought and expression. Now, that shared passion was viewed through the prism of Baxter's ultimate depravity.

The formal inquiry had been exhaustive, a brutal dissection of his professional and personal life. He had cooperated fully, laying bare his interactions with Baxter, his understanding of the man's intellectual trajectory, and, most damningly, his past involvement with the Aeon Society. He had not been a mere observer of the Aeon Society or The Infinite Discourse; he had, in his younger years, been a fervent participant. Its esoteric discussions, its exploration of ancient philosophies and the darker corners of human consciousness had once resonated deeply with his own intellectual curiosity. He had, at the time, believed it to be a harmless, if unconventional, intellectual pursuit. Baxter, too, had been a member, and Gibson had, in some ways, served as an informal bridge, guiding Baxter's initial explorations into the society's archives and its labyrinthine philosophical underpinnings.

But time, and Baxter's horrifying actions, had irrevocably altered the perception of the Aeon Society. What had once been seen as a quirky intellectual collective was now framed as a breeding ground for delusion, a crucible where Baxter's nascent obsessions had been nurtured and amplified. Gibson, as a prominent figure associated with the society's past, found himself inextricably linked to this new, terrifying narrative. He had provided Baxter with intellectual sustenance, had engaged him in discussions that, in retrospect, seemed to foreshadow the very descent into madness that had led to unspeakable violence. The investigation had concluded that Gibson had acted with no malicious intent, that his association with the Society and Discourse and his interactions with Baxter were born of genuine intellectual engagement, not a shared blueprint for destruction. He was cleared of any criminal wrongdoing. Yet, the clearance felt hollow, a legalistic absolution that did little to assuage the gnawing sense of guilt that had taken root within him.

He carried that guilt like a shroud. It was not the guilt of a murderer, but the guilt of a witness to a slow, agonizing unraveling, a guilt of insufficient foresight, of a failure to intervene more forcefully, more decisively. He replayed conversations, his own words, Baxter's responses, searching for the inflection, the subtle nuance, the unsaid phrase that might have served as a warning, a pivot point. He saw now, with the clarity of hindsight, the subtle shifts in Baxter's demeanor, the increasing intensity of his gaze, the way his pronouncements, once intellectually stimulating, had begun to take on a feverish, almost evangelical tone. He had dismissed these as the eccentricities of a brilliant mind pushing the boundaries of conventional thought. Now, he understood them as the harbingers of a dangerous obsession.

His academic reputation, once a source of quiet pride, now felt like a fragile edifice built upon shifting sands. The Society and Discourse connection, amplified by the sensational nature of Baxter's crimes, had become the defining feature of his public persona, eclipsing his decades of scholarship in ancient history. He found himself fielding questions not about Hittite cuneiform or the socio-political structures of Bronze Age civilizations, but about the "esoteric influences" on Baxter, about the "occult leanings" of the Society and Discourse, about whether Gibson believed "true genius" always bordered on madness. These were questions he felt ill-equipped to answer, questions that reduced complex intellectual pursuits to sensational soundbites.

The burden of guilt manifested in a renewed, almost desperate, dedication to his work, but with a profound shift in focus. Gibson felt an urgent imperative to steer the university's literary and intellectual discourse away from the precipice that had claimed Baxter. He saw, with chilling clarity, how the unchecked pursuit of extreme ideas, the glorification of intellectual fervor without a grounding in ethical consideration or a connection to human empathy, could lead to devastating consequences. He became a vocal advocate for a more balanced, more responsible approach to academic exploration, particularly within the humanities and arts departments.

He began by initiating a series of departmental colloquia, not focusing on the sensationalism of Baxter's crimes, but on the very nature of intellectual inquiry itself. He invited scholars from various disciplines – philosophy, psychology, ethics, literature – to engage in robust discussions about the boundaries of creative expression, the responsibilities of the intellectual, and the potential dangers of unchecked ambition. His own contributions were marked by a quiet intensity, a deep-seated concern that resonated with those who had also been shaken by the events. He spoke not of Baxter directly, but of the principles that had been compromised, the ideals that had been perverted.

"We must be vigilant," he stated during one such forum, his voice steady, though a subtle tremor betrayed the depth of his emotion, "not against the pursuit of challenging ideas, but against the allure of ideas that seek to isolate us, to detach us from the shared humanity that binds us. There is a profound difference between intellectual exploration and the construction of a solipsistic universe, a universe where the self becomes the sole arbiter of truth, and where the external world is merely a canvas for its own increasingly distorted projections."

He championed the integration of ethical considerations into literary analysis and creative writing programs. He argued for a curriculum that not only fostered critical thinking but also emphasized empathy, emotional intelligence, and a robust understanding of the societal impact of ideas. He worked with department heads, offering gentle but persistent guidance, suggesting syllabi that balanced challenging theoretical texts with works that explored the complexities of human connection and moral responsibility. It was a subtle, painstaking effort, a quiet rebellion against the kind of intellectual extremism that had consumed Baxter.

This new direction did not come without resistance. Some saw it as an overreaction, a pandering to public fear. Others, still reeling from the shock, were simply not ready to engage in such deep introspection. But Gibson persevered. He saw this work as his penance, his way of atoning for what he perceived as his own role in the tragedy. He wasn't seeking absolution from others; he was seeking it from himself, through the tangible act of safeguarding the intellectual landscape of Elmwood.

He found a strange kind of solace in this self-imposed penance. The hours spent poring over curriculum proposals, mediating faculty debates, and delivering lectures on the ethics of knowledge felt like a form of redemption. He was not merely an academic; he was an architect of a more resilient intellectual future, one that acknowledged the darkness but actively cultivated the light. The tarnished reputation was a heavy burden, but it was also a constant reminder of the stakes involved, a spur to continue his work with unwavering dedication. He knew that the shadow of Baxter would likely always linger, but he was determined that it would not define the future of Elmwood. Instead, he hoped to cultivate an environment where brilliance could flourish without succumbing to the seductive whispers of madness, where intellectual curiosity was tempered by wisdom, and where the pursuit of knowledge was always rooted in a profound respect for humanity. His own quiet reckoning was unfolding not in the courtroom or the police station, but in the lecture halls and seminar rooms, in the slow, deliberate process of rebuilding trust in the power of a responsible, ethical intellectualism.

Detective Maria Richards sat in the sterile quiet of her office, the faint hum of the fluorescent lights a counterpoint to the tempest that had raged within and around her for weeks. The Baxter case, a labyrinth of literary allusions, academic ambition, and ultimately, horrifying violence, had left an indelible mark. It had been more than a case; it had been a profound intellectual and emotional crucible, forging her in ways she was only just beginning to comprehend. The files, meticulously organized and cross-referenced, lay before her – a testament to the painstaking dissection of Julian Baxter's life and crimes. Yet, the true aftermath wasn't contained within those manila folders; it resided in the quiet recalibration of her own internal compass.

She traced the rim of her coffee mug, the ceramic cool against her fingertips. The initial thrill of the chase, the intellectual sparring with Baxter's carefully constructed narratives, had long since faded, replaced by a sober contemplation of the human psyche's darker currents. It was a familiar territory for any detective, but Baxter had elevated it, weaving his pathology into a complex tapestry of art and philosophy that had, at times, threatened to ensnare her own perception. She had prided herself on her sharp analytical mind, her ability to discern motive from misdirection, but Baxter had been a master of both. His elaborate literary defenses, his carefully chosen quotes, his very method of murder – all were designed to provoke, to challenge, to draw the investigator into his twisted intellectual game.

The line, she now understood with stark clarity, was not always visible. The fervent passion that drove an artist to create, that fueled a scholar's relentless pursuit of knowledge, could, with a subtle but catastrophic shift, morph into something dangerous. It was the same fire, merely a different fuel. Baxter's brilliance, once a source of awe for his peers and a formidable intellectual hurdle for the investigation, had become the very engine of his destruction. He had chased a phantom of ultimate expression, a distorted ideal born from ancient texts and amplified by his own burgeoning delusions, and in doing so, had trampled over the very humanity he claimed to understand.

Maria remembered the early days of the investigation, the sheer bewilderment that had accompanied the discovery of Baxter's first victim. The scene had been staged, a grotesque tableau intended to mimic a scene from an obscure Romantic poem. She had felt a disorienting disconnect, the stark brutality of murder clashing violently with the aesthetic intent. It had taken days of poring over Baxter's writings, his academic papers, his personal journals, to even begin to decipher the language he was speaking, the narrative he was imposing upon reality. It was a language she understood, a language of literature and symbolism, but it was a language twisted by a malignant purpose.

The Aeon Society and The Infinite Discourse, initially a seemingly innocuous academic circles, had emerged as a crucial element, a crucible where Baxter's intellectual inclinations had been solidified, perhaps even exacerbated. Dr. Aris Gibson's reluctant testimony, his own unease at his past association with the group and with Baxter, had provided a vital thread. Gibson, a man of intellect and gravitas, had unwittingly become a character in Baxter's final, macabre narrative, his past entangled with Baxter's present through shared intellectual interests and a youthful fascination with the esoteric. Maria had seen the genuine distress in Gibson's eyes, the deep-seated regret that he hadn't seen the precipice Baxter was hurtling towards. It was a sentiment she understood all too well.

She had felt it herself, that intoxicating pull of a complex mystery, the urge to delve deeper, to understand the perpetrator on their own terms, even if those terms were deeply disturbing. There were moments when she had found herself almost... captivated by Baxter's intellectual audacity, by the sheer audacity of his literary crimes. It was a dangerous fascination, a siren song that threatened to drown her professional objectivity in a sea of academic curiosity. She had to actively pull herself back, to remind herself that behind the elaborate prose and symbolic gestures were real victims, real lives extinguished.

The psychological toll of the investigation had been significant. Late nights spent deciphering obscure passages, early mornings poring over crime scene photos, the constant mental gymnastics of trying to anticipate Baxter's next move – it all weighed heavily. The literary ghosts, as she'd come to think of them, the characters and themes that had populated Baxter's world and, by extension, her own recent reality, had begun to haunt her sleep. They whispered in the dark, their voices echoing Baxter's own chilling pronouncements. She saw Ophelia's drowned form in the glint of moonlight on a puddle, heard the tormented soliloquies of a doomed prince in the rustling of leaves.

But the darkness was beginning to recede. The methodical process of piecing together the evidence, of building a concrete case against Baxter, had provided a tangible anchor. The arrest, the subsequent interrogation, had brought a measure of closure, not just for the victims' families, but for her own weary mind. The intellectual battle had been won, the literary deceptions exposed, and the perpetrator, finally, brought to justice. The quiet resolve she felt now was not the triumphant surge of victory, but the steady, unyielding strength of one who has faced a profound challenge and emerged, scared but not broken.

She looked at her hands, the faint tremor now gone. The investigation had demanded an almost obsessive attention to detail, a relentless pursuit of meaning in every word, every gesture. It had forced her to confront the boundaries of human creativity and the terrifying abyss that lay just beyond them. She had learned that passion, when untethered from empathy and reason, could become a monstrous force. The artist's fervor, the scholar's dedication, the detective's drive – they were all fueled by a similar intensity, but only when tempered by a fundamental respect for life could they serve a constructive purpose.

Maria stood and walked to the window, looking out at the Elmwood campus. The intellectual hub, once a sanctuary of learning and discovery, had been irrevocably touched by the shadow of Baxter's actions. The whispers among students and faculty, the hushed conversations about the events, were a constant reminder. Gibson's efforts to foster a more balanced and ethical intellectual discourse were a positive step, a necessary counterweight to the kind of intellectual extremism that Baxter had embodied. She hoped they would succeed, that the seeds of doubt and suspicion would not fester into a climate of fear, but rather into a more profound understanding of the responsibilities that came with the pursuit of knowledge and creativity.

Her own perception of justice had been reshaped. It was no longer simply about apprehending criminals and securing convictions. It was also about understanding the cultural and intellectual currents that could contribute to such acts, about recognizing the subtle ways in which ideas could shape reality, for good or ill. Baxter's case had been a brutal, high-stakes seminar on the power of narrative, on the seductive allure of a well-crafted story, even when it was a story of death.

She closed her eyes for a moment, taking a deep, steadying breath. The ghosts were still there, perhaps, but they no longer held the same power over her. They were lessons, etched into her professional memory, reminders of the delicate balance that humanity constantly navigated. The intellectual puzzles Baxter had laid out were solved, the literary mysteries unraveled. Now, it was time to move forward, to apply the hard-won lessons to the next challenge, whatever it might be. The quiet resolve within her felt like a newly forged weapon, honed by the fires of this extraordinary case. She was ready.

The hushed solemnity that descended upon Elmwood University was a stark contrast to the intellectual fervor that had once defined its hallowed halls. The echoes of Julian Baxter's crimes had rippled through the academic community, leaving behind a landscape irrevocably altered. The initial shock had given way to a profound sense of grief, a communal mourning for the lives so brutally extinguished. Across the sprawling campus, where ivy-clad buildings usually buzzed with the energy of discovery and debate, a palpable sadness now settled, thick and heavy as the pre-dawn mist.

The administration, under immense pressure from students, faculty, and the wider community, initiated a series of memorial services. These were not grand, ostentatious affairs, but rather quiet, introspective gatherings, intended to honor the victims and to begin the arduous process of collective healing. Small, intimate ceremonies were held in lecture halls, chapels, and even in the tranquil gardens that Baxter had so often frequented. At each gathering, a single candle flickered, its flame a tiny beacon against the encroaching darkness, symbolizing the lives lost but also the enduring spirit of the university. Speakers, their voices often thick with emotion, spoke of the victims not as names on a casualty list, but as individuals – bright minds, budding artists, promising scholars, each with their own dreams and aspirations, tragically cut short. They spoke of the void left behind, a silence that would forever echo in the spaces they once occupied. Students shared anecdotes, their memories painting vibrant portraits of classmates and friends, reminding everyone that behind the headlines and the intellectual machinations of the case, there were human stories of love, laughter, and shared ambition. The memorials were somber affairs, yet they also served as a powerful testament to the interconnectedness of the university community, a reaffirmation that in the face of unspeakable tragedy, they would not stand alone.

Beyond the grief, a more complex and unsettling dialogue began to emerge from the ashes of the tragedy. The intricate web of literary allusions and philosophical justifications that Julian Baxter had woven around his crimes forced a reckoning with the very nature of knowledge and its potential for perversion. The question hung heavy in the air: how could the pursuit of literature, an endeavor celebrated for its capacity to illuminate the human condition, become a tool for such profound darkness? Seminars, once focused on dissecting classic texts, began to pivot, their syllabi augmented with discussions on the ethical implications of artistic expression, the responsibility of the intellectual, and the fine, often blurry, line between passion and pathology. Professors found themselves leading discussions that ventured far beyond the confines of literary analysis, delving into the psychology of extremism, the dangers of unchecked ambition, and the societal factors that might contribute to the radicalization of thought.

One particularly poignant series of lectures, organized by the English department, was titled *The Shadow in the Text: Literature, Morality, and the Abyss*. Dr. Aris Gibson, still bearing the weight of his past association with Baxter and the Aeon Society and The Infinite Discourse, found himself at the forefront of these discussions. He spoke with a raw honesty about the intoxicating allure of esoteric knowledge and the dangers of intellectual isolation. He cautioned against the hubris of believing that one could master complex philosophical ideas without grounding them in a bedrock of ethical consideration and human empathy. Gibson argued that Baxter's descent was not an isolated incident, but a cautionary tale about a broader trend in certain academic circles – a tendency to intellectualize to the point of abstraction, to become so engrossed in the theoretical that the tangible realities of human suffering were overlooked or dismissed. He spoke of the Society and Discourse, not as a dens of evil, but as a breeding ground for unchecked intellectual curiosity, a place where the pursuit of abstract meaning sometimes overshadowed the importance of concrete ethical principles. His personal reflections on his own past engagement with such ideas served as a powerful, if uncomfortable, reminder to many that the potential for intellectual seduction existed within the very fabric of the university.

Other faculty members explored the historical precedents for the weaponization of ideas. Discussions ranged from the philosophical underpinnings of various totalitarian regimes to the role of propaganda in shaping public perception. The focus was not to equate Baxter's actions with broader political movements, but rather to understand the universal mechanisms by which potent ideas, divorced from ethical moorings, could be manipulated to justify violence and oppression. These were not easy conversations. They often involved confronting uncomfortable truths about the university's own intellectual history and the inherent risks associated with fostering environments of intense intellectual exploration. The ivory tower, once seen as a bastion of pure thought, was now being scrutinized for its potential vulnerabilities, its capacity to inadvertently nurture the very forces that could undermine its foundational principles.

The student body, deeply shaken by the events, was also actively engaged in this process of introspection. Student-led forums and discussion groups sprung up organically, providing spaces for open dialogue and emotional processing. Many students expressed a newfound anxiety, a sense that the familiar comfort of their academic pursuits had been shattered. They grappled with the unsettling realization that the abstract theories discussed in lectures could, in the hands of someone with a disturbed psyche, manifest in such brutal reality. This led to a heightened awareness of mental well-being, a growing understanding that academic pressure and intellectual rigor needed to be balanced with robust support systems.

The university administration, in response to the widespread concern and the clear lessons learned from the tragedy, pledged to implement significant changes. A comprehensive review of student societies and organizations was initiated, with a particular focus on groups that fostered esoteric interests or operated with a high degree of autonomy. The stated goal was not to stifle intellectual exploration or to impose undue restrictions on student life, but to ensure greater transparency and accountability. Mechanisms for reporting concerning behavior or rhetoric were strengthened, and clear protocols were established for investigating such reports. The aim was to create an environment where potential warning signs would not be overlooked, and where intervention could occur before any harm was done.

More significantly, the administration announced a substantial increase in funding and resources dedicated to mental health services on campus. New counseling staff were hired, wait times for appointments were reduced, and outreach programs were expanded to make students more aware of the available support. Workshops on stress management, resilience building, and recognizing signs of distress in oneself and others became a regular feature of campus life. This was a direct acknowledgment of the psychological toll that the Baxter case had taken on the student body and a commitment to prioritizing their well-being. The message was clear: the university recognized that academic success and personal fulfillment were inextricably linked, and that mental health was a crucial component of both. They aimed to cultivate a culture where seeking help was seen not as a weakness, but as a sign of strength and self-awareness.

Furthermore, the university began to explore new pedagogical approaches. There was a growing emphasis on integrating ethical considerations into the curriculum across various disciplines, not just in philosophy or literature departments. Students were encouraged to engage with the societal implications of their chosen fields of study, to consider the broader impact of their work on the world around them. This was a deliberate effort to move beyond purely theoretical understanding and to foster a more responsible and engaged form of scholarship. The idea was to equip students not just with knowledge, but with the wisdom and ethical framework to use that knowledge for constructive purposes.

Despite these proactive measures and the genuine commitment to healing and change, the scars of Julian Baxter's crimes remained a somber and indelible part of Elmwood University's history. The elegant architecture of the campus, once a symbol of intellectual aspiration, now carried a shadow of remembrance. Certain locations, once vibrant hubs of student life, were now tinged with an unspoken melancholy. The ghost of what had happened, of the lives lost and the darkness that had briefly consumed a corner of their world, lingered. It was a reminder that even in the most esteemed bastions of learning, the human capacity for both great good and profound evil existed, and that vigilance, compassion, and a steadfast commitment to ethical principles were paramount. The university was not the same place it had been before the murders. It had been tested, pushed to its limits, and forced to confront its own vulnerabilities. In its struggle to heal, it had also begun to mature to recognize that true intellectual growth must be accompanied by a deep and abiding respect for the sanctity of human life. The process of rebuilding was underway, but the lessons learned, etched into the very soul of Elmwood, would forever shape its future. The silence that had fallen was not just the silence of grief, but also the silence of contemplation, a necessary pause before the slow, deliberate work of rebuilding could truly begin, ensuring that the pursuit of knowledge would always be guided by the light of humanity.

The confession, a chillingly methodical account of his descent into madness, had been the linchpin. Julian Baxter, captured, incapacitated, and finally vocal, had detailed his crimes with an unnerving clarity. The five lives he had extinguished, each a meticulously chosen sacrifice within his twisted literary pantheon, had been cataloged with the same precision he had once applied to his academic research. Yet, for Maria Richards and Dr. Aris Gibson, the profound relief that had washed over Elmwood University was tinged with a persistent, almost imperceptible disquiet. It was a phantom limb of doubt, a whisper in the quiet aftermath that refused to be silenced.

They had pored over Baxter's journals, his digital breadcrumbs, and the fragmented poetry that had been his twisted manifestos. Each word had been dissected, each allusion traced back to its source, in a desperate attempt to understand the architect of such unspeakable horror. The five victims – Clara Bellweather, the doctoral student whose final act had been one of unwitting terror; Dr. Toby Bennett, the professor that was fascinated with morbid folklore and ancient death rituals met his fate in the library; Mary Underwood, the aspiring actress whose final stage had been reduced to a macabre tableau; Brandon Pendelton, the librarian whose life was permanently checked out; and Dr. Edgar Nevel, professor and critic – were undeniable. Their deaths were etched into the fabric of Elmwood's history, a dark testament to Baxter's warped intellect. But the nagging question persisted, a shadow cast by the sheer breadth and depth of Baxter's literary obsessions. Had his 'opus,' as he'd chillingly referred to his crimes, truly concluded with these five?

Maria, back in her dimly lit office, surrounded by stacks of research papers and the faint scent of stale coffee, found herself returning to the same passages again and again. Baxter's poems, particularly the later ones penned in the weeks leading up to his capture, were steeped in a dense, symbolic language. While he had explicitly linked specific victims to specific allegorical figures and literary archetypes, there were also recurring motifs and unfinished narratives that defied easy categorization. He spoke of "unwritten chapters," of "silences yet to be filled," and of a "grand narrative" that stretched beyond the immediate horrors he had confessed. These weren't mere poetic flourishes; in Baxter's fractured mind, they were integral components of his grand design.

"He saw himself as an author, Aris," Maria said, her voice barely above a whisper, as Gibson sat across from her, his own gaze distant. "And his life, his crimes, were his magnum opus. But what if he intended to write more? What if these five were just the prologue, or perhaps a single, albeit horrific, act in a much larger play?"

Gibson, his usual stoicism strained, ran a hand through his greying hair. The weight of their shared experience, of their proximity to Baxter's intellect and the darkness it harbored seemed to press down on him. He had been the one to initially dismiss the deeper implications of Baxter's intellectual proclivities, believing them to be the eccentricities of a brilliant but isolated mind. Now, the consequences of that misjudgment haunted him. "The sheer volume of his literary allusions, Maria, the interconnectedness he wove between his victims and the texts... it was breathtakingly complex. He didn't just *read* literature; he *lived* it, and then he *wrote* himself into it, in the most ghastly way imaginable."

He paused, his eyes flicking to a photograph on her desk – a younger, more hopeful version of himself, standing beside a student who was now synonymous with terror. "The question is, did his narrative extend beyond the five we know? He referred to his poems as 'chapters' in his confession. He spoke of *The Manuscript of Desolation* as his life's work. Did he have other 'manuscripts' in mind? Other 'chapters' that were never written, or perhaps, that he never intended for us to find?"

The idea was, on its face, terrifying. Baxter, though apprehended, had demonstrated an almost supernatural ability to manipulate, to deceive, and to orchestrate events. The possibility that he had laid dormant plans, weaving intricate threads of potential future violence into his literary tapestry, was a chilling prospect. Maria remembered one particular poem, discovered tucked away in a hidden compartment of Baxter's desk, that spoke of a "chrysalis of silence" and a "rebirth in shattered mirrors." At the time, it had been interpreted as a metaphor for his own fractured psyche, his hope for redemption or, perhaps, a foreshadowing of his eventual downfall. But what if it referred to something more tangible?

"He was obsessed with the idea of the unmade choice, wasn't he?" Maria mused, her fingers tracing the worn spine of a volume of Kierkegaard that Baxter had annotated extensively. "The road not taken. He saw potential in every diverging path, every alternate reality. He spoke about how a single textual ambiguity could ripple outwards, creating entirely new interpretations, entirely new worlds. Could he have applied that same logic to his victims? To people whose lives hadn't yet intersected with his in the way the others had?"

The fragmented notes found on Baxter's computer hinted at this. There were lists of names, accompanied by annotations that seemed to draw parallels to minor characters in obscure novels, or to figures from mythology whose stories had multiple variations. Some were crossed out, others left with question marks. Were these discarded ideas, the detritus of a fevered imagination, or were they dormant seeds of future violence, carefully cataloged and waiting for the right conditions to sprout?

Gibson recalled a conversation he'd had with Baxter during his time as a graduate student, a conversation that had seemed insignificant then but now echoed with a dreadful prescience. Baxter had been discussing the nature of narrative and character development. He'd argued that the most compelling villains were those who saw themselves as heroes, whose motivations, however warped, were internally consistent with their own worldview. "He said something about how an author has a responsibility to their characters," Gibson recounted, his brow furrowed in concentration. "That even the minor characters, the ones who serve a fleeting purpose, deserve a kind of internal logic, a justification for their existence within the narrative. He was talking about fiction, of course, but the way he said it... it was with a chilling intensity."

Could it be that Baxter had perceived individuals within the Elmwood community, or even beyond, who were destined to play a role in his grand narrative, a role that had not yet been fulfilled? The poems were a labyrinth of symbolism, dense with literary ghosts and half-formed allegories. One particular verse spoke of "a shadow in the library stacks, a whisper among the forgotten texts, a destiny unwritten by mortal hands." It was evocative, certainly, but also maddeningly vague. Was this shadow a reference to a specific person, a hidden threat, or simply another facet of Baxter's tormented inner world?

Maria sifted through a digital archive of Baxter's online activity, focusing on the months leading up to the murders. His search history was a testament to his encyclopedic knowledge, but also to his increasingly dark preoccupations. Beyond the literary research, there were searches for information on obscure poisons, on the historical use of ritualistic sacrifice, and on the philosophical justifications for extreme acts. But there were also more mundane queries: library records, course catalogs, student directories. These seemed innocuous, the tools of a diligent academic. Yet, when viewed through the prism of Baxter's actions, they took on a more sinister hue. Was he cataloging potential subjects, assessing their vulnerabilities, weaving them into the intricate tapestry of his planned narrative?

"He wrote about the 'cosmic irony' of certain juxtapositions," Maria murmured, her gaze fixed on a particularly dense passage of Baxter's poetry. "The idea that the most profound truths, the most significant events, often arise from the most unexpected and seemingly trivial connections. He saw patterns everywhere, Aris. The way a particular student's name echoed a minor character in a Dostoevsky novel, the way a professor's research touched upon themes he was exploring. He was always searching for resonances, for connections that would validate his worldview."

The chilling implication was that Baxter's narrative wasn't just about his intellectual journey or his personal demons; it was about the entire ecosystem of Elmwood University itself. He saw himself as a curator of meaning, a literary alchemist transmuting the mundane into the profound through the alembic of violence. If he believed that certain individuals held the key to unlocking further layers of his grand narrative, then their existence, their proximity to him, might have been as significant as any explicit threat.

Gibson remembered a fleeting encounter with a young woman in the philosophy department, a student who had once approached him with questions about a particularly abstruse essay Baxter had published. She had been fiercely intelligent, articulate, and possessed an unnerving intensity that had reminded Gibson, uncomfortably, of Baxter himself. He couldn't recall her name, nor the specifics of her query, but the memory resurfaced now, a flicker in the periphery of his consciousness. Had Baxter noticed her? Had he seen in her a potential player in a future act, a character waiting for her cue?

"The problem, Maria," Gibson said, his voice low and grave, "is that Baxter's 'chapters' might not have been written in ink. They might have been written in silence, in the spaces between his known actions, in the potential for harm that he perceived in the world around him. His obsession with literary archetypes meant he was constantly looking for individuals who embodied certain roles, certain thematic resonances. It's entirely possible he saw potential victims in people who never even knew he existed, or who only knew him as a brilliant, albeit peculiar, student."

The cryptic poems offered tantalizing, yet ultimately frustrating, clues. Phrases like "the ballad of the unanswered plea," "the tragedy of the unheard song," and "the final verse of the forgotten scholar" were so general that they could apply to countless individuals within a university setting. Was the "forgotten scholar" a reference to a specific professor whose work

Baxter admired, or a student struggling in obscurity? Was the "unanswered plea" a cry for help from someone Baxter had observed, or a literary device to emphasize his own isolation?

Maria felt a cold dread creep into her heart. The meticulous planning, the intellectual justifications, the sheer audacity of Baxter's crimes had been overwhelming enough. But the idea that his ambition had stretched beyond the tangible, that his literary edifice might have had unseen foundations, was a new and deeply unsettling dimension to the tragedy. It suggested that the threat hadn't been entirely contained, that the ghost of Baxter's narrative might still hold sway over the lives of others, whether he was incarcerated or not.

"He believed that certain lives were... poetically significant," Maria whispered, more to herself than to Gibson. "That some individuals were destined to be keystones in the grand narrative of human experience. He saw the world not as a collection of individuals, but as a vast, interconnected text, and he was the ultimate editor, the ultimate author. If he believed that someone else's life was crucial to completing his opus, to fulfilling his literary destiny, he would have found a way to incorporate it."

The thought was a chilling one, a dark echo in the halls of Elmwood. While the authorities had focused on the documented victims, the tangible evidence of Baxter's depravity, Maria and Gibson were left grappling with the intangible, the potential for violence that lay dormant in Baxter's fractured psyche, woven into the very fabric of his literary obsessions. The question of whether there were more victims, more chapters to Baxter's horrifying manuscript, remained an unanswered ellipsis, a lingering shadow cast by the specter of his genius and his profound, devastating madness. The university might have breathed a sigh of relief, but for Maria and Gibson, the unsettling truth was that Baxter's story, the true extent of his literary machinations, might never be fully known. The silence that had fallen over Elmwood was not just the silence of grief, but also the silence of untold stories, of potential tragedies that might have been conceived but never fully realized, leaving an invisible scar on the collective consciousness of the university.

CHAPTER 15

THE EPILOGUE OF MEANING

The air at Elmwood University, months after Julian Baxter's chilling confession and subsequent apprehension, carried a peculiar stillness. It wasn't the quiet of peace, but rather the hushed reverence that follows a cataclysm, a palpable pause as the inhabitants of this hallowed ground tentatively assessed the damage and considered the arduous journey back to normalcy. The grand stone buildings, once imbued with the comforting hum of intellectual pursuit, now seemed to hold their breath, each lecture hall, each shadowed alcove, a silent witness to the horrors that had unfolded within their very walls. Yet, amidst this pervasive somberness, a new narrative was beginning to take shape, a deliberate and determined effort to wrest the story of Elmwood from the clutches of Baxter's macabre authorship.

The faculty, a collective of scholars and mentors who had weathered the storm alongside their students, found themselves tasked with a profound undertaking: to reclaim not just the physical spaces, but the very essence of their academic community. The tragedy had cast a long, dark shadow, threatening to redefine Elmwood not by its rich history of scholarly achievement, but by the depravity of one former student. This was a narrative they refused to accept. The intellectual discussions that had once filled seminar rooms, the passionate debates that had ignited minds, the quiet contemplation that had fostered profound understanding –

these were the threads from which Elmwood's true story was woven, and these were the elements they resolved to re-emphasize, to reinforce, until they eclipsed the memory of terror.

This reclamation began subtly, in the hushed tones of department meetings and the earnest conversations that took place over warm coffee in the faculty lounge. It was a conscious pivot, a collective decision to foreground the inherent value of literary study, the very disciplines that Baxter had twisted into a grotesque justification for murder. The focus shifted from the 'why' of Baxter's madness, a question that had consumed them, to the 'what' and 'how' of literature's enduring power. They spoke of empathy, of the profound human connection forged through shared stories, of literature's capacity to illuminate the darkest corners of the human psyche and, in doing so, offer solace and understanding.

Dr. Aris Gibson, his lectures now carrying a more measured, introspective tone, began to weave discussions of narrative agency and the ethical responsibilities of the storyteller into his syllabus. He spoke of how authors, much like individuals, could choose to construct narratives of destruction or of creation, of despair or of hope. He emphasized the critical thinking skills that literary analysis fostered, the ability to dissect motivations, to identify propaganda, and to discern truth from manipulation – skills that had proven tragically inadequate against Baxter's sophisticated deceptions but were now more vital than ever in rebuilding the university's intellectual resilience.

The library, that vast repository of human thought and imagination, had become the epicenter of Baxter's final, horrifying acts. For a time, its hushed aisles and towering shelves had felt tainted, imbued with a chilling aura of dread. Students and faculty alike had felt a prickling unease, a phantom sense of being watched, a heightened awareness of the shadows that danced in the periphery. The scent of aged paper, once comforting, now carried an undercurrent of something darker, something that spoke of unspoken fears and violated sanctity. Yet, as the seasons turned and the academic calendar progressed, the library began to shed its spectral cloak. It was a slow, almost imperceptible transformation, akin to a scar healing, the raw edges gradually softening, the pain becoming a duller ache.

Students, initially hesitant, began to return. They came, at first, out of necessity – for research papers, for exam preparation, for the sheer practicalities of academic life. But gradually, they rediscovered the quiet sanctuary that the library had always been. The rustle of pages, the soft tapping of keyboards, the murmur of hushed conversations – these familiar sounds, once overshadowed by the specter of violence, began to reassert themselves, weaving a new soundscape of diligent study and focused intellect. The weight of Baxter's actions, though never truly forgotten, was slowly being offset by the persistent, life-affirming rhythm of academic endeavor.

The librarians, those silent guardians of knowledge, played a crucial role in this gradual reintegration. They maintained their routines with an unwavering dedication, their presence a steady anchor in the shifting currents of post-tragedy life. They fielded questions, retrieved obscure texts, and offered quiet guidance, their normalcy, a subtle but powerful testament to the enduring resilience of intellectual pursuits. They saw, in the students returning to their carrels, in the professors poring over manuscripts, a quiet defiance, a refusal to allow the darkness to extinguish the light of learning.

The university's literary journals, once the conduits for Baxter's twisted pronouncements, were now being re-purposed. New submissions poured in essays that explored themes of resilience, of confronting trauma through artistic expression, of finding beauty in the aftermath of destruction. Poetry that spoke not of despair, but of dawning hope, of the enduring power of human connection, and of the quiet strength found in shared vulnerability. These were the new voices of Elmwood, the literary counter-narrative to Baxter's destructive opus, a testament to the generative power of literature when wielded not as a weapon, but as a means of healing and understanding.

Academic conferences, once filled with the detached exploration of theoretical frameworks, now began to incorporate discussions that directly addressed the ethical dimensions of literary creation and interpretation. Panels were convened to discuss the responsibility of academia in shaping public discourse, the delicate balance between intellectual freedom and the potential for harm, and the role of literature in fostering a more empathetic and understanding society. These were not abstract debates; they were deeply felt conversations, informed by the visceral experience of having witnessed the catastrophic consequences of a warped literary vision.

The very act of studying literature, which Baxter had perverted into a justification for murder, was now being championed as an antidote to such darkness. Maria Richards teamed up with Dr. Gibson, to give lectures in their respective capacities, tirelessly articulated this perspective. They argued that literature, at its best, forces us to step into the shoes of others, to grapple with complex moral ambiguities, and to confront the full spectrum of human experience – from the sublime to the horrific. It was through this empathetic engagement, they contended, that individuals could develop a deeper understanding of themselves and of the world, a critical bulwark against the simplistic, destructive ideologies that fueled acts of violence.

The university bookstore, which had briefly stocked Baxter's published works alongside its usual fare, had quietly removed them. In their place, new titles emerged, books that explored themes of reconciliation, of community healing, and of the power of shared narratives. The covers, once perhaps stark and unsettling, now often depicted images of light breaking through darkness, of hands reaching out in connection, of the enduring resilience of the human spirit. It was a subtle but significant shift, a visual representation of Elmwood's collective effort to redefine its own story.

The recovery was not without its challenges. There were still moments of quiet anxiety, of sudden chills, of a lingering unease that would surface unexpectedly. The memory of Baxter, the chilling precision of his intellect, the sheer audacity of his crimes, remained a part of Elmwood's history. But these moments were becoming less frequent, less potent. They were being gradually subsumed by the resurgence of academic life, by the renewed engagement of students and faculty in the pursuit of knowledge and understanding.

The narrative of Elmwood was being reclaimed, not by erasing the past, but by building upon it, by infusing it with new meaning. The tragedy had undoubtedly left an indelible mark, a dark stain on its esteemed history. But it had also, paradoxically, revealed the profound importance of the very disciplines it had threatened. Literature, in its myriad forms, was not just an academic pursuit; it was a vital tool for navigating the complexities of the human condition, for fostering empathy, for critical thinking, and for ultimately, for constructing narratives of hope and resilience. The library, once a site of unspeakable horror, was slowly, deliberately, being transformed back into a sanctuary of learning, a testament to the enduring power of the written word to heal, to illuminate, and to rebuild. The story of Elmwood was no longer solely Baxter's; it was once again becoming the story of its people, their shared pursuit of knowledge, and their unwavering commitment to the power of narrative to shape a better future. The whisper of fear was being drowned out by the steady hum of intellectual inquiry, and in that gentle resurgence lay the promise of a future where meaning, not madness, would once again define the heart of the university.

Dr. Aris Gibson found a peculiar solace in the hushed, cavernous halls of the introductory literature lecture theater. The air, once thick with the anticipation of groundbreaking, albeit esoteric, discourse, now felt lighter, imbued with the earnest curiosity of young minds encountering foundational texts for the first time. His departure from the more prestigious, specialized seminars hadn't been a retreat, but a recalibration. The weight of what had transpired, the devastating realization of how his own intellectual passions had intersected with Julian Baxter's descent into darkness, had necessitated a profound course correction. He had once chased the intoxicating thrill of unlocking hidden meanings, of plumbing the depths of philosophical texts with an almost feverish intensity. Now, his focus had shifted, honed by a hard-won wisdom and shadowed by a deep, abiding regret.

His voice, once capable of soaring flights of intellectual fancy, now held a more grounded, deliberate cadence. He spoke not of obscure hermetic traditions or the intoxicating allure of forbidden knowledge, but of the fundamental ethical responsibilities inherent in the act of interpretation. "Every text," he would begin, his gaze sweeping across the sea of eager faces, "is an invitation. But an invitation can be accepted with respect, or it can be twisted into a demand. We must ask ourselves not just 'What does this mean?' but 'What is the *consequence* of my interpretation?'" He saw it now, with a clarity that still pricked at him, how his own relentless pursuit of deeper, darker truths had inadvertently created an environment where Baxter could find fertile ground for his warped perspectives. He had been so engrossed in the *how* of meaning-making, the intricate dance of symbols and subtext, that he had, for a critical period, overlooked the fundamental *why* – the ethical implications, the potential for harm.

He remembered the feverish discussions he'd had with Baxter, the shared intellectual spark that had initially felt so exhilarating, so promising. He'd mistaken Baxter's incisive intellect for genuine intellectual rigor, his obsessive focus for profound insight. Gibson had been a curator of ideas, a guide through the labyrinthine corridors of human thought. But he had, in retrospect, been a negligent guide. He had allowed Baxter to stray too far, to become lost in the shadows, without adequately illuminating the path back to reason, to empathy, to the simple, profound understanding that literature was meant to connect us, not to divide us, to illuminate the human condition, not to justify its brutal exploitation.

"There is a dangerous seduction," Gibson continued, his voice resonating with the gravity of personal experience, "in believing you have unlocked a secret that no one else possesses. It fosters an arrogance, a detachment from the shared reality that binds us. Baxter was brilliant, undeniably so. But his brilliance was untethered from a moral compass. He saw the texts, the philosophies, not as windows into the human soul, but as blueprints for its deconstruction. And in his obsession, he convinced himself that he was not destroying, but *revealing*." Gibson paused, letting the weight of his words settle. He spoke of how the very act of interpreting could become a form of control, a way of bending a narrative to one's will, especially when that will was fueled by a deep-seated need for power or a twisted sense of justice.

He steered his students away from the precipice he himself had once teetered upon. The intricate, almost arcane, philosophical systems that had once consumed him were now presented with a stark, cautionary framing. He would introduce a complex concept, tracing its historical development, but always with an emphasis on its limitations, its potential for misapplication. He spoke of how a philosophy that seeks to dismantle conventional morality, while intellectually stimulating, could, in the wrong hands, become a justification for barbarism. He didn't shy away from the darker aspects of literature or philosophy, but he approached them with a newfound caution, like a seasoned surgeon handling a volatile compound.

"Consider the concept of the 'Übermensch'," he might say, gesturing towards a well-worn copy of Nietzsche. "A powerful idea, certainly. The potential for self-overcoming, for pushing beyond limitations. But what happens when that 'overcoming' involves the subjugation of others? What happens when the 'master morality' is applied not to oneself, but to the world around you? This is where interpretation becomes not an act of illumination, but an act of violence. Baxter believed he was the Übermensch, and that his interpretations were the dictates of a higher law. He saw himself as divinely appointed to prune the 'weakness' of humanity. And he used the language of philosophy, the very tools we use to understand ourselves, to justify his horrific actions."

Gibson found himself dedicating an increasing amount of lecture time to the concept of narrative responsibility. He emphasized that authors, editors, critics, and readers all held a stake in the ethical landscape of literature. "We are not passive recipients of meaning," he'd stress. "We are active participants. The choices we make in how we engage with a text, the questions we choose to ask, the connections we draw – these choices have consequences. To embrace a nihilistic interpretation without considering its impact on our understanding of human value is a dangerous gamble. To champion a text that glorifies violence without acknowledging its potential to incite that violence is, at best, irresponsible, and at worst, complicit."

His own regrets were a constant, quiet hum beneath the surface of his teaching. He remembered the pride he had felt when Baxter had sought his counsel, the intellectual camaraderie they had shared. He had seen a reflection of his own intellectual fire in Baxter, a shared passion for the profound. But he had failed to see the conflagration that was building, the destructive potential that lay dormant beneath the surface of intellectual discourse. He had been so focused on the abstract beauty of ideas that he had, for a time, become blind to the very real human cost of their misapplication.

"The greatest danger," he confessed to his students, his voice tinged with a weariness that went beyond mere physical fatigue, "is not in encountering difficult ideas. It is in encountering them without the accompanying framework of empathy and ethical consideration. Literature, at its core, is about understanding the human experience in all its complexity. It is about walking in another's shoes, feeling their joys, their sorrows, their fears. When we divorce ourselves from that fundamental human connection, when we reduce characters and authors to mere pawns in an intellectual game, we risk losing our own humanity."

He would often use Baxter's own published writings, not to dissect their intellectual merit, but to illustrate the chilling emptiness that lay at their heart. He would present passages where Baxter eloquently argued for a radical detachment from societal norms, for a pursuit of truth at any cost, and then juxtapose it with the brutal realities of his crimes. "Here," Gibson would say, pointing to a particularly chilling sentence, "we see the theoretical abstraction. And here," he would gesture towards a news clipping detailing the discovery of Baxter's victims, "we see the horrific, undeniable consequence. There is a chasm between these two. And it is our responsibility, as readers, as thinkers, to ensure that our intellectual pursuits bridge that chasm, rather than widen it."

He no longer sought to find the ultimate, hidden meaning, the singular truth that unlocked the universe. Instead, he encouraged his students to explore multiple interpretations, to engage in respectful debate, and to always, always consider the human element. He wanted them to understand that literature was not a puzzle to be solved, but a conversation to be engaged in, a means of fostering understanding and connection. He emphasized the importance of literary history not as a detached academic exercise, but as a record of human struggles, triumphs, and failures.

"We study the past," he would explain, "not to repeat its mistakes, but to learn from them. We examine the works of authors who grappled with profound questions, not to emulate their conclusions uncritically, but to understand their journey, their context, and the impact of their ideas. Baxter sought to transcend human limitations, to create a new order. But true transcendence, I believe, lies not in imposing one's will upon the world, but in understanding and connecting with the shared humanity that binds us all."

His new role, teaching these foundational courses, was a form of penance, a deliberate turning away from the intellectual precipice he had once flirted with. He was no longer the celebrated scholar pushing the boundaries of interpretation; he was a humble educator, guiding his students through the essential terrain of literary understanding. He found a quiet dignity in this work, a sense of purpose that had been fractured by the events of the past. The applause he once received for his groundbreaking theories had been replaced by the quiet satisfaction of seeing a student's eyes light up with comprehension, or witnessing a nascent spark of critical, ethically-grounded thought.

He spoke of the dangers of obsession, not as an abstract academic concept, but as a visceral, lived reality. He described how a singular focus, unchecked by broader considerations, could narrow one's vision to the point of delusion. "When you dedicate yourself entirely to a single idea, a single interpretation, without allowing for external validation, without engaging with dissenting voices, you risk becoming imprisoned by your own thoughts. Baxter was so consumed by his particular reading of the world, by his self-appointed role as arbiter of meaning, that he became incapable of seeing the horror he was inflicting. His obsession became his reality, and it was a reality that ultimately consumed him and those unfortunate enough to cross his path."

Gibson's regret was a quiet companion, a constant reminder of the responsibility that came with intellectual curiosity. He had learned, in the most profound and painful way possible, that knowledge without wisdom, and intellect without empathy, could be a terrifyingly destructive force. His lectures, stripped of their former esoteric flourishes, now focused on the enduring power of literature to foster understanding, to cultivate compassion, and to serve as a bulwark against the very darkness that had once threatened to engulf Elmwood. He was planting seeds of a different kind now, seeds of ethical interpretation and responsible engagement, hoping they would grow into a more resilient, more humane intellectual landscape, a landscape where shadows could be illuminated, not amplified into instruments of terror. The introductory halls, once perhaps perceived as a step down, were now his chosen ground, the fertile soil where he could cultivate a new generation of readers, readers who understood that the true power of literature lay not in its ability to deconstruct, but in its profound capacity to connect.

The sterile interrogation room, once a theater of stark questions and guarded silences, now felt different to Detective Maria Richards. It wasn't that the fluorescent lights were any less harsh, or the scent of stale coffee any less pervasive, but her internal landscape had undergone a seismic shift. The raw, brutal reality of the Baxter case, a narrative that had burrowed deep into her psyche, had irrevocably altered the way she perceived her own profession, and indeed, the very fabric of human motivation. She found herself no longer just seeing crime scenes as collections of evidence, but as chapters in a larger, often tragic, story. Each victim, each perpetrator, was a protagonist or antagonist within their own unfolding narrative, driven by a complex tapestry of desires, fears, and, as she now understood more profoundly, by the stories they told themselves and others.

Maria had always been a pragmatist, her mind trained to dissect facts, to build logical chains of causality, and to pursue justice with an unyielding, albeit often weary, resolve. The world of psychology and literary theory had, prior to the Baxter investigation, seemed a distant, perhaps even frivolous, realm. It was the domain of academics like Dr. Gibson, brilliant minds who grappled with abstract concepts while she, Maria, dealt with the messy, concrete consequences of broken lives. Yet, Baxter, in his chilling meticulousness, had inadvertently become her most profound, albeit unwanted, tutor. His ability to twist philosophical discourse into a justification for unimaginable cruelty, to weave elaborate justifications for his heinous acts, had forced Maria to confront the sheer, terrifying power of narrative.

She recalled the initial dismissiveness she'd felt when Dr. Gibson had spoken, in hushed, regretful tones, of how Baxter had used literary and philosophical concepts to rationalize his violence. At the time, her focus had been on the tangible: the forensic evidence, the witness testimonies, the meticulous piecing together of a timeline that led to the discovery of Baxter's atrocities. The "why" had seemed secondary to the "how." But as the investigation deepened, as she delved into Baxter's journals, his correspondence, his elaborate justifications, she began to understand that the "why" was not just relevant; it was the very engine that powered the "how." Baxter's worldview, a warped and dangerous construct built from carefully selected texts and twisted interpretations, had been the foundation upon which his reign of terror was built.

Now, Maria found herself looking at her own case files with a new set of eyes. The meticulous detail Baxter had poured into his journals, his almost obsessive need to document and articulate his twisted ideology, struck her as a chilling echo of the very narratives she was now beginning to recognize in her own cases. It wasn't just about finding the smoking gun; it was about understanding the story that led to the gun being fired. She started to notice the subtle shifts in a suspect's language, the recurring themes in their statements, the way they framed their own actions. Were they painting themselves as victims? As avenging angels? As misunderstood geniuses? These were not mere linguistic quirks; they were windows into the internal narratives that shaped their reality and, consequently, their actions.

She found herself rereading transcripts, not just for factual inconsistencies, but for narrative coherence. Did the suspect's story hold up against the backdrop of their known life, their motivations, their psychological profile? She began to see how individuals, consciously or unconsciously, constructed narratives to make sense of their world, to justify their choices, and to present a particular version of themselves to others. This was particularly true in cases of domestic violence, where perpetrators often spun tales of provocation and self-defense, meticulously omitting their own aggression and cruelty. Maria had always recognized this manipulation, but now she understood it with a deeper, more nuanced appreciation, seeing it not just as a lie, but as a deliberate act of narrative control.

The case had also made her more empathetic, a quality she had always possessed but had often kept carefully guarded, believing it to be a potential liability in her line of work. Seeing the depth of Baxter's intellectual corruption had paradoxically led her to a greater understanding of human vulnerability. She saw how individuals, adrift in their own personal narratives, could become susceptible to dangerous ideologies, how a need for belonging, for meaning, or for power could be exploited by those who offered a compelling, albeit false, story. She remembered the interviews with Baxter's acquaintances, those who had admired his intellect, who had been drawn into his charisma, and she realized that even the most discerning individuals could be swayed by a well-crafted narrative, especially when it tapped into their own unspoken desires or anxieties.

Maria began to incorporate this new perspective into her interrogations. She would still be firm, still relentless in her pursuit of truth, but she would also listen more intently to the stories her subjects were telling, looking for the underlying threads of their personal narratives. She learned to ask questions that probed these narratives, not to trap them, but to understand them. "Tell me more about that," she'd say, her voice calm and non-judgmental, encouraging them to elaborate, to reveal the underlying beliefs and motivations that shaped their actions. She understood that sometimes, the most effective way to dismantle a false narrative was to allow the speaker to expose its inherent contradictions themselves, simply by giving them the space to speak.

She found herself drawn to the psychological profiles of offenders, not just as clinical assessments, but as narratives of descent. She saw how a single traumatic event, a series of perceived injustices, or a deep-seated insecurity could be woven into a personal mythology that justified deviant behavior. Baxter's narrative had been one of intellectual superiority, of a chosen few destined to transcend the limitations of ordinary humanity. He had, in essence, cast himself as the protagonist of a grand, philosophical drama, and the world, unfortunately, had become his stage.

This shift in her perspective wasn't always easy. It meant grappling with the ambiguity of human motivation, with the uncomfortable truth that the lines between good and evil were often blurred, smudged by the complexities of personal history and individual interpretation. It meant recognizing that sometimes, even the most heinous acts stemmed not from pure malice, but from a deeply flawed understanding of the world, a narrative that had gone terribly, tragically wrong.

She started reading more widely, not just police procedure manuals, but books on narrative psychology, on the power of storytelling, and even, hesitantly at first, on the literary and philosophical works that Baxter had so perversely admired. She wanted to understand the source of his twisted logic, to see the texts through his eyes, not to validate his ideology, but to better combat it. She found Dr. Gibson's perspective invaluable, his cautious explanations of how certain ideas, when divorced from ethical considerations, could become dangerous weapons. He spoke of the seductive nature of intellectualism untethered from empathy, a concept that resonated deeply with Maria's experience.

Her colleagues noticed a subtle change in her. She was still the dedicated, sharp detective, but there was a new depth to her approach, a more intuitive understanding of the human element. Captain Cushman, a man who valued results above all else, found himself relying on Maria's increasingly insightful assessments, even if he didn't always understand the precise methodology behind them. "She's got a knack for it," he'd grumbled to his Lieutenants, shaking his head in a mixture of admiration and bewilderment. "Sees things we don't."

Maria no longer viewed her job as simply the application of law, but as the navigation of human stories. Each crime was a deviation from a potential narrative of peace and order, a disruption that needed to be understood in its entirety. She saw her role as not just to restore order, but to understand the forces that had caused the disruption, to untangle the twisted narratives that had led to the crime. It was a more demanding, more emotionally taxing way of working, but it was also, she realized, a more profound and ultimately, more effective one.

She understood that Baxter's story, however horrific, was not an isolated anomaly. It was a stark, extreme example of a universal human tendency to construct meaning through narrative. Her own story, as a detective, was also a narrative, one of seeking truth, of fighting for justice, of trying to make sense of the chaos. And the Baxter case had irrevocably altered the chapters of her own unfolding story, imbuing it with a deeper understanding of the power and peril of the narratives that shape our lives, and ultimately, dictate our actions. The pursuit of justice, she now knew, was not just about apprehending criminals; it was about understanding the stories that drove them, and in doing so, perhaps, preventing future tragedies.

The heavy oak doors of the Aeon Society and The Infinite Discourse, once beacons of intellectual discourse and spirited debate, were now bolted shut. The scent of aged paper and simmering philosophical arguments that had once permeated the hallowed halls was replaced by the sterile air of finality. The Society's, a venerable institution that had nurtured generations of scholars, thinkers, and dreamers, had been formally dissolved, its assets and records meticulously cataloged and then sealed, destined for a silence that echoed the abrupt end of its vibrant existence. It was a stark, unavoidable conclusion, a somber epitaph etched by the chilling revelations of the Baxter case. The very intellectual curiosity that had defined the Aeon Society and The Infinite Discourse, once celebrated as the pinnacles of human endeavor, had, in its unchecked pursuit, veered into a terrifying abyss.

Maria Richards observed the process from afar, a silent spectator to the dismantling of a legacy. The uniformed officers, their movements precise and unfeeling, carried out their duty, each box of documents a piece of history being entombed. It was a tangible manifestation of a truth she had come to understand with a visceral, almost painful, clarity: that ideas, untethered from the anchor of ethical consideration, could become instruments of immense destruction. The Society and Discourse, in its purest form, had aimed to foster critical thinking, to explore the vast expanse of human thought without constraint. Yet, Baxter, a product of its very environment, had twisted its foundational principles into a rationale for unspeakable acts. His meticulous journals, filled with esoteric references and self-serving interpretations, were a testament to how abstract concepts, when wielded by a corrupted mind, could morph into justifications for barbarism. The society, in its unwavering commitment to intellectual freedom, had inadvertently provided fertile ground for such perversion. Its disbandment was not merely an administrative decision; it was a societal acknowledgment of the inherent dangers lurking within unchecked philosophical exploration.

The sealing of the Society and Discourse's archives was more than just the storage of books and papers; it was the deliberate act of interring a powerful, yet corrupted, narrative. The society's history, once a source of pride and intellectual lineage, was now recontextualized. It became a cautionary tale, a stark, undeniable reminder that the pursuit of knowledge, without the accompanying framework of moral responsibility, could lead down a path of profound darkness. The meticulous records, now hidden away, would serve as a silent testament to this perilous journey. Each document, each debate transcribed, each lecture recorded, represented a thread in the complex tapestry of thought that had once defined the Society and Discourse. Now, those threads were being carefully gathered, not to be woven into future understanding, but to be tucked away, a dark chapter closed. The void left by its dissolution was palpable, a somber testament to the intricate dance between intellect and ethics, a balance that, when faltered, could have devastating consequences.

The impact of Baxter's actions had rippled outwards, not just through the legal system or the lives of his victims, but through the very intellectual landscape he had so profoundly disturbed. The two Society's, once a hub of vibrant intellectual exchange, had become irrevocably tainted by its association, however indirect, with his depravity. It was a tragic irony that an institution dedicated to the elevation of the mind had, in the eyes of many, become synonymous with the corruption of it. The debates that once echoed within its walls, the passionate arguments about ethics, existence, and the human condition, now seemed hollow, overshadowed by the horrifying practical application of twisted philosophies. The very ideals the society championed had been perverted, their noble aspirations twisted into a justification for cruelty.

Maria understood that the dissolution of such an institution, even one that had strayed so far from its intended purpose, left a vacuum. The absence of a space for rigorous, open intellectual inquiry was a loss, albeit a necessary one given the circumstances. It highlighted the fundamental challenge of fostering critical thought without simultaneously cultivating a robust ethical compass. The danger lay not in questioning established norms or exploring radical ideas, but in divorcing those explorations from any sense of accountability, any grounding in human empathy. Baxter had demonstrated the terrifying efficacy of such a separation, constructing an elaborate intellectual edifice that shielded him from the moral implications of his actions.

The legacy of the Society and Discourse, therefore, was not to be found in its past achievements or its future potential, but in the stark lesson it now embodied. It was a lesson whispered in the hushed tones of those who had once frequented its halls, a lesson shouted in the pronouncements of the authorities who had decreed its closure. It was a lesson that echoed in the quiet contemplation of detectives like Maria, who had witnessed firsthand the devastating consequences of unchecked intellectualism. The Society's names would forever be linked to the darkness that had emanated from within its orbit, a dark shadow cast by the brilliance that had been so cruelly manipulated.

The sealed records represented not just the physical evidence of the Society's existence, but the conceptual evidence of its downfall. Within those boxes lay the genesis of ideas that, when nurtured and cultivated by a mind like Baxter's, had blossomed into instruments of terror. The philosophical texts, the treatises on existentialism, the debates on the nature of consciousness – all had been meticulously studied and distorted. Baxter had not merely read these works; he had consumed them, reinterpreted them, and ultimately, weaponized them. He had crafted a narrative of his own superiority, a philosophical justification for his brutal actions, and the Society and Discourse, in its open-minded embrace of intellectual exploration, had provided him with the raw materials.

The disbandment served as a societal pause, a moment of collective reflection on the potential dangers inherent in intellectual pursuits. It forced a confrontation with the uncomfortable truth that the pursuit of knowledge, while noble, was not inherently virtuous. Without a guiding moral framework, without a deep-seated commitment to the well-being of others, even the most profound intellectual endeavors could be corrupted. The Society and Discourse, in its final, unintended act, was a stark illustration of this profound truth. Its legacy was now a somber warning, a reminder that the architecture of thought, however grand, required a foundation of ethical understanding to prevent its collapse into chaos and destruction. The silence that now enveloped the institution was a profound, almost deafening, indictment of the dangers of intellect untamed by empathy.

The meticulous process of sealing the society's archives was a physical manifestation of a conceptual severing. It was an act designed to contain not just the physical remnants of intellectual discourse, but the potent, potentially corrosive ideas that had festered within its walls. The very notion of "legacy" for the Aeon Society and The Infinite Discourse had been irrevocably altered. It was no longer a legacy of enlightenment or intellectual progress, but a grim testament to the fragility of reason and the ever-present potential for its perversion. The papers, now locked away, contained the echoes of debates that had once been seen as vital to understanding the human condition, but which now served as a chilling prelude to unimaginable suffering. Each archived document was a potential spark, and the fear was that even in their sealed state, the embers of dangerous thought might still glow.

Detective Richards watched as the last of the boxes was carried out, a sense of profound melancholy settling over her. The Society and Discourse had been more than just a collection of intellectuals; it had been a symbol of a particular kind of human aspiration. Its downfall was not just the closure of a building, but the symbolic end of an era of naive faith in the inherent goodness of intellectual pursuit. The narrative of the two Society's, from its inception as a beacon of learning to its ignominious end, was a complex and tragic story, one that Maria would carry with her, a stark reminder of the ever-present need for vigilance, for ethical grounding, and for a profound understanding of the stories we choose to tell ourselves and, in doing so, shape our reality. The void left by its dissolution was a stark, enduring reminder of the inherent responsibility that accompanied the power of thought.

The weight of the Society's closure, a palpable absence in the intellectual heart of the city, pressed upon Maria Richards with a persistent melancholy. Yet, in the quiet aftermath, as the dust settled on the ruins of that grand edifice of thought, a different kind of meaning began to coalesce. It wasn't the thunderous pronouncements of Baxter, his twisted manifestos meticulously crafted to echo through eternity, that held the true resonance. Instead, it was in the hushed resilience of those he had touched, the survivors whose lives, though irrevocably scared, continued to move forward with a quiet fortitude. It was in the persistent, often tedious, work of investigators, poring over evidence not for sensationalism, but for the granular truths that would bring a semblance of closure to shattered families.

The university, once a vibrant nexus of youthful curiosity and scholarly pursuit, now bore the indelible mark of Baxter's depravity. His name, inextricably linked to the hallowed grounds, served as a dark annotation in its storied history. Each lecture hall, each library carrel, each windswept quadrangle, held the spectral echo of his actions, a chilling reminder of how easily the pursuit of abstract thought could curdle into tangible horror. But even within this somber recontextualization, Maria began to discern a deeper significance. The official narrative, the one splashed across headlines and debated in hushed tones, was a story of terror and intellectual corruption. Yet, the true meaning, she realized, was not to be found in the glare of that sensational spotlight, but in the quieter, more enduring spaces – the margins of human experience, where the seeds of resilience were sown and the persistent quest for understanding continued, undeterred.

And what of the students, those who had once looked to Baxter as a guru, a fount of profound wisdom? Many were left grappling with a profound sense of betrayal, their intellectual heroes shattered, their faith in the very nature of learning shaken. Yet, within this disillusionment, a new form of awareness began to emerge. They began to question not just the content of the ideas, but the context in which they were presented, the ethical underpinnings, the responsibility of the messenger. A new generation of thinkers was being forged in the crucible of this disillusionment, one that was more critical, more discerning, and perhaps, more profoundly aware of the potential pitfalls of unchecked intellectualism. They started forming study groups, not to dissect Baxter's warped ideologies, but to explore the very concepts he had twisted, to reclaim them from his perversion, to understand them through a lens of empathy and ethical responsibility. They debated not just *what* was true, but *how* truth should be pursued and *to what end*. Their resilience lay in their refusal to be defined by the darkness, but in their determination to illuminate it with the light of a more responsible, more humane, understanding.

Maria often found herself revisiting the shelves of the university library from time to time, not to find answers to the Baxter case, which had been meticulously dissected and documented, but to rediscover the solace and wisdom that literature offered. She would trace the spines of worn volumes, each one a vessel carrying stories, ideas, and emotions across time. It was in these pages, often overlooked in the clamor for definitive pronouncements and sensational revelations, that the true meaning of human experience was often found. The detective novels, with their intricate plots and their relentless pursuit of truth, mirrored her own investigative journey, but they also offered a sense of order, a narrative arc that brought resolution to chaos. Yet, it was in the poetry, in the novels of social commentary, in the historical accounts of human struggle and triumph, that she found a deeper resonance. These were the texts that explored the complexities of the human heart, the enduring power of love, the devastating consequences of hatred, and the quiet strength that emerged in the face of adversity.

She remembered a particular evening, after a long day spent sifting through Baxter's meticulously cataloged archives, the sheer volume of his intellectual narcissism overwhelming. She had retreated to the hushed sanctuary of her study, the air thick with the scent of old paper and brewing tea. Her fingers had alighted on a collection of essays by essayists who had themselves grappled with profound societal upheaval. One essay, in particular, spoke of how even in the darkest of times, art and literature served not as grand pronouncements, but as quiet acts of defiance, as whispers of hope in the face of overwhelming despair. The author wrote of how meaning was not always found in the loud declarations of those who sought to dominate, but in the gentle persistence of creation, in the shared experience of a well-told story. It was a revelation that echoed the very sentiments Maria had been wrestling with. Baxter had sought to impose his meaning, a twisted narrative of intellectual supremacy, upon the world. But the true meaning, the enduring meaning, was being written by those who simply lived, who loved, who grieved, and who, in their own quiet ways, continued to create and to connect.

The university's history, once a proud chronicle of intellectual achievement, was now irrevocably marked by the Baxter case. It was a dark stain, a cautionary tale woven into the fabric of its legacy. Yet, even this narrative was not monolithic. Within the official pronouncements of condemnation and closure, there were other stories unfolding. There were the stories of professors who, despite the tarnished reputation of their institution, continued to teach with passion and integrity, fostering critical thinking and ethical awareness in their students. There were the stories of administrators who, in the wake of the scandal, initiated new programs focused on mental health awareness and ethical leadership, attempting to mend the fractured trust and to build a more robust framework for safeguarding the intellectual environment. These were the stories that Elias Baxter could never control, the narratives that unfolded in the spaces he sought to dominate and destroy.

Maria realized that the true epilogue to the Baxter case was not to be found in the finality of his sentencing or the dissolution of the Society's, but in the ongoing, evolving narrative of the human spirit. Baxter had attempted to write himself into history as a tragic genius, a martyr to his own intellectual revolution. But his story, in its grandiosity, had missed the essential truths of human existence. He had focused on the apex, the dramatic climax, the definitive statement, failing to recognize that meaning is often found not in the thunderous declarations, but in the quiet hum of everyday life, in the enduring power of connection, and in the persistent, sometimes arduous, journey towards understanding. The margins of his horrific narrative were being filled with the quiet resilience of survivors, the dedication of truth-seekers, and the enduring power of literature to illuminate and heal.

The university, once a symbol of intellectual enlightenment, had become a stark reminder of its potential perils. Yet, even in its tarnished state, it continued to be a place of learning, a place where new generations grappled with complex ideas. The process of recovery, Maria understood, was not about erasing the past, but about integrating it, about learning from its darkest chapters to build a more resilient future. The Baxter case, a brutal annotation in the university's history, served as a profound reminder that every story, no matter how tragic, ultimately finds its meaning in the margins of human experience, in the quiet acts of courage and compassion, and in the ongoing, unwavering quest for understanding. The dramatic pronouncements of a deranged killer faded into the background, their power to define the narrative diminished by the enduring strength of those who chose to focus on the resilience of the human spirit, the pursuit of truth, and the profound, healing power of stories. The meaning, she concluded, was not a destination to be reached, but a journey to be undertaken, a continuous act of weaving together the threads of experience, both light and dark, into a tapestry of enduring human significance. The true legacy was not in the shockwaves of destruction, but in the quiet ripples of healing and the persistent, unyielding search for wisdom, found not just in grand pronouncements, but in the subtle inscriptions of a life lived with courage and compassion.

EPILOGUE

THE LAST LECTURE

The autumn wind carried the scent of old pages and dying leaves through the courtyard of Elmwood University. Beneath the bell tower, police tape fluttered like tattered streamers from a forgotten celebration. Students whispered in clusters, eyes darting toward the cordoned-off statue of Dante Alighieri. Blood had pooled beneath his stone feet—crimson against marble.

Inside the library, the air was still. A single desk lamp glowed, casting a circle of pale light over open books. On the table lay Dante's *Inferno*, *Macbeth*, *The Iliad*, and *Dr. Faustus*—each splattered with rust-colored fingerprints.

A note rested on top of *Inferno*, written in deliberate, elegant handwriting:

Abandon all hope, ye who misinterpret.

Detective Laura Haines studied the scene with a gnawing unease. The killer had struck seven times in three months—each murder mirroring a death from classical literature. A student burned alive for "the sin of pride." Another drowned, lashed to a desk labeled "Ophelia." A third, found frozen in a lecture hall, eyes wide and lips blue, clutching a note that read: *"To study without wisdom is to die without purpose."*

Now, the killer was gone. The final entry in the security log showed the library doors opening at 3:03 a.m.—but no one leaving.

The campus quieted, but the silence wasn't peace. It was anticipation.

Weeks later, a cardboard box arrived at the English Department of Harrowgate University, three states away. No return address. No postage stamp—just the word *TRANSFER* stamped in red across the top.

Inside were books.

All children's fables.

A copy of *Aesop's Fables* lay open, a line underlined in crimson ink:

"We hang the petty thieves and appoint the great ones to public office."

A faint scent of ash rose from the pages.

Dean Justin Norman frowned. "Is this some kind of prank?"

But the secretary, pale and shaking, pointed to the corner of the box. Scrawled there in the same ink were words that made her stomach drop:

Aesop understood what Dante began. The lesson continues.

Outside, the university bell tolled once—low and resonant—echoing through the courtyard like the turning of a page.

And far away, in a dorm room lit by flickering candlelight, someone whispered the next story aloud.

"The Fox and the Crow..."

Then came the sound of laughter—soft, amused, and utterly devoid of mercy.

www.ingramcontent.com/pod-product-compliance
Lightning Source LLC
Chambersburg PA
CBHW020459020726
47493CB00001B/101
* 9 7 8 1 9 6 9 7 7 0 1 6 6 *